How Old Was Lolita?

How Old

Was Lolita?

Alan Saperstein

Random House/New York

Grateful Acknowledgment is made to the following for permission to
reprint previously published material:

Coleco Industries, Inc.: Trivia questions appearing in this book are
taken from the Baby Boomer Edition of the Trivial Pursuit brand game
and used with permission. The Trivial Pursuit game Baby Boomer Edition
is copyright © 1983 by Horn Abbott, Ltd. All rights reserved.

Warner Bros. Music: Excerpts from the lyrics to "Perfect World"
by David Byrne and Chris Frantz.
Copyright © 1985 INDEX MUSIC, INC. & BLEU DISQUE MUSIC CO. INC.
All Rights Administered by WB MUSIC CORP. All Rights Reserved.
Used By Permission.

Library of Congress Cataloging-in-Publication Data

Saperstein, Alan.
How old was Lolita?
I. Title.
PS3569.A58H69 1987 813'.54 87-9611
ISBN 0-394-56372-7

Manufactured in the United States of America

23456789

First Edition

For Lynn

Create   Append   Revise   Include   Next
                —Fragments from a word-processing menu

"This is the saddest story I have ever heard."
                                —Ford Madox Ford

How Old Was Lolita?

1

IT'S FRANK'S TURN. He's really good. He always goes for the toughest categories. Lives and Times. Or Nightly News. Or RPM. Most of us tend to stick to what we know, but Frank extends himself. That's what we like about him.

"What graveyard smash buried the rest of the chart on October 20, 1962?"

"What *what?*"

That's Frank's way of buying a little more time. He pretends that the question is not clear or that the questioner did not read the question clearly. Frequently the question is not clear. The authors of the game are Canadian and their grammar is difficult to understand. But you just have to figure out the syntax. When you can figure out where the commas should be, what the verb really is, when you can spot the missing information and emphasize it in your reading, then there's no problem. I think I'm the best at reading the questions. I have such confidence in my reading that I refuse to repeat the question. I'll say something like "You heard me." That's because I take the little extra time to analyze the question before I read it and I know I'm making it absolutely clear. And so does the person I'm asking. Nobody ever challenges my readings.

"What *graveyard smash* buried the rest of the chart on October 20, 1962?"

" 'Monster Mash'?"

Of course Frank's right. He has the annoying habit of putting a coy little question mark at the end of his answer, but we all know that Frank knows.

David got here late. When he came in, he went right to the refrigerator to get ice for his eye. He said he'd been in a fight. With a cabdriver. Sort of a fight. He told the cabdriver to drop off Suzanne, his ex-wife, and then continue on to my address. When David's ex-wife got out, the cabdriver turned off his meter and David scolded him. David can't stand incompetence. It must be because of his job. Incompetence on his job can bring the entire airline industry to a halt in a few minutes. We were impressed when he told us that. He's a computer analyst and troubleshooter, and he has to wear a beeper twenty-four hours a day. He's always on the phone with the chairman or president of this or that major corporation: AT&T, IBM. Apparently the cabdriver had his own rules about split fares, and even though he had agreed to drop Suzanne, he wasn't about to lose the buck twenty-five or whatever it is he gets by throwing the meter again. David said he threatened not to pay and started to get out of the cab at Suzanne's apartment. The driver headed him off at the door and slammed David into a wall and said to give him his fare or else. David said he told the guy that he'd give him the money but that the guy ought to give David the number of his cab so David could report him. That's when the guy socked David. He punched him in the eye and knocked our friend down to the ground. David got up and the cabdriver knocked him down again. At that point there was no other recourse but to give the cabdriver the money. From down on the ground, David reached into his pocket and came up with a five. He knew the fare was three something, but he told the driver to keep the change. The guy could have had a knife or a gun. He could have had a tire iron under his jacket.

Most of us are married now. Except for Michael and Julia, we have all been married at one time or another. Julia is too caught up preparing for what we hope will be her breakthrough exhibit to worry about not being married, and we're pretty sure Michael is gay. The only other ones not married now are David and Barbara, and David still hangs out with his ex, and Barb has been married twice and is always engaged to some VP where she works. She works in an advertising agency. She's a planner. That's a job that didn't exist ten years ago. It didn't exist ten months ago. Not as it does now. Several people who had other responsibilities would do part time some of what Barb now does full time, but it took Barbara and another pioneer to recognize the value of having full-time planners on staff. Now, Barb tells us, all the ad agencies are turning their best account executives into planners. Pretty soon, she says, there won't be any decent account executives left and she'll reinvent that job and get another ten thousand-dollar promotion. She got the ten thousand as a bonus for her planner idea and took us all out to dinner at one of our favorite Japanese restaurants.

We all have jobs or specialties that did not exist ten years ago. We forced the world to create these jobs by how important and impressive and indispensable we made our specialties look on our résumés. I suppose I'm the only one of us who's an exception, since my professional status is still up in the air. I'm still vacillating between two basically traditional careers. I'm still determined to make it as a jazz musician and I go to the "office" every day to work on the communal jazz crossover symphony, but I'm growing more and more dedicated to my appraisal work, which has been sporadic but a real windfall when it comes, and I've been considering going into appraisals full-time. I appraise the financial opportunities of unreleased films, plays, and TV pilots and I earn ¼ percent of the appraised figure, which can amount to a lot of money. A well-marketed movie, for example, can earn millions, which can mean thousands to me. And I get paid up front whether the marketing works or not. Actually, both of these careers are quite different than they were ten years ago. I compose and perform on the synthesizer. And ten years ago, an appraisal did not have to take into account the complicated but enormous financial potential afforded by pay TV, videocassettes, and European distribution.

We do not have our share of kids. We tend to wait. We want to get plenty of living in before having kids ties us down. We all work and we all love our jobs. We all get to travel on business. We take vacations together. And we have more unofficial holidays than any generation before us. We celebrate all the usual calendar holidays with grand parties, of course. We observe all of our religious holidays with orthodox "rituals and victuals," as Dale puts it. Dale is a writer. A ghostwriter. He also specializes in writing novelizations. Of anything. TV shows, movies, concept albums. Also, we observe the births, deaths, and achievements of our own pantheon of cultural heroes, suicides, and victims—Elvis, Jimi, the Kennedys, Terry Fox, Jim Fixx, Ralph Nader, Steven Spielberg, Steven Jobs. And we commemorate the historic events that shaped our times—the war, the assassinations, Nixon's resignation, the first man on the moon, the last episode of *M*A*S*H*. God, we must have a hundred parties a year just getting together to watch our favorite TV shows—*Dynasty, Remington Steele, Wheel of Fortune, Saturday Night Live* reruns. We do everything together. We go everywhere together. We made it through schools and summers together. We made it through a war without getting called up. We made it through acid and pot and coke without winding up in body bags. We've rented beach houses and ski lodges, stood up for each other at our weddings, gotten each other jobs, given each other glowing references. These are my friends. I love them.

David's the only one of us with a kid. His daughter lives with Suzanne. Her name is Anjelica, but everyone calls her Angel. She's only fourteen but smart as a whip. She makes David look good. We used to let her sit in once in a while, but she was too smart for us. Even when we made her pick from the Baby Boomer Edition, somehow she knew all the answers to questions about things that happened before her time. Once we drove to Vermont for Christmas and Angel came with us in our rented car and she knew the words to every song that came on the radio. It was eerie, because all the songs were pop standards from the forties and early fifties. I remember I asked Angel how she knew those songs and she just shrugged her shoulders and said she didn't know how she knew, she just knew them. That was spooky. When she beat us at our own game, it wasn't spooky. It was annoying. And she knew it. And she enjoyed it. And so did David, because Angel's brightness reflected on him. But the rest of us didn't appreciate Angel's intelligence. Every one of us went to David and Suzanne separately and asked if we could keep Angel out of the game. We all used the same excuse, that we didn't feel comfortable saying what we felt in front of a twelve-year-old. And since we always played at David's and Suzanne's apartment (which became Suzanne's apartment after the divorce), and since Angel was always hanging around because she is as socially backward as she is academically advanced, David volunteered to have a long talk with her and ask her to butt out. It was a very good talk, he said. They talked all about us, David said, and even though Angel is too young to really understand how wonderful we all are and how interesting we are and how terrific we are at what we do, she understood that she made us feel uncomfortable and she said that she would let us play by ourselves if that was what we wanted. David told us that of course she had to remind him that "you and all your brilliant friends played the *Genius* Edition of your stupid game for a year before you realized it's called the *Genus* Edition." Kids.

After Suzanne divorced David, our apartment became the central gathering place. Victoria's and mine. My wonderful, shy, devoted, beautiful Victoria. So appropriately named. "After the age," Barb always says. God, where the hell is she? It's late and I'm scared, and I'm losing my patience. I don't know how much more of this I can take. I don't know how much longer I can keep making excuses for Victoria's behavior. It really isn't very fair of them. Never mind decency; what about simple fairness?

Our apartment is not only the most centrally located, it's the biggest, the cheeriest, it has the best selection of wine and beer, room enough for two or three to spend the night on the hide-a-bed in an emergency—at least that was true before Andrew showed up—plus we've got a Cuisinart, a microwave, a VCR, video games, an Apple, the synthesizer, a regular piano, just about anything we really need.

NeAndrewthal, Barb calls him. She should only know the

truth. She should only know what Andrew is doing to Victoria and me. To each of us alone and to the two of us together. God, if we can get through this one, there isn't anything I'd put past my friends and our generation and our patience and our ability to make things turn out for the best. It's comforting to know that if things get worse, I can turn to my friends and they'll know exactly what to do. They know so much. They have such style. They're always in the right place at the right time with the right answer. If I have to, I can tell them what's been happening, bring them into the whole sordid business, and I know that they'll understand and be supportive and come up with the perfect solution. They are my friends and I love them. They are my friends and we are the future. In fact, we may be the first generation that thinks of itself as the future rather than of its children as the future. Frank says it comes from having a tight grip on things, a sharp focus, from knowing all the possibilities and all the limits. We cannot be deluded. We know what can and cannot be accomplished and we know how to get the job done. Frank is an epidemiologist.

It's my turn. Frank's roll of the die has kept him out of the center. We know going in that when Frank's in the game we're playing for second, but it's still exciting. I'm securely in second place and so I can show off by trying Nightly News.

"Who was pope between June 4 and June 20, 1963?"

I am bad at popes. I am bad at geography, world wars, popes, and rock 'n' roll hits of the fifties. But I'm good at deduction, and I conclude that such a short papal reign must mean an unorthodox answer. It may even be a trick question. I guess that the answer is no one, and I'm right. Not because I know popes but because I identify with the sense of humor of the Canadians who invented the game. I have a good sense of humor and a good sense of logic. When everyone realizes that the hour is late and that Dale and Phyllis have not shown up or called, everyone instinctively turns to me for a logical explanation. I think about it for a second and then I say that they must have gone to TKTS to try to get tickets for What's His Name's play before What's His Name leaves the cast. My friends are wonderful because they know exactly who I mean. They have all read the review of the play and the article about

What's His Name's planning to leave the cast because he does not believe in doing anything for longer than three months, and they know that Dale and Phyllis are real fans, but they turn to me to synthesize this solution. Over the years, a wonderful personal shorthand develops between wonderful friends such as mine. Sometimes it is very flattering.

Julia asks if she should process another batch of her margaritas. Julia's in charge of margaritas. Before we got our processor, she used a small electric hand mixer that she always brought from home. We are all in charge of something. Julia's in charge of Mexican drinks and Mexican hors d'oeuvres. Barb is our resident Asian expert. She can make sushi. It is astonishing. The pieces of raw fish are perfectly formed and magnificently wrapped in seaweed. The green mustard is always perfectly diluted with soy sauce. She also has been known to make a pitcher of sake martinis just slightly more powerful than the bomb we dropped on Hiroshima. Victoria has the health food concession. She's great at making grains and sprouts and leaves and berries taste like ratatouille. Victoria is devoted to health. She swims and works out on exercise machines and won't eat fatty foods or red meat and insists on a minimum of eight hours' sleep every night. She's not a fanatic, though. She's smart. As a paralegal, she works with lawyers and judges. She assists in and out of court. She has to look good. She hasn't gone swimming or worked out on her machines since Andrew arrived. She's gone to her health club only once since Andrew arrived and that was to take Andrew with her to show him what the club was like because I thought it might be a good idea for him to join. He lit a cigarette in the men's weight lifting room and then when all the body builders complained, he flicked it into the whirlpool.

Tonight Julia is cook. Besides the margaritas, there are quesadillas, nachos, and a tacolike invention of Julia's that is so *picante,* you have to dip it into her fresh, garlicky guacamole to cool it down before you dare put it in your mouth. We all say "Yum" when we taste anything extraordinary like Julia's invention. "Yum" is what the gremlins growled in the movie *Gremlins,* which Steven Spielberg produced. Spielberg is the best. The absolute best.

2

NDREW ALWAYS HATED being called Andrew, which is why I call him Andrew now. He preferred to be called Nick. He thought Nick sounded rough and romantic and that it was the perfect *nick* name. I will not call him Nick. I will call him Andrew. I introduce him to my friends as Andrew. When I go out, I leave him notes addressed to Andrew. He has not complained. He does not seem to care any longer about being called Andrew. He does not seem to care what you call him or if you call him. Most of the time he doesn't answer. He just sits and stares at Victoria. Or he does something incredibly embarrassing, which my friends—who do not know the whole story—think is amusing. The other night, with everyone here playing our favorite game and digging into Julia's quesadillas and special taco invention, Andrew staggered in at midnight (fifteen minutes after Victoria finally came home) and sat down in the middle of everything, and then, when one of us warned him that the heaping handful of Julia's taco invention he was about to shove into his mouth was very spicy, he got up and staggered into the kitchen and came back with a jar of dried red chili peppers and proceeded to eat the peppers right out of the jar. He held the lip of the jar up to his own lips and chugged the peppers like candy. So amusing.

Andrew is my older brother. He is ten years older than I am—almost to the day. He is forty-four. Until he showed up at our door a month ago, I hadn't seen him for twenty-five years. He was bloated, sloppy, drunk, and much older looking than forty-four when I answered the door. Still, I recognized him immediately.

The last time I had seen Andrew was when he went away to college. Then he dropped out of college and out of my life for twenty-five years except for an occasional postcard from the Himalayas or New Zealand or Africa or some other desolate, undeveloped, backward, forsaken place. He always wrote the postcards in the native language. Whenever I asked one of my friends to help translate, a friend who might know that particular language or might know someone else who spoke Swahili or whatever it happened to be on the latest postcard, the response was always that the handwriting was too illegible. He wrote me illegible postcards and I wrote him off.

I began by worshiping Andrew. Then I envied Andrew. Then I became disappointed in him. Then I detested him. Then I forgot all about him. And now I'm thrown completely off balance by Andrew's return and by his outrageous behavior. I would like to throw Andrew out of my house, but I can't. I would like to confront Andrew with his behavior with Victoria, but I'm afraid the two of them will deny everything and make me look like a fool. I would like to avoid getting my friends involved if I possibly can, but I'm losing patience and don't know how much longer I'll be able to stand idly by and watch my own brother make a mockery of my life.

He is my older brother and I do not know what to do. Nothing about him is admirable. He has money—cash—but I don't know where it comes from or how he plans to earn more. His clothes might have been expensive and stylish when he bought them, but now they're threadbare, ill-fitting, soiled, and ridiculously old-fashioned. He wears a Mao jacket or a Nehru jacket. He arrived with a beat-up steamer trunk that he lives out of; he has been with us for a month, but there is not a single possession of his to be found anywhere in the apartment—he keeps everything in the trunk. There is no other trace of a guest except for the disarrayed hide-a-bed. He stays in our apartment during the day when we are at work and then leaves before I get home. There is a good possibility that he meets Victoria when she is through working and that the two of them spend the evening together. I do not have proof of this. Victoria says she's working late, but she has worked late every night since Andrew's arrival, and one or two times when I've tried to reach her at her office, there was no answer. Also, the two of them come home within fifteen minutes of each other, sometimes Victoria first, sometimes Andrew, usually around ten or eleven at night. Andrew comes back dead drunk, embarrasses me in front of our friends, who pretend he's amusing, opens the hide-a-bed after our friends leave, lies down for a while, and then goes out again the moment Victoria and I retire to the bedroom. In the morning, I leave for work before Victoria and usually "run into" Andrew in front of my building. It is obvious to me that he has been waiting for me to leave for work, but he always nods as though he arrived just that minute in front of the building on his way upstairs. He nods as if he has just run out to buy the morning paper. In one month's time, he has managed to arrange our three schedules so that the only time Victoria and I are alone together is when we are asleep. I have no proof of this.

In the month since he showed up at our door, Andrew has barely spoken except for grunting, grudging monosyllabic yes or no answers to practical questions. "Uh . . . yeah," he'll be staying indefinitely. "Uh . . . yeah," he'd like to use the john, have a drink, go to sleep. "Nah," he would not like to play in our game or go to a show or have dinner at a great new Thai restaurant. Consequently, there is a tendency to treat him as though he is sick or in shock. And yet there is something frighteningly healthy about him. Something seething under the surface threatening to explode if anybody crosses him. And so any tendency to worry about Andrew is nullified by awe of this simmering explosiveness.

Sometimes when he is silent and just staring at Victoria, she says that he is musing. Not amusing. Musing. One night during the eleven o'clock news, five minutes after she got home and ten minutes before Andrew stumbled through the door, Victoria said that we and our friends never muse. We are always too busy to sit with our thoughts. We are always watching TV or reading or playing games or going out to dinner or planning trips or plotting career moves or checking the movie timetable to see if we can squeeze three movies into a single evening. It did not sound like Victoria talking. It sounded like Andrew talking, although I don't really know what that sounds like. I know what Andrew sounds like when he belches and retches after he has come home stinking drunk and passes out and snores. But I do not know what a conversation with Andrew is like. I am sure Victoria knows. But I have no proof.

Victoria had been swimming and exercising when Andrew showed up for the first time in twenty-five years. When she walked in, she was wearing a sweat suit and a watch cap and leggings and she was carrying an overstuffed gym bag in one hand and an unwieldy bag of groceries in the other hand and her hair was sopping wet under the cap and her nose was running and all she wanted to do was drop everything right there on the floor and blow her nose and draw herself a hot bath and collapse into the bathtub and soak for an hour before our friends arrived. I have seen her come home like that a thousand times. But when she saw Andrew sitting in our living room, she just stood there and let him stare at her. I could see the skin whitening on the knuckles of the hand holding the bag of heavy groceries while she just stood there in front of my older brother, who stared at my wife as though she were some kind of miracle. I said something like, "Victoria, this is my brother . . . Andrew. You've heard me talk about Andrew. Andrew has just popped in out of the blue. Andrew, this is Victoria. My wife." God, it was like a scene out of some Pinter play or something the way they just stood there and sat there and stared and got stared at. It was spooky. Like when Angel knew all the forties songs on the car radio going up to Vermont.

3

I F IT WERE JUST ME and Victoria, then I could understand. But it's not. She's part of something so much bigger and stronger than just the two of us. She is x necessary degrees in our perfect circle of friends. She is a vital circuit in this flawlessly programmed board processing all of our lives and all of our work and all of our futures into a communal future that will never allow itself to be short-circuited; fail safe is built in. She is as much a part of David as his beeper. She is the only one Frank ever talks to about the work he's doing on AIDS. She has offered to help Dale research the James Brown ghost job he's negotiating with Simon & Schuster. And who would Barb play off of? And who would Lori and Phyllis go jogging and shopping and to B movies with? Victoria's the only one of us who's ever met Michael's alleged lover. It was by accident. At lunch. And she won't say a word about it to any of us. She still sees Suzanne occasionally. And she took Angel to the *Nutcracker* last Christmas, when David was out of town on an emergency airline reservations breakdown and Suzanne had the flu. That's the kind of woman Victoria is. Named after the age. Proper. Decent. Honest. Trustworthy.

I find myself lying in her behalf more and more, covering for her with greater imagination, as if I were hiding something about myself from my friends. Whatever Victoria tells me, I tell them with more detail, more flourish. I find myself defending her late hours, unfurling them as though they were a banner of her current success, when what I would really like to do is ask these wonderful people whom I love and who love us what can be done to stop this madness.

You would have to know Victoria to appreciate how strangely she has been acting since Andrew arrived. She, too, is my friend, not just my wife. She was my friend first and I know her and love her apart from sex. Originally, she was David's girl. The two of them dated the first two years of college. The three of us were inseparable, but they were boyfriend and girl friend, although I am sure they were never lovers. Sex has never been important to Victoria. That is, perhaps, her chief allure. She is above sex. Above the savage loss of control. Above the disorienting aftermath. Of all of us— David with his precision computers, Frank and his task force of emergency deductive pathology, Dale and his outlines for novelizations, me and my synthesized jazz and financial forecasts, Michael and his laser animation, Barb and her account planning, Lori, Phyllis, Julia—of all of us, Victoria is the most organized. Even in school she was able to crank the most out of herself. She knew what hours of the day she was most productive. She knew how much she could absorb at a sitting, at a reading, in a conversation, on a date. She had a clear image of herself, and there were never any surprises. Victoria always looked and sounded and acted and achieved exactly what was expected from her. Not that she's a robot. God, she's wonderful. Barbara may be earthier and wittier, Phyllis may be smarter, Lori may be more sophisticated, Julia may be more creative, but no one is Victoria. No one has her . . . I was going to say *hair*. No one is as . . . lovely. That's the perfect word for Victoria. She is the loveliest person I have ever known. Even her intelligence and energy are cloaked in loveliness. She exudes complete confidence and at the very same time she's delightfully shy about her many, many strengths. It is a lovely combination. The day we realized we loved each other was a lovely day. It was a lovely time in all our lives and careers and in our perfect circle when we realized that marriage was next.

Now I do not know what is next. Now Victoria is full of surprises. The second night Andrew was here, I put on a cassette and Victoria invited Andrew to dance with her in our living room. He waited for a slow song and then danced so close to her I thought I was hallucinating. I thought I was at the wrong prom, that I didn't know these two high school sweethearts. God, he had his head buried in her neck and she just let him drape himself all over her the same way she just lets him stare at her all the time. She never looks away. She bathes in it.

She has gained weight, too. In her belly. She has a little pot belly now. Her fingernails need filing and polishing. For the first time since I have known her, there is a stubble of hair under her arms and on her legs. Sometimes in bed, I can smell smoke in her hair. I have no proof, but I think I can smell red meat on her breath. Certainly red wine. She is not alternating her outfits the way she used to, either. The laundry and the ironing have piled up.

She is more talkative now, too. In the past, she has been a better listener than talker. Now she initiates potentially controversial conversations about sex and infidelity and the fact that none of us muses and all sorts of provocative topics, which so far I have been able to head off at the pass. Also, she has become Andrew's interpreter, so to speak. When he is silent, she speaks for him and he doesn't take exception. When he is out, she defends his absence and tries to steer the rest of us into talking about him. She seems to have an obsession with making Andrew the center of all our lives. Doesn't she see that I'm trying desperately to keep everyone else out of this—to spare our friends this madness?

Partly because Victoria is seldom at home anymore and partly because she does not act at home even when she is here, we have not had any down time to ourselves in a month. I do not know what's going on in her head. When any of our friends is here and Victoria has managed to come home early enough to spend an hour or two with us, she strikes me as being extremely nervous, on edge, impatient. So far, however, none of our friends has said anything. My imaginative excuses for her late hours and the fact that she does look haggard and over-worked when she walks in are enough to satisfy our friends that Victoria is simply agonizing over some difficult but promising new case at the firm. Anyone who knows Victoria cannot be expected to think anything else. Anyone who has known the real Victoria, anyone who has dated her or roomed with her or studied with her or worked with her or socialized with her or gotten involved in her projects, cannot help but think that her present behavior is prelude to some wonderful breakthrough in work or in life. Secretly I feel that way myself. I spend more and more time trying to resist the cynicism and suspicions my older brother has created in my home. But strangely, it is Andrew even more than Victoria who encourages this in me. He is, after all, my brother. My own flesh and blood. How can I think he would consciously, willfully undermine my happiness? How can I suspect him of betraying me simply because he dances too close with my wife? Or stares at her? God, sometimes he stares at me. When he first met Barbara, he stared at her until she was out the door. But it was not the same kind of staring. His eyes were amused by Barbara. When he stares at Victoria, his eyes are more serious. They exclude everyone and everything else. Me especially. It's almost as if he isn't really there. Only his eyes are there. Burning into Victoria's new flesh and stubble and appetite.

I was only nine years old when he left. But nine years was time enough to form a fraternal bond impossible to dissolve. Now everything else in my life seems to be dissolving. I am completely off balance. My work is suffering. My position in our circle is being compromised. My wife is being seduced away from all our silent commitments. But because I feel that I know Andrew and love him and that he is incapable of hurting me more than he has already hurt me by disappearing from my life for twenty-five years, it's difficult for me to believe that he is truly capable of threatening me and Victoria and our friends. The only possible answer is that he simply does not fit in. He is strange. He is an alien in our midst, and aliens are always menacing at first. But then when you get to know them, it turns out they are even more afraid of you than you are of them. Every book of science fiction I've ever read draws this conclusion. Every bit of intuition leads me to this theory. He has been away for a long time. He has been out of touch. And even before, when I knew him, he was strange. He was always dressing in costumes and communicating in grunts and disappearing into the basement, where he was allowed to smoke and drink beer. To someone of seven and eight and nine years old, Andrew was a dashing figure, handsome and mysterious and intense. But perhaps he was really overweight and foolishly dressed and sadly unable to express himself. Perhaps his aura of mystery and adventure was only the reek of nicotine, hops, and unwashed clothes.

But now—today, tonight, tomorrow, tomorrow night—Victoria should know better than to fall for his aura. She should know better than to stay out to all hours in his new basement and come home reeking of his smoke and his drink and the red meat he feeds her. If anyone is to blame it is Victoria, not Andrew.

4

I HAVE BEEN SO concerned with Victoria's behavior and with
Andrew's intrusion into our lives and with my own failure
to rise above it all and get on with my work that I have
forgotten I am not the only one who has problems. Frank has
failed to get a research grant. Barbara's fiancé is returning to
Pakistan for at least a year. Angel ran away from home and was
found sleeping on a bench in the bus terminal at six in the
morning. Julia postponed her exhibit. Dale did not get what he
wanted for the James Brown book and is thinking of pulling
out of the deal in favor of a novelization of *Superman V*, which
he really doesn't want to write but probably has to because the
money is so good.

We talk about our problems because it feels good to talk and
we comfort each other as no one else can. The last people I
would call about Andrew are my parents. They're three thousand miles away and would only be upset and would offer
absolutely no good advice other than "he's your *brother.*" Perhaps that's the only advice there is.

These are my friends and I need them and they need me.
It is a communal marriage of interchangeable parts and partners, except, of course, for sex. We know each other so well.

We are so comfortable with each other. There is nothing we cannot say or do in front of each other. It is by far the greatest testament to my friends' trust and compassion that they say and do absolutely nothing about Victoria and our houseguest.

It's Dale's turn.

It's my turn to read him his question. "What followed the graffiti 'To do is to be—John Stuart Mill; to be is to do—Jean-Paul Sartre'?"

Frank looks perplexed. I don't understand the question myself and look at the answer. Now I understand.

"What follows these two graffiti," I repeat. " 'To do is to be' by John Stuart Mill and 'To be is to do' by Jean-Paul Sartre? What comes next? There's a third one in the same vein. Only it's a joke."

I'm obliged to give Dale this hint because the question and the answer are rather obscure and none of us really has his mind on the game yet.

"Say them together fast," I tell him. " 'To do is to be', 'to be is to do,' and '. . .'?"

On his way from the kitchen to the john, Andrew accidentally upsets the game board. The plastic pie wedges used as tokens disappear under furniture and into guacamole dip. Andrew does not apologize. He goes to the john. He leaves the door open and we hear him pee into the water in the toilet bowl. We do not hear him wash his hands. Hands that may wind up on Victoria's body.

Our hearts are not in the game and we decide not to continue. The answer is: To do is to be—John Stuart Mill; to be is to do—Jean-Paul Sartre; and do be do be do—Frank Sinatra.

"I'm going out. I've got to go out for something," Victoria says.

"Where are you going, Victoria?"

"I forgot something at the office. Some papers."

"Can't you get them another time?" somebody says.

David says, "You're going to the office tomorrow, aren't you? Otherwise I wouldn't have asked you to have lunch with Angel."

"Victoria," I call after her, "if you really need them, I can get them for you later, honey."

But she is out the door. She has practically run out the door.

"Where are you going?" I ask Andrew.

He has put on his Nehru jacket and is heading for the door. He doesn't answer me.

Can't you even wait the customary fifteen minutes, for Chrissakes? I want to say, wondering how I can keep things from my friends much longer.

"She'll be right back," I say to Barbara, who looks the most alarmed by the sudden departures. "How long did you say Mohammad is going to be in Pakistan?"

These are my friends. When they hurt, I hurt. The problems they are able to share with me are my problems. The intelligence brought to bear is a communal intelligence, the force of our collective perspectives. Together we can solve anything. Together we can make everything turn out all right simply because we are together and that is solution and happy outcome enough. What saves time and makes it so easy and fills the air with respect is that we do not talk down to each other. Each of us uses his or her professional vocabulary, and the others understand completely. We have brought each other along right from the start. They all know that the symphony I am working on is an attempt to discredit polyharmolodics, the last major jazz innovation, although most people think that fusion is the last invention of jazz, and it is, but it is of no real consequence.

We all know the language of computers, of advertising, of publishing, of marketing, of Julia's art, of Michael's laser animations, of each of our specialties.

When it is my turn, I do not talk about Victoria and Andrew. I talk about the drum problem. The synthesizing of tympani. It's tricky. Though one would think percussion is the most easily and naturally synthesized, in fact it's the most difficult, for the very nature of percussion makes the synthesizer superfluous.

As it turns out, Frank has a similar problem. He keeps going around and around in circles because the state of laboratory art is far more primitive than what it's trying to analyze and conquer.

"Do you need more sophisticated equipment?" one of us asks Frank.

"We need less sophisticated diseases," Frank answers.

This is nothing compared to what he faces in his primary work as an epidemiologist. But he does not talk about that, because there is nothing to talk about. His next challenge is completely unknown. A minute before the first case of Legionnaire's Disease broke out, no one knew there was such a thing as Legionnaire's Disease. According to Frank, modern chemical technology and the resurgence of certain ancient sexual practices between humans have made the possibility and variety of new disease greater than at any time in history. We are in a golden age of epidemic.

Barbara's problem is one of the heart. She thinks she is truly in love with Mohammad, the Pakistani investment banker who is leaving for Karachi in one week. He's the first man Barb has claimed to be in love with who has not been a colleague. Or an American.

"I feel like I disregarded a no trespassing sign," she says. Mohammad is her first foreigner and there is a difference. Barb is finding it difficult to talk about him with her usual combination of acid and self-deprecating wit. We can sense that she is uncomfortable. "When I'm with him, I feel like I'm really a-broad," is the best she can do.

We all discuss the possibility of spending our traditional Christmas holiday ski trip in the Himalayas so that Barb can be with Mohammad. Michael is nominated to find out what kind of deal we can get on a charter and to coordinate the trip.

Julia does not believe anyone can solve her problems but herself. As an artist, she tends to be the most reclusive of us all. But we are able to prove to Julia that talking about the difficulties she is having in readying her exhibit can be productive. Phyllis says something that sparks Lori to say something and then as a result Barbara says something that Julia seriously considers. The theme of the exhibit has to do with the failed promise of feminism, and the females in our circle have more to offer on the subject than Julia had thought. When the men join in, there is even more for Julia to consider, for men of our generation are inveterate feminists, even more so than the women. We are determined not to become targets. We are fair and we know we are fair. That is wrong. It is not even a question of being fair. Fairness is not something we are in a privileged position to dole out. Fairness belongs to everyone equally. And it is only when we men are unfairly thought of as being men first and people second that we are even tempted to raise our voices about feminism. Otherwise it is not a problem.

What is a problem is figuring out how to talk to David about his daughter. None of us knows how to broach the subject, and David seems unwilling to bring it up himself. It is a good time for a new batch of margaritas. Dale has found a plastic pie wedge in the dollop of guacamole he has just scooped onto his tostado. Michael suggests we all go to the new Woody Allen movie, but fortunately, Dale and Phyllis have already seen it, otherwise how would I have coordinated the movie timetable with Victoria and Andrew's timetable. I overhear Dale ask David what he thinks Andrew keeps in that beat-up steamer trunk besides those two ridiculous jackets, and I panic. I do not want Andrew to become a topic of conversation. In my panic I come up with a question for David that not only opens the way for a discussion about his daughter but also entertains all of us for the rest of the evening. Where this question comes from I do not know.

"David, can you set up a program on a computer that will solve a personal problem? I mean, can you feed in certain observations, certain hypotheses, and then work it out so the computer will give you a probable solution?"

"You mean like Ann Landers?"

"No, no. I mean . . . well, supposing you were to feed into a program all the . . . this is really working backwards . . . all the indications you could think of that would have led to Angel's running away, all right? Now you've put all this data into the computer—fights with Suzanne, boyfriend trouble, whatever—and you have devised a program that will lead to a certain conclusion. Could that conclusion be *running away from home*, I guess is my question?"

"What you're talking about is predicting or anticipating an effect based on the causes you feed into the design."

"I am?"

"Sure."

"You mean, it's that easy? It's being done, is that what you're saying?"

"In theory, yes. But in execution it works only on an extremely unsophisticated basis. Like a computerized banking machine, for example. You punch in real money and it will result in a new balance. But you're going to get your new balance only if you put real money into the machine. What happens if you put a thousand dollars' worth of bananas into the machine? The trick is in making sure that what you feed into the design is relevant. One irrelevant piece of data will result in a completely specious effect. And you're talking about interpretable data. And one of a thousand possible effects. In theory you can probably do it. But in practice I think what you're talking about is as far off into the future as the Oracle of Delphi is in the past."

The subject has been raised. David is amused by it. He finds it easy to talk about the reasons for Angel's running away from home in terms of relevant and irrelevant input, proper and improper data. She is not doing well at school. Certainly relevant. However, Angel is extraordinarily intelligent and so her poor scholastic performance has to be analyzed further. Am I beginning to see how tricky and delicate and slippery the list of causes can be?

"I see what you mean."

We conclude that it's most likely the pressure of having to perform well that is compromising Angel's innate genius. That plus a natural spirit of rebellion. Are we beginning to see how much the program designer must assimilate and synthesize before he can produce a design that will be as useful to humanity as one good, intelligent friend? The rest of it is a piece of cake—banking statements, hotel reservations, library records, call reports, cross referencing, cataloguing, alphabetizing, sorting—the rest of a computer's work is old hat, nothing to it. But feed it a real exercise in human dynamics . . .

"It would make one hell of a Christmas novelty, wouldn't it? Computer Consultant."

"We'll call him Smart Alec."

"Or Chip."

"Tips from Chip."

David feeds Chip more information about Angel. She is probably feeling his absence. He cannot be a real father on alternate weekends, Thanksgiving, Christmas, and two weeks during the summer. He needs to be there when she needs him to be there, and that is not always possible. But that must be counterbalanced by the fact that she does not need him to be there brawling with Suzanne every night. They can only live peacefully together when they are not living together. What to do?

I am already thinking about the relevant data I can feed Chip concerning Victoria and Andrew. That, I realize, was the source of my inspired question about a computer's capacity to predict or anticipate the probable effect of certain causes. Certainly Victoria and Andrew's sudden disappearance is relevant data. Certainly the stubble of hair under her arms and on her legs is relevant. Certainly the bulge in her belly. Certainly his spooky staring and her bathing in it. Certainly her lack of exercise and late hours and less disciplined diet and . . . I was going to say her duller, more lifeless hair.

This is a good game. We are enjoying ourselves immensely. Two hours ago we were besieged by our problems. Now we are laughing at them. Assigning them relevance. Feeding them to a hungrier and hungrier Chip. Yum. We feel better about ourselves knowing the possibilities of our minor dilemmas.

Victoria is home. She came in with a notebook filled with papers. Andrew stumbled in behind her. He is drunk. He is disheveled. More so than usual.

"You won't believe what happened," Victoria says. She is out of breath with excitement. Her hair smells from smoke.

"We rode downtown to my office and asked the cab driver to wait while I ran upstairs for the papers I forgot. So then I come down and get back into the cab and we drive back here and he realizes that the cabdriver had turned off the meter at my office and then put it back on for the return trip. So he gives the cabdriver the six dollars showing on the meter and the cabdriver says it's twelve fifty because we have to add in the fare for the ride down to my office. Well, he's not about to pay that extra six dollars, so we get out of the cab and the driver comes out after us and says give him his money or else and pulls out a crowbar or something and starts waving it around and he hurries me into the lobby and walks up to the cabdriver and wrestles him to the ground and they fight and the crowbar goes flying down the street and the next thing you know the cabdriver is bleeding all over the place because his face is all smashed up and he puts the cabdriver into his cab and releases the emergency brake and puts the cab into drive and sends the cabdriver, who's practically unconscious, down the street in his cab, which is in drive, and the cabdriver just came to in time to keep from running the light and smashing into a bus."

Everyone is crowding around Victoria. They want to know more. They want to hear the same things again. It is not often they hear an eyewitness account of such a thing. The fare becomes fifteen dollars in the retelling. The crowbar becomes a tire iron. She never mentions Andrew by name. No one but me is thinking about the two hours that elapsed between the ride to Victoria's office and the ride back to the apartment.

5

I HAVE FOUND THREE pieces of evidence this week. I do not know what to do with them.

The first piece of evidence I am ashamed of finding. It was the middle of the night, Victoria was sleeping—snoring, I should add—and I was walking around the apartment because I could not sleep. There on the living room floor was Victoria's bag. I kept staring at the bag. I'd go into the kitchen for a drink of water and come back and stare at the bag. I'd sit down for a while to read and by the end of every paragraph I'd find myself staring at her bag. Never in my life have I spied on Victoria. Never in my wildest dreams would I consider invading Victoria's privacy. Yet I kept staring at her bag as if it contained the antidote to my misery, and before I knew it I was going through the contents of her bag like a burglar.

I found a diary of sorts. Loose pieces of notepaper torn from a pad, sloppily folded, crammed into an envelope. Judging from the handwriting, the thoughts looked to be as desperate and disorganized as the diary itself. I read four words of one entry—not even the first four words, not even four words in a row, just four random words that leaped out at me—and then I stopped myself. It was bad enough I had gone into her bag.

Bad enough I had found this secret diary of sorts. Bad enough I had begun to read something that was never intended for my eyes. Bad enough I had seen my own name in the entry plus three other words, which made little sense by themselves. I could not continue. Tantalizing as my discovery was, I resisted making sense of the four words I should not have read. Resisted any further invasion of Victoria's privacy. Sentenced myself to reconstruct my own sentence out of Victoria's four words.

I found the second piece of evidence the next evening when I came home from yet another unproductive day at the studio those of us who are working on the symphony call the office. I was depressed by my increasing lack of energy and creativity and especially by my sudden lack of basic skill; three times I had misplayed the notes of a certain phrase and thrown everyone else off. Three times we had to regroup and retape. That was just simple lack of concentration, and it depressed me. I poured myself a drink while I played the phone messages. Victoria was going to be late again, of course. Lunch with Angel had been very nice. A colleague at the office phoned to suggest that maybe we should spend a little time away from the symphony since we seemed to be at a dead end at the moment. He had a chance to go to Chicago for a week on a club date and thought going would clear his head. I was not sure what it would do for my head. Angel called to thank Victoria and Nick for lunch.

God.

I sat down on the unmade hide-a-bed. Fell down, rather.

Victoria and *Nick*?

God.

And then I found the third piece of evidence.

My hand was absently roaming the hide-a-bed while I was imagining Andrew and Victoria and Angel at lunch together, and my fingers came upon something silky and moist. It was a pair of Victoria's panties.

There were sticky, half-coagulated bloodstains in them. Also, slightly lighter colored stains of another kind.

The night before—right after Andrew went out again because Victoria and I had gone into the bedroom—I had made a modest overture to Victoria and she told me that she had just gotten her period. And then the next day I come home and find her bloodstained panties in Andrew's hide-a-bed.

God.

I took the panties down to the basement. I put them in the washing machine and waited. Then I put them in the dryer and waited. Then I took them back upstairs and put them in Victoria's drawer.

I folded up the hide-a-bed and moved the furniture back in place.

I erased the phone messages.

I went to the Apple and booted up a new file.

For an hour, I typed in every scrap of relevant data I could think of. I divided the file in half, one half for Victoria, the other half for Andrew. Under their respective names I listed every bit of respective data. Some data, such as their dance together and their lunch together with Angel and their ride to Victoria's office together and his staring and her being stared at and other acts in which they equally participated, I did not know whether to assign to Andrew or to Victoria. Finally, I decided to assign such data to both halves of the file, changing only the pronouns, so that if I typed "He rode with her from our apartment to her office and back" under Andrew's name, I would then type "She rode with him from our apartment to her office and back" under Victoria's name. However, when I reread what I had typed, the communal data proved unsatisfactory. I overtyped the following substitution: "He offered to take her from our apartment to her office and back" and "She invited him to come with her from our apartment to her office and back."

In an hour I had built my file to five pages, single-spaced, Victoria's half almost twice as long as Andrew's. And then my friends began to arrive and I had to leave off. In the few minutes between the announcement that David had arrived and his elevator ride from the lobby to our floor, I had to think of a code name for the file so I could save it and store it. I did not want the code name to look suspicious, and yet I wanted it to reflect the awful nature of the file itself. Something in me made me want this file to stand out from the others and strike terror in my heart every time I called up the list. I took the initial letters of the four words I had glimpsed in Victoria's diary, arranged them and rearranged them in my head, and named my file RAWN, which also stood for RAW Nerve as in striking a raw nerve, and as in the raw nerve Andrew and Victoria were exhibiting by their behavior.

Dale and Phyllis arrived next. And then Julia. And then Frank and Lori and Michael. And then Victoria, of all people. She came in full of energy, full of apologies for being late, full of genuine friendliness and good spirit so typical of the old Victoria.

"Don't worry," she called out as she hurried into the kitchen, "I didn't forget the humble."

Then I remembered: We were celebrating the anniversary of Nixon's resignation. The party menu always consisted of crow and humble pies, and it had been Victoria's turn to provide a humble but edible pie. Someone else, Barbara I think, was responsible for this year's crow, a much more difficult assignment.

"Well, where's Barb?" Victoria asked, poking her head in from the kitchen. "We can't have desert before the main course."

It was such an unexpected and overpowering pleasure to see and hear and feel Victoria's familiar, rightful, comfortable, nearly punctual presence among our wonderful friends that all thoughts of RAWN were driven out of my head. And fifteen minutes later, when the doorman announced that Barbara was on her way up (not Andrew), yet another wave of pleasure and contentment washed over me.

I still cannot believe the crow Barbara served us. There on a huge platter sat not one, but one hundred crows, an assortment of one hundred Japanese tekka maki and kappa maki, each bite-size piece of raw tuna or cucumber and rice rolled in its own sheet of crow-black seaweed out of which Barb had somehow formed little wings and a head. It was a marvel.

We crowded around the platter and with every bite of crow toasted Richard Nixon's political demise, washing away his checkered career and Barb's spicy meal with the Kirin beer I always have on hand, quoting famous Nixon lines, cheering

Sam Ervin, Samuel Dash, Judge Sirica, Archibald Cox, Peter Rodino, booing the bad guys, singing my special parody, "Hell to the Chief," challenging one another to recall who said such and such or what was said by so and so, and then each of us recalling his or her favorite Watergate moment while we rested before dessert. It was like a *Son et Lumière* show: each of us in turn reclining in the spotlight of the game and reenacting another historic scene in this evil, farcical, but finally retributive pageant of democracy in action. I was portraying John Dean, coolly explaining that there was a cancer in the White House, when Victoria came in with her piping hot humble pie.

"God, what the hell is that smell?" someone called out.

"Hey, this is a critical moment in history," I objected, but the spell had been broken.

"What is it?"

"It smells weird."

"Jesus, Victoria."

"Is that what I've been smelling all night? I thought it was coming from outside."

"It's authentic humble pie," Victoria stated proudly. In her slightly pixillated condition, she said "humple pie."

As it turned out, Victoria was correct. It was authentic humple pie. She insisted that we look it up in the compact edition of the Oxford English Dictionary, which Dale and Phyllis had bought us two Christmases ago to settle such disputes. Technically, humble pie is filled with the "umbles" or "inwards" of a deer. The entrails of another animal may be used instead. Victoria used the entrails of a deer. She would not say where she managed to find the entrails or why she bothered to find them. When we reacted to her pie as if it had been a not-too-funny joke, she became defensive. It was no joke. She meant for us to eat her humble pie. She meant for us to understand what it really must have been like for Richard Nixon to resign. She meant for us to truly know what a self-humbling experience life can be.

Barbara took her into the bedroom for a talk. The rest of us tried to play What Kind of Tree, a game in which one player goes out of the room and the remaining players select one of themselves to be "it." Then the player who left the room comes back and has to identify who "it" is by asking a series of questions along the lines of "If this person were a tree, what kind of tree would this person be?" All the other players answer, and from these answers, the questioner must figure out who "it" is. But we could not concentrate.

Andrew came home. The doorman did not announce him. Andrew has his own key. He shrugged in response to our hellos and made directly for the john.

Victoria and Barbara came out of the bedroom. Victoria looked as defensive and disconnected as she had when we rejected her humple pie. Barbara looked a bit ill at ease as well. But in typical Barbi fashion, she made a gesture to us indicating that whatever Victoria's problem was, it was not serious and would take care of itself.

There had been a few hours of blessed relief, of high-spirited fun and food and friends, during which there had been a complete remission of madness, but the day ended as maddeningly as the day before, when I had found Victoria's diary, and that afternoon, when I could not play notes a beginner in a marching band could play, and that evening, when I listened to Angel thank Victoria and Nick for taking her to lunch and I found Victoria's period-stained panties in Andrew's hide-a-bed and I opened up a raw nerve.

"Oh you're not leaving, are you?" Victoria asked with genuine disappointment. And then, with genuine sarcasm, she added, "You haven't touched your dessert."

"Cute," Michael said, kissing Victoria goodbye and blazing a trail for the others to follow.

"I think you should leave, too," I said to Andrew after my friends were gone.

Andrew sat cross-legged on the floor, ignoring me.

"I said I think you should leave."

"You can't throw your own brother out," Victoria shouted at me.

We proceeded to have an awful fight, Andrew and myself, but with Victoria standing in for Andrew.

"He embarrasses me in front of our friends!" I said, wishing I could have summoned up the courage to tell Victoria that it was she who was embarrassing me in front of our friends and now it would be impossible to keep our friends out of it.

"How can your own flesh and blood embarrass you?"

"He makes a spectacle of himself," I said weakly. "He staggers in at all hours dead drunk and makes a spectacle of himself. You ask him a simple question, he doesn't say a word. He doesn't even have the common courtesy to say hello when someone says hello to him. He leaves the door open when he goes to the john. He's drunk and sloppy and vulgar and I want to know why he came here and what he thinks he's doing."

"And he wants to know what in the world he could have possibly done to you that makes you turn against your own brother, your own flesh, your own blood!"

I did not have an answer. I did not have an answer I was brave enough to give. I got up and moved the furniture so that the hide-a-bed could be opened.

"Are you coming to bed, Victoria?"

"Soon."

"I'll wait up for you," I said, and went into the bedroom, leaving the two of them alone.

An hour passed. An hour of maddening silence. At last the bedroom door opened and Victoria came in and I knew Andrew had gone back out again to wherever he goes when Victoria and I are alone together in our bedroom.

I pretended I was asleep. I watched her undress. She was moving slowly and in darkness and my eyes were pretending to be closed; she looked like a dream. First she unbuttoned her blouse. Then she stepped out of her shoes. Then she took off her blouse and reached behind her back and unfastened her bra and her breasts fell ever so slightly and the air filled ever so slightly with the smell of her naked breasts. Then she unhooked her skirt and let it fall to the floor. She was not wearing panties.

Except for her jewelry, she was completely naked. Victoria does not wear a lot of jewelry. She usually wears a watch, earrings, her engagement ring and wedding ring. Sometimes she wears a gold chain around her neck. She was not wearing the gold chain that night. She took off her earrings. She took off her watch. She took off her rings. She sat on her edge of the bed for a moment. Then she lay down. No brushing of her teeth. No washing of her face. No fifty strokes with her hairbrush. No fresh tampon. She lay there very still but breathing very heavily. On her right wrist there was a thin gold bracelet, which I had never seen before. On her breath was the unmistakable stench of authentic humble pie.

6

E VEN IN THE MOST complicated jazz composition, one in which the untrained listener is mostly lost in calculated departures and extemporaneous flights of the soloist's fancy, there are oases of clarity, precious moments of plain and simple melody, riffs of recognizability. These moments are what keep the untrained listener going until he can attune himself to the larger composition. Similarly, any ordinary, recognizable moments with Victoria, with my friends, with my colleagues, are what will keep me going while I try to attune myself to the larger composition, while I try to fathom the soloist's unpredictable flights of fancy. With the exception of Andrew's arrival and Victoria's behavior, the rest of my world is moving along perfectly; it is quite normal, quite recognizable, quite comforting. My friends are still my friends, still working as dilligently as ever on their projects, still making things happen, good things. Victoria and Andrew are but a few unexpected notes in the symphony of life; nothing more than an out-of-place phrase, a discordant phase, bound to blow over, bound to elaborate on itself and rectify itself next time around. What I must do is cling to the greater evidence of sanity. I must preserve the sanctity of sanity. And now that my friends have been drawn into the picture by Victoria's own hand, I can count on their wisdom and support and love.

For the second night in a row I could not sleep. Victoria lay there snoring, reeking of humble pie, leaking onto the sheets. Still, her face was a face I recognized. The delicate eyes, the sharp nose, the thin lips, the fair skin, the fan of her fine blond hair spread upon the pillow in a million single waves. If this person were a tree, I thought, she would be a soft but sturdy white pine in autumn. If she were a flower, she would be the graceful, hardy tulip. If she were a symphony, she would be the Jupiter. But my eyes found hair beneath an outstretched arm and along her calves and venturing down the insides of her thighs, where usually she kept the skin smooth and clean, and none of this hair was familiar to me. Nor was the bulge in her belly. Nor were her uneven nails. Nor was the thin gold bracelet on her wrist familiar to me.

For the second night in a row I roamed the apartment. Again I was drawn to her bag. Again I resisted. I made up a game for myself. I called the game How Then. The hide-a-bed had never been opened and I stretched out on its sofa incarnation.

We fell in love slowly, over a period of five years, after we had become wonderful friends, after we knew ourselves, after we had chosen our paths and traveled irrevocably ahead: How Then could she abandon in such a short time a life she had so carefully and intelligently constructed?

She could not.

She has told me a thousand times how much she loves my ability to converse, to talk to anyone, to tell jokes, recount anecdotes, summarize books and movies, to pontificate on jazz and science fiction, to elaborate, expound, expand, explain, and that more than anything else, this is what she prizes in a man, his ability to say what ought to be said, and that this is what attracted her to me, and that sometimes, at a party, she just sits back like an audience and enjoys watching me perform: How Then can she be attracted to someone who mutters, mumbles, grunts; whose only recognizable oral offerings are the stench of cheap red wine, garlic, spittle, belching, vomit; who, if he converses at all, more than likely talks to himself like the psychotics you run into on the street who are carrying on conversations with imaginary friends and enemies, conversations started twenty-five years ago in smoky, beery basements and are still raging and are still no further along and are still no closer to being brought to a reasonable conclusion?

She cannot.

In matters of sex, she has always been shy, quiet, almost embarrassed by the subject and the act, and yet not frigid, not prudish. The last time we made love—it must have been a month ago—was no different than the first time. We undressed in the dark and lay down next to one another and touched each other intuitively, tentatively. She never made a sound. Sometimes her mouth moved, but no sound came out. Afterward, we held each other very close without saying a word. Once when I asked her if what I was doing to her felt good, she became embarrassed and said that everything felt good. Once I wanted to ask her if she had climaxed, but I knew that she would not be able to answer. Not that she has been cold. Not that she has been unloving. Not even that she has been passive. We have made love in different positions, in different rooms of the apartment, on weekend trips to country inns, in a rented car once, in a sleeping bag once. She is often too tired, but then so am I. She is a slave to the proper amount of sleep and can't stay up much past the hour when the last one of our good friends usually leaves. On a late night of partying, it is not unusual for her to go to bed while our friends are still eating and drinking and playing. They understand. And in the morning, I leave first and she is always rushing through her shower and putting on at least two outfits before she decides which one to wear. But when we have the time and the energy, she is more than a willing, if silent, partner. It is just that sex has never been all-consuming for either of us. It has never been overpowering. It has always been lovely, though. She will wash herself before and after. She will perfume her breasts. She will gargle if we have had stir-fried beef and garlic. She will shift her body according to the slightest pressure of my hand. She will wait for me patiently, or preempt her own quiet passion if I am too quick and cannot go on any longer. She will whisper "I love you" at least once during the act of making love. A

month ago she looked at me so tenderly, so lovingly, so con-
tentedly, and she scrunched up her nose and crinkled her eyes
and put her hand on my cheek and whispered, "I love you"
with such happy sincerity: How Then can she scream an un-
pent passion into the brutish, slobbering face of some lumber-
ing, filthy bear who would manhandle her, invade her, force
her into acts I can't even imagine, defile and devour her, make
her soil herself in his face, make her stink in her sleep, drug
her with deer intestines and thick red wine, and then drag her
off, night after night, past her bedtime, into dark alleys and
back seats of gypsy taxis and seedy motel rooms where the
sheets are still damp from the previous couple, and then pull
her down, morning after morning, onto her own hide-a-bed,
and crouch over her and lick his lips because she has her period
and she is glad she has her period, glad she does not have to
ever wash herself again, glad she can stink and bleed and moan
and scream and break her nails by raking them down his back
in her very own living room?

No.

No, she would not.

Not Victoria.

Her parents were due to arrive. I had forgotten. They were
flying in to spend their daughter's birthday with her. They
were arriving in the afternoon, and we were all scheduled to
have dinner together at her father's favorite restaurant. I wondered if Victoria remembered. I was tempted to wake her and
remind her, but it was five o'clock in the morning. I would
remind her later. I would not have to remind her. She could
not possibly forget that her parents were coming to town. She
is devoted to her parents. She adores her father. She is a friend
and confidante to her mother. I was delighted that they were
coming. I was hopeful that their visit would provide the precious moments of plain and simple melody that Victoria
needed. That I needed.

Family.

Continuity.

Completeness.

I was too hopeful, too excited to go to sleep. I had a sudden
surge of energy. Creative energy. I had an idea for the sym-

phony. So what if it was five o'clock in the morning. Why not go to the office immediately? Why not take advantage of this oasis of clarity? Why not leave before Andrew returned to lurk around the building at my usual hour of departure?

I showered, got dressed, and left Victoria a note. Then I went to the door and, as I was unlatching the lock, heard a key at the other side. Andrew and I opened the door together. My bag was over my shoulder. My hair was blown dry. I looked like I was leaving. I could not pretend that I wasn't.

How did Andrew know?

7

T HOUGH ONLY AN HOUR EARLIER I had tapped a reservoir
of energy, creativity, and hopefulness, Andrew's uncanny timing threw me farther off balance than ever.
How could he have known I would be leaving the apartment
at precisely that unpredictable hour? And yet he had known.
And as a result, when I got to the office, I was predictably
uninspired. There could not have been a more desolate, un-
suitable place for my mood. Surrounded by unlit equipment
and unassembled instruments, I felt disconnected, untuned,
powerless. The tympani problem, the loss of faith by at least
one and maybe all of my colleagues, the increasing attractive-
ness of a more manageable and profitable career in appraising
unreleased cinema, theater, and TV shattered the silence with
shriek after shriek of mental feedback.

I sat down at the disconnected synthesizer and trilled the
soundless keyboard. God, I felt so alone. I could not remember
ever feeling so alone.

I found myself wanting to phone David, wanting to call upon
the intelligence, counsel, and support of my friends. But at the
same time I felt an obligation to protect my friends from this
. . . cancer in my house. I could not expose people I loved and

respected to this contagion. I could not weaken our ranks and jeopardize the sure, bright future we promised.

I decided to approach my friends individually, to give them each a separate, appropriate part of my problem and let them work on it independently and exclusively, like scientists working on a top secret project; in the end, only the one person who can be trusted with knowing the complete secret, who has been cursed with knowing it, sees all the pieces at once and puts them together and has the answer. David's section would be "haywire behavior." That was his specialty. Also, he was once Victoria's boyfriend and he was the only decent person I knew who could tell me if she had played that role—the role of girl friend—differently with him than she played it with me. The question was how to get him to tell me what I wanted to know without compromising our friendship.

I phoned David. He had Angel for the day. Suzanne had asked if he could take her a day earlier so Suzanne could spend a three-day weekend with her ailing mother in Boston, and I told David that I would really like to see him and that it was fine with me if he brought Angel along; she might enjoy the office.

"Does she play an instrument, David? We've got dozens of instruments and pretty fancy recording equipment."

He must have sensed an urgency in my voice because he agreed to come right before lunch, right after he picked up Angel. He had to work in the morning and then he was going to take the afternoon off.

"They owe me some time. Besides, they can beep me if they need me. Unless I can get myself a hundred and twenty-six miles away."

David's beeper has a range of one hundred and twenty-five miles.

"Then I'll see you around noon."

No one is more punctual than David. No one is faster and more precise and more on target than a person whose job it is to keep vital operational and communications systems on line for companies like AT&T and IBM and the whole airline industry and who knows what other powers that be. Of all our friends—in fact, of all the people I have ever known in my life—David is the one person who comes closest to singlehand-edly being responsible for the continuing, smooth, uninter-rupted operation of our society. I mean, if David fucks up, then AT&T and IBM fuck up, and if they fuck up, everything grinds to a halt. He's always talking about moving up into systems design, but he admits that he loves the responsibility of being one of the few people on call in case society breaks down.

At 12:05 I saw the red light bulb in the studio flash on and off several times, which meant someone was ringing the bell on the street. Only three of my colleagues on the symphony were there, and we called a two-hour lunch break. Then I buzzed David and Angel inside. I hadn't seen Angel in a year or more. She had grown into an imposing teenager. Tall, taller than her father, that was the first impression. Very full figured, large breasts, wide shoulders; I could not figure out where she got her bigness from. Her face was not unattractive, but hardly pretty. Angel wore thick glasses and kept her hair in an unflat-tering style for a person her size, and the expression on her face was one of extreme discomfort. She did not look like she wanted to be where she was. Probably she never looked like she wanted to be where she was. When I said hello, she an-swered in a formal, monotone alto. I showed her around the studio. She played piano and I gave her enough of a quick lesson on the synthesizer so she could experiment while David and I went into the engineer's booth for our talk. I only wish now that when I was talking to David I had already had the benefit of having talked to Victoria's parents about the unnerv-ing events that took place that evening. Perhaps then I would have been braver with David. Perhaps then I would have been more candid.

"Listen, David, I just wanted to apologize about the humble pie. Victoria hasn't been herself lately."

"Hey, she was right. We always say we're eating humble pie, and we're eating apple pie or potato pie or chicken pot pie. Victoria put it to us. She was right."

"Have you noticed that she hasn't been acting like herself?"

"What do you mean?"

"Well, I think she's been going through a lot at work. But you know Victoria, she'd never admit that she was under a lot of pressure."

"I hadn't noticed."

"She's put on a little weight. And I think she's probably drinking a bit more than she's used to."

"She's in a booze-intensive business."

"Did you ever know her to put on weight? To let herself go a little?"

"What do you mean did *I* ever know her? You know her as long as I know her. She's your wife."

"But you were her first real boyfriend."

"Anyway, she's always had a weight problem, you know that. She was chubby when I met her and when you met her, too, don't you remember? And whenever she got depressed, she ate her weight in junk food. Hell, doesn't she eat berries now and go to the gym all the time?"

"What do you remember? What was she like those first two years? Do you think she's changed, David?"

"We've all changed."

"I don't mean *grown up*, I mean *changed.*"

"You want to know the truth? Of all of us, I think Victoria has probably changed the least."

"You think so?"

"She was always quiet and shy and full of energy and ambitious and extremely centered and this really great organizer of other people's lives—and she still is. She's the one who kept us all together after graduate school, when it would have been pretty easy to lose touch. She's the one who organized our first few ski trips and that house on the island two summers ago. She's an inspiration, Roger. I'm not so sure the rest of us'd keep our ends up if it weren't for the fact that we'd feel so bad about disappointing Victoria. You know, she's not very aggressive, she doesn't ever want to be or try to be the center of attention, but in her own quiet way Victoria is a force. A real force."

"I know that."

"Well, what's the matter then? Why all the questions? Haven't you two been getting along?"

"Oh no, it's nothing like that. I told you, I think it's just that she's under a lot of pressure at work. And at home, too. You know, it's pretty awkward having my brother around all the time. I think he's getting to her."

"What's his story, anyway? Is he staying with you guys for the duration or what?"

"I don't think he knows himself. I think he's hanging in until someone says that's it."

"Why is he here? Is he working on something? What does he do?"

"He must be working on something, he's always got plenty of cash. Victoria says he's given her a hundred dollars for room and board every week that he's been with us. But I have no idea where he gets the money or what he does to earn it. You've seen what he's like. Ask him a question and somehow he just dismisses it with a grunt or a yes or a no and you wind up right where you started. He's a mystery, David. I'd love to tell you more about him and see what you make of it, but I'm telling you everything I know. He's a mystery. And he's my brother."

I was not sure how to continue talking to David. He hadn't noticed Victoria's odd behavior, and I was not about to spell things out for him. What should I have done, tell him about the hair under her arms and the blood in her panties? It was consolation enough that he had noticed nothing, had suspected nothing, even at my prompting. After all, if a system was breaking down, David would be the first to know. The first to come beeping to the rescue.

David's beeper sounded.

"Duty calls," he said.

He depressed the silencer button, and the number he had to call displayed itself on his beeper.

"Can I use this phone?"

I debated asking him whether or not he could help me design the kind of computer program we had all been talking about the other night, something that could predict the probable effect of the relevant data fed into it. Of course, what I really had in mind was asking if *he* could predict the probable effect if I fed *him* the relevant data. But there was just so much relevant data I could allow myself to reveal. I debated making up the plot of a movie I had a chance to appraise, making the plot comparable to the recent plot of my own life, but I decided that would be too transparent.

"Maybe that'll hold them," David said, hanging up the phone. "We'll know in about five minutes."

When David is beeped, he calls the number shown on his beeper and tries first to solve the problem by giving directions over the phone to the staff facing the problem. If that doesn't work, they will beep David again, and if he can think of no other suggestions to give over the phone, he will have to go to the trouble spot himself and solve the problem in person.

"Anyway, David, he's my brother and I guess I've got to put up with him. And I guess Victoria will just have to put up with him, too."

"Well, what does she say?"

"Actually, I think Victoria likes him. I think she sees something in him we don't. Some kind of dangerous charisma."

"Well, he's certainly not going to win any awards for charm."

"No, but maybe he has a sort of perverse charm that's even more seductive to a woman like Victoria. She has not known many men in her life. Certainly not *any* like my brother. I really think she's amused by him. I mean, Victoria is used to men like us, David. She thinks of us as good, bright people who can make good things happen. She thinks of us as respectful, supportive, appreciative friends. As sensitive and considerate lovers."

"Speak for yourself on that one."

"Well, I'm sure she does. I mean, you were boyfriend and girl friend for two years, David."

"What is that supposed to mean?"

"It's not supposed to mean anything."

The beeper sounded. David depressed the silencer. While the number came up, I asked him if it was so odd for me to think that he and Victoria had been sensitive and considerate lovers for two years.

"Jesus, what the hell kind of question is that to ask me?"

He dialed the number. Through the soundproof glass separating the engineer's booth from the studio, his daughter was watching our mouths move.

"Jesus," he said, waiting for an answer.

"Well, if the two of you weren't sensitive and considerate, I wish you'd tell me, David. It wouldn't matter. It wouldn't matter a bit between us. I would just like to know if Victoria was always . . . reserved. Or if she's only reserved with me. I would just like to know whether she could be completely different with another man than she is with me, and you're the only other man I can think of who might know the answer."

He did most of the listening and reacted to what must have been a very serious and desperate plea for help and said he'd be there as soon as he could.

"What are you asking me?"

"Just to analyze a situation. I feed you certain relevant data and you give me the probable effect."

"I really have to go."

"Just tell me, do you think Victoria is different with me than she was with you?"

"If you're asking me if she's different in bed, then it's a ridiculous question and don't expect me to answer."

"I don't want to know that. What I want to know, in your personal and professional opinion, is if a person like Victoria, a creature of so many fine and dependable habits, can ever betray those habits. Isn't there an analogy in computer language? Aren't there habitual strings that will never malfunction? Aren't there certain indestructible givens, certain *a priori* facts of form, that cannot be changed no matter how haywire a system goes? What I want to know is whether a woman like Victoria, a woman you once knew better than I did, can such a woman change her basic character from situation to situation? Or does she have to be the kind of woman we all think of her as being: solid, unwavering, still the shy, quiet, ambitious, energetic organizer she always was and will be? And however you are able to judge that, whether from two years of dating, fucking, whatever, or from the last fifteen years of wonderful friendship, or all of those years together, I don't care, however you're able to judge, just tell me if you think—if you *know*—whether or not I should be worried about her overeating and her drinking too much and her late hours and that business with the humble pie and Andrew and any other evidence of a change in Victoria's character—should that worry me? Man to man, David, have you ever known

Victoria to be wild and abandoned and disorganized and everything else we would never think of calling her?"

He looked at me like a true friend. He was not angry. He did not look as though I had compromised his privileged information about Victoria. He put his hand on my shoulder and looked radiantly self-assured and said that perhaps I was the one who was under a lot of pressure.

"My guess is that you're overloaded. The symphony, your brother, whatever it is about Victoria that's upsetting you. To answer your question: No, I do not think Victoria is the kind of woman who changes from situation to situation. She is the same wonderful woman today that she was when I first met her. Only better. Smarter. More successful. Happier. But that's just fine-tuning. The system's the same and it's still working perfectly. She is so reliable that the least little glitch seems like a major breakdown to you. That's my personal and professional opinion. Now I really have to go. They're waiting for me."

It was a good beginning. I felt reassured. That's what a friend like David is for. And I'm sure I looked reassured, which must have satisfied him. Our conversation could have gotten out of hand, emotional, even nasty; it could have forged a gulf between us, but instead it brought us closer together. Together we found oases of clarity, precious moments of plain and simple melody, and we clung to them. We are smart. We are in control. We are in the right place at the right time. David is my friend and I love him.

8

DAVID ASKED IF ANGEL COULD hang around the studio while he went troubleshooting, and I was more than happy to repay him for his good advice and support.

I asked Angel if she'd like to go out for some lunch.

"Don't feel you have to entertain me," she said. "I'm fine."

I watched her test the keyboard on the synthesizer and experiment with the controls. She had good reach and excellent dexterity. Perhaps she inherited her agility from David's agility on the computer keyboard. Otherwise there was not much in how Angel looked or carried herself or in the way she talked or acted that suggested her parentage. As a baby, she had had David's curly hair and squinty eyes and Suzanne's cranky disposition. But she had outgrown those traits. At only fourteen, she looked and acted like a person who had come on the scene full-blown, with no history.

"Everything okay now?" I asked her. "I mean about your great adventure the other night?"

"We talked it to death," she said, still fiddling with the keys. "Who?"

"David, Suzanne, me. We've been through it and through it. We must have logged a hundred hours on the subject."

I was collecting sheet music, puttering around the studio,

packing up instruments. She was playing chords, switching channels, varying frequencies.

"And?"

"And they're happy. Nothing makes them happier than the sound of their own voices."

"And you? Are you happy?"

"Sometimes."

"Well, that's something."

"You want to know when I'm happy?"

"When?"

"When most people would be unhappy."

She was on to something on the synthesizer. She had figured out how to warp a classical piece—Wagner, I think—into something that sounded . . . Egyptian maybe. Middle Eastern, anyway.

"When is that?" I asked her.

"When I'm dumb."

"But you're not dumb. Not according to your father."

"I'm not allowed to be dumb in front of David." The synthesizer wowed, and Angel knew exactly which control to ride in order to fix the wowing. "I have to have at least two major thrusts in my life." The Wagner whined. "I have to be at least ten years ahead of myself." It sounded like "Lohengrin" being played on a sitar. "I have to talk to him for hours and hours about things that stop being real as soon as you talk about them."

"What? Like why you ran away?"

"Like anything. Like this conversation."

"You don't really mean that. How are you going to figure anything out if you don't talk about it, Angel?"

"You're right. It's too late for me. I'm a compulsive talker. It's in my blood."

"I know you had a good talk with Victoria at lunch yesterday. You phoned to thank her."

"Is that what you think?"

I stopped whatever I was doing and stared at Angel. She stopped playing.

"You're as bad as David."

I didn't say a word.

"You both think words are these great magical solutions to

everything. If you can put enough words together into enough sentences and paragraphs and put enough sentences and paragraphs together into some theory, then that's all there is to it. You take a simple statement like 'I am not happy' and turn it into a hundred-page analysis that bears no resemblance whatsoever to the simple fact that there is a person who is just plain not happy. She doesn't have a problem. She doesn't have an emergency. She's not into drugs or cults or anything like that. She's just not happy. Except when she's dumb. Except when she stops examining everything and planning for everything. When there isn't one single idea in her head, then she's happy. Then she's just out there . . . all by herself . . . in the silence."

She was the one who mentioned drugs, not me. I moved toward her nonchalantly. Her eyes looked clear. She was neither sluggish nor hyperactive.

"Well, if I'm wrong, then why *did* you call to say thank you for lunch?" I asked, moving close enough to see if there were track marks on Angel's arm. On her right wrist there was a thin gold bracelet identical to the one Victoria had slept in the night before.

"Because nobody said a single word. The three of us sat there for two hours in total silence."

9

I BOOTED UP THE APPLE and loaded RAWN.

Nobody called me about dinner. I had phoned Victoria earlier, but she was out at meetings all afternoon and she never called back. I did not know when Victoria's parents were scheduled to arrive or where they were staying.

It was after seven when I loaded RAWN, and I thought about calling the restaurant Victoria's father would want to go to, an Italian place way downtown specializing in very little atmosphere and enormous portions, but I couldn't remember the name of the place. I did remember where the place was, though, and I thought about just showing up. But then I got lost in my file and before I knew it, it was nine o'clock and there was no point in trying to meet the three of them. Besides, Victoria's birthday wasn't until Monday. I was not missing her birthday celebration. We had theater tickets for Monday night.

I amended RAWN to include the fact that Angel had a gold bracelet like Victoria's and Andrew's. Then I composed possible sentences using the four words I had found in Victoria's diary. From the beginning, I had not been sure whether to read one of the four words as *weak* or *wreck,* and half of my hypothetical sentences used *weak* and the other half used *wreck.* My own name was unmistakable, as were the words *against* and *nature.*

At ten o'clock the doorman called up to announce that Victoria's parents were downstairs. I exited RAWN and waited for them to ring the bell.

Victoria's parents are the greatest living example I know of the theory that opposites attract. Victoria's mother is small; her father is large. Her mother is shy; her father is outgoing. Her mother is pious, realistic, and reveres the world and everything and everyone in it, while her husband places his faith primarily in the almighty dollar and what it can buy you and where it can get you and what it can prove. Consequently, even though Victoria's father is more extroverted, Victoria's mother is more open, more trusting, a quicker, truer friend. And yet it was Victoria's mother who was a bit surprised and unsure about the events of the evening.

"Well, where have *you* been all day?" she said as she came in.

"I was at the studio except for a half hour. And I've been home all night. My friend David came by the stu—"

"How's David?" Victoria's father asked.

"He's fine. He came by with his daughter and left her at the studio while he went on an emergency ca—"

"He still keeping AT&T firing on all four?" her father asked.

"Something like that. Anyway, I brought his daughter to where he was working, and I went right back to the studio. I was there all afternoon," I said, suddenly realizing that Victoria's parents were alone.

"Victoria tried and tried. She called three times from Fontano's," her mother said.

Fontano's, that was the name of the Italian place.

"Where's Victoria?" I asked as casually as I could.

"Oh, they went to the hotel to pick something up for us," her father said.

"They?"

"Victoria and Nick," her mother said.

"Great guy," her father said.

"You had dinner with my brother?"

"Great guy."

"You had dinner with my brother and then you sent him and Victoria to your hotel?"

"Well, we sort of had dinner." Her mother laughed uneasily. "Your father-in-law and Nick disappeared for an hour. They went around the corner to bring back wine before the dinners came . . ."

"How did I know they had a bar in the liquor store?" Victoria's father joked.

". . . and when they got back, their dinners were ice cold," continued her mother.

"But we ate them, didn't we?" her father said triumphantly.

"And took the leftover rolls for the cab ride, too," he was reminded.

"But why did they have to go to your hotel?" I asked.

"We forgot Victoria's birthday present," her mother said.

"Couldn't it have waited?" I asked. "You're going to be here all weekend. Couldn't you have brought the present over tomorrow?"

"We wanted her to have it tonight. She can use it tomorrow. We all can."

"Well, where are they? How long does it take to pick up a package?" I said.

"Oh, they're probably having trouble finding a taxicab at this hour," Victoria's father said as he poked around the living room looking for something new. I never met anyone who loved new purchases as much as he did.

"The remote controller is new," I said. "You feed the information from all your other remote controls into it and this one unit controls everything—the TV, the tape deck, the Apple, the microwave, everything."

"Now, this is something useful," he said, examining the unit. "This is terrifically useful."

"I never saw him take to anybody like he did to your brother. It was a regular reunion. The two of them were like old friends who hadn't seen each other in years and years."

"I wouldn't have thought you two would have all that much in common. What did you talk about?" I asked.

"Oh, you know. The usual thing. Men talk," her father said, still examining the remote control unit.

"I think I'll call. What's the name of the hotel?"

"The Continental," Victoria's father said, looking for something else that was new.

"Would you like something? Tea? Coffee? A drink?" I asked while I dialed information for the number of the Continental.

"Not me."

"I'm fine."

I phoned the hotel and asked for room 714. Victoria answered after the seventh ring.

"Where the hell are you?" I whispered.

Victoria told me where she was.

"Obviously I know where you are. I meant why are you still there. Why aren't you leaving? Your parents are here waiting for you, Victoria. Is Andrew with you?"

Andrew was in the shower. They were going to leave as soon as he was finished.

"Oh that's fine, Victoria. Just fine. Don't we have a shower? Listen, I think we better have a talk about something. Later, tomorrow, first chance, I don't care when. But soon."

Twenty minutes later, Victoria arrived home without Andrew.

"Where is he?" her father asked with more disappointment than I had ever heard in his voice.

"You sure you wouldn't like something?" I asked everyone again. "How about you, Victoria?"

She said she wanted a beer. At eleven o'clock at night. A beer. Victoria, who reluctantly used to agree to a sociable glass of beer or wine now and then, who was always watching her weight, who was always ready for bed by the first commercial break in the eleven o'clock news, that same Victoria wanted a bottle of beer at eleven o'clock. Eleven-oh-nine.

"Well, then I'll have one too," her father said. "Victoria, I love the new remote controller," he added in the same breath.

"Don't you want to open your present, darling?" her mother asked coyly.

"Why didn't he come back? Where did you say he went, Victoria?" her father asked again, still not over his disappointment.

"Open it up, Victoria."

"I figured he'd come back with you."

"You can use it tomorrow. We all can."

"I'm sure you'll see him again, Daddy," Victoria said, climbing onto her father's lap and mussing his hair and tickling his ear. She adored him, but she never behaved that way with him.

Her mother got up and went over to the large shopping bag Victoria had brought back from room 714 in the Continental Hotel. The room she had gone to with Andrew. Andrew and my wife. In her very own parents' hotel room. With her very own parents' blessing.

"What's this?" her mother asked. "Where's your present?"

"Isn't it in there? Don't tell me we forgot it after all that?" Victoria said innocently, cuddling with her father.

"There's just bedclothes in here. I don't understand."

"They're yours. Since I was coming back alone, we thought the two of you might as well stay here tonight, Mom. Like always."

"But what about your present?"

"I guess we forgot. I'll run over for it tomorrow. Anyway, we can still open a present. There's a present in this apartment for me," she said, climbing out of her father's lap and going into the foyer, where Andrew kept his beat-up steamer trunk, "and I've got permission to get it and open it right now."

I was not angry. I was not confused. The background of madness that had been plaguing me since Andrew's arrival had finally become foreground. Instead of being angered and baffled by every little evidence of madness, I suddenly felt drawn into the whole sordid machinery of madness. Whatever had gone haywire had taken over. No longer was I looking for square pegs; I was looking for square holes to fit them into. Suddenly I felt like a player instead of an observer. I, too, was disappointed that Andrew had not come back with Victoria. Not because he was an old friend I hadn't seen in twenty-five years, but because I wanted to verify the entry I had found in RAWN; I wanted to see if he was wearing a gold bracelet on his right wrist that matched the one on Victoria's wrist and the one on Angel's wrist. And I wanted to see the present Victoria had gone to get from Andrew's trunk. And I wanted to read

Victoria's diary. And I wanted to talk to my friends, because
suddenly shame and danger were not factors, to find out what
my friends had to say, particularly Frank, who could tell me if
people who find out they're going to die—AIDS victims, for
example—if suddenly they develop a curiosity and then a fasci-
nation and then an obsession with the disease that is destroying
them. Do they suddenly feel as though they are an integral
part of the disease itself and therefore deserve the right to be
let in on every little twist and turn the disease takes, on all the
ways it survives and thrives and spreads?

"I bet you're wondering why I of all people am willing to let
a hotel room that I'm paying for go to waste. Because I'm *not*
paying for it. I did business this afternoon and I'm doing business Monday and the office is paying for the whole shebang."

Victoria came back into the room with a package as big as
her head. It was carefully wrapped in a foreign newspaper, and
Victoria unwrapped it just as carefully, finding each little snip
of tape, peeling it back as though she were defusing a bomb,
slowly, slowly trying to avoid tearing the old, yellowed, fragile
paper printed in an incomprehensible alphabet.

"What is it?" her father wanted to know.

"Who is it from? Is it from you?" her mother asked me.

"Who do you think? It's from Nick," her father said. "Look
at the paper. That's Indian writing. Nick was there. He's been
places."

When Victoria finally removed the last piece of tape, the
wrapping came apart into two sections. She managed to keep
the object within the paper out of our sight for a small eternity
while she cast first eyes upon her present. From the expression
on her face, she was flattered and unnerved.

"Well, let *us* see it, Victoria," her father whined.

She placed the present in her lap and let the newspapers fall
away. Now it was our turn to be unnerved.

The present was clearly an ancient artifact, a carved totem
of a face, and the face was even more clearly Victoria's.

10

I AM BEING TOLD NOTHING. And yet nothing is being kept from me. The morning after Andrew sat in for me at dinner with Victoria and her parents and then warmed up room 714 in the Continental Hotel and then one-upped everyone else with his extraordinary birthday gift, I awoke to find Victoria gone. The note she left explained that she had gone to the hotel to get her parents' present and would be back soon. What the note did not say was that on a rainy Saturday morning, Victoria and Andrew were not at home and the legitimate tenants of room 714 were blissfully and ignorantly asleep on our hide-a-bed.

Her parents must have been tired out by their flight of the day before. They were still asleep after I awoke, read Victoria's note, showered, dressed, and put up Mr. Coffee. They were forced to touch each other in their sleep by the narrowness of the hide-a-bed, the same hide-a-bed that had nudged Victoria and me into each other's arms in the early days of our marriage, the same hide-a-bed, no doubt, that had nudged Victoria and Andrew into thrilling stolen moments while I was on my way to the office.

After her parents woke up and I gave them a small breakfast

of toast and fruit and coffee, Victoria returned. Her present was a large straw picnic hamper filled with heavy plastic wineglasses, wicker holders for paper plates, stainless steel utensils, blue and white checkered linen napkins, and luxurious provisions such as French mustard, Spanish olives, and Swiss chocolates. Unfortunately, the chance of a picnic was rained out, and Victoria spent the day shopping with her mother. I went to lunch with her father, who talked about the great career David was forging in computers and how it was too bad that opportunity hadn't existed for him when he was David's age. I think fathers always best remember the first real boyfriend their daughter brings home, even if she winds up marrying someone else. After lunch, Victoria's father went to the hotel and I shopped for dinner and then went home and cooked pasta primavera for the four of us. It was a delightfully uneventful evening. We ate, played Hearts, talked about terrorism, the Japanese automotive industry, Victoria's aunts, uncles, and cousins, the one movie all four of us had happened to see over the past six months, the promised excitement of the networks' ceaselessly promoted new TV lineup for fall, and other harmless topics. Andrew's name never once came up. Nor Nick's. The forecast for the next day was sunny, and we decided to make it an early evening so we could get off to an early start in the morning. I called Frank and canceled our plans for a Sunday evening birthday party and asked him to call the others.

We did get sun the next day, and the four of us piled into the car I had rented and drove out of the city to a public park complete with picnic grove, hiking trails, biking trails, a lake with boats for rent, a small mountain, lovely lookouts, and expanse enough to feel uncrowded by other refugees from the city.

By the time we got ourselves settled, it was almost time to open the picnic hamper. Victoria had shopped early for barbecued chicken and deli sandwiches, and I had packed leftover pasta primavera into one of the handsomely designed plastic containers that came with the hamper. It was a lovely summer's day and we luxuriated in the late morning sunshine and fresh air. We had a cassette player with us and books and the picnic lunch, and there was a place just beyond the lake to buy cold drinks. All of us felt contented and quiet. It was almost too good to be true, and more than once I shuddered, the way you shudder and wake up when you're dreaming that you're falling, because this peaceful, comforting countryside seemed the perfect setting for the sudden disruptions I had gotten used to in my life since Andrew showed up at our door. Though I hadn't felt so relaxed since he showed up, there were several moments all during the day when I half expected Andrew to spring out from behind some beautiful big shade tree and drag Victoria off into the woods. But he never did. I hadn't seen him since early that day when somehow he had known that I would be leaving for the office almost three hours ahead of schedule. Except for those moments when I shuddered, I was not thinking about Andrew. Not directly, anyway. But even in tranquility, even in his absence, Andrew found a way to make his presence felt.

I watched Victoria. She looked very much at home in the outdoors. I watched her walk by herself and then with her father. At one point, he put his arm around her. She seemed thoroughly happy and carefree, like her old self, with her family. She wore khaki shorts that flattened the bulge in her stomach and a skimpy black halter that showed off her breasts. But the halter revealed the unshaved hair under her arms, and that depressed me until I could divert my attention. I watched her face for an hour while she napped, and I marveled at the uncanny resemblance between Victoria's face and the ancient totem Andrew had given her for her birthday. The whole time I stared at Victoria's face, I could not get the carved face out of my mind.

I am not very good at describing things. I leave that to Dale, who can blind you with a description of the glint off Superman's teeth. I am better at taking a good story and improving it in the telling with metaphors and similes and anecdotes. I need the help of references. I need the whole of my knowledge, my entire store of memory and information, from which I can summon up another picture or another experience to enliven the one I am trying to communicate. How then can I describe Victoria's face in a manner that will make anyone who does not know her appreciate the uncanny likeness captured in Andrew's totem?

The things I can say have nothing at all to do with an accurate description of Victoria's face but rather of how her face, at certain times and in certain situations, has made me feel. While watching her dozing or peacefully lying in the grass listening to one of the cassettes we brought along on the picnic, I realized that whenever I look at her, I am actually looking at remembrances of her.

There have been times, many times, when her eyes have made me feel larger than my real size. Their openness and the wonder pouring out of them have magnified me to unreal proportions, have made me feel that I am enveloping her like the sky and that I am floating above her and all around her and that she can see nothing but her husband no matter where she looks. It is flattering but also unnerving, for some of those times I have felt as though I could not escape her gaze.

In a photograph I remember, Victoria is smiling broadly. It is a photo of just her face, and her smile overpowers everything else. She is not laughing; she is smiling to herself. Her teeth are like a gate no one can enter. I do not like when she smiles like that. I like it when she is serious. I can't be sure of her smile, I can't trust it.

There are other photos. Childhood snapshots she keeps. Pictures of herself as a little girl, her face practically unchanged except for the length and style of her hair. Her hair is her most wonderful feature. It is very thin and usually very curly because Victoria has it permed. But what I am most attracted to about her hair is the fact that it reveals her rather than conceals her. It tends to disappear from her face when she is lying on a pillow. Her hair fans out and away from her forehead and ears. She cannot wrap herself in her hair and conceal the little looks of pleasure on her face. Or the little looks of dutiful compliance. Unlike her smile, which obscures the woman behind it, Victoria's hair illuminates her. By its tendency to recede into the background, it outlines the true proportions of her head and what is going on inside it.

Once on a beach, I took off my sunglasses and looked at her face. The sun revealed clusters of faint freckles on her skin.

Ordinarily I would not describe Victoria as being freckled. But on that beach in the glare of the sun, without my sunglasses, the freckles were there. Even in their faintness they were so vivid to me that ever since, I've been unable to stop expecting to feel them when I touch her cheek. I expect her skin to be faintly bumpy with them. But it never is. It is always amazingly soft and smooth.

There are only two things I can say about her nose: one, that it is ever so crooked, and two, that she scrunches it up when she tells me she loves me.

Were her open, magnifying eyes and her broad private smile and her halolike hair and freckled cheeks and scrunched up nose carved onto the totem Andrew had given her? That is not important. What is important is that the totem reflected these images of Victoria so accurately that I could not imagine the artist did not know her. I could not imagine that Andrew did not know her.

We stopped for hot dogs on the way back and got home late. I dropped Victoria off at the apartment and dropped her parents off at their hotel on my way to return the car. The rain the day before had moved our picnic forward a day and made us call off the birthday party we were going to have that night. All our friends would have been there. Lori would have cooked Spanish. We would have played our games. We would have toasted Victoria and celebrated her birth and all of our good fortunes in knowing one another and being with one another at such a joyous time. But instead, Victoria and I spent the balance of the evening by ourselves. It was the first time in a long time that we were alone. Neither of us had much to say. By the first commercial break in the eleven o'clock news, Victoria was fast asleep.

11

A S USUAL, THE NEXT MORNING I awoke before Victoria, left while she was in the shower, and met Andrew outside the building on his way home.

"Haven't seen *you* for a while," I said casually, sarcastically, barely stopping, suddenly extending my hand to shake his without giving him time to think. His hand shot out automatically. I shook it and saw the thin gold bracelet beneath the frayed cuff of his Mao jacket.

I decided to buy another birthday present for Victoria. Originally, the theater was going to be her present, that and dinner afterward. But Andrew's outrageous gift and the fact that obviously he had given her the bracelet as well made me want to give her something else. Something more.

I had an idea I hated, but I tried selling it to myself and it kept me from thinking of anything better for most of the morning. The idea was a ring inset with Victoria's birthstone. I looked up her birthstone in my pocket calendar. It was a carnelian or sardonyx, neither of which I had ever heard of. I had to look them up in a dictionary. Carnelian wasn't in the dictionary. Sardonyx was a form of chalcedony, and I had to look that up. Then I got the Yellow Pages and looked up jewelers in the neighborhood of the office.

I called four jewelers and plotted my course of shopping according to their addresses. That done, I tried to keep my mind on the drum problem. But I was bothered by the idea of a birthstone. There was something obviously personal about such a gift—personal to at least one twelfth of the population—but there was also something stupid about it. Something as arbitrary and unrealistic as one's horoscope. What made a carnelian or a sardonyx more suitable for Victoria than any other stone? I looked up the birthstones of my friends to see if theirs suited them. David was not particularly an opal. Julia was more the deeper red sardonyx than the emerald she was supposed to be. Frank was definitely not a ruby. I did not see myself as a garnet. Only Barbara's diamond was a possibility. The rest seemed about as appropriate as those gift ideas for specific anniversaries, a list of which followed the birthstone listing in my pocket calendar. Why, for example, was something made of wood the proper gift for a fifth anniversary? Even a horoscope made more sense than that. At least horoscopes were written cleverly enough so that you could read your real personality traits into the analysis. I was sure that the whole idea of birthstones had been devised by an association of jewelers to promote the year-round sale of their gems. Nevertheless, I did not have a better idea for a gift. Right before lunch, however, I received a call from my Wall Street contact, who asked if I was interested in appraising three unreleased films, and that gave me the better idea I was looking for.

I had met my contact five years ago through one of my colleagues. The colleague and the Wall Streeter were old friends, and the Wall Streeter had called to ask my colleague if he wanted a shot at an appraisal. The movie in question needed to be appraised by someone well versed in the trends of popular music. The movie was one of the first to be built around an assortment of rock songs, and my colleague played rock and jazz and just about everything else. But my colleague was not interested in churning out a ten- to fifteen-page financial appraisal. His friend told him that it was relatively easy, that prototypes existed, and that this was not a bad way to earn good money. But my colleague took one look at the prototype and ran the other way. When the Wall Streeter asked him if he knew anyone else in the music field who might be interested, my colleague suggested me. And when I took a look at the prototype, I jumped at the chance. I knew it was something I could do. I knew if I ran into trouble, I could count on David's computer know-how and the fact that Dale, who at one point in his life wanted to be an actor and then wanted to be a producer, had read and saved every issue of *Variety* for all the years that I had known him. So I took the assignment and worked it out on David's computer and, with his help and with Dale's help, in one month I made eleven thousand dollars.

I discovered that that appraisal and all appraisals are needed for bookkeeping reasons. Theoretically, an accountant or a tax lawyer can do the job, but the producers always seem to want a creative touch, and, I suppose, a good accountant or a good lawyer does not want to deal in theoretical numbers. Ultimately, the appraisal hardly ever influences what actually happens to the product. It is something required by law and then filed away while the producers do whatever they were always going to do to earn back their investment. I guess that in a really good appraisal there might be an idea or two for profit opportunities that the producers overlooked, but basically an appraisal is something that exists for the sake of worried investors.

For two years I have been toying with the idea of quitting my music and working full time at appraisals. I earn a very small income from my music. Occasionally I play recording dates that require a synthesizer, but unless you get in on a big-time, multimarket commercial with a heavy media schedule, the residuals are only moderate. And the big-time commercials are usually made by conservative companies for conservative products, and no one wants the highly contemporary, sometimes jarring sounds of a synthesizer interfering with slice-of-life marketing for soap or dog food or whatever. As for the symphony, we have a sort of vague promise from someone at Verve that when we are done with it—and if it has a successful performance—it will be recorded and released and distributed. But when is the last time a jazz symphony went platinum? That work is really for art's sake and I never counted on its bringing in much money.

The only two things preventing me from appraising full time are the lack of assignments and the time it would take away from the symphony to build myself a dependable clientele. But the symphony was not going well and now suddenly there were three appraisals and I had a terrific chance to build a portfolio and a reputation in the business. Victoria is up to thirty-two thousand in her job as a paralegal. I average fifteen thousand from my recording dates and whatever more I can make when an appraisal comes my way. But so far I haven't gotten more than two appraisals in one year and they are not always worth eleven thousand dollars. So at best we can expect a combined income of less than fifty thousand. That isn't bad, but it's undependable. And my contribution is not enough to support us if Victoria should become pregnant and want to quit and if we should want to buy a house. She will not come right out and say it, but she would love me to develop a clientele and go into appraising full time. I could still play recording dates and probably develop at least a fifty or sixty thousand-dollar appraisal business as well. She will not say it, though, because she knows how important the symphony is to me. But if ever the time was right for me to make the decision, it's now. And what an excellent birthday present it would make.

I wanted to present my decision to Victoria in some wonderful way. I wanted her to be able to unwrap it the way she unwrapped her carved totem. But instead of some mysterious relic from the past, my gift would be a clear and unequivocal symbol of the future. It would be a business card. It would be white and rectangular and official. ROGER ABEL, THEATRICAL APPRAISALS, MY ADDRESS, MY ZIP CODE, MY TELEPHONE NUMBER. I would have a thousand printed up and put in a box and wrapped in gift paper.

The Yellow Pages listed dozens of printers in the neighborhood of the office. I remembered that one of the questions in our game was What is New York's largest industry? and that the answer was the printing industry. First I called all the companies that had bought ads in the Yellow Pages. But none of them could print and deliver business cards in an afternoon.

Eventually I called every printer, in alphabetical order, regardless of where they were located, and not one of them could do the job in time for Victoria's birthday. Not even for a price.

I was not at the office in the afternoon. I was with my Wall Street contact. He gave me the three films on three VHS cassettes. He gave me formal and informal background regarding the three productions and he gave me my schedule for each one. If Victoria had called the office to tell me she would be late for the theater, she would not have found me in. I was going over the details on the three appraisals and cultivating a more professional rapport with my contact. I told him I had decided to do this work full time. He thought it was an excellent idea and assured me that I could depend on him for more and more assignments while I was developing a broader range of expertise. So far he had only given me music-oriented projects to appraise, but he said he had every confidence that I could branch out and would try me on the first appropriate project that came along. He gave me suggestions and offered to lend me copies of appraisals he thought were well done so that I could study them. I was also greatly encouraged when he mentioned that I did not have a whole lot of competition in the field, that there were only a handful of people who appraised full time and they were all very successful.

I was actually thinking about how I would spend my first million when the lobby lights flashed. Victoria still hadn't arrived; the show was beginning. I left her ticket at the box office and went inside. The lights went down and six actors took the stage. They played three married couples, characters roughly our age, living in the city, all of whom were having marital difficulties. One couple was honeymooning and already questioning their decision to have gotten married. Another couple was celebrating a second blissfully successful year of separation. The third couple was waging a furious and hilarious nonstop war of insults and threats. The play was in two acts, and the first act introduced these relationships. Interestingly, I found myself making the kind of mental notes a reviewer might make on paper. Things like *the dialogue is contemporary and funny.* And *lampooning of self-help groups is right on target.* And *the characters are really caricatures, but the audience, myself included, seems to recognize and empathize with every one of them.* Things like *wonderful set, good props, great choice of incidental music, likable actors, especially the newlyweds.*

I realized I was looking at the play as if it were the subject of an appraisal, and I was terrifically excited by how quickly and dramatically my decision to go into appraising full time had sharpened my perception. I felt in control of the play, in control of my life, in control of the future.

By intermission I was still sitting next to an empty seat, and I went outside with the smokers to wait for Victoria. The theater was all the way downtown; she would have to arrive by taxi from her offices uptown. Because of all the little pocket parks and squares and traffic patterns in the area, I determined that the taxi would have to come east on the side street down the block from the theater, and I strolled in that direction. Traffic was heavy. There were a lot of occupied taxis that did not stop. A lot of people were out walking in the sticky summer night. After five minutes I strolled back toward the theater and caught sight of Victoria heading for the theater from the opposite direction. She was not, I thought, walking very quickly or purposefully. Her hair was incredibly windblown.

"I called you, but you weren't there. I had to work late," she said without apology.

"Happy birthday," I said. I kissed her on the cheek and gave her the package that I had in my pocket. "This is for you," I said sweetly.

We still had a few minutes before the second act and I told her to go ahead and open the package. She tore away the glossy red wrap in an instant and let it fall onto the street. I was picking the torn wrap off the street when she opened the little box and said, "Oh, how pretty." She said it as if it weren't hers, as if she were looking at it in the window of a shop.

"If it doesn't fit, we can have it resized," I said as I walked toward a nearby trash receptacle.

Victoria slipped the carnelian ring onto a finger and admired her outstretched hand.

"It's a carnelian. That's your birthstone."

"Is it? I never knew what my birthstone was."

"Do you like it?"

"It's lovely," she said somewhat more enthusiastically.

"If you don't, I can return it."

"It's lovely," she said, trying the ring on another finger. It was loose on that finger, too.

"There's something nice about having your birthstone, don't you think?"

The lights in the lobby began to flicker.

"The play's terrific," I said as we followed the smokers back into the theater. "I have another present for you, too. I'll tell you about it over dinner."

We took our seats and I gave Victoria a quick synopsis of the first act, but the second act turned out to be so completely dependent upon everything that had come before it that I found myself whispering explanations all the way through. My part was almost as big as the actors'. Victoria did not ask for these explanations; I volunteered them. I kept leaning over and whispering into her ear. She sat looking straight ahead. Occasionally she laughed politely. That was all right. The second act was not as funny as the first. Once in a while she touched the ring I had given her.

In the end, the three couples had exchanged roles. The couple that had been separated finally divorced; the man married an incidental character, and on their honeymoon they began questioning whether they should have gotten married. The original honeymooners grew to despise one another and began waging their war of words. The third couple, of course, wound up separating and improving their relationship, although the audience knew it wouldn't last. Most interesting to Victoria, she said, was that after all the theatrical smoke had cleared, there was still one woman whose future was unaccounted for. The divorcee.

As we filed out of the theater, I asked Victoria what she felt like eating. But we were not to make our own plans. Outside the theater, we were surprised by a loud, off-tune ale house rendition of "Happy Birthday, Dear Victoria" sung by David, Dale, Phyllis, Frank, Lori, Michael, Julia, Barbara, and a short, slight, dark-skinned, well-dressed man who did not know the words. That was Mohammad.

Victoria loved her birthday song and the surprise of all of our friends and the huge carrot cake Phyllis had baked and carried through the streets, the thirty-four candles flickering in the night, waiting to be blown out. Even some of the theatergoers and passersby stopped to sing along and wish Victoria a happy birthday. God, I thought, what a good bunch. Always in the right place. At the right time. With the right idea.

"Hey, this is just the beginning, gang!" David shouted. "We've got big plans! First to Charlie's!" And David began hailing cabs.

"Just wait," Lori said to me, laughing and teasing.

Frank and Michael and Dale helped David hail cabs to take us to Charlie's, a new mesquite restaurant Dale and Phyllis had heard was terrific. The restaurant wasn't far, and Victoria kept saying we should walk. We'd have to walk through a rough neighborhood, but there were eleven of us, and nine of us had been drinking all night, and the mood and the moon and the beer emboldened us.

The women walked together and the men walked behind, the two obstreperous groups shouting, laughing, singing, swaying, prancing and dancing along ominously quiet streets. The shadows across the street or coming at us or sneaking up from behind probably belonged to hustlers, dopers, youth gangs, and other *wonderful* characters. But we were pretty wonderful ourselves, and no one bothered us.

The parade turned into a party at Charlie's. We took over a corner section of the back room. The decor reminded Dale of Los Angeles, with its mirrored walls and wicker chairs and murals of swans and palm trees. We ordered carafes of red and white house wine and studied the chic menu. Although everyone wanted one of the three highlighted specialties of the house, we agreed to order eleven different appetizers and entrees so we could sample more of what Charlie's mesquite grill had to offer. Mohammad was the exception. He only wanted an appetizer. He was very definite about that. We could see that he was a person of very definite ideas, and that once he made up his mind about something, it would be useless to try to change it. He spoke quickly and correctly in a high voice and sounded excited when he talked. And yet, in his pale blue three-piece gabardine suit, he looked the picture of a calm, cool, and collected businessman. Barb had told him we were considering taking our traditional Christmas ski trip in the Himalayas, and Mohammad had done a little research for us. The place to go, apparently, was a resort called Shangri-La. They had just put in a ski lift and trails; the accommodations were the best in the area; it was not expensive (except to travel there), and a cousin of Mohammad's was part owner.

Between courses, we played a round of Botticelli. Mohammad said he preferred to watch. One of us—that night it was me—had to think of a famous person and provide the others with only the first initial of his last name. Then each of the others had to think of a famous person whose name began with the same initial and give me a clue to his person's identity. If the clue was broad enough that I could come up with an acceptable answer, even the wrong one, then no one got to ask me a question to discover my mystery person. For example, if my famous person's name began with the letter S and a clue given to me was "an English poet" and I guessed "Shakespeare," then even if the person who gave me the clue had been thinking of Shelley, no one got to ask me a question. But if the clue had been "author of 'To A Skylark,'" and I said "Shakespeare," or if I had no answer at all, then the group had a chance to ask me a question that could be answered by yes or no. No one knew why the game was called Botticelli; maybe the originators of the game happened to use Botticelli as their first mystery person.

The letter I gave was V—in honor of Victoria's birthday, I said—and my mystery person was Gloria Vanderbilt; but we were all so giddy that the clues were silly, and it took us until dessert to go around the table once, and still no one had guessed Gloria Vanderbilt. The game ended in a friendly dispute about whether or not Vincent Van Gogh was an acceptable V or should have been a G.

"This was not a particularly good game of Botticelli to watch," someone apologized to Mohammad.

But it was all in great fun, and we all loved the restaurant and the food and the night and each other. It was nearly midnight and not even Victoria was tired. I had totally forgotten about talking to her about my plan to go into appraising full-time, although I'm sure that decision contributed to my good mood and energy, along with the fact that I was surrounded by my friends. And that Victoria was there. And Andrew was not.

Over coffee I brought up the subject of birthstones. Victoria showed everyone her ring. I took out my pocket calendar, and we went around the table talking about each of our stones. Barbara said she was going to wear a diamond in her navel from now on. Everybody laughed but Mohammad, and Barbara quickly changed the subject. When the bill arrived, David made his announcement.

"And now for the evening's final entertainment . . . Big Tubs!"

He reached into the leather shoulder bag he always carries and produced a handful of prepaid admissions to Big Tubs, the California-style hot tubs we sometimes frequented, although all of us had never gone at once. At most, six of us had gone together. The plan to go to the tubs was a surprise only to me and Victoria, although Mohammad looked as though he didn't understand what in the world David was talking about. I looked at Victoria to see her reaction. We had gone to the tubs maybe a half dozen times, and Victoria had never said she didn't enjoy going, but I always felt she just tolerated the tubs for the sake of not spoiling everyone else's enjoyment. There was a whirlpool she always used at her health spa, which could explain why going to Big Tubs never appealed to her the way it appealed to the others. But she was smiling when I looked at her. Wide awake and smiling.

Our friends divided the check, and our party turned back into a parade. This time we walked in smaller groups. Barbara walked with Mohammad and talked to him the whole way. It sounded like she was explaining Big Tubs to Mohammad, what you did there, how relaxing it was. It sounded like she was trying to convince him to come along with us. Michael left us at a subway station. No one was surprised. He had said all along that he had to be uptown for an all-night editing session. He was working on a rock video, and in order to keep expenses down, he had to book the studio after hours. He kissed Victoria goodbye. Michael has never gone to Big Tubs with any of us.

Big Tubs was in a friendlier neighborhood. We went inside through the attractive, well-lit facade and were warmly greeted by the Oriental hostess, who had been expecting us. She handed us our towels. Mohammad looked particularly out of place in his three-piece gabardine suit, a pink terry cloth towel thrown over his shoulder like one end of a toga. The hostess led us down a long hallway toward room 6, which was the largest and could accommodate twelve people comfortably. On the way, we passed all the other rooms and a bathroom. Although we had been a rowdy bunch only minutes before, the soft lights, the faintly perfumed air, the exotic music, and the submissive behavior of our costumed hostess relaxed us and quieted us as we walked the length of the thick Oriental runner extending down the hallway. Our hostess opened the door to room 6 and turned on the lights. Then she began to remove the lightweight tarpaulin that covered the tub. Frank and I made a start to help her, but she became very embarrassed and politely insisted that she uncover the tub by herself. She did so quickly and easily, folding the tarpaulin into a size she could carry under one arm, while she pointed out the tape deck, the shower, the lights, and the controls for the tub. When she pressed a button, the water in the tub bubbled up immediately.

"Please keep door locked," our hostess said as she set our timer for one hour and left us.

David had brought tapes and inserted a Talking Heads cassette into the deck. Mohammad excused himself and went to the bathroom. By the time he came back, we had all undressed and slipped into the tub and were submerged in the hot and churning water up to our collarbones. Mohammad was still dressed, the towel still slung over his shoulder toga-style.

"Come on in!" Barb said. "I saved you a spot." She was referring to the space next to her on the built-in wooden platform along three sides of the tub. At its greatest depth the water was probably only three, three and a half feet deep. If you sat on the platform, you were underwater up to your neck. There was another platform, outside the tub, a wooden deck area for lounging, because you weren't supposed to stay in the hot water for too long a time.

"I don't think so," Mohammad said, but his voice left room for him to be persuaded.

"Come on, it's fantastic," Dale said.

"Somebody said that it happens all over the world/I do believe that it's true," Talking Heads sang.

"Haven't you ever tried it, Mohammad?" Lori asked.

"I could use about three days of this," Julia moaned.

"I don't think so. Not for me," Mohammad debated.

"And the sun's coming up/And we're doing all the things that we should," sang Talking Heads.

"Come on, Mohammad," Barb said with her eyes closed, her head resting on the outer deck, the water bubbling up around her long hair, pulling it in all directions. "We only have an hour."

"Doesn't everybody here believe in the things that we do?" the song continued, about to bubble into the chorus.

"Well, I'm here, I suppose," Mohammad said. He went looking for an available hook on the wall.

"Hey!" we all shouted together. The lights had gone off. They stayed off for almost a minute while some of us protested and some of us decided it was interesting in the dark. Then the lights went on again. Mohammad was standing by the switch, the gabardine suit gone, the pink towel still over his shoulder but extended down the front of his body so that it covered him to his knees. Mohammad sat down on the outer deck and in one smooth movement slipped out from behind the towel and into the space on the ledge next to Barbara.

"Well, what do you think?" somebody asked him.

"It's not as hot as I thought it would be," Mohammad said in his high excited voice. "It's comfortable."

"(And she said) This is a perfect world," sang Talking Heads.

We were all easing into deeper and deeper states of relaxation. There were looks of blankness, in varying degrees, on the faces of my friends. The water rocked us and settled us. The jets of whirling water buoyed our bodies and blanked our minds. The hotness in the water and in the air wrung us out. Big Tubs also had rooms with isolation tanks, but this was better; here each of us was isolated in his or her own relaxation, and yet we were enjoying it together.

"I'm riding on an incline," the chorus continued.

"You look like Meryl Streep," David said to Victoria, whose head, like Barbara's, was resting on the deck, her thin hair fanning out in the foam at her neck.

"I'm staring in your face," sang our favorite group.

"She does," I said.

"You do, Victoria."

"You'll photograph mine," the chorus ended.

"Who do I look like?" Phyllis wanted to know.

"Everybody looks like somebody," Dale said.

"Who do we all look like?"

A new game. We went around the tub from head to head and decided who everyone looked like. I looked like Dustin Hoffman. David looked like Timothy Hutton with a beard. Barbara looked like Joni Mitchell. There was an awkward silence when we got to Mohammad, but luckily we could not think of anyone for Julia either, although there was a half-hearted mention of Cher, which was immediately hooted down. Dale looked like the guy who played the young, smart-alecky reporter on the Lou Grant show, but no one could remember his name. Phyllis looked like Billie Jean King. Frank was a sick Al Pacino or a healthy Ralph Nader. And it was agreed that Lori looked like a female David Letterman, mostly because of her teeth, although Lori said she was going to enter a formal protest against the decision.

By the end of the game, it was time to take a break from the terrifically hot water. A couple of us dragged ourselves up onto the deck and collapsed on the spot as though we were unconscious and had been beached. David took a cold shower. A few more climbed out of the water and consciously collapsed. Victoria and Barbara stood by the stall shower waiting for David to get through. Frank turned over the cassette. Mohammad never came out of the water. Frank told him what the temperature could do to his veins and arteries, especially if he had been drinking, but Mohammad ignored him. After rests and cold showers, we were all back in the tub again, livelier than we had been before. Barbara and Julia stood up in the middle of the tub and started dancing to the Talking Heads. They both had long hair, which was soaked and clung to their shoulders and upper backs no matter how wildly they moved their bodies to the convulsive rhythm. By the end of the song they were exhausted again. It seemed to be darker and hotter in the room. Sleepiness and heat weighed on our bobbing heads. The blankness on our faces approached euphoria, and all the troubles in the world, all the mysteries, seemed no more threatening or more difficult to dissolve than the short-lived bubbles at our chins. It was a perfect end to a perfect evening. To a perfect birthday celebration. The peaceful, famous faces surrounding me belonged to my friends, wonderful, wonderful friends, every single one of them, and I loved them.

"It's going to take us forever to use the shower," David said. "We better start now, a couple at a time. They charge you extra if you're not out of here in an hour."

"I'll go first," Julia said. "I've had enough anyway." She and Lori got out and showered. Over the next twenty minutes, we were all either showering or toweling or dressing or waiting to take our turn in that progression. Eventually everyone was out of the tub except Mohammad and Victoria.

"First we couldn't get you in. Now we can't get you out," Barbara said.

"I'm coming," Mohammad answered.

Mohammad climbed out of the tub, Victoria right behind him, and he started to walk to the shower at the far end of the room. Then he remembered Victoria and turned around to offer her the shower first. I thought I was the only one who noticed. But as I sneaked looks at the faces of my friends, I saw that all of them had noticed.

"You go ahead, Mohammad," Victoria said.

"If you don't mind," Mohammad said. He said it politely and as though everything were perfectly normal, as though he had not forced us to think about something we did not want to think about.

The mood was suddenly different. Everyone seemed embarrassed. People turned away from one another and finished dressing quickly. Victoria was the only one who did not seem embarrassed, and I assumed that she had been looking away when Mohammad turned around to offer her the shower first. She wrapped her towel around her shoulders and stood by the stall. When Mohammad came out, no one dared look at him. Half of us were dressed and waiting out in the reception area by then anyway.

On the street, those of us who were heading in different directions said goodbye and hugged each other and wished Victoria happy birthday again. At that late hour it was easy to get a taxi; three lined up in front of us. We drove off subdued and still embarrassed. Victoria fell asleep in the taxi. Dale and Phyllis dropped us at our apartment. I woke Victoria and we rode the elevator in silence.

Andrew was not at home, although he must have just left; a cigarette was still smoking in the ashtray on the coffee table in front of the unopened hide-a-bed. Victoria tore off her clothes and fell onto her side of our bed. I could still smell the chlorine on her skin. While I undressed, I stared at her naked body, which was face down on the bed. I wanted to make love to her. The ends of her hair were still wet. With each deep breath, her body rose and fell. I wanted to make love to her, but she was already sleeping. I was naked myself, standing over her body, watching it rise and fall. I wanted to make love to her. I looked like Mohammad when he came out of the tub.

"Where's the ring I gave you?" I whispered, shaking Victoria awake.

She looked up dazedly.

"Where's the ring, Victoria?" I asked again, holding up her hand to show her that the ring was not on it.

"Mmmust have taken it off," she said into the pillow.

"It's not on your dresser."

"Mno?"

"I bet you lost it."

"Hmmm?"

"I bet you lost it in the tub."

12

I WAS HOPING TO BEGIN WORK on the first scheduled appraisal. I intended to boot up, open a new file, and get to work. But I have wound up in RAWN. I did it without thinking. Even though I have no expectation that the file will resolve anything, it has been recorded and therefore must be kept current. I had new data that needed to be included—Victoria's late arrival at the show, her messy hair, her not being embarrassed by Mohammad's erection, her lack of enthusiasm for her birthstone ring, the loss of the ring, her sudden irritability and argumentativeness—so I automatically called up RAWN instead of beginning the first appraisal.

In the morning, Victoria and I entered a new phase. She was visibly upset that I wasn't going to the office as usual. Ordinarily, when she wakes up, I'm already dressed to leave. I have a cup of Mr. Coffee when she goes into the shower and I'm gone by the time she comes out. But this morning I was still in my pajamas when she awoke.

At first she was surprised and asked if I was okay. She thought I might have been ill.

"I'm fine."

Then she became suspicious.

"Nothing is the matter," I said. "I'm not keeping anything from you."

Then she seemed on the verge of anger. She didn't believe me.

"Not anything bad."

I told her I was staying home from now on. That that was the other present I had wanted to tell her about last night over dinner.

"Simon called me with three appraisals," I said. "I'm going to try to set myself up, Victoria. The hell with the symphony. It's time to earn a living. It's time to make some money. It's time to get on with it, Victoria."

"What do you mean on with it? On with what?" She was more nervous and defensive than I had ever seen her.

"With us. Our lives. The future."

"I thought that's what we've *been* doing," she said. She had been standing in the foyer the whole time. In her silky saffron-colored robe. Suddenly she turned and went into the bathroom, half closing the door behind her. During the rest of our conversation—or our argument—she never once looked me straight in the eye. I could see her through the half-closed bathroom door. She was bending over the tub to regulate the temperature of the water as it poured out of the bath tap. While she was bent over, the saffron robe fell open. When she liked the temperature, she stood up, closing the robe and tying the belt.

"Well, we've been doing that, yes. You have," I said.

"And what have you been doing?" she asked, taking a new bar of soap from the medicine cabinet.

"Less than my share."

"That's not what you've been saying. That's not what you've been saying. You've been saying that the symphony is wonderful. You've been saying that the symphony is revolutionary," she quoted me, tearing the paper off the bar of soap as haphazardly as she had torn the paper from the birthday present I had given her in front of the theater.

"Yes, but do you want to live like a revolutionary? What about a family? A house?"

"I have to take a shower."

"Can't we talk about it?"

"Why? We didn't talk about your decision to stay home and work on appraisals."

"It's not too late."

"I'm late."

"We'll talk about it tonight."

"I'm going to be late tonight."

Victoria closed the bathroom door. Ten minutes later, she opened the door and found me virtually in the same spot. She edged past me to enter the bedroom. She had already combed her hair and made up her face. I never heard her run the shower.

"You've been late every night for weeks."

"I told you I called yesterday. You weren't there," she said, searching the closet for the outfit she wanted to wear.

"I was with Simon."

"Right. Deciding what you were going to do with our lives."

"Hey, what's going on? What are you so upset about? I said we can still talk about it. We've got a lot to talk about."

"It doesn't sound that way. It sounds as if you make a decision and then you want us to talk about it afterwards. What's the point?"

I was sure I had not done that. I was sure that I had only acquiesced to what Victoria had wanted all along. She put on her underwear behind the closet door so that I couldn't see her. When she came out from behind the door, she was wearing a skirt and bra. Our discussion was over as far as she was concerned.

"What about the ring?" I asked. "Do you want me to call the place?"

"Sure," she said coolly. "I don't know if that's where I lost it. It was too big. I shouldn't have left it on. Maybe I lost it in the theater."

"You had it at dinner. We talked about it. You showed everybody."

"Then call the place."

"I'll stop over there. I have to go downtown anyway to talk to the guys at the studio."

"Oh, so they don't know either," she said, as if that clinched her case. I let it go. She was buttoning her blouse, her back to me.

"It wasn't cheap, Victoria. You could have been more careful."

"I'm sorry."

She said she was sorry with no more enthusiasm than she had mustered when I gave her the ring.

"What's bothering you?" I said. Everything I said seemed to irritate her and make her defensive; I had nothing to lose. "Is it Andrew?"

"What does Andrew have to do with anything? You're the one who can't stand him. He's your own brother and you can't even talk to him." She should have whirled around and confronted me, the way she said that—angrily, self-righteously— that's the way it happens in the movies. But she didn't.

"Are you kidding?" I said to her back. "Who the hell can talk to him? Can you?"

"Look, this is silly. I have to go; I'm late. I'm sorry I lost the ring. I hope they found it. Is that what you're so upset about?"

"I'm not the one who's upset. I'm fine."

She checked her briefcase and edged past me again. As she was going out the door, I gave her a parting shot.

"I notice that you haven't lost the bracelet Andrew gave you."

"Maybe that's because it fits," she snapped. And she slammed the door behind her.

Like everyone, we have had our arguments. But they have always been logical, understandable disagreements, and we have always come to logical, understandable settlements. We have never screamed, thrown things at one another, stormed out, held grudges. I don't remember either of us ever slamming a door before. But this morning's argument was different. Victoria was different. I had to be different, too, in order to stay in the ring with her. Everything that was said seemed to be covering up something else that should have been said. Subjects were avoided . . . by both of us. Neither of us was apologetic. In the past our arguments had been specific disputes that were kept separate from personalities. The dispute itself, the issue, was always the enemy, and starting from our opposite sides, we could not run fast enough toward each other until the enemy disappeared in the loving compromise of our embrace. But this morning *we* were the enemies. And the closer we moved toward each other's camp, the more dangerous we became. We were antagonistic. Evasive. Indignant. Somehow Andrew and the lost ring and my decision to quit the symphony all seemed beside the point. We would have fought about anything. We were the issue.

All during my shower and while I got dressed and on the long bus ride downtown to the office, I reassured myself that I had made the right decision. It was true that I hadn't discussed it with Victoria or with our friends, but I had acted as I believed they all wanted me to act. They had supported my music, but they had supported my appraisal work even more, especially David and Dale, who threw themselves wholeheartedly into helping me with my first appraisal. God, for every one time my friends have asked how the symphony is coming along, they have asked five times about when I'm going to get another assignment from Simon. And every time the subject of buying a house or starting a family has come up between Victoria and me, it has always ended with one of us pointing out that the only way we could afford either of those dreams was if, by some miracle, I made a killing with the symphony or if I went into appraisals full time.

My colleagues sensed that something was wrong. It was unusual for me to disappear for a whole afternoon, as I had done yesterday, and then to come in late the following morning. I told them point blank that I was through. I didn't want to leave any room for them to try to persuade me to continue. Fortunately, Rich was not there. He was the one person who would have tried the hardest to change my mind. But Rich had taken the out-of-town playing date he had mentioned a couple of days before. The others tried their best in Rich's absence. They appealed to me to wait at least until Rich came back from his date so we could all talk about it. Chuck, who is our engineer, said my timing was ironic. It was the sixteenth anniversary of the first public recital of electronic music. Someone had given Chuck a musician's calendar for Christmas, the kind that lists an important musical event or birthday or death for every date of the year.

I said I would certainly talk to Rich but that my decision was final. I wound up telling them more than I had intended, but my fight with Victoria had made me defensive, and whatever I told my colleagues was a rehearsal of what I would tell Victoria when she was ready to listen.

"I'm a trained musician," I explained. "Seventeen years of classical theory and technique. And what I've been doing is trying to make the most of that training, to capitalize on it. I've been trying to make seventeen years of practice pay for itself with a symphony that isn't getting anywhere and, even if it does, probably won't earn back our expenses. I am not obsessed. I am not the kind of person who stays up all night every night jamming because his music is more important than life itself. I'm a professional. I'm a union member. This is my job. This is my office. And right now it's the wrong job."

I convinced me.

Then I stopped at Big Tubs to ask about the ring. Instead of the lovely Oriental hostess, a big burly man was standing behind the counter. I figured he must have been the owner. He was wearing an Hawaiian shirt and a thick gold chain around his neck.

"I can't look now, there's people in there," he said when I asked if he would check the tub in room 6.

I said I would wait until the hour was up, and he said, "How am I going to see anything anyway? You can't see anything on the bottom like a little ring."

"Don't you ever drain the tub?"

"No. You don't have to in New York. Anyway, if I drained the tub, you'd never find it. It'd go right down the drain."

"Well, what am I supposed to do?"

"Maybe someone'll turn it in. Maybe someone'll step on it and turn it in."

"Look, why don't I just rent the room myself. Maybe *I'll* step on it. How much is it?"

"Twenty dollars an hour."

"I'm not really going to use the tub. Can't I just rent it for fifteen minutes?"

"I can't . . ."

"I just want to look for the ring."

"You're going to take a towel and get undressed and lock the door and get in the tub just like any other customer. Somebody comes in and wants the room, I can't give it to 'em. Maybe they don't want to wait fifteen minutes while you're splashin' around steppin' on rings. I can't do it. I'm not the owner."

I was sure he was the owner.

"You have a card? I'll call you. In case somebody finds it," he lied.

If the city's biggest industry had been able to move a little faster, I'd have had a card. Not that I believed anyone would turn in the ring or that the owner would actually call me if someone did.

"Here," I said, handing him a twenty. "I'll take the room for an hour."

In a half hour, two men my age came out of the hallway. Both were wearing tight shorts and see-through T-shirts. They had their arms around each other's lower backs. Their hair was short, shiny wet, and brushed straight back. One of them was carrying a lightweight bright green gym bag. I think I was not so much startled by the fact that they were obvious homosexuals as by the fact that they were able to visit a hot tub in the middle of the workday. It always startles me to see adults look and act like they're on vacation during business hours. Even though I've always been able to set my own hours, I have purposely set them from nine to five to discipline myself. It would have been easy to get into the habit of sleeping late or taking in midday movies or not going back to the office after a particularly languorous lunch—especially when the symphony was not going well. But these were unproductive habits, and I wondered whether they were tourists or between assignments or self-employed writers or artists or in some other line of work that could excuse the tub break they had taken. It wasn't until I was actually in the tub that I thought about their homosexuality, and when I did, I shuddered at the filmy feel of the still water.

Being in the tub alone was odd and depressing. Dinner and wine and companionship had made it wonderful last night, but today it was sad and eerie. Like walking through your high school when it was empty. The ghosts of good friends were all around, soaking and laughing and telling me I looked like

Dustin Hoffman. Instead of the high-spirited rhythms of the Talking Heads, the lonesome wailing of sitar music was being piped into the room. I walked all through the tub, dragging my feet flat against the bottom, back and forth, back and forth, covering the entire surface of the floor with my feet. I stared down through the water as I walked, but even my slow movements churned the water and made it difficult to see bottom. Also, the floor of the hot tub was painted to resemble mosaic tile, and if the carnelian was down there, the many tiny squares of color camouflaged it. My eyes found nothing. My feet found nothing. They dragged bottom three times. Twice I ran my hands across the built-in ledge submerged along three sides of the tub. I found nothing there, either. I got out of the tub and searched the stall shower at the far end of the room. The ring was not there. I searched the outer deck, the floor, everywhere. The ring was gone. Either someone had found it and kept it or Victoria had lost it somewhere else. I considered turning on the whirlpool jets for the forty-five minutes still owed to me, but the idea of sitting in an empty tub in an empty room without the company of my friends seemed more like a term of solitary confinement than an hour of wonderful indulgence, and so I showered, toweled off, got dressed, searched the hallway on my way out, and went home.

When I let myself into the lobby, the doorman on duty was not there to greet me. He and two other building attendants were in back, talking Spanish a mile a minute. The object of their animated discussion was a huge motorcycle parked by the entrance to the storage rooms. The motorcycle was big and black, and the handlebars and windshield were covered with flags, decals, foxtails, pinwheels, skulls and crossbones, all sorts of gaudy ornaments and decorations. It had thick mag wheels, a long black saddle seat, a wraparound rearview mirror, and a tangle of shiny metal pipes, rods, shocks, and springs. The engine was covered by a black and chrome shell that looked like a weightlifter's chest, all contoured and puffed up and powerful. It sounded like the attendants were arguing, and when I shouted hello, Manuel, the doorman, turned around and gestured with his hands first to me and then to the motorcycle and then to himself as if to assure me that everything was under control. But everything in my life was not under control.

When I got upstairs I checked the phone messages, hoping Victoria had called to apologize, but there was nothing from her. There was a frantic call from David; Angel had run away again. I called him at his office, but he was out on an emergency. I left word for him to call me back and hung around the phone for two hours without beginning work on the appraisals. I listened to tapes, read the paper, did the crossword puzzle, and read two chapters of Asimov's newest novel. Finally, David called.

"They won't do anything until she's missing for twenty-four hours."

"Even if she's done it before?"

"They won't do anything for twenty-four hours."

"Well, how long has it been?"

"It's been five or six hours since Suzanne woke up and went into Angel's room and she wasn't there. But who knows how long she was gone before that."

"You should have told them she's been gone for twenty-four hours."

"That's what I should have told them, but I didn't. And now I can't."

"You're sure she's gone?"

"She's gone, Roger. Suzanne's been on the phone all morning. She's not anywhere we can think of."

He needed me. I told him to come to my apartment. He needed me, and I was anxious to help. We agreed to meet in an hour at a Mexican restaurant near his office. Then his beeper went off and he had to hang up. He told me that if he saw he couldn't make it to the Mexican restaurant, he'd call me in a half hour. Half an hour later David hadn't called, and I left. The attendants were still jabbering over the motorcycle. I hailed a cab and told the driver where I was going. There was not much traffic and I got to the restaurant early. At three in the afternoon there was a crowd inside, but there was room at the bar and I stood there waiting for the woman bartender to bring me a Carta Blanca. The iced glass she brought me was dirty, and I asked her for another one. This Mexican restaurant was dark and the tables were wooden and the atmosphere was almost medieval. The newer Mexican restaurants, which we preferred, were lighter and airier. The food, too, seemed lighter and fresher and as tasteful as the pastel earth tones of the walls and tablecloths and uniforms. This place was somber, and the brown globs of food piled on pewter plates all looked as heavy and bland as bad chili.

David was fifteen minutes late. When he came in, he immediately ordered two more of whatever I was drinking.

"You still haven't heard anything?" I asked him.

"What am I going to do, Roger?"

"You're absolutely sure she ran away? It's not possible that she's at a friend's hous—"

"What friends?"

"—or that she went to the movies or the library or the museum or something like that?"

"I'm telling you she ran away. She said she was going to run away and she did."

"She told you she was going to run away?"

"The first time she did. And when I asked her to promise me that she wouldn't ever do anything like that again, she said she couldn't make that promise. What would you think? What other conclusion is there, Roger?"

The woman bartender brought us two beers and updated the bill.

"Do you want to talk about why?"

"Why what?"

"Why Angel wants to run away."

"I don't know why. She's at that age."

I did not want to make the only suggestion I had. I did not want to bring up the fact that Angel had gone to lunch with Andrew and that he might have had something to do with her running away. I didn't want to implicate Andrew because I didn't want to implicate Victoria. But I had to offer David something.

"Look, I've got an idea," I said.

"Fuck."

A high-pitched signal came from the small leather holster clipped to his belt. It was David's beeper.

"I'll be right back. I have to find a phone."

When he came back, I told David that I had quit the symphony.

"To do what?"

"I got three appraisals yesterday."

"From Simon?"

"I'm going into it full time."

"What about the symphony?"

"Nothing. I'm just going into appraisals full time."

"Well that's fabulous."

"And I've got three right away."

"If that's what you want, I think it's fabulous. I mean I always liked what you were doing with the symphony, but to be perfectly honest, I think this is what you ought to be doing."

"What I thought, David, is that mayb—"

"Victoria must be happy."

"—maybe Ange—"

"Why didn't you say something last night? Jesus, Roger, you make a decision like that and you don't even say anything."

"Listen, I thought maybe Angel could help me and—"

"Angel?"

"—and I could help her."

I was in the middle of telling David that I thought Angel could be helpful to me in judging the appeal of the three movies I was supposed to appraise when his beeper sounded again.

"Fuck. Hold your thought."

I held it.

He came back smiling. It had been a phantom beep. Someone dialed his classified number by accident.

"Angel's the market," I said. "She's the right age, the right education, the right geographic location, the right everything. Essentially, my appraisal is based on how many Angels I think are going to want to see these movies."

"I think it's a great idea. A great idea."

"And maybe, I don't know, maybe if she feels that she's doing something responsible, that somebody values her opinion, that it's not just school or you or Suzanne telling her what to do but somebody asking her for her opin—I could even pay her, David. I could even pay her. A percentage of what I'm getting. There's plenty of money in the deal."

"I think it's great. Really, Roger. All we have to do is find her."

"Two more," I said to the bartender.

"All we have to do is find her."

We finished our beers and I paid the bill.

"What's mine?" David asked, but I couldn't let him pay for his beers.

"You sure you don't want to come by for dinner?"

"I told Suzanne I'd be over there. She's hysterical."

"Well, I'll be home. I'm not going anywhere. I'll be home all night and if you hear anything, call me, will you? Please don't forget to call me. I'll call you at Suzanne's anyway."

"Roger."

I turned back to David.

"Thanks," he said. Then he got into a cab that had just pulled up.

I closed the back door of the cab behind him and told him I was sure Angel would be home and that he should remember to ask her about reviewing the movies for me or to tell her to call me so I could go over the whole thing with her.

When I got home from the Mexican restaurant, the doorman greeted me. It wasn't Manuel. It was Freddy, who worked the early evening shift. The motorcycle was gone. I was anxious as I rode upstairs in the elevator; I was hoping Victoria had called to apologize. But when I listened to the phone messages, only Frank had called. He left a number and I called him back.

"Great news, Roger."

"What?"

"Guess where I'm going?"

"I don't know. Did you hear that Angel ran away again?"

"No. When?"

"I don't know. David doesn't know. He thinks last night, in the middle of the night. The police won't even start looking for her until she's missing for twenty-four hours."

"Did you talk to him?"

"I just had a drink with him. He's all right."

"Will you let me know?"

"I asked him to come over, but he's going to Suzanne's. She's hysterical."

"Well, will you let me know what happens?"

"Sure. If I know. I quit the symphony, by the way. I'm doing appraisals full time now. I got three from Simon yesterday. I called Dale, but there's no answer. You don't know where he is, do you?"

"No, but that's terrific. You made the right decision, Roger. I mean it. I was going to talk to you about it. I was going to tell you to do that. That's great, Roger."

"So where are you going?"

"Christ, are you ready for this, Roger? I'm going to Pakistan."

"What do you mean you're going to Pakistan? Does Mohammad have something to do with it?"

"No, this is through WHO, the World Health Organization. When we were all talking about going to the Himalayas, I applied to go there with a team of epidemiologists. Shit, Roger, Pakistan is a fuckin' laboratory for an epidemiologist. They got epidemics up the ass. They get plagues the way we get pimples. It's a way of life. And it's all expenses paid for me and Lori."

"God, that sounds great."

"You know how much money there is floating around in any world organization? The tax benefits? Not only that, but it's great on the résumé, Roger. I could head up a government task force or something when I get back."

"Absolutely."

"What are you guys doing tonight? We should celebrate. Me, your new career, we should celebrate, Roger. What's everybody doing?"

"The problem is David."

"Christ, I forgot."

"Maybe she'll come home."

"Look, will you let me know? Let me know about David and see if you can round up Dale and everybody. I'm still trying to get hold of Lori."

"Jesus," I said, "Pakistan."

"Can you believe it? The trick now is to get the rest of you guys over there for New Year's."

My early morning fight with Victoria was still controlling my emotions. It prevented me from feeling as bad as I should have for David and as good as I should have for Frank. It prevented me, also, from getting down to work. I should have started screening the movies. I should have started developing my own appraisal. At least I should have opened up a file in the Apple and entered my notes from yesterday afternoon's meeting with Simon. Instead, I read another chapter of Asimov. And then I tried Dale again. And then I put two frozen tortillas into the microwave on "thaw," and when they were soft, I grated extra spicy Monterey Jack cheese onto one, covered it with the other, and put the whole thing back into the microwave on "high" for a minute. It came out bubbling and steaming and too hot to eat right away. Two minutes later, it was cold and starting to get stiff. But I ate it. It was all I wanted for dinner.

At five o'clock I called Suzanne.

"She's home."

"She's home?"

"She came in about an hour ago."

"Where was she?"

"She won't say."

"Is David there?"

"He's on a call. I haven't been able to reach him."

"What do you mean she won't say? She just came home all by herself? Is she all right?"

"She just blew in, Roger. Just like that. I really mean blew in, too. Her hair looked like she just stuck it in a fan or something. It was blown all over, standing straight out, like the bride of Frankenstein. Other than that, she looked fine. But not a word. No explanation, no nothing."

At six o'clock I turned on the news. Victoria still hadn't called. She didn't call to apologize or to tell me that she would be home late again. Michael called and wanted to know if he could come over and talk to me about something. He said he'd be over in an hour. Then an hour later he called back to say he couldn't make it after all, maybe tomorrow.

The TV has been on since the six o'clock news. I've been half watching every show. I did not even play along with *Wheel of Fortune*. At ten, *Remington Steele* will go on. I don't know if I can make it up. I'm tired. It has been an exhausting day. To counteract my tiredness, I tried to start a file on the appraisals. But I got caught in RAWN and I can't get out. Angel runs away and comes home with messy hair and somehow it becomes an entry. Frank calls to tell me that he's going to Pakistan and somehow it involves all of us, particularly Andrew and Moham- mad. Victoria is still out. I can't reach Dale to tell him about my decision and ask about borrowing his last few issues of *Variety*. Frank wanted to celebrate tonight, but he never called back. The ring is still missing. The carving of Victoria's face is still sitting on her dresser, mocking me. I have not done a scrap of work on the appraisals. I do not know whether to be conciliatory or sullen and resentful when Victoria comes home. I do not know how she will be. I *do* know that I don't want her to find me in RAWN. Sometimes she will stand over my shoulder and watch what I'm working on. If I save and store the file in the computer's memory on whatever page I happen to be working, the screen will show only the name I gave the file and some basic instructions regarding command options. I can do that quickly, as soon as I hear her key in the door. If she comes in and sees the name RAWN and asks about it, I can tell her that it stands for *R* oger's *A* ppraisal *W* ork *N* ew. Or I can just turn down the light on the screen until the screen is blank. But that might arouse her suspicion. God, the last thing we need is more suspicion around here.

Even with the television playing, I can hear the elevator stop at our floor. I can hear footsteps approaching our door. Quickly, I hit the keys that will save RAWN. I can turn the Apple off now without losing anything. I will just turn it off, seeming to be ending the night's work on my appraisals when Victoria comes in. If she is still in an irritable mood, I can stay at the Apple and ignore her. If she's calm, I can turn off the computer.

I won't be able to see her until she comes through the front hall into the living room, where I'm sitting. The door will open, close, she will put her briefcase down and put away any out- door gear she may be carrying or wearing. Then she will pick up the briefcase again and walk through the living room on her way to the bedroom.

There is the key. She is inside. The door closes. She is not stopping in the front hall. I do not look up from the Apple. Without planning it, I am waiting for her to say something— hello, sorry, did you have dinner, whatever—before I even acknowledge her presence. I am suddenly filled with the anger left over from this morning. Victoria is in the bedroom. She has walked past me without saying a word. Now I am forced either to continue working on the Apple or say something to Victoria.

"Your ring wasn't at Big Tubs."

I call it out to the bedroom. I call it out coldly, a declaration inviting no reply. It is this morning again. We are arguing again. Fourteen, fifteen hours have passed futilely.

It is apparent that Victoria is not going to answer me. She is not even going to come out of the bedroom. She is going to bed without washing her face or brushing her teeth or saying a word to me. I have brought RAWN back onto the screen. I hit the "end" command accidentally and the file forwards itself to the very end.

Ten minutes have passed and there is another key at the door. Andrew lets himself in. He hangs something solid and heavy on the coat tree. He, too, comes through the living room without saying anything, but that is not unexpected. He goes into the bathroom, leaves the door open, and pees loud and long. Then he goes to the kitchen and takes a beer. He opens the hide-a-bed and flops down onto it, swigging the beer, still dressed in his Nehru clothes. The eleven o'clock news is just coming on. Andrew flips through the channels until he finds a local cable station that features outrageous sexual programs. A completely naked woman is being interviewed. The set and the manner of the host suggest the Johnny Carson show. But the questions the host asks are disgusting.

"So you know exactly where your G spot is, huh, Candy?"

"Sure, want to see it?"

The camera pans down and moves in for a close-up while the naked woman parts her legs and spreads herself apart with her hands, leaving a forefinger free to point out the precise location of her G spot.

"I'm not bothering you, am I, Andrew?" I ask him sarcastically. But he's asleep, the beer bottle still in his hand, a cigarette burning in the ashtray on the floor next to the hide-a-bed.

I have not seen Andrew sleeping since he arrived. He has never gone to sleep before Victoria and I have gone into the bedroom. I have never found him in bed when I have woken up in the morning. His beer belly rises and falls. He grinds his teeth. His stomach growls. He snores. I stare at the Apple.

Victoria and Andrew's file precedes my hypothetical sentences made from the four words I glimpsed in Victoria's makeshift diary. If a file is loaded without hitting the "end" command, the screen displays the beginning of all its data. If the "end" command is entered, which I accidentally did, the final entry in the file appears on the screen, in this case my hypothetical sentences. I get up and walk around the living room, trying to remember when and why I could have entered the sentence: The forces of human *n*ature are *a*gainst *R*oger; and I am *w*eak.

I walk into the front hall and see what Andrew hung on the coat tree. God. I go into the bedroom and see Victoria's body almost completely covered by our summer blanket, and I cannot believe my eyes. God. I go back into the living room, over to the hide-a-bed, looking for the remote controller so I can switch off the TV. I can't find it anywhere. Perhaps Andrew has rolled over on top of it.

I backtrack on the screen to the last entry made in Victoria and Andrew's file and update it. I type in that Victoria has cut off almost all of her hair, that it's like a boy's haircut. Next to that entry, in Andrew's column, I type in that my brother has come home with a black motorcycle helmet.

13

I AM NOT GOING TO GIVE UP my basic beliefs. They are being tested beyond anything I could have imagined, but they are going to survive. I know they are. We have worked too hard and come too far to permit an opponent to dictate tempo and strategy. What the opponent does not realize is that we can play a waiting game. Because we have faith. Faith in ourselves, faith in each other, faith in the beliefs we share. And first among them is the belief in and respect for one another's territorial prerogative. A person has the individual and absolute right to do whatever he or she must to defend, protect, and preserve his or her own space. That is the underlying basis of our faith. Victoria has the absolute right to be irritable, to stay out late, to let herself go, to race around on the back of a motorcycle like some Hell's Angel's old lady, to cut off her hair, to join whatever weird confederacy she likes with Andrew and Angel. I know that she is acting in good faith, with intelligence and purpose, and that she cannot help but do what she must for our common good.

A relationship is based on trust. My friends and I trust that none of us would knowingly do harm to any other. Never in history has such solidarity been so natural and strong, because never before in history has a society of people been so focused, so targeted, so completely and precisely borne along the same wavelength. It's as if we're each a note in a continuing chord. If there's a wrong note, the overwhelming rightness of the chord will cover it, and the wrong note will soon correct itself because it cannot escape the chord. Now the chord is luring us all to Pakistan. We are our own Pied Pipers. Barb already has Mohammad checking out accommodations for us. Frank has already arranged his and Lori's trip through WHO and I can't question his decision. He's too good at what he does. He has the absolute right and the absolute right stuff to make Pakistan the next stop on his professional agenda. Much as the thought of going to Pakistan troubles me because of Andrew's association with that part of the world, going there is becoming the right thing to do. First Barbara, then Frank and Lori, and now Michael.

Three times Michael made a date to meet me to discuss a personal matter, and three times he canceled at the last minute. When finally we got together at my apartment, it was two days after he first said he wanted to talk to me.

Michael was incredibly nervous. Usually he is very relaxed. Even when our conversation moves toward his private life, he keeps himself removed and somehow out of reach of embarrassment or nervousness. We all take his homosexuality for granted. We accept it, we understand it, we never mention it. We talk around it with tacit approval. If Michael chooses not to tell us about his personal life, that is good enough for us. It's his right. But when he came to my apartment, it was to tell me about his personal life, that much was clear, and he was under a great deal of pressure.

"Want a beer?"

"Sure."

I poured two Kirins and took the foamy one for myself. Michael's had no more than a half inch of foam.

"What's up?" I said cheerfully. "How's the video coming?"

"Good. I worked on it last night," he said cautiously. "That's why I had to cancel dinner. Some studio time got freed up."

God, his hands were trembling.

I tried to make it easier for him by telling him about my

decision to go into appraisals full time. I told him about the three assignments and quitting the symphony and my idea of having Angel help me judge movies marketed for her peers. Michael was visibly grateful for this preliminary conversation. He calmed down. His hands stopped shaking somewhat. His voice did not waver when he congratulated me.

"We're on the move, Mikey," I said. "We're getting there."

"Listen, Roger, what I want to talk to you about," he began, "is . . . listen, I assume you know I'm . . . not like you."

It suddenly occurred to me that Michael and I had never had a conversation alone, just the two of us. I'd known him for years, since college, but the two of us had never been alone together. Although what he said was the absolute truth, it was impossible for me to answer his question nonchalantly. I tried. I spoke as nonchalantly as I could, hoping the embarrassment in my voice and the flush I felt on my face were not as noticeable to him as they were to me.

Now that he had broken the ice, his nervousness completely disappeared. Now I was the one who was uncomfortable. He was asking me to deal with something he knew intimately and I did not know at all.

"I'm not gay, Roger."

I couldn't imagine what he was going to tell me.

"I'm the wrong person."

I finished my Kirin without wiping my mouth.

"I don't understand, Michael."

"I'm in the wrong body, Roger. I'm the wrong gender. I'm a woman, Roger. I know I'm a woman."

All I could think to say was, "Would you like another beer?"

Michael was excited now. He followed me into the kitchen, jabbering about men and women and genes and mistaken identity.

"I'm not gay. I'm not a man who likes men. I'm a woman who likes men. I don't want to go swishing around like a woman; I don't want to pretend to be a woman; how can you pretend to be something you really are?

"I've got a woman's mind and heart and soul, Roger. And everything's stuck inside the wrong body. I'm a monumental case of mistaken identity. It's like somebody got the wrong baby at the hospital, only in this case, it was the baby who got the wrong baby."

"Well, so what are you saying?" I said, sensing that there had to be more, some decision Michael had come to that he wanted me to endorse, which I, of course, was ready to do. "Here," I said, handing him another glass of beer. This time, mine was poured without a head, too.

"What I'm saying is that I'm going to fix it, Roger. I'm going to have an operation."

"Jesus."

"Look, if you had a tumor or something growing inside you—or between your legs—and it was going to kill you if you didn't take care of it, wouldn't you take care of it? Wouldn't you have an operation?"

"Sure, bu—"

"It's the same thing, Roger. It's the same thing. I promise you. This is going to kill me if I don't do something about it."

I really could not comprehend the dimensions of Michael's despair, his problem was too alien to me. But I could understand this much: he had been suffering tremendously and now he had figured out a way to be happy, and I was all for that. Anybody would be.

"Well, then do it. Do it, for Christ's sake, Michael. Absolutely do it."

But that was not what he wanted from me. He wanted to unburden himself. He wanted to share his pain with me. He did not want me to endorse his decision, he wanted me to arrive at it vicariously.

"Have you ever gone into a men's room and died of embarrassment, Roger? Or had to shake a man's hand when you wanted him to kiss your hand? Or been reminded of your curse and your misery every morning in front of the shaving mirror? Little things, stupid things, Roger. But they're like death sentences. When we're all together, how I wish I were in the kitchen or shopping or gossiping or showing off a new dress with Victoria and Barbara and Lori and Julia instead of drinking beer with you and David and Dale and Frank."

I could not keep myself from looking at Michael's glass of beer and wishing I could take it back.

"I'm nothing. I'm neither here nor there, this nor that. I'm just nothing. Thank God I've got my work; thank God I can lose myself in my work. The other night when everybody went to Big Tubs to celebrate Victoria's birthday, thank God I had to work all night. Thank God I didn't have to go with you. I wouldn't have gone anyway, but thank God I had a place to go and work to do and didn't have to think about it. Can you imagine what it would have been like for me to go with you?"

I couldn't.

"Can you imagine me looking at the bodies of the men and loving how strong and rough and handsome they all are and hating my own for being exactly the same? And then looking at Victoria and Barbara and Julia and Lori and Phyllis and loving them and wanting them in a completely different way, an impossible way, wanting to be them, knowing I am them, wanting to be soft, wanting to be graceful, wanting to be beautifully weak, wanting to be swept away? It's a joke, Roger, a cosmic joke. Only there's no punch line."

I kept trying to picture Michael as a woman, but all I could succeed in picturing was him and the rest of us as sort of neutral beings, not men or women, just forms that were all basically the same. Hair, sexual organs, facial features were just accessories, something these basic humans might wear. Yet I could not really imagine Michael putting on anything different than his usual black close-cropped hair, his smoothly shaved jutting jaw, his slightly bulging eyes and small ears. I couldn't imagine him making a very attractive woman. I wondered if the operation he was going to have included cosmetic surgery.

"Anyway, I am going to have this operation."

I did not really want to know what the operation entailed. I imagined the obvious and it made me squeamish.

"In India."

"India?"

"In New Delhi."

"You're kidding."

"I'm going the end of September. The Kama Rawni Clinic in New Delhi. It's the only one like it in the world, believe it or not. And I'll be there through the holidays. If you all go skiing in the Himalayas, Michelle will join you."

He had come to tell me his news and he had told me. He had trusted me with his torment and his solution. He had tried to make me understand, and I suppose he succeeded, although there was no advice I wanted to give him, no questions I wanted to ask him, no philosophical observations that leaped to mind. He would go to New Delhi as Michael and meet us in the mountains as Michelle. We would love him still. Love *her* still. It was his wit and charm and style and creative talent that mattered.

Michael finished his beer and stood up. He had to go. He was glad we finally had gotten together. For some reason, I shook his hand. As he was leaving, I called his name and he turned around to hear what I had to say. I meant to tell him how overwhelmed I was by his frankness and trust. I considered it a great honor and a great testament to our friendship that he had chosen to confide in me, that the first private conversation we had ever had, just the two of us, should have been such a momentous and intimate one. The fact that he had chosen me to confide in made me want to pay him back in kind. Now, partly out of gratitude and partly out of appreciation for Michael's candidness, I wanted to ask his advice.

"I want you to know how much I appreciate your telling me this, Michael. I understand how . . . I know how . . ."

"I do feel better now. I'm doing the right thing, Roger."

". . . and if you don't want me to say anything to anybody . . ."

"It's all right. Everybody knows."

"Everybody knows?"

"I told everyone. One by one. I had to. You're the last."

14

"HOW OLD WAS LOLITA?"
Frank dipped a boiled Chinese dumpling into a thin hoisinlike sauce and popped it into his mouth.

"Mymeam the mook?" he stalled.

If he answered the question correctly, Frank would have an additional roll of the die to get himself into the center section, where one more correct answer would win the game for him.

"What do you think?" I said. "Of course I mean the book."

We are all here except Victoria. We seem to be going through the motions. There are other things on everyone's mind. Frank and Lori are arranging things for their impending trip. Barb misses Mohammad, who returned to Pakistan yesterday. Dale and Phyllis can only stay until nine-thirty. They have tickets to a ten o'clock performance of What's His Name's new play at the newly converted theater two blocks from our apartment. Interestingly, Julia is involved in the game more than anyone. She thinks she has to take a break in order to work through her artist's block. She's eager to rest her weary mind by competing with someone other than herself. David, of course, is still worried about Angel. He spoke to her about my offer, and she said she would think about it. Still, he is not himself. Nor is Michael. Literally.

No one has mentioned Michael's operation to me. I know they all know, and I assume each of them knows that all the rest of us know. But it is not a matter for conversation. That reassures me. I feel that whatever I have said to David and whatever I might say to any of the others will not be discussed between them.

No one seems to mind Victoria's absence. By now, her absences are expected. They think she's working hard and they all know what that's like. Time and place stop mattering. The few minutes you have put your friends on hold for turn into hours, days, weeks, months, and that doesn't matter either.

Some of them like Victoria's new boyish haircut and some of them don't. The ones who don't have not offended her. They have only said that they liked her old haircut better. As for me, I despise it. She looks like an entirely different person. She does not match the images of her I see in my mind. But neither does her personality these days.

We have hardly spoken to each other for three days. We have seen little of one another, and when we have seen each other for a few minutes in the morning or late at night, the atmosphere is either equatorial or arctic. Whatever I say triggers either a quick, boiling retort or an absolutely ice cold silence. In between, I have managed to screen the three assigned movies and I have begun to research the market potential for the first scheduled appraisal.

"Thirteen."

"Wrong."

"How old?"

Julia wants to guess before I reveal the answer. So do the others.

"Fourteen."

"Twelve."

"Fifteen."

"I'll take eleven."

"Sixteen."

"Who said twelve?" I asked.

"I did," Phyllis said.

"It's twelve," I said.

"How did you know that?"

"Jesus, twelve, no wonder the book was such a scandal."

Lolita's age seemed to revive enthusiasm in the game. Also, Frank was no longer one answer away from winning.

At 9:30, as Dale and Phyllis were leaving for the theater, Victoria came home. She begged them to stay, but understood. She had something she wanted to ask them and would call tomorrow. Victoria seemed to be in a good mood, but I had seen that look turn suddenly into anger or indifference over the last three days, and I had to wonder how long it would last. When she passed by where I was sitting, she bent down, and I thought she was offering her cheek for me to kiss. I tried to peck it and surprised her. She was bending down to reach for a sparerib.

"Why don't you take Dale's place; his token's in second place," Frank suggested to Victoria.

"You guys play. I want to get out of these clothes."

I hated myself for wondering how many times she had already gotten out of them today.

Like clockwork, Andrew arrived fifteen minutes later. There was a roaring in the hallway, accompanied by excited shouts in another language. It sounded like we were under attack. We all ran out into the hall. Andrew was trying to maneuver his motorcycle down the hallway, two building attendants trailing his exhaust and cursing at him in Spanish. He was too drunk to hear them.

I helped him park the motorcycle out of the way, made him shut it off, and then I helped him out of the long black saddle. Frank and David took it from there and brought him into the apartment while I quieted down the building attendants by promising them that we'd take care of getting the motorcycle out onto the street. What finally calmed them down was my willingness to accept all responsibility for damages.

Victoria was not with us when we ran out into the hallway. She was still in the bedroom getting out of her clothes. When I got back inside, Andrew was in the bedroom, too. David and Frank had deposited him in my bed to let him sleep it off until everyone left and he could be transferred to the hide-a-bed.

"Where's Victoria?"

"I guess she's tucking NeAndrewthal in," Barb said. "You know, you ought to have that guy committed," she added.

"He's a menace to himself and everybody around him. What's his story, anyway? Is he just a drunk?"

"Well, are we all going to Pakistan or not?" Frank asked.

"I mean, Jesus, Rog, he drove a goddamn motorcycle up the elevator. That's not just a kid having fun." Barbara would not give up.

"Come on, Barb," Julia said. "Lay off."

"I'll go see what's going on," Barbara said. She got up and started for the bedroom.

"Please do," I said.

Barbara left the bedroom door open. Under the pretense of going to the bathroom, I walked into the foyer, where I could see into the bedroom. Victoria was lying on top of Andrew on our bed. Andrew was holding her against her will, holding her on top of him with one hand and pawing at her with the other, trying to force her head close enough to his so he could kiss her, grabbing at her ass, trying to get his hand up the pant leg of the khaki shorts Victoria had put on. Barbara was also holding Victoria, trying to pull her away from Andrew. When she succeeded, Andrew grabbed Barbara and pulled *her* down on top of him. With all the thrashing around and struggling, as violent as the scene was, it was played out in dead silence. Andrew was thrashing about wildly and the two women were struggling to get free, although they were treating him as though he was not responsible for his actions. When they finally broke loose and Andrew's body went limp, Barb and Victoria headed back into the living room like mothers who had finally succeeded in getting a colicky baby to sleep. Before they saw me, I dashed into the john and closed the door. I waited a few seconds, flushed the toilet, ran the tap, waited another few seconds, and rejoined the party.

The game was over. We tried to talk about going to Pakistan, but no one besides Frank and Lori and Michael was ready to make a final commitment—not even Barb. Frank was trying to talk it up, of course, and Barb said it all depended on whether Mohammad was too busy to get away for five or six days. David was concerned about being away from Angel, although he relished the prospect of being so far out of beeping range, and Julia was lukewarm about the whole idea because she still had to produce an exhibit for the gallery and going to Pakistan meant being away just when her show was starting to take shape; at Frank's insistence, though, she acknowledged that there would still be enough time to set things right if the gallery happened to fuck up. Victoria was silent. I really didn't know if she wanted to go to Pakistan or not; we had never discussed it. I did not want to go, but I felt that everything that was going wrong in my life was mysteriously connected to this alien land. I was thinking about Andrew's gift wrapping and his Nehru suit and Mohammad's erection and Michael's operation and Frank's assignment from WHO, and all I said was, "I don't know, I'd like to go, but I don't know," in case Victoria refused to go or in case I needed the time to work on the appraisals or in case it turned out that for some unforeseen reason, going to Pakistan for Christmas and New Year's would further complicate my already complicated life.

By eleven o'clock, everybody was gone. David left last and promised that Angel would call me about assisting me with the appraisals. He offered to help me figure out what to do with the motorcycle. The two of us spent half an hour trying to start it up, but neither of us knew a thing about motorcycles. We took turns sitting on the monstrous bike and jumping up and down on what might have been the starter. It took half an hour before it occurred to us to move the motorcycle back into the elevator and down to the lobby without starting it. We rolled it backward down the hallway, pushed for the elevator, and when it came, managed to position the big black Harley in the car so that there was room not only for us, but for two more passengers, if necessary, on the way down. The building attendants were delighted to see us. They came to our assistance immediately and took the motorcycle from us, rolling it out the front door and onto the street.

"You going to put it out on the street?" I asked them.

"On the stree! Jes! We haff to," said Tony; he was not about to listen to any other suggestion.

They parked Andrew's motorcycle head-on in a small space across the street from the building. David hailed a cab and promised again to have Angel call me. "It's a great idea, it'll do her a world of good."

It was not until I was back in the elevator, halfway up to my floor, that I realized what had been bothering me about the motorcycle, what was different about it from before. I got off at the next floor and pushed for a down elevator. I had to wait for the car I had just left to reach my floor and then return before I could ride down to the lobby. I walked outside. Even from as far away as across the street, I could see what I had unconsciously suspected. When the light changed, I crossed the street and went directly to the handlebars of Andrew's motorcycle. What movie had it been? What was the name of that movie? Tied to the bars and the bracket of the headlight was a silver statuette. What movie? Another hand-carved totem of some kind. At first it had fooled me because it looked like a hood ornament, but now I saw that it was a hand-carved statuette of a naked woman, her body not unlike Victoria's and her hair shorn like a boy's. Marlon Brando. The movie with Marlon Brando where he's the leader of a motorcycle gang. I couldn't remember the name of it, but I remembered that Marlon Brando stole some racing trophy and pretended he won it and always kept it strapped on to the front of his motorcycle.

When I got back to the apartment, the hide-a-bed was open and Victoria was sleeping in it. I had no choice but to undress and get into the hide-a-bed with her while Andrew snored and ground his teeth in our bedroom.

15

IN THE MORNING I AWOKE TO find myself in the living room and Andrew in the bedroom. Victoria had already left for work.

There were still Chinese take-out cartons on the coffee table near the hide-a-bed, an ugly sparerib sticking out of one, a congealed layer of mu shu pork in another, chopsticks all over the place, empty beer glasses, small containers of hot mustard and soy sauce, tea bags, and broken pieces of fortune cookies, the fortunes sprinkled about like confetti.

I had slept soundly, and my first thought was whether or not Victoria had awoken in the middle of the night and gone back to her own bed. I never would have known. He has intruded into my house, cast his insidious spell over my wife, and now he has changed places with me, stolen my bed, perhaps my wife. Andrew has always taken things away from me. But I have been able to tolerate his intimidation and greed by knowing always that whatever he succeeded in stealing, he stole because of the weaknesses of others, never through any fault of mine. From the time he left college for his mysterious life on the road, he usurped all the attention from our parents. Because they were sure of my progress, they concentrated on his, making up grand stories from the occasional postcards he sent them. His cards from Africa, in our parents' interpretation, had him teaching bridge-building engineering skills to aborigines. In Libya he drilled for oil. In Greece he excavated ancient treasures from the Aegean. In India he erected huge power plants in the northwest frontier. And all of this could be attributed to two things my mother and father remembered about Andrew. When he was a little boy, Andrew had a penchant for constructing with his Erector set. And for a sixth grade assignment he had painted a map of the world on a wooden board, hammered nails where the major world capitals were located, hammered a column of nails to the side of the map where he listed the names of the capitals, and then cross-wired all the nails coming through the back of the board so that positive and negative wires connected to a battery pack completed a circuit when touching the name of a world capital and its correct location on the map, causing a red bulb to light up. My parents still keep this sixth grade project of Andrew's. They still cart it out as evidence of his genius. Andrew was eleven or twelve years old when he made it, and he has lived off it for more than thirty years.

Because of the ten-year difference in our ages, when I was born, there was an entirely new philosophy of child-rearing, but for my parents the newer theories were abnormal. If the rule when Andrew was born was to feed an infant upon demand and when I was born to feed only on schedule, then feeding on demand was normal, but the newfangled theory of feeding on schedule was not. Consequently, whatever Andrew did, thought, or believed became the rule by virtue of its having happened first, and whatever I did, thought, or believed became the exception. The clothes I wear are abnormal departures from the way Andrew dresses. The foods I eat can't stick to my ribs or lead a woman to my heart the way Andrew's blue plate specials do. When I ask Hertz for a small, safe economy car, I'm defecting to the Japanese (and my parents would enjoy knowing how Andrew has literally driven that point home on his Harley-Davidson). To our parents, Andrew stands for the way things should be. But only for the time being. Only until David is president of IBM and Frank is surgeon general of the

United States, and Dale is the Book-of-the-Month Club's main selection. We are on the cusp of the future and one day it will be ours and everything we say and do will be the rule.

He was still snoring, still grinding his teeth. I got up and went into my bedroom to look at him. He was spread-eagled across my bed, the covers tangled in his legs, the pillows bunched beneath his neck and hips. He was big and sloppy and noisy. His hair was long and dirty. He hadn't shaved in a while, and his beard was stubbly. He slept in his clothes. His drinking and smoking made his breathing sound congested. There were nicotine stains on his teeth. His nails were bitten down.

He was living without apparent purpose and coming home when he was drunk or exhausted. He was living out of a beat-up steamer trunk that held the contents of his life after forty-four years. It could be filled with rupees or bracelets or the architectural plans for African bridges and Grecian excavations, but on this particular morning he was where *I* belonged and I felt I had a right to that trunk. I walked into the foyer and attempted to open it. It was unlocked. Andrew had nothing to hide.

At first glance, the contents of the trunk looked like junk, a thousand odds and ends from Andrew's travels, thrown together into a portable garbage heap. There were pieces of wood, cloth, paper, metal; there were wrappings, sheets of newspaper, packing materials; there was an array of fabrics, colors and shapes that blended into an abstract collage smelling of mildew and dampness. But then, as I poked and probed into the heap, the different objects began to take on individual significance, and I became aware that everything in the trunk was related in the most incredible way.

I picked out a wooden hand the size of a doll's hand and held it in my palm. It had not been broken off something larger, it was meant to be only a hand; and it was exactly like Victoria's hand. The fingers were long, the knuckles a bit too large, the thumb bent back disjointedly at the top. I picked out a large bronze coin; on one side was an engraving in profile of the head of some ancient goddess, and the profile was unmistakably Victoria's. Everything in Andrew's trunk eerily evoked the image of Victoria—drawings, carvings, masks, puppets, photos torn from magazines, newspapers, and books, her face, figure, and limbs depicted in every way possible by an unconscious confederacy of artists, artisans, and craftsmen. I opened a small jewel-studded box and found a tress of hair the color of Victoria's. I opened a leather pouch and found a swatch of silk the color of her eyes. There seemed to be no stone that Andrew's obsession had left unturned. I picked up a crudely made picture frame that displayed a page neatly cut from a novel—I didn't know which novel—and read a description of a character that could have been Victoria. And yet the language was not modern. It was full of *thee*'s and *thou*'s. Everything in Andrew's trunk was old, like the carving he had given Victoria for her birthday.

I didn't have to examine everything. It was all the same. Andrew's trunk contained countless unrelated depictions of women throughout history, yet the result was a collection devoted to one face and figure. It was a tribute to Victoria. Or to someone who looked like Victoria. Certainly Andrew had never laid eyes on my wife until he showed up at our apartment. No wonder he stared at her. No wonder he was speechless. All his life he had gone around with a picture of this dream woman in his head, collecting every kind of image of her, carrying around a portable shrine to her, and then quite by accident he had come face to face with her in his brother's house. Something from Kismet should have been on the tape deck.

I had had it wrong right from the start. Andrew hadn't been controlling Victoria's mind; it was Victoria who had been controlling Andrew's. For some reason I wanted to laugh. I picked out a familiar looking little box from Andrew's trunk and took it to the window opposite the hide-a-bed and looked outside. It was a terrifically bright day. The sun reflected blindingly off passing cars. Commuters trudged east toward the bus routes and the subway; others tried to flag down off-duty taxis. The scene outside was filled with such brilliant simplicity. Everything was as it should be. Even the stripped motorcycle parked head-on across the street.

"Jesus Christ!" I heard myself say out loud.

Inside the familiar looking box was the carnelian ring I had given Victoria.

16

NGEL CALLED ME. Trying not to sound enthusiastic, she agreed to help with the appraisals if the price was right. I told her I had no way of knowing for sure what I would earn because it depended on the final appraisal figure but that she could have three percent of whatever my ¼ percent amounted to; reluctantly, I speculated that she might wind up with several hundred dollars for just six or seven hours of her time. Plus she would have a chance to see three movies before her friends at school got to see them. "What friends?" she said, but she agreed to screen the movies with me. I told her to come over right away, we could spend the afternoon, I even had a box of Orville Redenbacher's Microwave Popping Corn. She said okay, and then before she hung up, I don't know why, I asked, "How old are you, Angel?"

"Fourteen," she said, "going on a thousand."

I knew she was fourteen. She was old enough to get to my apartment by herself. She could get her own taxi and pay her own fare. She was old enough, and she looked even older. She reminded me of that very tall girl in women's tennis, I can't remember her name, Pam Something, I think, the one with the great serve and great reach and terrific net game and a temperament as tightly strung as her racquet. She's wonderful to watch and everyone always hopes things go her way so that her raw talent isn't compromised by her raw emotions. Once I saw "I'm sure her name is Pam Something" play in person at Forest Hills, and it was amazing how nervous the crowd was. No one wanted to do anything that might upset her. If someone spoke too loudly or cheered inappropriately, there was a chance Pam might lose it right then and there, and the match would not be worth sitting through. That is what happens when I'm with Angel. I find myself being overly careful not to upset her. It's unnerving. It must be like being a surgeon—I'll have to ask Frank if I'm right—I'm terrified I'll make a fatally wrong move.

I even harbor some doubt that Angel will arrive as scheduled. Since her last disappearance, Suzanne and David have been trying to keep her on a shorter leash, without antagonizing her, of course. But I know there's always the chance that Angel might use getting out of the house alone and coming to my apartment as an opportunity to run away a third time.

However, she arrived promptly, wearing prescription sunglasses, a black headband, and a black jump suit. She had no handbag, and the thought occurred to me that I had never seen a woman who didn't carry some sort of bag. But Angel was traveling light.

"Right on time," I said. "Come on in."

She came in and plopped down on the closed hide-a-bed without a word.

"Is this where we watch?" was the first thing she said, referring to the TV monitor.

"That's it."

She did not take off her sunglasses.

"You want some popcorn? Something to drink?"

"Daddy says I'm fat," she said without expression.

She was large, not fat.

"Popcorn isn't fattening," I said.

"It is when you pour butter all over it and I can't eat that shit without butter."

She said "shit" as though it were no more offensive than the word *popcorn*.

I made popcorn for myself and poured myself a Kirin.

"I've looked at the movies already, Angel," I called out from the kitchen. "I really need your input."

Silence.

"I guess I'm just getting old. I don't understand half of what's going on in these movies."

"Maybe next life," she said.

At first I thought she had said "Maybe next time," meaning that you had to watch these movies twice before you could understand them, but then I realized that that was not what she had said.

"What? What did you say?"

"Nothing."

"Anyway, the music's pretty good rock, although I'm not quite sure what most of it has to do with what's going on in the film. I mean, it should, shouldn't it? Shouldn't a soundtrack mean something? Shouldn't it create an appropriate mood? Haven't you ever wished there was a soundtrack in your own life? You know, a clash of cymbals when you have a brilliant idea or a crescendo of violins at some particularly poignant moment? Somebody gives you a beautiful gift, maybe jewelry, gold maybe, a necklace, a bracelet, and all of a sudden there's this crescendo. I don't know." I knew my references to a gold bracelet were meant to be provocative, but I was really just being chatty. I didn't even necessarily believe what I was saying.

"No," Angel said.

She could not remember ever wishing for the sound of violins in real life. Nor could I.

I carried the bowl of popcorn out of the kitchen and set it down on the coffee table in front of Angel.

"It's got a buttery flavor," I told her, "but no butter."

I had already set the VCR; the first movie was in the machine, the counter at zero, the channel selector on three.

"Now, you understand how this works? All you have to tell me is how you like the movie. Whether you'd go to see it because of the actors, the subject matter, the music, whatever. It would help, of course, if you could tell me why you like it or don't like it, but it's okay if you don't know. I'm really interested in your gut reaction, Angel. Anything you can tell me above and beyond that is a bonus."

She still hadn't taken off her sunglasses. She reminded me of a fighter after a brutal fight, and I wondered if surrendering and coming back home after running away had been a pulverizing defeat for Angel; I wondered if there were swollen purple eyes behind her sunglasses. I pushed "on" and "play," and said I wished I could find the remote controller, then I could turn the sound up or down or stop the movie at any point and go back or rerun a scene in slow motion or freeze a frame. I could do any of those things without the unit, but it meant getting up repeatedly to work the controls on the machine itself. Remote control was so much easier.

While Angel watched the movie, I watched Angel. The movie started energetically with quick cuts of teenagers waking up, getting ready for school, going to school, attending classes, having lunch, getting out of school, and going home again. One entire typical school day was compressed into two minutes of film. The titles were chalked on the classroom blackboards. Gimmicky. Counterpointing the pictures was a corruption of Chuck Berry's "School Days," renamed "School Daze" and sung by the Dropouts, a popular rock band that was renamed Onan in the movie. Angel moved her head slightly to what I thought was uninfectious rock 'n' roll. I thought I saw her lips moving. I wished I could see her eyes.

The plot developed quickly. The student community wanted Onan to play at the big school dance. But the band had been associated with satanism, a reputation enhanced by the appearance and stage behavior of its members and by the sacrificial murders that had coincided with their last three concerts. Students at three schools where Onan had played were found dead in neighboring woods, their mutilated corpses marked with chicken heads and the word *Kthuru* written on their bare chests in chicken blood. *Kthuru* was one of a string of apparently nonsensical words in a popular Onan song. In the song, when students were questioned by their teachers, they were encouraged to answer the ridiculous questions with the equally ridiculous refrain "Shfkagbka-Kthuru-Rlu," a refrain almost as unpronounceable as it was unintelligible. These were not typical rock concert deaths attributable to an overwrought or overdosed audience. These were ritual murders, premeditated acts of evil. The question was whether the band was only inspiring the murders with its music and performances, or whether it was literally killing its audiences. Beyond the conventional question of whodunit, I knew the moviemakers were asking a larger question about the moral responsibility of those people in a position to influence and incite teenagers. Should these people be censored? It was a hotly debated subject at the moment. There were hearings going on in Washington. Rock 'n' roll celebrities were being interrogated about their song lyrics and record album jackets. One citizens' group was lobbying for the institution of a rating system similar to the one used in movies.

If ever a movie deserved an R rating, it was *Song in the Key of Death*. According to Simon, this working title of the movie would probably be changed because it was too close to the name of a Stevie Wonder album. There was sex, violence, bloodshed, devil worship, mutilations, and explicit language. But each of these elements was treated lovingly by the director, one of the two things about the movie I couldn't understand and was hoping Angel could help me with. Why would the director choose to film scenes of such obvious evil in a way that idealized them? It reminded me of a famous public service TV commercial that had won a million awards. The commercial was supposed to warn against the terrible consequences of heroin addiction. Ninety percent of the commercial consisted of the camera's slowly panning along the horizontal body of a nude young man. The lighting—the commercial was filmed in black and white—bathed the nude body in a sort of celestial glow. The body itself was beautiful, like a Greek statue, slim and smooth and graceful as a sleeping David by Michelangelo. The music was subtle and enchanting and seductive. Maybe just strings or a single oboe. In hushed, hypnotic tones, the voice-over described the incomparable tranquility and euphoria the heroin addict experiences. BUT! The punch line was a jarring shot of the body suddenly being slammed into a refrigerated drawer. The door clanged shut and the point was made—what might tempt you to use heroin is not what you are going to get. And yet for most of the commercial, the viewer, like the addict, finds himself getting high on this cinematic splendor. So it is in this movie. The viewer finds himself inexplicably attracted to the slow-motion bludgeoning of small animals, the methodical rape of a high school cheerleader, the growing collection of severed fingers and toes hidden beneath the skin of a conga drum. Why? I hoped Angel could enlighten me.

I hoped, too, she could help explain the other thing in the movie I didn't quite understand—the relationship between the students and the teachers. When I went to school, teachers were unapproachable figures of absolute authority. We would not think of calling a teacher by his or her first name or chatting about anything other than schoolwork or having any relationship other than a professional one. And yet in the movie it was difficult sometimes to tell the teachers from the students. They dressed alike, talked alike, acted alike. Teachers and students were allied against the principal, against the board of education, the police department, the local politicians, and the committees advocating censorship. But their alliance went beyond the mere political. They seemed to be emotional allies as well, and I hoped Angel could help explain this to me.

At the end of the movie Onan was absolved and allowed to play at the school, the berserk killers were uncovered and apprehended. The moral seemed to be that evil could not be attributed to the provocations of rock 'n' roll. This point was emphasized in an epilogue. But a second epilogue showed the Dropouts, as themselves, at work in their palatial West Coast mansion. Surrounded by exotic paraphernalia, they sang the title song of their next album while the final credits ran, the words of the song invoking the devil and leaving the audience unsure of whether Satan had indeed been defeated.

All through the movie, Angel was quiet and attentive. She asked me to stop the movie once so she could go to the bathroom. She asked me to turn the volume down on two occasions when the music was overbearingly loud. She never touched the Orville Redenbacher Microwave Popping Corn. She never took off her sunglasses.

"Well? What did you think?"

"I thought," she said, not taking her eyes off the now blank screen, "that it was perfect."

"You liked it?" I marveled, unable to conceal my surprise.

"It was perfect."

"What was?"

"Maria."

Maria was a minor female character, a student who did not fit in with the other students because she was "out of it." In one of the contrived subplots, Maria began to hear strange voices through her Walkman. Nobody believed her because nobody could hear the voices when they listened to her Walkman. Eventually these voices persuaded Maria to kill herself, which she did in an erotic scene filmed in excruciating slow motion. Through much smoke, we watched reflections in a mirror that grew steamier as Maria committed suicide in her bathtub, slowly, serenely slitting the veins behind her knees. To me this suicide could only have been committed by someone as obviously deranged as Maria. To Angel it was perfect.

"Do kids and teachers really act like that?" I switched the subject.

Angel did not seem to understand my question.

"I mean, do you call your teachers by their first names and talk about their personal lives, things like that? Do you have that kind of relationship with the teachers at your school, Angel?"

She looked at me seriously through her sunglasses.

"Roger, there are kids in my class who have been sleeping with their teachers for two years."

I was stunned. God, even Lolita was more discreet than that.

We decided that one movie was enough for today. We talked about the soundtrack, which Angel liked. We talked about the director's idealized treatment of brutality, which Angel said she could understand without being able to explain why, like life after death, which led us into a discussion I could not have anticipated and have not been able to forget.

"Do you believe in an afterlife?" I asked her.

"Many."

"Many?"

"If you promise not to tell David or Suzanne, I'll tell you what I really believe in."

"I promise."

"Reincarnation."

"Are you serious?"

"If you patronize me, I'll never talk to you again, Roger."

"I'm not patronizing you. I'm just . . . surprised, that's all."

"I haven't told anyone."

"Then why are you telling me?"

"Because you deserve to know."

"Reincarnation isn't something you know, Angel; it's something you believe in. Do you really expect me to believe in it?"

She just stared at me through her dark glasses. After a long long minute, she said, "Do you have everything you need from me on the movie?"

"Well, no. No, I wanted to find out what you thought about the actors and whether or not you'd see it more than once or buy the soundtrack or buy the videocassette when it comes out, things like that."

"Don't you get it, Roger? I don't care about your stupid appraisals. That's not why I'm here. I'm here to tell you, Roger. I have been many people before this and I will be many people after this. But don't you see who I am now, Roger?"

"What are you talking about, Angel?"

She got up abruptly. I saw a quick thin flash of gold on her wrist as she got up.

"I'm Victoria, Roger. The reincarnation of Victoria."

17

IF THE RECENT OCCURRENCES IN my life were happening to a stranger, if I were reading about them in the newspaper or a book or watching them on the eleven o'clock news, a sex-change operation, reincarnation, a wife's probable infidelity with her husband's brother, a trunkful of mysterious relics, a secret diary, a missing ring, and a Himalayan holiday would seem much more unbelievable. Yet when experienced personally, they are real, believable, even natural. They began; they will end. This is the second act.

"Hello! Roger! Hello! Anyone home in there?"

"Huh . . . uh what? I'm sorry. My mind was just—"

"It's your turn, Roger."

"Sorry."

"Ready? What Yippie said in 1968: 'My goal is at the age of thirty-five to act like I'm fifteen'?"

I am tempted to go through Victoria's diary when she is asleep. I find myself awake in the middle of the night staring at her handbag. I realize that it's an act I should not commit. It's a betrayal of my belief in the territorial prerogative. It's treason; yet I'm tempted. And losing resistance. I'm beginning to feel that it's my prerogative to do what I must to preserve our friendship, our love, our marriage. It's not as easy as it was, because now Andrew sleeps the night on the hide-a-bed, if he hasn't been put into my bed to sleep off a colossal drunk. Victoria is in one room; Andrew is in the other. I walk the high wire in between. Each night I sneak closer and closer to the bag like a curious cat, brushing against it, kicking it, moving it from the floor to a chair, from the chair to her dresser, from her dresser back to the chair. "What are you doing with my bag?" I imagine Victoria saying. "Just putting it on the chair so nobody steps on it." I try hard to be heard over the pounding of my heart. In my imagination, Victoria has been insulted. Her eyes look disappointed and angry like they are now, after our argument about going out tonight to the new Italian place Dale and Lori found. Victoria didn't want to go; I did.

"If you hate it, I'll eat it," Lori told her at the restaurant.

"What are you making her order?"

"*Pancetta,* Italian bacon. But it tastes like balled up little pieces of fried chicken skin. Yum."

"Another carafe of white wine, please."

Dale: "It's not certain, but I'm working on it. If I can convince them that I need to be on location, the studio will send me to the Khyber Pass. And maybe I can get Twentieth Century-Fox credentials for all of us."

Pakistan again. Perhaps there is black magic in all of this. Like in *Song in the Key of Death.* The bracelets, the relics, reincarnation . . . Pakistan, India, voodoo. I do not want to think about it, but I am thinking about it.

"Think about it, will you, Angel?" I had suggested the next day.

"You think about what I told *you*."

"I owe you some money, and you owe me two more screenings. As far as I'm concerned, you were helpful, and all that business about reincarnation, well, if you want to talk about it, fine."

"Not today. And if you tell anyone, I'll deny it."

Andrew has had his motorcycle repaired. I don't know where he parks it now. Not on the street. There's been a change in his attitude since he started sleeping nights while Victoria and I are in bed in the next room. He's become moody and even less communicative than before, if that's possible. I wonder if they've had a fight. Maybe it wasn't kismet after all.

Not that it matters that Victoria and I are in bed together, does it, Victoria?

"Don't."

"It's been a long time."

"Your brother is right outside."

"What about when he wasn't right outside?"

"I'm angry, Roger. I've been angry."

What can she be angry about? She is angry because it is convenient for her. I have done nothing to make her angry. Yes, I quit the symphony without consulting her, but I know in my heart that was what she wanted all along. There is really nothing I can do to make her stop being angry. It will be over when it is over. That's what Frank is talking about.

"I hope I'll have done what I can in time to get my ass over to Pakistan. But I don't know. A thing like this is unpredictable. It could take days. It could take months. It'll be over when it's over."

"I always thought an epidemic was something that only happened to people."

"It *is* happening to people. Indirectly, anyway. Those poor damn fishermen. And it's not just this clam cancer they're worried about. They're getting screwed all the way from Massachusetts to Chesapeake Bay. There's the clam leukemia, hemapoietic sarcoma. There's some new parasite called MSX that's killing off fifty percent of the oysters. Plus there's this snail that they've always had called the drill that's killing another twenty percent of the oysters. That's seventy percent of the oysters—gone!"

"That's like having an epidemic of impotency!"

"What are you talking about?"

"Oysters are supposed to be an aphrodisiac."

"Don't believe it. I had a dozen oysters last night and only eight of them worked."

Tomorrow it will be September. Victoria is going away. A business trip to California. Except for a few small trips, none of us has ever gone anywhere at his own expense.

"You're staying home and I'm going out of town," she said

when we got home, still arguing the first of our recent pointless arguments.

"What do you mean, on a case?"

"California."

That was what she had wanted to talk to Dale and Phyllis about the other night. They go to California whenever Dale can trump up a meeting with the studio about a movie he's novelizing. Victoria wanted them to recommend some restaurants, shops, sights.

"That Mineo business. Twenty-two sworn statements. I've got to find them, sit them down, and take twenty-two sworn statements."

She enjoyed describing her assignment to me in a cold businesslike manner. She knew it annoyed me because I was powerless to object. What could I say? What could I accuse her of . . . doing her job?

"How long?"

"Depends. Two weeks. Three. But I have to have them by the first week in October."

"Well, when?"

"When am I going? I don't know. Soon. I've got to coordinate it with everybody. Not before the weekend, anyway."

She left the next day. She came home in the afternoon, packed in an hour, and phoned for a taxi. Then she explained the sudden urgency of her trip. Three of the people she had to track down were going out of town on *extended vacations.* If she didn't get to them before they left, the case would be delayed again, and time was on the side of the defendants. Victoria's firm couldn't afford another postponement.

"They're playing games with us," she said.

I feel like my life is a game. It's like this round of *Wheel of Fortune* I'm watching. There aren't enough letters filled in for me to arrive at a solution, but I can't stop thinking about what I've already uncovered.

18

SPRING IS WHEN NATURE renews itself. Fall is when humans renew themselves. If April is a harbinger of new prospects, then September is when the work starts. It's like our night in the hot tub. After a summer spent in hot and whirling communal play, September is the jolt of a cold shower.

Victoria is collecting sworn statements in California. Frank has left for Maryland, Virginia, and Massachusetts to consult about the clam epidemic before preparing for his trip to Pakistan under the auspices of WHO. Because Frank will be busy with the clam problem, Lori has taken a free-lance assignment from Barbara's advertising agency and will style the wardrobe for a pool of six commercials that have to be shot in two weeks. This means a frantic shopping spree for Lori so she can fashionably outfit the six men, eleven women, and three Afghan hounds who are in the commercials. Dale is on his second draft of *Superman V.* He is also negotiating with the studio for a location meeting on the new Khyber Pass movie and trying to wangle Fox credentials for his good friends, who all might happen to be in that part of the world during the holidays. Phyllis is back at the UN School to teach her course in women's history, a course she created. Julia is busily organizing her late January art show. Barbara is account planning at the agency for a new product launch. Michael is working forty-eight hours a day trying to finish his video before he has to leave for the Kama Rawni Clinic. David is up to his ears in beeps because of a new reservations system the airline he works for is installing in travel agencies up and down the East Coast. And I am facing a mid-December deadline on the three appraisals. The only one of us who is not hard at work at some new enterprise is Andrew. Now that Victoria is out of town, he sleeps until ten, doesn't brush his teeth, takes off on his motorcycle for the day and most of the night, and comes home no earlier than the beginning of the eleven o'clock news. He is always roaring drunk, disheveled, and covered with new food stains on his Nehru jacket. He switches off the news and switches on the porno cable channel and passes out in his clothes on the hide-a-bed whether I have thought to open it ahead of time or not. For Andrew, September is no different than any other month.

I have not heard from Angel at all. With the apartment empty so much of the time and September in my blood, I have made terrific progress on the first appraisal. Angel's help was invaluable. Just knowing that the movie appealed to her elevated its worth in my eyes. In my appraisal what I might have rated one star, I gave three, and those two extra stars translated to more than a million dollars extra in forecasted revenues. Angel's reaction had increased my estimate of the movie's value and consequently the size of my fee. At this point it looks like when I finish the first appraisal, my percentage is going to amount to about five thousand, if Simon accepts it, which I can't believe he won't. He has accepted every appraisal I've handed in so far. I don't think I would have quit the symphony and gone into this full-time if Simon and I weren't in sync.

I thought the fee for the first appraisal would more than cover a trip to Pakistan, but a week after Victoria left for California, Lori called with news that promises to wipe out more than just the five thousand dollars.

"I'm crazy, Rog, I haven't got a minute. I tried calling Vic-

toria three times at the hotel, but she was out. Do me a favor
and tell her if she calls that I can't do any better on that coat.
I don't think I could even find one like it here. But tell her it's
worth it. That's what they cost."

"What coat?"

Victoria had called Lori to ask about a natural lynx coat she
had seen in some fancy Beverly Hills shop. Lori is our resident
expert on clothes. She's a commercial stylist. It's her job to
dress actors and actresses for parts in commercials and sometimes plays or TV shows. Once she did a TV pilot. She has to
know what's in fashion and what things cost. That's why Victoria had called her from California. Victoria had seen the coat
in a shop and had fallen in love with it even though it cost a
fortune. Lori described the coat to me; it was called a Victoria
Lynx.

"Are you sitting down, Roger? It's seven thousand dollars."

"Is she crazy?"

"She said she's been in the shop every day. She drives past,
has to stop, goes inside to try on the coat, and then leaves
without buying it. It's a lot of money, Roger, but it's worth it.
That's what she wanted to know, if it was worth it."

"Jesus Christ, Lori, she's a fucking antivivisectionist or whatever the hell you call it. Don't you remember that night she
said we ought to write a goddamn letter to Fred the Furrier
telling him how they kill minks and torture baby seals so he can
go on television and make his millions?"

"Hey, I gotta run. Give her the information anyway, will
you? You know Victoria, she'd never spend seven thousand
dollars on a coat. She's just amused by it. It's even got her
name. By the way, Frank called. He says where he is is like
Auschwitz for clams. They're just piled up in these huge pits
along the bay. It looks hopeless, which means it looks good
for him to be able to get away to Pakistan. If he can't do any
thing more there, what's the sense of staying? I really gotta go.
'Bye."

God, if something's bothering her, why can't she just go out
and buy a hat like everybody else? Why does she have to be
"amused" by a seven-thousand-dollar coat?

Even though it was eleven o'clock in the morning in Califor-

nia, when she'd most likely be out taking sworn statements, I
called Victoria's hotel. I was counting on her being out. Considering the fragile nature of our relationship recently, I didn't
want to forbid her to buy the coat. I had never forbidden
Victoria anything. But she had never wanted anything so outrageous before. Also, it would only fuel her persistent argument about my arbitrary decision to go into appraisals full time
if suddenly I objected to the kind of expenditure my new
career was supposed to make possible. But I didn't want her
to buy the coat. There was something about her sudden desire,
her change of principle, that made me think of Andrew.
And so I composed the perfect message to leave at the hotel
desk. I dictated it to the switchboard operator slowly and carefully: *Lori says the coat is a lot of money. Roger.* Not only
had I quoted Lori accurately, but the message succeeded in
keeping me out of the matter entirely. I was not forbidding
Victoria to buy the coat. I might not even know what it was
all about.

Fifteen minutes later, while I was still congratulating myself
on the message I had left at the hotel, Andrew staggered
through the door. With Goldie.

"Hi, baby bro, Ah'm Goldie," the black girl said cheerfully.
She sniffled, loud and wet, as though she had a terrible cold or
a heavy cocaine habit.

She was young, hard to guess how young, and very thin, but
not sickly thin. She had long legs and high heels and skin-tight
black pants that made her look even thinner and taller. And
she wore a low-cut leotard sort of top that made her breasts
look lethal.

"We gon' have us some fun, babe?" she asked me sweetly,
professionally, helping Andrew and his crash helmet over to
the closed hide-a-bed, where he crashed.

When I got a good look at her face, I saw that Goldie had big
bright buck teeth and big bright eyes and that all that sniffling
noise came from a very tiny nose. She wore a stiff, shiny, or-
ange-colored wig as unselfconsciously as a football player
wears his helmet; it was part of the uniform.

I did not like the decision I had to make. On one hand, I was
allowing Andrew to stay with me, which meant that my apart-

ment was his home for the time being. It was hardly my place to reprimand my older brother for bringing home a hooker. On the other hand, he had been an obnoxious, insensitive bum from the minute he had shown up at my door. Now he had finally gone too far. But I knew that if Victoria wasn't out of town, Andrew never would have risked her finding out that to him love was something you paid for by the hour. And so I felt I was holding something over Andrew. And Victoria. Some weird kind of proof that he was cheating on my wife. Some weird kind of consolation that if Victoria ever decided to leave me for Andrew, she would be making the biggest mistake of her life. All this ran through my mind while Goldie explained the sweeping terms of her contract with Andrew.

"Big bro be real genrus. You two git Goldie all day long, babe. You git han' jobs, blo' jobs, fuckin', dancin', Ah don't care what, long's you let me put pr'tection on you," she said, digging a prophylactic out of her purse and flashing the unfamiliar black and white tinfoil wrapper, " 'n s'long's Ah don't drop dead, baby." She sniffled and laughed a big buck-toothed laugh that made me think of a snorting horse, but a beautiful sleek black horse.

Andrew revived for a second and mumbled something completely unintelligible, which Goldie seemed to understand perfectly. Obediently, she laid him out on the hide-a-bed and unzipped his fly. She held the square of tinfoil between her teeth while she exposed Andrew. With quick, professional movements, she unwrapped the prophylactic, unrolled it, checked it for flaws, rerolled it, excited Andrew's penis, rolled the prophylactic onto his penis, which even in a semierect state was bigger and thicker than Mohammad's erection at Big Tubs, and then she bent down to go to work, slurping and sniffling and bobbing her head as casually and automatically as if she were performing the most natural act in the world. Again Andrew mumbled something unintelligible, and she understood him by verifying that "You wantcher balls, baby?" and then reached her hand into his open fly and started playing with them.

I did not want to look, but except for youthful horsing around in locker rooms or at sleepovers or at camp, guys don't ever get to see other guys when they're aroused, and I was interested. I tried to keep my eyes on the screen of the Apple to pay complete attention to the final edit of my first appraisal, but I must have watched everything that took place between Goldie and Andrew.

He was incredibly drunk. His hands flopped around uncontrollably. His face was screwed up into a squint that made him look as though he were blind and in terrific pain. Goldie earned every penny of whatever Andrew had paid her. She did all the work. She stood him up or sat him down or laid him out or bent him over, whatever was required; she undressed him, aroused him, satisfied him, dressed him, brought him a beer, brought him leftovers, undressed him again, aroused him again, satisfied him again, and then repeated the process, sniffling the whole time, calling him baby the whole time, occasionally asking me if I'd like something, too. But, of course, I remained loyal. And despite the events of the day and then the night, I succeeded in finishing the editing of the last pages of the first appraisal, although how I did it I'll never know. Except for those awful moments when Andrew's ecstasy embarrassed me and sent me into the kitchen, I stayed at the Apple and worked almost automatically, typing, overtyping, deleting, inserting, proofing, checking, amending, appending, and storing as though in a trance, all the while watching Goldie perform out of more than the corner of my eye. Andrew remained oblivious until reaching each climax, when he would moan and scream like someone being hanged, his arms and legs flapping and twitching and then stiffening like in rigor mortis. Goldie sniffled and giggled in accompaniment because she was thrilled when he lost all control and screamed and died—it meant she had done her job. But his grotesque death scenes filled me with nausea and made me run from the Apple to the kitchen sink, where I could splash cold water on my face.

"You sure, baby?" Goldie kept asking me.

I was sure.

Andrew couldn't go on forever. He fell sound asleep on the closed hide-a-bed. Goldie asked if she could watch TV.

"Why don't you go home?" I told her.

"Ah'm paid for, baby," she said indignantly. "Ain't you never worked for nobody?" she said with mock shock that I didn't understand this elemental rule. Then she laughed at us both.

"How old are you, Goldie?"

"How old you think?"

"I don't know. Twenty-five?"

She could have been any age. Her appearance camouflaged all possibilities.

"Seventeen, baby."

God, she was a baby herself.

"Why do you do this?"

"Ah got to sind money for mah little girl."

She was still bright-eyed and smiley as she told me all about the "scumbag" who had loved her and left her and the pregnancy that forced her out of school and the adorable little girl she named after Coretta King and the aunt in New Jersey who offered to raise little Coretta until Goldie saved enough money to take care of her daughter herself.

"But Ah see her ever weekend, 'n she sure 'nough know who she belong to, baby. She sure 'nough know that."

Then she wanted to know what I was doing. I showed her the Apple, how it worked, and gave her a simple explanation of my assignment, which led her to believe that I had something to do with making movies.

"Ah had me a movie star one time. You'd know him, too. He paid for a blo' job but he just wanted a han' job, know what Ah mean? While we was driving. He never told me who he was, but I reckonized him under his hat and shades, baby. It was him all right. But Ah wouldn't tell nobody nothin', baby. I wouldn't tell nobody nothin' 'bout you neither. You sure you don't wantcher balls or somethin'?"

She was sitting next to me at the Apple and reached down and touched me and I glanced at the hide-a-bed to see if Andrew was still asleep. I knew she would listen only to him. He was her boss.

"Why don't we wake him up," I suggested, gently pulling Goldie's hand out of my lap. "It's his money. Why don't you wake him up and take him out on the town?"

"You too?"

"I've got work."

"You been." And she attempted to switch off the Apple.

"No, don't. First I've got to save what's on here. Otherwise everything's lost."

"How could if you do somethin' it be lost?"

"Because it isn't real until I save it."

I stopped pretending that I didn't want to go out on the town with Goldie and Andrew. I would go as a witness. I was building a case against Andrew to prove to Victoria how unworthy he was. I had watched him all afternoon and saved every detail as evidence. Now I would go out with him and his paid hooker and gather even more evidence. About his hangouts. About the kind of people he associates with. About the kind of life he leads. I was the private detective Victoria should have hired to follow Andrew around while she was in California. God, do I have to do everything myself?

Gently, I pushed Goldie toward the hide-a-bed. She woke Andrew by unzipping his fly and reaching in and arousing him. I couldn't believe that he was ready again. Wasn't liquor supposed to be a depressant? But he was ready, and he was more sober now, too, after his little nap. He mumbled something and Goldie answered him so quietly I couldn't hear. For the first time, Andrew was an active participant. He tried to kiss her, and I made a mental note of his clumsy but tender expression of affection. It would go into my private detective's report to show Victoria if she ever decided to choose Andrew over me. Andrew's tenderness did not last very long. Angered by Goldie's reluctance to let him kiss her, he got rough with her. He threw her down on the floor and stood over her, his pants down around his legs, his penis standing out over her like a weapon. He tried to stand astride her, but he couldn't get his leg over her body because his fallen pants acted like leg irons. His excitement disappeared and along with it his weapon. It hung over her like a sprig of withered mistletoe, and Goldie couldn't help but laugh. Andrew glowered at her and then aimed himself at her with a very familiar thumb-and-first-two fingers grip that looked familiar to Goldie, too. She rolled onto her side just in time, clutched Andrew's leg, and slithered out from under him without being hit by a drop. She was behind him now, and she reached up between his legs and gently squeezed his balls while at the same time she licked and kissed and sniffled at his tensed rear end. I was too stunned to say or do a thing. I was too stunned to be angry. I could not take my eyes off the two of them and the puddle darkening the carpet below them. All I could think of was whether the stain would be permanent.

"Soap 'n wahter and Lysol," Goldie said to me when he was finished. "Take it right away like puppie pee. C'mon, getcher shoes, baby. Big bro want to take us on the town, dontcha, big bro?" Andrew had already hoisted his pants and half tucked in his shirt and squeezed into his rumpled Nehru jacket and was looking for his crash helmet.

"We can't all go on his motorcycle," I protested. "Look, I've got to clean this up. Why don't you two go without me. Tell me where you're going, and I'll meet you there later."

"We goin' everwhere, baby."

If they didn't want to wait for me, that was too bad. After putting on my shoes, I soaked up most of the pee with paper towels, holding the drenched towels by the corners with the tips of two fingers and breathing through my mouth so I didn't have to smell Andrew's puddle. I trashed the towels and went into the bathroom and got a washcloth, wet it and rubbed soap into it and came back out and rubbed the stain. Then I threw out the washcloth, too, and sprayed Lysol all over the darkness on the carpet. I washed my hands with the bathroom cleanser, dried them, and applied Vaseline Intensive Care Lotion. At some point during this procedure, Andrew and Goldie had gone out into the hallway to press the button for the elevator. The door was open and I looked out into the hallway. Goldie was standing in the vision of the elevator's electric eye, keeping the door from closing, letting it bump into her and then open again, causing it to buzz angrily because someone on another floor kept pushing the button. I patted my back pocket to make sure I had my wallet, patted my front pocket to make sure I had my keys, felt for my sunglasses, closed the door, locked it, double-checked that it was locked, walked down the hallway, and pushed into the elevator behind Goldie. Andrew was not inside.

"Let's go, baby," Goldie sniffled, putting her long pink fingernail against the button marked Lobby. "Big bro give us cab fare," she said, showing me a handful of disorganized dollars. "We goin' to meet him at Cherokee's, baby." And we were off.

Sometimes I pretend I'm a reporter covering a story. When I went to Big Tubs looking for Victoria's lost ring, I pretended I was working on an assignment for a newspaper or for TV. I wasn't personally involved; I was just doing my job. That was how I felt riding down the elevator with Goldie, going out into the street, hailing a taxi, listening to her give directions to the driver. I was just along for the story, for more evidence. By the time the taxi was probing the deserted downtown west side looking for our address, the driver had turned on his headlights. As the cab made a right turn toward the river, the headlights caught the small beat-up sign announcing the Cherokee Bar.

Outside, it was quiet and desolate. Inside, the noise was deafening—jukebox, shouting, laughing, arguing. It was packed with boisterous drinkers, most of them somehow familiar looking. The customers were mostly men, but there were several women in the bar, too, and they were extremely young looking. I realized what was familiar about the crowd. It was like a scene from the past filmed for today's audiences. Everyone's clothes were out-of-date and looked like a costume. There were motorcycle jackets and wool jackets with the names of schools or clubs scrolled on the backs. The people without jackets wore black turtleneck shirts or Italian T-shirts. Ties were wide and dress shirts were short-sleeved. The young girls had long hair and white complexions and moved their heads in time to the old rock 'n' roll songs blaring out of the art deco Wurlitzer. Andrew was already inside, his arms around two of these young girls. It took a full five minutes for Goldie and me to work our way through the three- and four-deep crowd at the bar to reach him. He ignored us, but he signaled the bartender to take care of us. I ordered Goldie a Manhattan and myself a dark beer. Considering the number of customers and their constant shouts of "Beer," " 'Nother round," "Hit us again," "Seven and Seven," our drinks came faster than I expected. There was not much else to do but drink in the Cherokee Bar, and the organization of taps, bottles, glasses, and ice was brilliantly designed never to keep a single customer waiting. The three bartenders were in constant motion—pouring, stirring, adding garnishes, delivering drinks, tabulating checks. The noise was so loud that conversation was virtually impossible. In no time at all, the big redhead waiting on us poured us two more drinks. Goldie was used to drinking. My beers were very smooth and went down easy.

What do I remember from the Cherokee? I remember the music, song after song mentioned in our favorite game all come to life in booming bass and whining falsetto with roller coaster interludes on sax. The words that were recognizable were always the same: young love, lost love, found love, true love, broken love, impatient love, April love.

I remember watching the two young girls Andrew was fondling laugh and bat their eyes every time he kissed them on the cheek or squeezed them around the waist or buried his face in their cleavage. And then some guy took exception to Andrew's familiarity and pushed him—there wasn't room enough to do more than push—and Andrew pushed him back and spit into his face, and the guy backed off and disappeared into the crowd. Andrew was finished with these girls anyway. He dumped them in favor of two others, leaving the first pair just standing there wondering what *they* had done to offend *him*.

I remember switching to whiskey. I remember drinking and watching Andrew all night. He was crude and obnoxious, but something about his expression when I could catch a glimpse of his face made him look as though he was just going through the motions, acting out a part for some private audience. Now I know that I was that audience, and it makes me feel good that without realizing it then, I was an attentive and sympathetic one.

We stayed at the Cherokee for an hour or so, and then Goldie told me we were going uptown. I was beginning to feel the three beers and two whiskies.

We went to one of those overdecorated singles bars on the Upper East Side with fake Tiffany lamps that keep bumping into your head and antiqued mirrors everywhere and no room at the bar and not a lot of room at the table you're forced to sit at because there's a huge lazy susan filled with salad toppings and a big fancy silver caddy for the oil and vinegar and an enamel ashtray and salt and pepper and giant water goblets and oversize wineglasses and book-length handwritten menus and carafes of the special house red and the special house white and table tents advertising happy hour and brunch and special wine-tasting parties and special entertainment and special appetizers and special entrees and special desserts.

Andrew, who beat us to the restaurant on his motorcycle, had succeeded in getting up to the bar, of course. If he had brought us here to see meat on the hoof, he had timed it perfectly. Five minutes after we arrived, every unattached career girl from the city and the island streamed into the bar. They looked like members of the same sorry sorority, and Andrew looked like he was pledging.

I watched him work a small circle of these desperate women, buying them drinks, leering at them, being brash and crude and charming them with his chauvinism. As he had at the Cherokee, Andrew moved in on these women, inflating them with his attention, and then burst their balloons by turning his back on them, suddenly buying drinks for someone else. NeAndrewthal, Barb calls him. And all my friends would agree. But the girls he so casually but carefully picked out of the crowd found this attractive. NeAndrewthal was a link to something that had been missing from this place and time and from the lives of these anxious women. Here was a man who was not afraid to make a wrong move.

"What's he doing?" I asked Goldie.

"Whatever he want," Goldie said jealously.

But his behavior was self-destructive. What did he want? What was he after? I had two more drinks, Bloody Marys, served in steins with big black beads of pepper floating on top, wedges of lime crammed in among the tiny ice cubes, and long, thick stalks of celery flowering up over the brim. Goldie sipped and sniffled at a snifter of brandy. She was not happy. She was not used to being paid to do nothing. She only felt worthwhile when performing sexually. Being the date of someone more interested in watching Andrew than in her depressed Goldie. She may have been thinking about the money she could have been making by slipping out and flagging down a few cars. In the last two hours, she might have earned an extra hundred dollars or more for little Coretta by giving blow jobs at fifteen dollars apiece. But she made no attempt to leave. Goldie, too, was one of the girls Andrew bought and discarded. She went to the ladies' room, carrying her snifter of brandy with her. On the way back to our table, she stopped for a quick exchange with Andrew. As I munched another stalk of celery in an attempt to fight off becoming too drunk, she informed me that we were leaving. This time we were going to a private party Andrew had just arranged. Goldie paid the check with a messy pile of bills and we left.

Again, Andrew was there before us. Our taxi passed his motorcycle, parked down the block from the address written in tiny handwriting on the back of the cocktail napkin Goldie was holding. Six B was three long flights up, on a red door with a brass peephole. We knocked, were peeped at, and let into a foyer that was wide with a high ceiling and walls handsomely papered in a warm, subtle print. But what could have been a dramatic display of old world charm had been turned into a counterculture gallery of punk poster art. There were pictures of atomic blasts and posters that parodied other famous posters and posters of slogans and sayings all arrogant and defiant.

A sweet, demure young lady let us in. She was one of the several girls Andrew had been charming at the bar. Another one was in the living room carefully forming rows of cocaine on a makeup mirror. Andrew was stretched out on a reclining chair, a bottle of French wine in one hand. He was drinking the wine right out of the bottle.

"Hi, I'm Pam, and this is Kelly."

In my growing intoxication, I did not think it at all strange to introduce Roger and Goldie as though we were a married couple.

Kelly did not look up from the lines of cocaine. Pam asked if we wanted a drink. Goldie said yes. I was brought one while I was still deciding if I wanted one. I had no idea what it was, but it was clear and I assumed it was vodka. It turned out to be tequila.

"Ready?" Kelly asked, still bowed over her lines, fixing the misalignments only she could see, protecting her little field with a cupped hand against an errant breeze or sneeze.

I do not do drugs much. Marijuana occasionally. Drugs make me lose control. We do not like losing control.

"Do you two live here? I mean, like roommates?"

"Actually, I subleased the apartment from Kelly when she moved to L.A. to start her color salon—tell them about your color salon, Kelly—and then it didn't work out, although it was a great idea—it was the people, wasn't it, Kelly, weren't the people all wrong for the idea?—and she came back to the city, although you can never do a color salon in the city, the city is just not the right place, L.A. is still the place to do it, but not for another year or two, and so anyway Kelly came back, and all of a sudden I had no place to live and Kelly had no job, and I go, 'Look, why don't you come to work in my office,' because I knew they were looking for someone to be an assistant pro- ducer, it's Saks, in the advertising department, and I figured she knows so much about colors and has such good taste and she's certainly smart enough to pick up all the paperwork, so why don't they just give Kelly the job, which they did, and now Kelly's the casting director, too—I'm a copywriter—and I was going to find my own place, but we get along so well, we figured why bother? So we live together and work together . . ."

Goldie's wide eyes were spinning like pinwheels. Andrew kept sticking the bottle of wine into his mischievous smile. Kelly snorted the first row of cocaine through a cocktail straw she had brought back from the bar. I gulped my tequila in frantic time to Pam's nonstop account of how she and Kelly are so compatible even though Kelly is "cra-a-zy" sometimes and how they wear each other's clothes and never go after each other's guys and so on and so on and so on, until finally she talked herself onto the subject of cocaine and how much she liked it and how expensive it was, although someone at Saks gets it for her at a great price and sometimes gives it to her for free, because this guy was practically a millionaire anyway and was grateful when Pam paid a little attention to him and was generous when he was grateful and so on and so on, and I could see that she was ready for another line of cocaine but felt that if she kept talking, no one would think she was as addicted as she evidently was.

Goldie was next and she, too, snorted with casual professionalism. She obviously did not have a cold.

When it was my turn to snort, I tried the first thing I could think of to postpone the event. I asked Kelly what a color salon was. Pam answered.

"Everybody has colors that emanate from them. The right colors are more than just picking this to go with that, you know what I mean—am I telling it right, Kelly?—I mean what Kelly does is actually chart your colors like someone would chart your horoscope. There are colors you should wear on certain days, for certain activities, if you're relaxing, working, going out, having sex, if you're sick—Kelly can chart your colors and tell you all that. She can tell you what your personal colors are. She even gives you swatches. It's all part of the analysis. Then you go out and match your clothes and your makeup and your upholstery—everything—to your swatches."

None of us was interested in Pam's offer to have Kelly chart our colors.

"Come on, baby," Goldie said to me, pointing at the mirrored rows of cocaine. "Try some. You feel better than ever."

"I really don't think so. I don't know how even." But I was fully drunk now on a second tequila, which had magically appeared and just as magically disappeared, and I had very little resistance.

"You, too, big bro." Goldie winked at Andrew. "Not that you need help, honey." And she leaned over into Andrew's lap and started to rub him between the legs.

"Who's hungry?" Pam suddenly asked everyone. "I'm going to make the most fantastic meal you've ever eaten. I am probably the only person in the world who's not a professional restaurateur that can cook out of *The Cuisine of Fredy Girardet*."

Everyone told Pam not to bother, but she was already up looking for the cookbook.

"He's only the greatest French chef in the world," Pam shouted to us from the kitchen.

Kelly meanwhile took a special interest in initiating me into the joy of cocaine. She scooped a bit into her thumbnail and came toward me.

"What are you doing?" I slurred.

"This is easy. This is good," she kept saying. "Open your mouth."

"Why?"

"This is easy. Open your mouth. Come on."

I opened my mouth a little, like a kid being threatened with a spoonful of bad-tasting medicine.

"I'm just going to put this on your tongue and blow it down your throat. It's easy. It's good. Come on."

I felt myself get on my feet and cautiously, blindly backpedal.

"Don't run away. It's easy."

"I'm drunk. What happens if you take that stuff when you're drunk?"

"You'll be sober."

The promise interested me.

"That's it, open wide and stick out your tongue for me."

I'm sure my tongue leaped out of my mouth of its own accord. Kelly daubed the cocaine onto the tip and it felt cold. Then her mouth came at me like a scene from some horror movie when the camera makes a killer's eye or a vampire's mouth look fifty times bigger than it really is.

"Put your tongue back in your mouth," she whispered, and her voice, too, was tremendously magnified because her mouth was almost against mine. For a split second our mouths connected, although mine was wide open and her lips were pursed to blow the cocaine down my throat. My eyes were closed and I anticipated a pleasurable whoosh of warm fragrant breath. But suddenly she was gone. Andrew had pulled her off me into his arms. He was kissing her with the passion Goldie had just aroused and Goldie could not hide her disappointment. Andrew grabbed at the mirror and came up with a handful of the white powder, which he licked out of his palm and off his fingers, and then he kissed Kelly again, pulling her, as he kissed her, toward another room. She did not resist.

"We don't have *crème fraîche*," Pam shouted from the kitchen, "but I know how to do a great substitute."

I stood there with my tongue literally hanging out. Then I realized the cocaine was probably boring a hole straight through it and I spit the stuff out into my empty tequila glass, wiping my tongue with a handkerchief until it was so dry I thought I was going to gag.

Goldie and I sat there licking our wounds. From the kitchen came the clatter of busy enterprise. From the bedroom came undisguised noises of female ecstasy. The moaning and groaning were so descriptive, I could visualize their progress. This was the first time I had ever actually heard a woman give voice to her private excitement during sex. These were the sounds I always imagined when Victoria silently moved her lips during her climax. There were short shrieks and then longer and longer ones. Once in a while I could distinguish a word, such as "Yes!" or "Christ!" or "God!" always in a female voice. Goldie was bored and looking for more brandy. I continued to listen to the longer and longer moans until they got so loud I was embarrassed. Then at what had to be the very height of Kelly's ecstasy, when the yelling seemed to be coming through loudspeakers, the ecstasy abruptly turned into the saddest wail I have ever heard, and then into a cry full of terrible anguish and terrible pain, and then into an agonized rush of snarls and screams. Andrew appeared at the door, came out, whispered something to Goldie, picked up his crash helmet, and left.

"Come on, baby, we goin'," Goldie said sadly.

Pam was still going full speed in the kitchen. Irresistible but unidentifiable aromas were beginning to sneak out into the living room. Kelly was still screaming. As we got up to go, Kelly burst out of the bedroom, her dress and her underclothes and her shoes and the sheets in her arms.

"Get out of here! All of you! Get the hell out of here!" she screamed at us. Goldie led me back through the gallery of posters to the front door.

"That son of a bitch pulled out of me!" she screamed at us,

throwing her shoes at us. "That goddamn son of a bitch pulled out of me! Nobody pulls out of me! Nobody pulls out of me!"

In our panic to escape, I still managed to read and remember one of the posters in the foyer. "Fuck *me*?" it read, "fuck *you*!"

Three endless flights of stairs later, we were on our way to a famous sex club where everyone did whatever everyone felt like doing. I had heard about the club and always wondered about it, but I had never satisfied my curiosity. Now Goldie and my drunkenness and my desire to gather incriminating evidence against Andrew swept me to this seedy club. Goldie said something to the person collecting the hefty admission charge that let us in without paying. Apparently, Andrew had left tickets for us under a name he had given Goldie. I could barely hear the name, but I knew it wasn't Abel.

There were several rooms inside and no way to know which one Andrew was in. The rooms were planned and decorated for different activities. One room was for dancing. It was dark except for two powerful beams of light that kept moving and crisscrossing around the room. Disco music and wall to wall dancers were pulsating. Some of the dancers had removed some of their clothes. When the two klieg lights swept across the dance floor, I caught quick glimpses of small, flat breasts and well-muscled male torsos. All the breasts looked smaller than Victoria's, but I think that was because everyone was dancing with raised arms, like in an ethnic folk dance.

Goldie wanted to dance, but I said no. I told her I was too tired and too drunk, but I just wanted to find Andrew.

One room led to another. The next contained a bar area with unlit banquettes all around the room. Only the bar and a buffet table were lit. On the table were platters of hot hors d'oeuvres that looked Greek. I ordered Goldie a brandy and made a plate of meat wrapped in grape leaves so that we had a legitimate reason for searching the banquettes to find Andrew. But it was so dark I practically had to sit down in someone's lap to tell whether anyone was sitting there. The couples we disturbed were kissing, hugging, petting; at least two of the couples were homosexual.

Goldie and I had to separate to go into the next area. It contained a swimming pool, and men's and women's locker rooms preceded it. I walked around the room looking into lockers that still had keys in them when I came upon Andrew's Nehru jacket all balled up and thrown into the bottom of one of them with his other clothes, his shoes, and his crash helmet. He had not bothered to use his key.

I found an empty locker near Andrew's and began to undress. The signs posted on the walls warned against indiscriminate sexual contact, masturbating, urinating, as well as running, roughhousing, bringing food into the water. The safekeeping of all valuables was not the responsibility of the club. Patrons had to be twenty-one years of age. The steam room, sauna, and shower stalls were for hygienic and therapeutic purposes only. Used towels and house swimsuits were to be placed in the appropriate laundry bins. Only one towel to a customer. A vending machine dispensed body oil, talcum powder, toilet water, mouthwash, combs, prophylactics, and a fungicide for the treatment of athlete's foot. No one else was in the locker room, but there were voices coming from the showers. I placed my clothes neatly onto the hooks and shelf of my locker. The house bathing suits were really only loose fitting cotton shorts that looked like something provided in a hospital. I put on the shorts and wrapped a towel around myself. It was big enough to cover me like a robe. As I passed by the steam room, I glanced through the sliding glass doors and saw stray limbs and movement behind the steamy, streaked glass; I heard echoes of moaning. The doors to the sauna were as clear as a newly washed window. Inside the sauna were the same sounds, but no imagination was necessary. Three male bodies were engaged in a twisted act of sex on the redwood deck. None of them seemed to care that I was watching. One of them invited me inside with a wave of his free hand, a wink and a lip-smacking smile. It made me think about Michael and his secret longings. And it made me wonder if Michael secretly longed for one of us, his dear friends. I had to believe that he didn't. I had to believe that none of us longed for each other sexually.

The showers, too, were being used for purposes of sex. Men were in the stalls together under the running water. It made me think of copulating dogs that had to be sprayed with a hose to separate them. Two and three pairs of feet were visible under the doors. In one stall there were only two feet under the door and I imagined that his partner had his legs wrapped around the guy's waist.

The entrance to the pool was at the end of a small, carpeted hallway that reminded me of the hallway in Big Tubs. Big Tubs seemed like paradise compared to this place. The carpeting was soaking wet, and I walked on my toes to avoid contact with whatever it was that had drenched the floor. I opened the heavy door to the pool room. The circular pool looked like a green fluorescent UFO that had landed in a field in the dead of night. Tangerine Dream was whining out of powerful speakers. I recognized the synthesizers. Strong footlights illuminated the bar and the lounge area. The footlights also illuminated the small arcade of video games; the screens lit up the interior of the arcade like the dashboard of a huge mothership. The lemon and lime footlights cast a weird light that made everyone's skin glow. The pool was bright but cloudy, and the water reeked of chlorine. The people in the water were indistinct black or white forms. They looked like fish. No one in the water bothered with anyone else in the water. But in the areas surrounding the great glowing green cloud of water, people were engaged in all stages of lovemaking. Pads were especially provided, on which bodies writhed and pumped and rested. Some people reclined in lazy foreplay. Others shared the give and take of sex with multiple partners, servicing one while being serviced by another.

It was impossible to identify anyone. As I futilely scanned the room for a glimpse of Andrew, I felt a hand squeeze my ass. I turned around and heard Goldie's familiar, "Baby."

"How the hell did you find me in this light?"

"Gotta have good eyes, baby," she said, "if you workin' the night shift."

"I'm looking for Andrew."

"Oh he here all right. After all this afternoon, Ah can smell him."

But I couldn't find him. And then Goldie moved away, and I couldn't find her, either.

Suddenly I felt sick to my stomach. There were pads of slimy

people and their disgusting puddles everywhere, and I
threaded my way through them toward the safety of the closest wall and practically collapsed. I sank down to the floor and
breathed heavily, trying to inhale the fumes of chlorine to help
sober myself. What felt like an hour passed. Finally Goldie
found me.

"You okay, baby?"

"Not really."

She reached her hand under the towel and touched my
thigh.

"Not here. I couldn't do anything here," I said. "I couldn't
do anything anywhere."

"Sure you can." And she tried to move her hand under the
shorts.

I felt sorry for her. I felt sorry for both of us. This place
couldn't have been any easier for her than it was for me. I felt
a certain kinship with her. After all, we had both been dumped
by Andrew. We had both been bought and paid for and
dumped.

She bent down and put her head in my lap, and I felt too
exhausted to protest. When she loosened the towel, I let her.
And when she began to lick my thigh, I let her do that, too. And
when she exposed me through the fly of the shorts and worked
on me and kissed me there, I let her. My mind was not on
Victoria and I did not judge what was happening. It was all too
much like a hallucination.

I felt myself get excited, but it seemed to be happening to
someone else. The little twinges of pleasure melted into something hot and fluid that rose like mercury. At the same time
something rose up over the pool. As it descended, my excitement ascended and both met with an incredible splash.

An attendant switched on a dim but effective overhead light.
In the middle of the pool, the shadow was doing the dead
man's float. All around the edge of the small pool, naked people were swearing and shouting for the light to be turned off.
Two bouncers pulled Andrew's limp, naked body out of the
pool; the lights had to be kept on until they could escort him
to the locker room. They dragged him until he decided to
wrest himself free and leave the premises on his own. He was

defiant but willing, having already accomplished the disruption that he had had in mind when he cannonballed into the water.

I looked down into my lap at Goldie. But the girl who looked up at me was not Goldie. She was a total stranger.

"You really liked me, didn't you, baby?" she said.

19

A LONG TIME AGO, my mother punished me by not letting me watch Mr. Wizard on television. I went outside to play. It was a few minutes before the program was supposed to go on. My friend, who also liked the show, invited me to watch it at his house. I told him about my punishment, and he asked me how my mother could ever find out. She couldn't, I thought, and so I went to his house and we watched Mr. Wizard show how you could fit an egg through the narrow neck of a milk bottle without hurting the egg—first you hard-boil the egg. Then I went home. When I walked into the kitchen—God, I'll never forget this—my mother was waiting for me with her hands on her hips; her eyes were narrow and her lips were tight, and she was glaring at me and screaming at me without even raising her voice. "So you disobeyed me." I was so startled I never even bothered to deny my guilt. All I could do was ask how she knew. She told me, "Mothers know everything." Later, I found out that I had left my mittens at my friend's house when I was there and that his mother had called mine to let her know. Coincidence? Sure. But my need to believe in my mother's omniscience superseded everything else, and to this day I believe that certain people—my mother,

Victoria, David, for example—know everything. Whether it's their strong intuition or purely coincidence or my own poorly disguised guilt that gives me away, there is no point in my trying to cover up. I leave those damn mittens at the scene of every crime.

Last night I left mittens in bars, somebody's apartment, a sex club, taxicabs. This morning I woke up in my own bed, but I had no idea how I had gotten there. Or when. My clothes were half off, as though someone had tried his best to undo me. I was unbuttoned, unzipped, unshod, rolled up, pulled down, tucked in, yanked out. My head throbbed and my heart pounded. No one else was in the bed, thank God. No one else was in the apartment.

I did all the usual things—shave, brush my teeth, shower, put on clean clothes, make myself breakfast. After two cups of Mr. Coffee and three aspirins, my headache, nausea, and fatigue disappeared. My guilt, however, still throbbed and weighed on me. I had been unfaithful to Victoria. I had been unfaithful to my good reputation, to my friends' expectations, to my own expectations of myself. And for no good reason. For the alleged reason that I was spying on Andrew. No fucking reason at all.

God.

I found myself walking around the living room in smaller and smaller circles. I was worried. I wanted to apologize to Victoria, to tell her that what I did I did in order to keep her, in order to prove to her that Andrew was unworthy of her, that he was without guilt or remorse, that he cared only about revenge. But this morning, as I traced diminishing circles and tried to get rid of the remorse that filled my heart with guilt as thick as Mr. Coffee grounds, I worried that inadvertently I had proved my own unworthiness. Somehow I had to make Victoria understand. Somehow I had to feel her close to me.

I opened Victoria's closet and went through her clothes. Just holding them made me feel a little better. I knew I could not concentrate on my appraisals until I was feeling better, and brushing her pastel silks and linens and cottons against my cheek, smelling the faint trace of her perfume or talcum powder, began to distract me. Each article of clothing reminded me of a sweeter time in our life together. As I caressed a pale blue dress, I was able to remember a lovely day before Andrew came into our lives—pre-NeAndrewthal. I recalled her strong, graceful body outlined beneath the clingy blue fabric, her sunlit hair grazing her shoulders as she walked beside me through the city. We stopped at an outdoor café for something cool to drink and stayed two hours on the strength of one Tom Collins and three glasses of beer while the city paraded by. We felt content just sitting there sipping our drinks, two true New Yorkers, no less a city landmark than the statue of Simon Bolivar just across the square, the majestic horse soldier poised, like us, for the next wave of Japanese tourists to surround him and snap him.

God, I felt idiotic waltzing around the bedroom with her clothes. I stopped. What I needed was an antidote, not an anesthetic. Maybe then I could get to work.

I had to communicate with Victoria. I would not call her. It would have been too early anyway, not even six o'clock in the morning California time. Instead I went to the Apple and looked for the diskette labeled "Victoria." I had one, too, marked "Roger." We used these disks to store all sorts of information. Mine, for example, contained business and personal correspondence, a gift list from last Christmas, a list of classical recordings I wanted to buy, a list of classical recordings I already owned at the time, a short story I keep thinking I'm going to finish writing, a reading list, ideas for appraisal techniques, different résumés emphasizing different abilities, a record of birthdays and birthstones, all our credit card numbers and who to contact if the cards are lost or stolen, those sorts of things. Her disk, I always imagined, contained similar information, and it was important that I feel her presence.

I booted up the Apple and displayed the list of all of the data on Victoria's diskette. There were more than twenty names. I chose the one the cursor happened to be highlighting: WORK. It consisted of memoranda, letters, reports, and notes for more of the same. I read through ten more files, some as short as a single sentence (usually a reminder to expand the thought in that sentence into a more developed plan); some were lengthy systems of organization, including a partial attempt to catalogue all of our books according to the Dewey Decimal System;

one was a travel diary that logged all the places she had visited on business trips, what she had seen of interest, where she had eaten, what she had ordered. I was enjoying all this very much. I felt closer to her. I heard her talking to me and reassuring me with each entry. But I also felt like a trespasser. I had no more business invading the privacy of her diskette than I had going into her handbag or using her toothbrush. What if I found something I wasn't supposed to find? Or something I *was* supposed to find?

The secret file was named PENDING, not very intriguing, not something I would have checked into if I wasn't determined to read everything. But PENDING was more than I had bargained for. I could not have asked for better proof that Victoria loved me. Or worse news. Or more confusion. There it was, in fluorescent green letters, the cursor pulsing like my heart, daring me to read beyond the first three words . . .

"My Darling David"

I had to get up and walk around the room before continuing.

For those few moments I tried desperately to avoid the conclusion the file's opening words implied. I searched my memory for evidence of a secret liaison between them. What had I missed? Had they loved each other more than I had realized? Could they still be in love?

I read the letter once only. It began as a sensitive rejection of some drunken advances David had made to Victoria one night when the two of them had found themselves alone in our apartment. From certain key references, I was able to pinpoint the exact night. It had been a Friday. I had called to say I was going to be late. David had spent the afternoon drinking because he was upset about Angel. I had spoken to David, too, in the late afternoon, and I was the one who probably suggested that the two of them have dinner together. I thought it might do him some good to be with Victoria, that she might be able to make him feel better about Angel. I also thought it might be a clever way of keeping Victoria and Andrew apart.

Apparently, they never did go out for dinner. David got to our apartment drunker than Victoria had seen him in a long time. David doesn't drink much more than a beer or two now. He used to drink a lot in school, scotch mostly, and he smoked a lot of grass. But then he quit everything when Suzanne got pregnant. Ironic, he stopped drinking because of Angel and then he gets stinking drunk because of Angel. Anyway, he had had a lot more than a couple of beers by the time he got to our apartment, and then Victoria opened up a bottle of Johnny Walker Red Label for them.

What happened was that David told Victoria he still loved her. That he had always loved her. That he would love her to the day he died. They kissed on it, too. At least one good long kiss for old times' sake. And then they both felt so frightened by David's confession and by the response Victoria felt stirring in her heart that they could not say another word. They sat in total silence "waiting for whatever was going to happen next to come and get them."

Major. God, was it major.

And Victoria thought so, too. Enough to write David a letter. Enough to confess that she had often thought about how their lives would have turned out if the two of them had stayed together. Enough to tell him that she still cherished lovely memories of their romance, that it was easy for her to imagine herself bearing his children and sharing his life, that she still found herself admiring his character and success and sensitivity, that she was flattered and attracted by his love, but that they had to remember all three of us loved each other and what a shame it would be to upset that wonderful three-part harmony.

I don't think she ever sent the letter to David. There was too much additional information in it that had nothing to do with David. The first part of the letter dealt with what happened that Friday night, how nice it was that they had gotten it all out in the open, how special their few tender moments together had been, and how lucky for everyone that David's beeper went off when it did.

Then the letter was all about Victoria. About her mysterious obsession and her struggle to remain true to me.

"You asked me if there could ever be someone else in my life besides Roger," she wrote to David, "and the answer, sad to say, is yes. Not only could there be, but there *is*. There has been. There continues to be. There is someone who wants me so desperately, who loves me so much in so many ways I never knew existed and still don't understand, someone—or some-*thing*—whose hold over me is so strong that I feel as if I'm being torn in half. It's awful, David. He wants me to run away with him. He begs me to leave Roger and run away with him to this wonderful place he knows halfway around the world. He wants me to leave Roger and my work and my friends and just sail off into the sunset. I tell him no; I tell him we can't ever see each other again, and then the next day I'm back again, against my will, against everything I believe in. I tell him that I love Roger, that I can't do anything against Roger, that I will not wreck Roger's life—and my own, too, for that matter—and he just smiles at me. He knows I can't stay away. He knows I'm overwhelmed by the awful, evil world he has dragged me into. Words don't work. Reason is meaningless. Values disappear. Plans disintegrate. Nothing I trust matters when I'm with him. I might as well be crazy . . . that's what it all is—craziness! And yet . . ."

But she wrote that she was determined. She wrote that she would never give in to her obsession—or his. She would never run away with him no matter how much he begged and pleaded. She wrote that she would absolutely stop seeing him. She wrote that she was trying to arrange a business trip for herself—alone, without me—sometime in September/ October, and that she would use that trip to purge herself and free herself and get back to real life, hers, ours. She knew what she had to do to succeed: she had to convince herself that *he* had entered *her* life, not that *she* had entered *his,* and that her life was already wonderful and complete and there was no room for him.

It seems as if I have been sitting in this chair with my hand on the telephone receiver all day. I removed Victoria's disk-ette from the Apple and put it back into its sleeve and then put it back into the plastic case where we keep all our diskettes. I acted automatically, blindly flipping through the diskettes until I found the one containing my first appraisal, inserting it into the Apple, displaying the file names, and loading "OCT14." I was stunned to find that the appraisal had been completed. I reread it in its entirety and couldn't remember having finished it; I could only remember sitting at the keyboard watching Andrew and Goldie. And yet the final edit was done. Finished. Satisfactory.

I got up from the Apple, went into the kitchen, reached for the telephone, and sat down with it. I have been sitting here like this all day. Waiting. My hand on the phone.

I think I am about to call David. I think I am angry. I am not sure. I am waiting. My conclusions are incomplete. I am relieved but depressed. I cannot believe any of this is really happening. It makes no sense. Life usually makes sense. When it doesn't, I'm usually able to force it to make sense. Even my name means "everything is okay." Over and out. And so I will call David and say . . . what *will* I say? What is there to say?

Suddenly Andrew's behavior yesterday makes sense. Victoria has told him she's through with him. And yesterday he retaliated. Not just against Victoria, but against all women. It was not enough to act against her, he had to punish an entire generation of women. But it's over between them. She has won. I have won. Andrew has lost.

David, too, has lost. But not everything. Even if his beeper had not gone off, he has a built-in beeper that keeps him from making the wrong move. It was just all that scotch that got them crazy. Like me last night with all those drinks and that girl blowing cocaine down my throat. Who can blame me for what happened? I was crazy. Like Victoria. She said so herself in the letter. "I might as well be crazy . . . that's what it all is—craziness!" Who can blame her? I've been crazy myself. Andrew can do that to you. But now she's gone to California to recover. And when she comes back, she will be my wonderful, perfectly sane Victoria again. And I will be my old self again, too. And David will be David. And life will go back to what it should be. Heh . . . maybe there's something to all that reincarnation business. Maybe you have to go away and be possessed and then you come back and everything is all right again.

"Hello?"

It's David.

"Hello?"

I called him.

"Hello?"

"David?"

"Who's this? Rog?"

"Yeah. How's everything?"

"I don't know. Fine, I guess. You're lucky you got me. I've been in a hundred meetings today. I'm not even supposed to be here. I'm supposed to be in Miami. This new reservation system thing's a real bitch. Is Victoria still in California? I haven't seen anybody. I feel like I've been away for a year."

"Victoria? No, she's still there. Anyway, that's not why I called."

"What?"

"I called . . . I mean I just . . . I called really just to find out if Angel . . . about Angel. How she's doing. Is she back in school yet? Because I'm wondering if she's going to help me anymore with my appraisals."

20

I'M HAVING DINNER WITH DALE and Phyllis at a new Mexican restaurant Dale found. They make the guacamole right at your table. I haven't seen Andrew since he got bounced from the sex club. For all I know, he's in jail. Angel is coming by after school tomorrow to look at the second movie. Victoria phoned and left a message on the machine that she's doing better than she thought and expects to be home before the weekend. I am in a cheerful, hungry mood. I want to talk about Dale's Khyber Pass project. I want to hear all about the women's history course Phyllis is teaching. I want to eat hot food and drink tart margaritas. I'm really up for this evening.

The restaurant is elegant for a Mexican restaurant. No gaudy serapes and multicolored sombreros on the walls. No paper pennants strung along the ceiling like in a used car lot. The room we're in is fashionably dim and stark. The only decorations are Georgia O'Keeffe-type posters tastefully framed and hung high on all four sides of the four pillars dividing the room into more intimate sections. The posters are without detail and vaguely western in subject matter: beautiful, smooth, airbrushed desert landscapes minus the O'Keeffe skulls, rock and cactus. The waiters wear their well-tailored black and white uniforms proudly. There is no odor of garlic and cilantro hovering around them like flies. The waiter remembers our orders instead of writing them down on a grease-stained pad.

Dale asks for the guacamole to be brought to our table. He is thrilled by the procedure. He talked about it in the cab on the way over, and he pointed it out to us twice here in the restaurant when the guacamole cart passed by. Now the cart will be pushed to our table by the handsome maître d'. He will ask how many of us desire guacamole. Then he will ask if we prefer it mild, hot, or very spicy. We prefer it very spicy.

During the maître d's preparation of the guacamole, our waiter sneaks up on us with a plate of tender piping hot chips for dipping into the guacamole as soon as it's placed on the pale pink tablecloth. None of us is used to this kind of efficiency at a Mexican restaurant, and we are wondering if all this uncommon elegance and service will suddenly go south of the border.

The guacamole is delicious. Incredibly, it's spicy and soothing at the same time. Yum. And the frozen margaritas are even better. They're thick and tart and ice cold. Phyllis and I have to drink our margaritas through thin straws, drawing from the bottom of the glass, where the drink is more liquidy. Mine is so cold that the first few sips give me a headache. Dale, who is a more accomplished drinker, is able to cut through the froth without a straw or a headache. He will finish two margaritas before we are done with our first and then switch to Carta Blanca or Dos Equis beer. But he is a Hollywood drinker in that he never gets drunk. He only gets more talkative. The closest he gets to losing control is revealing something he shouldn't, usually something that doesn't mean a thing to us but was told to him confidentially by some business acquaintance. So Dale makes us swear not to say a word to anyone else, as if we knew anyone who'd be interested or as if we'd ever jeopardize the sacred trust of our friend no matter how irrelevant his secret. I love Dale. And I love Phyllis. I would rather be with them tonight than with any of the others. They are just a little bit more solid, a little bit older and more reassuring. Dale's stories are so glamorous and he tells them so colorfully that they take my mind off everything else. Phyllis's stories are so intellectually demanding that I find myself working at concentrating so I can follow along and contribute. Dale makes me dream and Phyllis makes me think, and being with both of them tonight keeps me from worrying about Victoria and David and Andrew and whether Victoria is succeeding with her California plan to rid herself of her obsession with Andrew. I know I'm very anxious about Victoria's return home. But I'm not thinking about that tonight. I'm thinking about swordfish.

The menu is simple and unusual, with fish a specialty. Every item is followed by a wonderful description. It's an old restaurant trick, I'm sure, but it always works. Even in Howard Johnson's. My mouth is watering from these descriptions, and I'm filled with a wonderful anticipation of the swordfish I will probably order and the stories Dale will tell and Phyllis's update on her new class and the confidence Dale will accidentally leak and then make me swear not to repeat.

Dale is in rare form. Phyllis is smiling behind the academician's face she always wears. I'm feeling the effects of half a margarita.

"Your titer is up," Dale says.

"What does that mean?" I ask Dale.

"T-i-t-e-r. I heard it last time I was in Hollywood and had to look it up and figure it out. Titer is the strength of a solution. From what you said you drank last night, your titer must be very high. All it takes is one little sip and all the alcohol you drank last night is back to full strength."

"Well, I can tell you that I'm getting *titer* by the minute, if that's what you mean."

The three of us are laughing and eating our guacamole and sipping our margaritas, and the last thing on my mind is Andrew and what's become of him or Victoria and how she's doing in her battle with her obsession or David and the goddamn fucking pass he made at my *wife*.

"So what's this Khyber Pass thing all about, Dale?"

"The Pathan. Did you ever hear of the Pathan?"

"No."

"They're unbelievable, Rog. I swear, there's not a society like the Pathan anywhere in the world. I'm sure you've seen 'em in a million movies—baggy pants, long coarse shirts, heavy woolen fezzes, Mongolian beards, belts of bullets strapped across their chests, a long rifle or a stripped and oily machine gun slung over one shoulder. They pop up from behind a rock and blow the ash off Stewart Granger's cigarette at a hundred paces. That's their claim to fame; they're the best damn sharpshooters anywhere. But there's never been a movie *about* them, only movies where they're a kind of backdrop, you know, like African natives or American Indians. This is actually a story *about* the Pathan."

"Tell him the story, Dale," Phyllis encourages her husband. She is proud of him. Proud of the way he tells a story. Proud of his Hollywood connections. Proud that he was chosen to write the novelization. Proud that he found such a wonderful restaurant for us. She is sitting by Dale's side the way Victoria sat by my side at that outdoor café across the square from Bolivar's statue two summers ago. Her husband is in command, holding court, center stage, a young, attractive, successful Manhattan burgomaster who seems to be responsible for all the fun everyone in the world is having.

"Well, you need some background. You need to know something about the culture and history of these people, Roger. Here they are, living for centuries in this one tiny little area of Pakistan, all rock and heat and flying bullets, beyond the last really civilized outpost, here they are guarding the gate of the famous Khyber Pass. Why? I don't know. They just do. They always have. They always will. They're a sort of natural resource, a rock people, a tribal evolution as natural and as formidable as the terrain in keeping trouble in or out of Pakistan—invaders, refugees, treasure seekers, soldiers of fortune, smugglers, gunrunners, troublemakers, they all have to negotiate the heat and the mountains and the Pathan."

I'm looking at the posters hung high on the pillars and the terrain pictured in these posters is of no help in imagining the Pakistani rock people hiding in their brutal landscape. In these posters there are no places to hide. Everything is flat, one-dimensional, like the surface of an ocean that has no depth.

"The population—even the government—thinks of the Pathan as an indigenous police force—like that subway gang, what do they call themselves? the Guardian Angels—and basically they leave the Pathan alone. I mean the Pathan can kill with impunity. The Pathan have an unwritten immunity from the written law of the rest of the land. They're treated the way we treat wild animals in their natural habitat. If a grizzly kills some poor sap who goes down the wrong road in Yellowstone National Park, nobody issues a warrant for his arrest, you know what I mean? It's like, 'Just don't mess with the Pathan.' Or 'Mess with the Pathan at your own risk.' They're human mountain lions."

"God."

"Oh, here comes something," Phyllis says, noticing our waiter making his way to our table with the order of chili peppers stuffed with shrimp we agreed to share for an appetizer.

"Anyway, that's sort of what the Pathan are like, Roger. Fierce, proud, self-appointed guardians of the great gate. God, this is fantastic."

"Yum."

"Yum."

"And their credo, Roger, is 'hospitality and revenge.' That's their golden rule. And that's what the whole thing is based on. Everything, the movie, the book, the plot, everything, hospitality and revenge."

A frosty Dos Equis arrives for Dale. The waiter pours it down the side of the chilled glass and leaves less than a half-inch of foam. Phyllis takes a sip of Dale's beer and decides to order one for herself. I am still working on my first margarita, although it is warm and unpleasantly diluted now.

"The central image is of the *hujra*. The *hujra* is a room in a Pathan house, always the first room that is built. It's a guest room. The Pathan, and most everyone in Pakistan, although not to the extent that the Pathan do, regard a guest as a blessing. If a Pathan's worst enemy shows up seeking refuge, he will be welcome to stay in the *hujra* indefinitely—that's what it was built for—but in payment, the guest must earn his keep by contributing his labor for as long as he stays. He has to raise livestock or garden or cook or clean or fight on the side of the Pathan or whatever else he can do to earn his keep. Otherwise he's out on his ass. And because the law of the land doesn't apply in Pathan territory, all sorts of criminals and escaped convicts and guys on the lam hide out with the Pathan, because the Pathan don't give a damn what you've done so long as you do what you're supposed to do when you're staying with them. And if you disappoint the Pathan by not doing your fair share, either they'll hand you over to the authorities, or, if you do something that really offends them, they'll shoot the eyes right out of your head. But it will be for leering at one of their women, not for the mass murder you may have committed last week in Islamabad. And because everyone knows this, life with the Pathan is better at rehabilitating people than prison. There are stories about convicts who have hidden out with the Pathan for twenty years, and every day they were on perfect behavior, or else."

The few months Andrew has been at my house seems like twenty years. I have been only hospitable. I have not thought about revenge. I have not thought about popping up from behind the Apple, a band of bullets slung across my chest, a machine gun at my hip, squinting like a marksman, like Clint Eastwood with a Mongolian beard, and pulling the trigger until all the buttons are blown off his fucking Nehru jacket. That's just a warning, Andrew old pal. Next time I'll shoot all the dirt out from under your nails. And if there's a next time after that, we'll go through your extremities, all of them, one by one, until you're as goddamn smooth as you think you are.

"So with this as the background, Roger, we've got an American newsman-turned-freedom fighter deciding to join the Afghan resistance in Pakistan—a character loosely based on Dan Rather when he snuck into Afghanistan dressed like an Afghan freedom fighter, remember?—and our hero winds up killing one of the Pathan because he gets drunk and can't tell the difference between them and the Russians and the Pakistani and the Afghans or anybody else. It's the old 'they all look the same' story, but turned around to show what can happen when your heart is in the right place but your mind isn't. Anyway, to make a long story short, and this really is a long story—the studio wants a fuckin' Michener out of me on this one—the newsman-turned-freedom fighter-turned killer finds himself on the lam, and the only place he can take refuge is with the

Pathan, and he winds up going to the *hujra* of the family of the Pathan warrior he accidentally killed."

"And, of course, he falls in love with the beautiful daughter of the guy he killed," Phyllis interrupts a bit sarcastically.

"It's not my idea. That's the way it happens in the screenplay. But I promised you, she won't be a gratuitous character when I get hold of her. I promise you, Phyllis."

Evidently, they have talked about this before.

"She will be very real, a victim herself. Of the land, of the culture, of international politics," Dale is thinking out loud, plotting out loud. "A little *For Whom the Bell Tolls,* a little *The Far Pavilions,* a little *The Jewel in the Crown,* a little Cecil B. DeMille."

"It sounds great, Dale. It sounds like a lot of work," I tell him respectfully.

"I figure we'll be in Pakistan at least three months. It's the kind of thing where you really have to soak in it for as long as the studio is willing to keep the water hot. Local color, details you don't find in brochures . . . flora, fauna, food, clothing, that's what I need, the real details. You know, Mohammad told me that in India, spring and fall happen at the same time, even in the same tree. You can see leaves falling and blooming on the same tree. You can read a thousand books on India and never come across that kind of information. They suck on some kind of leaf after they eat, I forget what kind, they suck on this leaf instead of having an after-dinner drink like we do. That's because Pakistan is a dry country, no booze. Mohammad carries these leaves around with him."

"Well, praise Allah this isn't a dry country," I tell Dale. "I think I'll have an after-dinner drink. You put me in the mood."

"And a good mood it is," Dale says, hailing our waiter with a flamboyant wave of his arm. The waiter spots him and hurries over.

"What would you like, Rog?" Dale asks.

"I don't know, a Black Russian."

"A Black Russian and a Stinger . . ." Dale tells the waiter, " . . . and for the lady?" he asks Phyllis.

"Nothing. A glass of water."

"And a glass of your best water for the lady, thank you," Dale finishes ordering. "She has an early class tomorrow," he tells me, referring to Phyllis.

"I wanted to ask you, how's it going?" I ask her.

"It's going. It's only been a couple of weeks, but I think we're going to be okay. The girls and *boys* are really responding."

Over our drinks, Phyllis tells me exactly what her students are responding to. The course she teaches is entitled Women's History, but it is not what you'd expect. It is not, for example, a series of portraits of outstanding women in history. It is a more comprehensive, well-researched treatment of the role women have played in the development of history, like what the impact was when women were first allowed to own land or what women contributed to medicine, like what was learned from the study of pregnancy, or the effect of women on educational standards. It is a study of women not unlike a study of air or microbes or evolution or some other force that has shaped today's world, and the fifth graders Phyllis teaches at the UN School, the sons and daughters of diplomats, ambassadors, and emissaries from every country in the world, are responding in a most encouraging way. By the end of Dale's first Stinger, Phyllis is talking about espionage.

"Do you have any idea how important women have been in the whole area of foreign intrigue? It's the whole Mata Hari thing, and it's true. Treachery is a particularly feminine talent. And governments have always known it and have always used it to their advantage. Whether witting or unwitting accomplices, women have been responsible for more overthrows of governments, more takeovers, more revolutions, more war and terrorism and assassination—and I'm not talking about Helen of Troy or Cleopatra or Eva Perón, I'm talking about the wives and mistresses and sisters and mothers of kings and soldiers.

"Dale didn't explain in detail, but the daughter of the murdered Pathan in his movie is a crucible of intrigue. Through her, three nations nearly collide. And if the studio does it right and if Dale does it right, it will be entirely plausible."

I have lost Phyllis. I sort of know what she's talking about, but *I* can't talk about it. I am grateful to Dale for changing the subject.

"Yeah, but you know the real intrigue in life is not something you can ever research, Phyllis. It's not for publication."

"What are you talking about?" Phyllis asks Dale, a little annoyed, I think, that he cut in on her.

"Do you know who this movie really belongs to, who the real sponsor is, where the idea really came from, who stands to make the most out of this project? Certainly not me. Certainly not the studio. You've got a guy from American Express, some guy who's responsible for the whole subcontinent, this VP from American Express just sitting around in the Far East somewhere in a plush hotel suite dreaming up ways of protecting American interests that Reagan can't even think of. It's *his* project, for God's sake. His and American Express's. His and a hundred unairconditioned offices where dirt-poor would-be hajis convert their life savings of a few miserable rupees into a once-in-a-lifetime ticket to Mecca—steerage. You don't know what I'm talking about, do you? Well, it's just as well because I'm really not supposed to be talking about it anyway. If the MasterCard people ever get wind of this—shit! Listen, I'll tell you, but you got to swear to keep it absolutely to yourself. I don't even want you to tell Victoria. Do you swear?"

"I swear."

"Look, the whole deal is a banking thing. American Express. We could do the interiors in Hollywood, but how the hell are you going to build the Khyber Pass on a back lot? So American Express finances the whole deal for the minister of tourism— planes, hotels, a temporary movie town—and don't think PIA and Intercontinental and General Zia aren't in it up to their gold teeth; they're all in it. But so could MasterCard be in it. If they knew. It's all top, top secret. This is the way things get done in the international infrastructure, Roger. This is the way you keep your offices open without an eighteen-year-old national guardsman machine-gunning you down because he thinks the Ayatollah maybe has a point. This is how you take a pilgrim's few rupees and make an American penny on the currency exchange and wind up with millions every day, week in and week out. This is how you turn the northwest frontier into the Ginza in one easy lesson. This is intrigue with a capital *I*, only you can't look it up in any card catalogue, Phyllis. How do I know? Because I had lunch with that American Express guy from the Orient and he told me. It's *his* idea. The whole movie is his idea. The Pathan, the newsman, the girl, the Russians, everything. It's his marketing plan for the nineties. Don't think you're going to get to do an appraisal on this one either, Rog. This one's a hit. This one's predestined, Roger. You know who's in it? I shouldn't tell you this . . ."

"Who?"

"You swear?"

"I swear, come on, who's in it?"

"I'll just say this, it's the number one American actor and the number one Russian actor."

"Who?"

"I don't want to say, because *they* don't even know yet."

"Well, the Russian has to be Baryshnikov, right?"

"I don't want to say. I want to talk about you, Roger. I've been talking all night."

Dale is as close to being drunk as Dale gets. He knows he has talked too much, although I don't feel like I've just been let in on some fantastic top secret, and now he wants me to bail him out.

"You've got a lot to talk about, I don't," I tell him. I do have a lot to talk about, but none of it is as exotic as Dale's news.

"What have you heard from Victoria?" he asks me. "Did she ever buy that million-dollar coat?"

"How do you know about that?"

Phyllis is looking daggers at Dale.

"Well, you must have told me. You told me she was thinking about it."

"I never told you, Dale. Lori must have told you."

There is an awkward attempt by Phyllis to divert the conversation to Michael's bon voyage party. When the check comes, Dale pays with his credit card. He claims he can write the dinner off because I do film appraisals. Otherwise there is silence. My head is still filled with squinting sharpshooters and spies who look like Marlene Dietrich, but the image of Victoria wrapped in the skin of a dead lynx is beginning to take over. It is not the image I had been waiting for Dale to let slip out.

21

I FEEL AS THOUGH MY LIFE is in other people's hands, that everyone knows what's going on in my life except me. Days go by that seem to be normal; I seem to be having a wonderful time with my friends at a new Mexican restaurant and then all of a sudden something happens or something is said that makes me feel all alone in the middle of my circle of friends and no one along the perimeter will talk to me. There are whisperings. There is guarded conversation. There are awkward slips of the tongue that are ignored or casually dismissed. I know I never mentioned Victoria's coat to Dale or Phyllis.

I'm being treated like Michael after he confided in everyone about his operation, except I have not confided in everyone. I have only talked to David, and knowing what I now know about him and Victoria, I am sure David has not said anything to anyone.

Or has he?

Maybe Victoria has been talking?

Never.

Maybe everyone has guessed that there is something wrong?

I doubt it.

It's fortunate that Angel is coming by after school. At least then I will feel more in control. I will be able to lose myself in the screening of the second film and the discussion of its prospects. Thank God for work. Thank God for all the small and predictable challenges in life that stretch out into the distance like railroad tracks.

I have been waiting for Angel all day, passing time by straightening up, doing the laundry, ironing, reading, listening to tapes, updating RAWN. At noon I went out for lunch. I went to the Thai restaurant that just opened in the neighborhood and ordered coconut soup with shrimp and red curry. I don't remember how it tasted. I don't remember what I read, what tapes I listened to, whether I ironed shirts or pants. I had wanted to include Victoria's letter to David in RAWN, but I couldn't remember her exact words. I think it's important to use her exact words. I'm thinking about copying Victoria's PENDING file into RAWN. I can do that with one simple computer command. It's like making a Xerox, not like stealing.

At two o'clock I could not stand the wait and watched the second film. I had already watched it once before, when Simon first gave it to me, and I remembered admiring its technical accomplishment but hating the story. It was too surreal, too disjointed, too unbelievable. I doubted that the movie would make much money and told Simon so during a phone conversation a week later. He disagreed. He thought the movie had a good chance of becoming a cult film.

I had the feeling I might have appreciated some of the weird images more and not cared so much about making sense of it all if I had been stoned. God, the soundtrack started off with "Voodoo Chile" by Jimi Hendrix! What more encouragement to get stoned did a viewer need? It's common knowledge that the director's heavily involved with drugs. He came out in favor of marijuana in the sixties before he was a director, just an aging character actor. Then he wrote an autobiography admitting to being high every day of his life for something like thirty years. He was higher than the Sierras all during the filming of *Cheyenne Pass,* one of those classic Hollywood westerns that "they don't make 'em like" anymore. Then, after the book, he dropped out of sight for a while, and now he's back, probably in his late sixties, with a movie that, to me, is more of a case history on the latent danger of drug abuse than the impressive debut of some great new auteur who thinks he's clued into the yearnings and alienation of today's youth, which is what Simon thinks. I'm not sure, but I think Simon is involved with the old guy in some way, some business deals. I vaguely remember reading something about him and drugs and an air freight business between the Keys and the Caribbean, and I know that Simon has a house down in the Keys. Anyway, I think Simon may have some personal investment in the director's future. I don't think he has a percentage of the movie, but if the movie does well, then it may mean they can pump more money into the other business, if there is one. But I wouldn't want that to influence my appraisal, and I'm sure Simon would be disappointed in me if I let it.

The movie continues. There are elements of science fiction that insult my affection for the genre. The best sci-fi is epic, moralistic; it presupposes that life is governed by extraordinary universal laws that we may not comprehend but that we are persuaded to believe. Not in this film, though. There are no laws; there is no brave new world worth entering for an hour and a half. Instead, there are supernatural occurrences in what is supposed to be a real world, but these events seem nothing more than theatrical contrivances, the director's indulging his hallucinations. I love sci-fi because it makes the unreal real, because it turns imagination into logic. I hate this movie because it takes what is real and makes it unreal; at the first sign of logic, it beats a mad retreat to pure fantasy. But the movie is not being marketed for someone like me. It is being marketed for someone like Angel.

She will be here any minute. I'm anxious to see her. I realize I've been straightening the apartment for her. I've showered and shaved and combed my hair. I've put on clothes I wouldn't ordinarily wear. We're going to the movies.

The phone rings. It is not the doorman announcing Angel's arrival. It's Barbara. She's crying. She's more than crying. She's hysterical. She wants Victoria's number in California. Julia isn't home, Phyllis isn't home, Lori isn't home; maybe she can reach Victoria at the hotel, she has to talk to someone. That someone is obviously not me.

"What's wrong?"

"I've got to talk to Victoria, please give me her number."

"What happened? What's the matter?"

"Nothing. Everything. It's terrible. Please, Roger."

"Hold on a second, I'll get it. Wait a minute, I don't even have it. I had to call information. The hotel's the Bel Epoch. I don't have the number, Barb. Barb, for God's sakes, why are you crying like that? What's wrong?"

There's a click. I'm talking to a dial tone.

It's frightening to think of Barbara out of control. Of all of us, she's the toughest. When a great-uncle of hers was dying a horribly slow and painful death, Barbara volunteered to take care of him. She *volunteered*. Her aunt couldn't. Her great-uncle had cancer and was being fed through a tube in his neck. One day her uncle wrote Barbara a note asking her to stop feeding him. Barb made double entries in the feeding records and allowed her uncle to starve to death. It took three weeks. Luckily, there was no autopsy. If they had found evidence of starvation, like a hole in her uncle's stomach, Barb could have gone to jail for murder. Then, after her uncle died, she arranged the whole funeral. Nothing gets to Barbara.

The phone is ringing again. Maybe it's Barbara calling back, willing to tell me what happened. But this time it's the door-man. Angel is on her way upstairs.

The movie is rewinding on the VCR. I turn on the tape deck and stick an Elvis Costello cassette into the machine. The sound starts in the middle of a song. I can't make out the words. He is known for his clever and incisive lyrics, but I can never understand them. Maybe the heads need to be cleaned.

Angel knocks. It doesn't sound as if she's knocking with her hand.

"Come in. Hi."

Her arms are full of school books.

"Can I help you with some of those books?"

"I got them," she says, and dumps them all onto a chair. On her back is a pack with more books in it. She wriggles out of the backpack and lets it fall to the floor.

"They're really working you, huh?"

"You like Elvis Costello?"

"He's all right. Victoria likes him."

"She likes . . ."

"What?"

"Nothing. Are we going to watch your movie?"

"That's what we're here for."

While I fast forward Elvis Costello to the end of side two, Angel unzips her backpack and starts searching for something.

"Is his name really Elvis?" I ask her, but she's too engrossed to hear me.

Angel is wearing what I assume are her school clothes. She's wearing a dress instead of her customary jump suit. The dress is belted, simple, ample, the arms widespread as wings, the whole enormous expanse of blue flowing from the loose cowl collar to the ankle-length flare of the hem. Her large awkward body resides uncomfortably inside the dress and makes me think of a restless sleeper in a tent. Below the hem are scuffed black boots. Above the collar is a face that is hers and hers alone, a face given to her free and clear by my best friend.

Angel finally finds the brown paper bag she has been looking for among all the things crammed into her backpack.

"Want a piece?" she asks indifferently. The bag is filled with taffy. It's thick and soft and pink and looks like it could rip a tooth out by its root. She stuffs a wad of it into her mouth.

"I thought your father objected."

"There are forces in this world even more powerful than parental authority."

The statement would have sounded more sarcastic if it didn't have to fight its way out through taffy.

"In that case, I still have Orville Redenbacher's Microwave Popping Corn. Want some?"

"Why not."

It gives me a certain satisfaction to go against her father's wishes. I don't mean to be jealous or angry, but I'm happy nevertheless to be fattening up his daughter for whatever kill David is guarding her against.

The movie has rewound. Angel has plopped down onto the closed hide-a-bed. The microwave is mobilizing Orville Redenbacher's molecules. My mind is everywhere but on the movie; I turn down a light that's making the TV screen glare,

I wait for the microwave to ring, I advance the movie cassette to the opening credits and freeze the frame. Angel's mind is not on the movie either. Both of us seem to be here under some pretense.

The popcorn is ready, and I put a bowl of it and several napkins down on the coffee table in front of the hide-a-bed.

"I'm going to have a beer. Do you want something?"

"Could I have a beer?"

"Do you drink beer?"

"Sometimes."

"At home?"

"Sometimes. When no one's home."

With the same satisfaction I derived from feeding her popcorn and watching her stuff taffy into her mouth, I pour each of us a Kirin beer. Angel immediately guzzles half a glass.

The remote controller is still missing and I have to get up to release the freeze frame. I take my place again on the hide-a-bed next to Angel, who has curled her large legs and large scruffy boots up under the wide hem of her blue dress. There is a lump in her cheek from a wad of taffy. She's holding her glass of beer in the hand resting on the arm of the hide-a-bed. She smells like a child, coppery and sweet. I have moved the bowl of popcorn between us on the hide-a-bed and repeatedly reach into it without looking. At some point, she will reach into the bowl, too, and our hands will touch.

Simon's friend, the actor-turned-director, has started his movie off wildly. To the exotic, erotic electric guitar of "Voodoo Chile," a UFO in the shape of a glowing pink cloud descends into a suburban backyard. There are frequent cutaways to a red moon as the song's lyrics refer to the fire-red the moon turns on the night the Voodoo Chile is born. The credits are superimposed over each shot of the red moon. Then back to the birth of the Voodoo Chile. Then back to the red moon. Then back to the birth, which is all smoky and shimmery and pink like the music as a human form takes shape in the middle of the cloud. The form becomes more and more human, finally taking on the unmistakable appearance of the star of the movie, J. Kennedy Dodd, whose great popularity is owed to his long and lovable run on a TV sitcom. He's a clean-cut, good-looking teenager who's probably five years older than the roles he plays. But beneath his good looks and midwestern appeal lurk tension and danger. These are new emotions for J. Kennedy Dodd, and the producer and director of the film are no doubt banking on the success of their stroke of genius in casting J. Kennedy against his expected grain. Angel seems to fall for it completely. She is mesmerized by the images on the screen. The lump in her cheek has not moved. The half glass of Kirin beer remains untouched, its color perfectly matching the thin gold bracelet around the hand holding the glass.

"Recognize him?" I ask her. She nods her head without taking her eyes off the screen. She continues to nod her head throughout the Voodoo Chile's birth, as if in tacit agreement with each new fantastic scene. She is mesmerized by something that, frankly, I cannot see. All I can see are bizarre, meaningless images.

The air in Backyard Suburbia, Planet Earth, is alien to the newly born teenager. It makes him drunk. He reels around in his pink cloud. The camera cuts away to the branches of an ominous tree. A hummingbird flits through the branches, humming louder than the electric feedback from Hendrix's guitar. This is another image from the lyrics of the song. Quite effectively, the hummingbird dissolves into a teenage girl and, by means of a jarring zoom out to a long shot, the audience is made to see that the tree is actually growing in the adjacent backyard but that some of the branches overhang the wooden fence dividing the two properties. I assume this is the way boy meets girl next door in the eighties, and my face takes on a pained, exasperated expression. The hummingbird transformation causes Angel to curl up tighter under her blue dress. During some boring exposition revealing the kind of household J. Kennedy will enter, Angel says something like, "They didn't show the sleep." I ask her what she said and she ignores me. She reaches into the bowl of popcorn and our two hands touch, which brings her back to earth. She pulls her hand back to wait her turn.

"No, go ahead," I tell her, and she does. There is now taffy and popcorn in her mouth. She attempts to wash it down with a slug of beer. I picture it: a pink and yellow hunk of goo, the kernels of corn extruding like pig's knuckles.

The third main character is introduced. He's younger than J. Kennedy and the girl next door. He's a mad computer scientist. No need to surround Aristotle, his nickname in the movie, with bizarre images. The pain and hate in his eyes foretell his fate. It's obvious he's going to kill somebody and then suffer a horrible death himself. The movie never makes clear what Aristotle is doing with all his computers except that it's something seditious involving intercepting and rewriting classified government data. He keeps talking about "changing the qualities" and "reuniting our planet with its brothers and sisters in the heavens" by reducing everything to "pure beingness." His pseudo-philosophical double-talk makes him sound like someone on *Saturday Night Live* doing a Dr. Strangelove impersonation. Except it isn't funny.

The real world is symbolized by the three main characters' fathers. J. Kennedy's father is ineffectual and doesn't understand his son. J. Kennedy is an alien in his father's world of middle-class values and preprogrammed responses, a latter-day flower child who actually stops in one scene to smell the flowers along the road. The hummingbird girl's father is a strict, no-nonsense puritan who thinks that growing up is the same thing as sinning, and he discourages his daughter from being affectionate even toward him. Aristotle's father is absent. Having left the family long ago, his existence is made known only by his monthly child support checks.

"I have no friends," the hummingbird girl confesses at one point, and I'm reminded that each of the main characters says this same line and gives it a personal meaning. When J. Kennedy says it, it is a plea for someone to befriend him. When the hummingbird girl says it, it's a realization that the kids she hangs out with really mean nothing to her. When Aristotle says it, it's with triumph and pride.

In this my third viewing of the movie, I have given up trying to make much more out of the plot. There are scattered moments when I can understand what's going on, but I cannot relate them to other moments that are comprehensible, so I have decided to concentrate on the soundtrack. After the Hendrix beginning, a dreamier score takes over that is all textural and repetitive and insinuating. It makes me want to close my eyes and conjure up my own images.

Angel's eyes are closed. The wad of popcorn-infested taffy is still in her cheek. Her hand has fallen asleep around the glass of Kirin. Her eyeballs are moving under the lids, up and down, side to side, as if she's watching the movie through the thin skin. Her eyes are closed and her head is tilted and she is breathing as if she's asleep, but there's something about her face that is wide awake. I want to watch her instead of the movie. This is the third time I have not been able to concentrate on this damn thing. I can't even remember how it ends. I think I shut it off before the ending the first time. I must have been on the phone with Barbara the second time. And this time I'm more interested in watching Angel. But I feel an obligation to see it through to the end.

J. Kennedy dies from an overdose of heroin. He's brought back to life by the hummingbird lighting on his chest. Aristotle dies, of course, but first he realizes the past error of his ways and reprograms his computers to intercept the worldwide destruction he has already put in motion. He diverts a missile and detonates an incredible explosion, which should have ended the movie. Instead, the blast dies down and the music starts up and a sparkling fairy dust kind of radiation rises from the ashes of Aristotle's laboratory and floats toward the adjacent homes of J. Kennedy and the hummingbird girl. The fairy dust settles on the UFO and the backyard tree, disintegrating both of them, and J. Kennedy puts his arm around the hummingbird girl and walks her across the yard to where his father is standing. "This is Mary," he tells his father. "She's my friend." Swell of music. Closing credits.

I don't know why, but I rewind the cassette back to the beginning of the explosion, and I freeze the picture at the first frame of the blast. Then I go back to the hide-a-bed and touch Angel's arm lightly.

"You were sleeping."

"No."

"Your eyes were closed."

"I wasn't sleeping."

"What just happened then?"

"You touched my arm."

"I mean in the movie."

"I don't know what just happened, you're talking to me. You touched me and now you're talking to me. I only know what happened up to when you touched me."

"It's okay if you were sleeping. That's valuable criticism."

"I wasn't. I was in the explosion and then I was in the tree."

Her eyes are open, but she is still in her trance.

"Angel . . ."

And then suddenly she snaps out of it and continues chewing on the wad of taffy like an oblivious cow. Suddenly she's a teenager again, more of a teenager than she usually is, certainly more talkative.

"What?"

"What did you mean when you said you were the reincarnation of Victoria?"

"I meant I'm the reincarnation of Victoria. Do you believe in reincarnation? If you do, then I'm the reincarnation of Mary, too, in the movie, and the hummingbird . . . or they're all the reincarnation of me, however it works. All I know is we're all the same person. Do you believe in it?"

I honestly don't know whether she's pulling my leg or not.

"Well, no, I don't. I don't think I do, anyway."

"Think about it. Read the *Tibetan Book of the Dead*. You have any more beer?"

"I don't want you to get drunk," I tell her. But I do. I bring in another Kirin and fill her glass.

"I don't know much about reincarnation, but I know what it means. By definition. And according to my compact edition of the Oxford English Dictionary, if you're the reincarnation of Victoria, one of you should be dead."

"One of us is."

"Funny."

"Did you like the movie?"

I don't answer her. Suddenly she's quiet again. In a semi-trance.

"What do you mean one of you is dead?"

"Did you like the movie?"

Everything she says sounds as if it's been dictated to her and now she's repeating it.

"What did you mean when you said 'they didn't show the sleep'?"

"Nothing."

There is pain on her face like the pain on Aristotle's face.

"What did you start to tell me about what Victoria likes when we were talking about Elvis Costello?"

"*Imperial Bedroom.* I didn't know we'd be talking about reincarnation. *Imperial Bedroom* is the only album by Elvis Costello she likes. We like. It's his Cole Porter album. She likes the internal rhymes. So do I. Do you like internal rhymes? Did you like the movie?"

"I hated it. Did you like it?"

"Yes, but nobody else will. It won't make any money this time."

"What do you mean 'this time'?"

"That movie already made its money."

"I don't understand."

She drinks her Kirin before she answers.

"When it was *Rebel Without a Cause.*"

"When what was?"

"The movie."

"This movie?"

"It's a remake. Check it out. Same story. Same names. Some of the same dialogue. No James Dean, though. They're all dead. James Dean is dead. Natalie Wood is dead. Sal Mineo is dead. All of them. Until they come back."

When it's on pause, the VCR turns itself off after five minutes, and regular television comes back on. A quiz show comes on like gangbusters. I like quiz shows. I like beating the contestants and counting up all the money I would have won. I always beat them to the answer and I'm almost always right. The questions are so simple. Even on the tough quiz shows like *Jeopardy* or the tricky ones like *Wheel of Fortune,* the questions aren't that difficult. Victoria always says they're tougher when you're there, that everything's easier when you're sitting in your living room with your friends.

I turn the VCR back on and fast forward to the end. I watch

the credits closely and freeze frame on any credits that say
"from" or "based on." I write down two names. When I have
the chance, I will look up *Rebel Without a Cause* and see if the
names correspond.

Angel is getting itchy. She's up now, walking around. Nobody's keeping her here, but she's pacing around as though she
has no choice.

"I'll give you another beer if you tell me more about you and
Victoria."

"You know everything."

"I do?"

"You know about them, don't you?"

"Them?"

"Talking is stupid. Souls don't talk, they commune."

"Maybe, but I'm not a soul. Not yet. And I'm not commun-
ing."

"Nobody does. Except the souls. Where's my beer?"

"I'll get you another one if you talk to me. Who do you mean
'them'?"

"Talking makes me . . . hysterical."

"Maybe it's what you're talking *about* that makes you hysterical."

"Let me have another beer. Please? Pretty please?"

She's looking at me differently. I could swear she's batting
her eyes at me.

"What did you mean when you said 'they didn't show the
sleep'?" I'm trying anything now.

"Nothing. It's just a line from the song. It's just another line
from 'Voodoo Chile.' Pretty please with sugar on top?"

"What did you mean 'you know about them'? Them who?"

The phone rings. It's Victoria. This is the first time I've
talked to her since she left for California. It's a poor connection; her voice sounds distant, weak.

"Did Barbara call you?" I ask Victoria.

Angel stops pacing. She stops squirming in her skin. She
stares at me and talks to me while I'm trying to listen to Victoria on the phone. "I ought to tell you," Angel says to me. "I
want to tell you. But without words." I put one hand over my

free ear and shake my head and gesture to Angel to wait until I hang up, but she keeps talking.

"No. I don't know. I'm not in the hotel," Victoria answers my question about whether Barbara called her.

Angel says something like, "She's not coming home, is she? She's going away from there. She can't help it. We can't help it."

"She was hysterical . . ." I tell Victoria.

"Hysterical?"

". . . but she wouldn't say . . ."

"What happened?" Victoria interrupts.

". . . she wouldn't say anything. Whatever it is, she didn't want to talk to me about it. She's all right. Hey, we're talking about Barb. She'll be all right. But you ought to call her."

"Okay."

"I want to tell you without words," Angel keeps talking, "like in the movie. Only they didn't show the sleep."

In her weak, distant voice, Victoria tells me why she called: a minor setback, back off schedule, a guy hiding out saying he's out of town to avoid giving a statement . . .

"They didn't show the sleep when I crawled into Daddy's bed and tried to kiss him without waking him up."

. . . not going to make it before the weekend . . .

"Crawled under the covers with him and put my face by his mouth so I could feel his breath on me."

Gesturing like mad for Angel to wait a second, trying to hear Victoria tell me it'll have to be the following Monday or Tuesday . . .

"And made my love to him on his face and his neck and his hands until even my feet were warm and everything was light when I closed my eyes."

. . . depending on how good a hiding place . . .

"And he breathed differently . . ."

. . . depending on airline schedules . . .

". . . and snorted . . ."

. . . depending on what the office says . . .

". . . and tossed once and turned . . ."

. . . sorry.

". . . but never woke up."

"Okay, it's okay, Victoria. I'll see you when you get back. Angel's here. We're looking at the second appraisal. Let me know. Call and let me know what plane. And call Barbara."

Angel's eyes are on the receiver. They follow the receiver back to the cradle.

"I couldn't hear a word you said, Angel."

She's putting on her backpack.

"You heard me."

"Victoria's talking into one ear, you into the other one . . ."

"I told you and you heard me. You just don't want to know. You don't want to know about us."

"I'm telling you, Angel, I swear . . . about who?"

"About people like us. Me. David. Victoria."

"Your father?"

"You heard me. You know who I'm talking about."

"I'm sorry, Angel, but I couldn't listen to you and Victoria at the same time."

"Then . . ." she says, buckling her backpack, opening the door, smiling goodbye, ". . . don't."

I still see the blue of her dress. I still hear her say her father's name, David, and it sounds strange for her to call him that instead of Daddy.

When, I wonder, did it happen?

How old, I wonder, was Angel?

22

ONCE AGAIN A DEAR FRIEND has sought me out to confide in me and receive comfort from me. She's tough, bright, and famous for her sharp-tongue and no-holds-barred straightforwardness. Dale once described her as the kind of person who can't wait to tell you that you've got something hanging out of your nose. This is Barbara. This trembling, red-eyed, hand-wringing person sitting on the hide-a-bed trying with all her might to compose herself is Barbara. She tried all of her women friends, and none of them was home. She tried calling Victoria and couldn't get through to her at the Bel Epoch. There was some kind of mix-up. They couldn't find anyone staying there under the name of Victoria Abel. I suggested to Barbara that she should have asked for a party in the name of Victoria's firm, but it makes little difference now. Barbara is here. In desperation, she has come to unburden herself to me. That's what friends are for.

When she can bring herself to talk, our conversation is like the text of a play before it is acted. There are no shadings to the words we speak. Everything is on the surface. Perhaps that's because Barbara still holds back even when she's baring her soul. So do I, for that matter. And so I can hear the two of us talking as though we are walking through our parts rather than feeling them.

BARB   I got a call from Mohammad this morning.

ME   Where? From Pakistan, you mean?

BARB   His sister killed herself.

ME   Shit. How? Did you know her? Did you ever meet her?

BARB   She was walking through a bazaar and a man with a pet monkey that played a drum made from an empty coffee can insulted her.

ME   What do you mean?

BARB   He was a beggar, Mohammad said. Just a street beggar with a trained monkey.

ME   What did he do to her? What happened?

BARB   He whistled at her or something. Called out something dirty. Complimented her ass or her tits or something. And the monkey stuck his tongue in and out and played with himself and then did a rim shot on the coffee can and then a double somersault and then covered his eyes with his hands. It was a little routine. To entertain the crowd. A few laughs, a few rupees tossed into the empty can when the monkey passed it around.

ME   And?

BARB   She kept walking—this is according to the crowd—she kept walking through the bazaar like she was in a trance. She didn't say anything or do anything right away.

ME   What did she do?

BARB   She got to a small two-story house and went inside. It looked like she might have lived there, but she didn't. Nobody knows how she knew the house was there or that there was an empty room upstairs or where the gasoline and the matches came from . . .

ME   What gasoline and matches?

BARB   ... and she poured gasoline all over herself and lit the matches and set herself on fire.

ME   Oh Christ, Barb.

BARB   Her dress and her veils must have gone up like that (snapping her fingers)—you know those thin dresses, almost like nightgowns—and then she threw herself out of the upstairs window.

ME   Jesus, Barbara. Jesus Christ.

BARB   Mohammad says it took them ten minutes to put out the fire.

ME   What a way to die.

BARB   Yeah, what a way to die.

ME   Shit, maybe the fall killed her.

BARB   The fall didn't kill her. The fire didn't kill her, either.

ME   What do you mean?

BARB   The insult killed her, Roger.

ME   No one ever whistled at you on the street? A construction worker?

BARB   She's a Moslem, Roger. She was degraded. That fucking beggar and his goddamn monkey should have known better. They should have known she would kill herself.

ME   Come on, Barb, we're talking about a religious fanatic. Only a fanatic would set herself on fire and jump out a window because some monkey sticks its tongue out at her.

BARB   And only another fanatic would think she did the right thing.

ME   You're not telling me you think she did the right thing?

She is beginning to lose her composure again. As what she says makes less sense, the drama increases.

BARB   'Mohammad, why aren't you crying; why isn't your voice breaking with sorrow or anger; why aren't you asking me to fly right over to be with you? Don't you want to be with me?' I asked him. 'With someone you love who can comfort you? I want to come. I want to be there for you. I also want to burn that fucking beggar and feed him to his monkey.' 'What did they do?' he says. 'They didn't do anything.'

ME   Mohammad said that?

BARB   'They didn't set her on fire, Barbara. They didn't throw her out the window. She did that to herself. She was disgraced, and she did the only thing she could do.'

ME   You mean Mohammad goes for that shit?

BARB   I don't even remember what he said after that. He was quoting from the Koran or something. You know how you can find something in the Bible to support just about any goddamn stupid thing you want to believe? Well, you can do that with the Koran, too.

ME   So he thought she did the right thing?

BARB   He thought she did the only thing. If you're a woman, you have to watch out for an insult on the street the way you have to watch out for a scorpion or something.

ME   And the guy? What happens to him?

BARB   What did he do? (Imitating Mohammad's earlier incredulous response) Unless he was drunk, what did he do? If he was drunk, they'd cut out his liver. But not because he insulted Mohammad's sister. Because he was drunk.

ME   Well, what are you going to do?

BARB   I don't know what I'm going to do.

ME   Are you going to go over there? To the funeral, I mean.

BARB   There is no funeral. She was disgraced. It took them a long time to put out the fire because they didn't want to put out the fire. There wasn't anything left to bury. And you can't cremate somebody who's already been cremated. The family goes through some kind of formal ceremony disowning her. Like cutting off a dead branch. And that's that. Next step, get Barbara ready to be married in a year. Except Barbara isn't sure she can go through with it. Barbara isn't sure she can marry a man who disowns his sister because she happened to be walking down the wrong street at the wrong time. Barbara isn't sure of anything any more. Except that she loves that fucker.

Here she suddenly breaks down and cries. It isn't called for in the script, but she cries anyway. Not only does she cover her face with her hands, she turns away from me. When I touch her shoulder, she pulls away angrily. She's angry at herself for letting me see her this way.

ME   What can I do? Can I get you something?

BARB   No. I'm fine. I ought to get out of here.

ME   Isn't there anything I can do?

BARB   No. I'm all right.

She is now completely composed again. She is the old Barbara. She is not about to discuss how Mohammad's acceptance of his sister's suicide will affect her engagement to him. That is a discussion for her and Victoria or Julia or Lori or Phyllis or all of them. Not me. Our discussion is over.

"Do you want to go out and have some dinner?" I ask her. "There's that new Argentinian place."

"Don't you know how to reach Victoria?" she answers with unrelated questions. "Why isn't she at the hotel? And where's NeAndrewthal, by the way?"

"I don't know where he is. I don't know where Victoria is, either, if she isn't at the hotel. Last I heard, she was there through the weekend. Maybe they ran off together."

"That's not funny, Roger."

"Why isn't it funny?"

"Because it isn't."

"Why, because it isn't that ridiculous?"

"Because you have to be blind not to see what's going on in his ape head. Not that I really think you have anything to worry about, but stranger things have happened than a guy's wife falling for his brother."

"You think Victoria is falling for my brother?"

"I think NeAndrewthal would just love that. I'm sorry, Roger, but you know how I feel about him. When Mohammad was telling me about his sister, all I could think of every time he mentioned that stupid little monkey sticking his tongue in and out was NeAndrewthal."

"Maybe you know something I don't. Maybe you've been talking to Victoria."

"Maybe I've got eyes."

"Well, I'm not going to worry about it."

"Well, I'm not going to go out to dinner with you," she says playfully, ending our conversation, getting ready to leave. "But thanks anyway."

She is up from the hide-a-bed, smiling as though no one has just immolated herself, smiling as though no one has just been accused of trying to steal his brother's wife, smiling just like the old Barbara, only behind red eyes.

"Why do I want to marry that guy anyway? You know what he does when he wants to make love to me? You know what he says, Roger? He looks at me and leans over and says, 'Chchchch.' I tell him to stop making that disgusting noise and he looks at me like I'm crazy. He claims that's the way they say 'psst' in his country. Well, what the hell do I want to marry a guy who's going to get me psst off everytime he wants to make love?"

Before she closes the door behind her, I hear myself ask her one more question.

"How old was Mohammad's sister?"

But she doesn't know.

23

VICTORIA CAME BACK THIS MORNING (at last! at last!).
She took the red-eye and called from the airport at 6
A.M. I was wide awake as soon as I heard her voice. (I was
dying to see her and afraid to see her. What if she hadn't
succeeded in ridding herself of her obsession?)

She said she was going to meet Barbara (red-eye to red-eye)
for breakfast, there was something important they had to talk
about (Barbara's news or Victoria's?) and then she'd be coming
home. I told her I'd see her late in the afternoon (I decided to
be cautious) because I absolutely had to go to the library to do
research for the appraisal I was finishing up, but that I missed
her and couldn't wait to see her (I couldn't help being anxious),
and did she want to go out for dinner to her favorite Mexican
restaurant or the new Thai restaurant or the new Mexican
restaurant Dale and Phyllis took me to?

She was eager to see everyone (I'm eager to see the two of
us) and said she'd call everyone and arrange something at our
place for tonight. It was no bother. (She wanted the bother.)

"Can't we be alone tonight, Victoria? I haven't seen you for
almost two weeks," I said to her on the phone (I haven't *seen
you* seen you for so long!)

She hesitated, then said sure (but I can wait, I don't want to upset you, I can wait until after everyone leaves), and I told her to go ahead and call everyone.

All day I have been wondering how she looks, if she has gotten a tan (a *pink*, considering her skin), and whether she'll be smiling again instead of being in that strange, miserable, distant state she was in when she left for California.

There's a young woman sitting at the end of the table who has been here as long as I have and has demonstrated truly amazing concentration. I have never seen anyone sit in one position for so long a time without fidgeting. Her research is piled high on the table in front of her and the pile keeps getting lower and lower as she takes one periodical after another from the stack, reads, makes notes, and puts it in the other stack, which is getting higher and higher. From where I'm sitting I can see her entire body, because her chair is pulled back from the table. Her lower body is facing me up to her lovely cinched waist, where it turns toward the table. She's wearing a flimsy, clinging dress that seems tight and loose at the same time. The silky fabric of the dress outlines her thighs and flows between her legs where they are spread slightly apart and then come together again at her crossed ankles (such beautiful bony ankles and bare tops of feet in low-cut loafers).

I feel I've known this young woman all my life. I can see through the dress and imagine her nude and getting ready for bed (the way Victoria gets ready). Her shoulders are sharp and strong and her neck is long (And oh! it arches back as she applies cream. Oh! she strains her head from side to side to relieve the tension in her neck and shoulders at the end of the day. She pulls her hair off her face and dabs her cheeks with something invisible to the eye, and oh! she is as smooth and polished as an apple, gleaming in the poor bathroom light). The woman stretches forward to add another completed periodical to the growing pile, and I can peek into her loose sleeve at that wonderful long expanse of flesh from under her arm (and all the way down the side of Victoria's body past her small waist to the start of her leg, a stretch which includes the first hint of breasts and the only fat of her back and the tapering sweep of shorter and shorter ribs descending to the bottom of the rib cage and to the sharp indentation of her waist and back out to the jut of her strong hip) and I can smell this stretch all the way at my end of the table, the familiar perfume coming from a beautiful glass bottle, tapered like her body, and from her own glands, clean and rancid, like the smell inside a dishwashing machine.

It's strange and frustrating to be sitting at the same table with this young woman and know her so well yet not know her at all, unable to say a single word to her for fear of being rebuffed.

It is difficult to concentrate. I try to read the 1955 year-end issues of several national magazines. Articles about James Dean and Jack Kerouac abound. This was my brother's generation. He was ten, eleven, twelve. The young woman sitting at the end of the table was not born. She is younger than Victoria. I have matched a name from a review of *Rebel Without a Cause* to one of the names I took down from the credits of the movie I'm appraising. Angel was right: the movie *is* based on *Rebel Without a Cause.* I'm old enough to witness the remake of a movie made in my lifetime. J. Kennedy Dodd is the reincarnation of James Dean. Aristotle and the hummingbird girl are reincarnations of the other two main roles. The three original actors, who would have been Andrew's age or older now, are all dead, one in an automobile accident, one by drowning, and one by violent murder.

In twenty minutes the library will close. It's time to return all reading materials to the front desk. The young woman at my table is even more beautiful when she stands, walks.

I pack my things and leave for home. Sitting across from me on the bus is the most beautiful black woman I've ever seen. The thought of her in my arms makes me weak. She's been shopping. A new dress? New shoes? A new coat (fur) (lynx) (NeAndrewthal) (missing) (link) (bracelet)? The black woman is like dark water personified as she flows down the aisle of the bus, her dress tight and loose at the same time, her legs spread and closed, spread and closed, her hair pulled back away from her face (as she prepares for bed) (smiling, not distant) (tan, not pink).

"You look terrific," I tell Victoria when she answers the door.

"Thanks."

I want to move toward her and hug her, but I'm paralyzed. Although we're only inches apart, I feel as if she's at the far end of the glossy surface of a library table, a distance measured by two weeks' time as well as space, and by secrets.

After a few seconds I notice that music is playing. *Imperial Bedroom,* by Elvis Costello. Around the room are bowls and dishes and cartons of Chinese food that I suddenly smell, and all our friends are eating buffet-style. One by one, I notice them. Everyone is here, everyone but Barbara. My God, Frank is back from Massachusetts. Michael is here. David is sitting in my chair.

I put my briefcase on the floor in the narrow space between the tape deck and the Apple, slide it back to the wall out of sight, and join my friends.

Victoria is burned, not tanned, like a deep blush. The sockets of her eyes are white from swimming with goggles. Her body is larger, more fluid, more inviting than any other in the room, but something in her shy glance keeps me from feeling that she is mine and mine alone. At the moment she belongs to the gathering of women who are talking about Barbara's absence and about Mohammad's sister's suicide. From what I can gather from the bits of their conversation I hear, they all agree that Mohammad's passionate defense of the suicide is the real problem. How can an independent and successful woman like Barb marry a man who espouses Moslem chauvinism? Is this the man for whom Barbara must forever forsake all other men?

Phyllis argues from a historical perspective, removing her wire-rimmed glasses and using them like a prop to emphasize her professorial approach. Without her glasses, her face looks soft and pretty. Julia stands alone on the abandoned prow of the good ship Women's Lib, her black hair and serious eyes and bohemian sexiness undermining her condemnation of Mohammad's sexual politics. Lori says, "Jesus Christ, all you have to do is look around at what's happening today, look at clothes, look at TV, look at the biggest movie stars, I mean it's a woman's world, girls." I look at the woman's world that is in my living room and it excites me. Women I have looked at a thousand

times before suddenly look like strangers to me, and I wonder
how they look in bed, how they feel, how they smell, what they
whisper in the dark. Victoria's only contribution to the discussion seems to come from as far away as Pakistan itself. "But she
loves him," she says sadly.

While the women move their conversation into the kitchen,
the men begin to talk about the plan to spend the holiday week
in Pakistan skiing the heady Himalayan slopes overlooking
Shangri-La.

"I don't know, I still haven't gotten an okay from the studio,"
Dale says with frustration, and then with confidence adds, "If
they don't come through with the deal I want, they can get
someone else to write their book."

"Well, I'll be there," Michael says. For perhaps the first time
in his life, he's enjoying the fact that his secret is out and his
plans have been made.

"It'll be nice to treat human epidemics for a change," Frank
jokes.

"What was it like, Frank, in Massachusetts?"

"Garbage. Ever go to the shore after a rainstorm? I've just
spent what, two weeks, three, hip high (yet his hand is at his
throat to approximate the height of the pile) in dead bivalves.
If I never see another clam for the rest of my life, it'll be too
soon for me."

"Is it over? I mean, can we eat that stuff now?" David asks
as he dips a shrimp into the thick oyster sauce, immerses it, and
works it into the goo with all the dexterity of our most accomplished chopstick wielder. It's a different kind of hunger that
makes me watch the flight of the tiny pink shrimp from the foil
plate up to David's open mouth. Oyster sauce drips onto his
pants, just missing the chair. My chair.

Our conversation is headed for Pakistan, but it's taking the
scenic route, going off on tangents that will eventually get back
to Pakistan. Michael insists that we throw no big bon voyage
party for him when he leaves next weekend for the clinic in
New Delhi, but we convince him that we are never going to
see "him," again and that such an occasion is certainly worthy
of a bash. He agrees only if it is held at his loft so his other
friends—people none of us has ever met—can come, too, and

not feel out of place. Frank digresses to a discourse on epidemics, and we all join in to discuss Malthus and Darwin and whether a plague might not be the best thing that could happen to Pakistan. David's talk wanders to his daughter. He's worried about her. She's letting herself go, overeating, not studying, going through the motions of obeying David and her mother, but not the emotions. But he turns the conversation back to Pakistan when he voices his concern for Angel's well-being and safety if he were to be so far away. My eyes dart to the beeper David keeps in a holster on his belt. Is Angel just another nervous system likely to break down? He's still sitting in my chair, his fashionable sport jacket caught behind his holster, probably thinking about Victoria. In my chair, thinking my thoughts.

Inevitably, the discussion of going to Pakistan leads to the subject of terrorism. No one will allow some kamikaze lunatic to intimidate him even in that controversial part of the world. Dale is serious when he suggests the idea of making and marketing a joke antiterrorist kit as a Christmastime novelty item. He doesn't know exactly what items the kit would contain, but, "You know, it could come with a little book of instructions that's funny and insulting and would be the only real work we'd have to do. Like the Pet Rock. That was just a box with a rock inside and a funny little booklet on the proper care and feeding of the rock. The booklet was the gimmick."

Frank guesses that none of us has ever been anywhere truly exotic or romantic or even fascinating except on business. Turns out he's right. The women have come back to the living room and they join us in remembering places we've traveled and whether it was on business. It becomes a little game, with one of us naming a place and the others guessing what the purpose of the trip was. I can't wait for the game to end. We decide that traveling on business is preferable to traveling on one's own. An expense account, of course, is a prime reason, but even more important is the overriding sense of purpose that makes the traveler feel like a citizen of whatever part of the world he happens to find himself in and keeps him from becoming an alienated, aimless, vulnerable tourist.

As for Pakistan, nothing is settled. The fun has gone out of going because no one knows what Barbara will do. She should have been here an hour ago. She said she was going to be late, but it's past what she promised.

"I'm not worried. She's probably planning her way out of this mess right now, or back into it," Julia reassures us by reminding us of Barbara's great resourcefulness and fortitude.

I am hoping Barbara doesn't show up. The evening is winding down and oh, I am anxious to be alone with Victoria. Oh, she is looking more and more beautiful the later it gets. She is still on California time and does not appear sleepy at her usually sleepy hour. I catch her eye and her shy look returns. Someone mentions Andrew, wonders where he is. I say I haven't seen Andrew for several days. "For all I know he's gone for good." I say this loudly and clearly directed at Victoria, to capture her attention. I'm trying something I've never done before—trying to give her a signal. A signal between two people who do not take each other for granted.

"What's with him, anyway?" David asks about Andrew. He is in my chair, asking my questions.

"He's a throwback." This is Frank's evaluation of Andrew.

"To what?" Lori challenges him.

"To a germ of a disease that almost ruined this country, okay?" Frank does not like Andrew.

"Well, I think he's just a boozy, sleazy bum who would rather play with himself—or anything else he can get his hands on—than do one minute of honest work." This is Dale's evaluation.

Phyllis talks about moments in history and how people get caught in them and nobody understands exactly what she means except that it sounds like she's defending Andrew. The women, it turns out, do not despise him; the men do. Michael doesn't have an opinion, he hardly knows the man. Victoria escapes choosing sides by cleaning up the empty cartons and dishes. A sudden beeping saves David from having to add to the discussion, in fact ends it and the party as well. David must go. Dale and Phyllis really ought to go, too. Julia is tired. Michael has two weeks' work to finish before he leaves for New Delhi next weekend. Frank still hasn't unpacked and Lori has an early call on the set of the third commercial in the pool of six she's been styling. I love my friends, but I'm glad to see them go.

Victoria and I will be alone (at last! at last!). I do not even look at her. My back is to her as I close the door on the last of our friends. I lock the door, turn off the tape deck, turn off the foyer light, and I know she is behind me, the shy look coming over her face like my own shadow approaching.

It has been a long time since we have been nervous together. A long time since we have looked at each other in a way that can only lead to a kiss. I kiss her and taste the shyness. I expect her to follow me into the bedroom and she does. In soft light we undress.

"I missed you," I whisper. She will not say a word. Her eyes are watery, the pupils dancing. I cannot tell whether the expression on her mouth and in her nervous eyes is still shyness or has turned into something else. (Can this be what guilt looks like?)

Her body seems to be operating independently of what's going on in her mind. Her arms and legs go wherever I want them. A former awkwardness in our embraces has disappeared. It's as if Victoria has already climaxed, already surrendered. She will only react. But her limp body is wonderful. It is all softness and heartbeat beneath me. The color she got in California seems to have toned her skin. The whiteness where she wore her swimsuit is startling and virginal and tremendously erotic. All day I have been waiting for this moment. From 6 A.M. this morning, I have been caressing her and kissing her and moving slowly toward the places I can enter. She is mine and not mine. I know her and don't know her. Our motions are both fluid and clumsy. The inside of my mouth is dry. Wherever I put my tongue, it meets with dryness. Victoria's skin is chalky and dry. Some of my foreplay hurts her. Some hurts me. The deeper I go into lovemaking, the dryer the terrain. I cough. My own cough excites me in her motionless hand, and she closes her hand around me when she feels my excitement. I am trying to prolong my desire. Partly because it is going to be over too quickly and partly because I think I can tunnel through the dryness if I last, I force myself to think sobering thoughts (I watched her and David closely tonight and they hardly looked at each other. Could it have been an act?). My imagination is working overtime. Now it's dredging up images of the young woman at the library. The images will not go away. They will outlast me. Victoria, too, will outlast me. She will last forever while I give myself to her because she is home (at last! at last!), and I cannot last a second longer.

The little noise is not mine. Usually it is mine, and usually it is not so little. I cannot keep quiet at such moments. But this time the noise comes from Victoria, who has always kept quiet at such moments. During all our lovemaking, she has never made a sound. Her lips have moved and her body has cried out, but she has never uttered a sound. Now she has whimpered—it is no more than a quick, harsh, barely audible whimper—and at precisely the moment when I should have been calling out in ecstasy. Her timing is too exact. Her little noise too unbelievably on cue. She has lied to me at love.

We are finished. I am standing at the window. There's a draft. Fishing for my robe in the dark closet, my hand finds that the hanging clothes are uncharacteristically close together. They do not move very freely along the bar. Something has been added that takes up much of the previous space. A garment bag. The feel of the bag, soft as a chamois, is expensive. What's inside must have cost a fortune.

24

ANDREW IS BACK.
Victoria was asleep when I finally went to bed last night and was gone before I woke up this morning. A sleeve of the lynx coat was hanging out of the unzipped side of the garment bag. She did not tuck it back in and rezip the bag. She did not bother to cover up what I had found, knowing we would have to have a major conversation, a conversation I am now waiting to have with her the moment she arrives home from work.

When I went into the living room and saw the opened hide-a-bed and Andrew's wheezing, bloated body sprawled over the top sheet—still in its clothes, still in its shoes—something compelled me to look beyond the stubble and muss, to lay bare what I thought I saw peeking out from collar and cuffs, pushing through the gaps fat forced in his shirt.

Careful not to disturb him, I dared to unbutton his shirt, nervous as someone defusing a bomb, one button, and then another, careful, careful, and then another, until at last I saw the evidence I had dreaded all along—the quick roast red of an hour or two in the California sun.

I stood over my brother and watched him breathe, hoping the thin gold bracelet around his wrist would strangle him as a rope around a tree trunk will strangle the whole tree by stopping vital circulation. Then I did not care about waking him. I rattled things in the kitchen, slammed cupboard doors, turned on the morning news, left the door open when I showered, but nothing disturbed him. I decided to print out Victoria's PENDING file and then enter selected information from her letter to David in my RAWN file. The noisy printing did not awaken Andrew; he didn't even roll over.

When the printer was quiet, I separated the printed pages, aligned the sheets, and removed the margins of sprocket holes by tearing along the perforated edges. The stack of papers was bigger than I expected it would be, and I checked to see if the printer had been set to triple space. But it had not been. Victoria's letter was longer because she had replaced it with a startling new entry. Yesterday! While I was in the library! Not being able to get her out of my mind!

"Mexico called to me," PENDING now began, "I heard it calling to me all day and all night. Wherever I went, on business or on time off, Mexico called to me like a beautiful little folk song drifting in from another room, a haunting song, so pretty and pleading, a melody I could not get out of my head, words I could not understand, calling calling calling to me in the streets and offices and restaurants and shops, everywhere I went, whatever I did, whoever I was with, pleading pleading pleading with me to come to Mexico, now, forever, take the car and drive, Victoria. 'Don't you hear that?' I kept wanting to ask passersby, waitresses, shopkeepers, gas station attendants, witnesses I had tracked down for sworn statements, 'Don't you hear that beautiful song?' But only I heard it. Only I had to resist it. For I had no business in Mexico.

"And yet I gave in. I finished my work, got into my rented car, and began to drive the San Diego Freeway south, the song playing as clearly as if it were coming from the car radio, the singer calling to me from the passenger seat. Past cities and beach towns and the setting sun, I drove as though in a trance, Mexico calling to me, Mexico whispering to me through the driving wind, Mexico touching my hand, stroking my arm, gently forcing my leg to apply more and more pressure to the accelerator.

"I could not make the entire journey nonstop. We pulled

into the ample parking lot of a low, sprawling Mexican restaurant, Mexico and I, and walked into a cavernous front room with stucco balustrades and parapets and several smaller back rooms. Inside, it was dark and gaudy. Brocaded sombreros and spangly serapes hung all over the walls. We were the only customers, Mexico and I, and it had been Mexico's idea to stop here, Mexico's idea to order the sickeningly sweet margaritas and catsupy salsa, to show me the difference between this and what was waiting for us one hundred miles south. I got woozy from the drinks and the salsa stuck in my throat. I got dizzy and a little sick and started to perspire as though I had been whirling and dancing to Mexico's song. My heart beat to the song, my head reeled to the song. The margarita in front of me was a hundred miles away, like a barely visible landmark in the distance.

"Mexico asked the waitress to convert a twenty-dollar bill into small change for the telephone. The telephone was near the entrance, and finding my way back through the maze of terraces, tables, and wrought-iron chairs was impossible. Without Mexico's leading me, I would have gotten lost forever. Without Mexico's singing to me, I would not have known what to say into the phone. But I heard myself singing along into the mouthpiece. A verse about me. About my job. About my schedule. About my having to chase down one last fleeing witness for one last sworn statement before returning home.

"Even before I went outside, the light stunned me. Mexico opened the door and the California light came in like a dense, expanding geometric shape, like a monster of light, white hot rays shutting my eyes. But the blinding, painful light also awoke me. By the time we were back in the rented car, I was refreshed, sober, alert, ready to drive the remaining one hundred miles to the border with the windows wide open, the strong wind and the day's last sun pouring in like water rushing through the ungated spillways of a dam. My obsession roared like the engine. We were speeding toward the border, Mexico singing faster and faster, Mexico coming closer at the rate of seventy, eighty, ninety miles an hour, America receding behind me. In that incredibly awake and aware state, we sped through remaining light. Along our right, the coastline went from dazzling to glowing as it swallowed the sun. Some of the road signs were in Spanish now and the hidden hill towns and plunging cliffside resorts turned into a last stretch of ugly, oily highway. There were naked white lights and foreign words in reflective lettering and rigs and generators and the smell of dirt and sea and oil all pouring in on the wind, the rented car eating up the tar and slick and cracks of the road, Mexico sitting beside me, Mexico looking straight ahead toward home, Mexico's eyes and Mexico's song as haunting as the twilight.

"The Friday night traffic leaving Mexico was backed up for miles. The beat-up vans, the gaudy panel trucks, the groaning station wagons and rusted, rebuilt, half-painted old Pontiacs and Cadillacs waiting to be inspected by customs agents were stopped in the inspection plaza, parked there, *señores* and *señoritas* sitting outside on folding chairs, eating, laughing, drinking colorful juices from large plastic jugs, waiting, partying, hundreds of them, thousands of them, their *niños* roaming the plaza like scrawny stray animals, more than one family barbecuing, others patiently seated around card tables playing out their hands, everyone resigned to the inevitable delay in getting out of Mexico for the weekend. Getting in, however, was no problem at all. We passed through the checkpoint as quickly and easily as if we had been going through an exact-change tollbooth. It was only after passing through and seeing the endless line of backed up traffic waiting to prove it was bringing no contraband into watchful America that the fear gripped me. Tomorrow that would be me, my rented car caught in the endless, motionless, timeless line of return. What was so easy to enter would be so difficult to escape.

"As soon as we passed through the inspection station, we pulled over to the side of the plaza and looked for a road map in the glove compartment. Instead, we found the car rental agreement. It specified in big bold letters and in no uncertain terms that taking the car across the border was STRICTLY FORBIDDEN; the knowledge that we had done something STRICTLY FORBIDDEN chilled us in the already cool and frightening night. It was too late. The crime had been committed. We had crossed the border. We were about to drive a strange road into a strange country in an illegally operated vehicle. We were headed for Tijuana, anticipating the hell town depicted in movies and novels and gossip columns, a lawless, degenerate carnival full of tequila-ravaged hell raisers, scar-faced desperadoes, toothless harlots, pitiful consumptives, fat and sweaty policemen drooling and grinning at our alien car and native panic. Yet we met none of these characters. For the first mile or two, the road was quiet. We met only the suspense of darkness.

"When we came upon the Friday nightlife of Tijuana, it was nothing but a brightly lit bazaar overcrowded with battered vending machines and broken-down cars and stand-up bars and stall after stall of one-man concessions offering newspapers, beer, ice cream, souvenirs, sacks of rice, automobile parts, cheap shoes, pants, belts, shirts, blouses, sheets, pillows. The traffic crawled, but we moved steadily enough so that no one approached the car. Even so, we kept the windows rolled up and the doors locked. And then in less than a mile, the bright lights were behind us and we drove deeper into the darkness, on toward the next town, always taking the forks and bends and turns that would keep us close to the sea.

"Halfway through the town of Ensenada we needed to stop . . . for something to eat or drink or to rest . . . but there was no place, only empty shacks or vacant lots or private houses or small shops closed for the night. We kept circling the same streets; three times we took the same shortcut through a long-abandoned gas station, thinking we had missed something or that a lone house lit on the second floor might have been a cantina of some kind and that if we continued to pass it, perhaps we would see guests coming or going who would give us the confidence to knock at the door. But when we encountered the same cruising car for the second time, we were afraid we had aroused suspicion or that we had marked ourselves as lost or drunk or fleeing and vulnerable, and we wasted no time speeding away toward the next town.

"The road was new and empty and wound through low hills and the cool moonless night and the stronger and stronger smell of the sea. Occasionally we saw one or two men walking, the ashes of their cigarettes as bright as flashlights in the darkness. I don't remember the name of the next town. In my mind, it was a town entirely comprised of the cantina we found. There was darkness and fear and then a sudden grand, sweeping bend in the road, and in that bend set back upon the beach was the cantina. It was big as a barn and partially supported by pilings so that the wooden terrace attached to the main structure overhung the crashing of waves in the night.

"We knew it was open to us. There was light and faint music and a huge hand-painted sign announcing the Marlin. On the sign was an illustration of a bounding boat at sea and the leaping namesake of the cantina. We parked where there were no other cars and locked our belongings in the trunk so no one would be tempted to break in. The wind off the sea was strong enough to keep customers from ever reaching the Marlin, but we put our heads down and fought hard and made it across the highway and the long narrow path through the sand and rock of the beach leading to the entranceway of the Marlin.

"To get to the door we had to climb a rickety stairway that ended at the landing of an outdoor hallway. We made our way along the hallway's creaking floorboards around back to the seaward side of the barn, where we eventually found a second stairway, this one shorter and sturdier than the first, and we took it to the canopied terrace of the dining room. The terrace and the dining room were completely open to the sea and the wind whipped and swirled and roared through them. Napkins anchored by pewter cups of salsa flapped noisily on every table. Paper pennants strung along the ceiling fluttered and ticked and tore. The canopy held fast behind us, but the wind rapped against it like a thousand fists at the door. There were no customers, but there were five young waiters standing lazily at their stations, their long hair blowing in and out of their eyes, their string ties flapping like birds attacking their throats, their aprons ballooning at the hem. Except for the light, which was bright and constant, except for the warmth and aroma from the huge ovens visible at the rear of the dining room, except for the scratches of music coming through a staticky speaker, standing there was like standing on the deck of a ghost ship.

"An old man in a sea captain's hat appeared from the kitchen and came toward us. Somehow the wind did not disturb him. 'Where would you like to sit?' the captain asked us, gesturing toward the best table. We took his advice and sat there, and one of the five young waiters brought us a basket of tortilla chips. The chips were hot and doughy and did not have to be guarded from being blown out of their basket by the wind. 'We only want drinks,' we told the captain. 'It is just as well,' he said, 'because the food is not ready for another hour.' The young waiter brought us two margaritas rimmed in salt. The mix was tart and the tequila was harsh and the thick salt around the rim of the glass was less a decorative tradition than a necessity to counterbalance the woody, fruity taste of the margaritas. Slowly we sipped them and greedily ate our chips and tried to analyze the recipe for the salsa, which was the spiciest and most delicious I had ever tasted. There might have been fish in it. And something resembling onion, but not onion. And several spices I couldn't identify. Together the ingredients burned slowly on my lips and in my mouth and throat and inside my chest, building with each first cool lemony fish flavor into a cumulative fire which, for all its rage, was not unpleasant.

"This was Mexico. These ferocious tastes and this wild wind and restless sea. And the lizard eyes and smooth brown skin and cocked hat of the captain, and the five young waiters stationed throughout eternity against the wind, this, too, was Mexico. Without my realizing it, the haunting little folk song I had heard all through Los Angeles and en route to Mexico had turned into the soulful wailing of *los mariachis.*

"We moved our seats right up to the railing under the canopy on the terrace. From there we could see the dark shape of the sea and the phosphorescent foam of waves breaking on rocks. On the terrace, Mexico talked to me, asked me questions. Where had I come from? How had I come to be so far away from that place? What language did I speak? What language did I wish to speak? Mexico interrogated me, tested me, determined whether I was worthy of citizenship. At one point, Mexico reached across the windswept table and took my hand. Mexico's hand was large and warm, and mine completely disappeared within it.

"We ordered two more margaritas each and worried about finding a place to stay the night. Staying the night was no

longer a contingency, it was our destiny. The waiter did not
know of a place. He sent the captain out to us, and we asked
him where the nearest, largest hotel was. He turned and
pointed away from the sea and I noticed that his white hair was
so long beneath his hat that he had it tied in a ponytail. 'I don't
know if she is full,' he apologized as he pointed the way and
indicated his sketchy directions with his hand, 'but you go
there, to Rosario, two more towns,' to look for El Rio Playa,
'beeg, modren, mucho dinero.'

"Despite the effects of the salsa, it was cold on the terrace,
and I wanted my new coat, which was locked in the trunk of
the rental car. Mexico would have been glad to get it, but we
had had enough to drink and decided to leave immediately to
give ourselves time to search for Rosario and the hotel. We had
not known it when we arrived, but there was a separate entrance to and from the terrace, another stairway leading—as
it looked in the dark—directly into the sea. *Los mariachis* still
wailing in my ears and heart and throat and chest, I followed
Mexico down the wide wooden stairs onto the beach. The sand
there was finer than in front. There were no rocks or patches
of scrub grass . . ."

My God, where has she learned this . . .

". . . or fallen trees that had tried their best to thrive in the
wind and sand."

. . . she writes like an angel.

"We wished we could walk the beach. I sensed that Mexico
might put its arms around me. But it was too cold and too late.
Instead, we hurried around the Marlin, back to the front path,
and across the highway to the car. In the car I put on my new
coat. We unpacked the trunk and I unzipped the bag and
snuggled into its warmth. Fur and Mexico wrapped themselves around me. I reclined the seat, let Mexico drive, and we
continued on the highway toward Rosario. The road straight-
ened and widened as it entered the next town. There were
streetlights. There were narrow sidewalks. There were gar-
ages on both sides of the street with row upon row of hubcaps
nailed to the facades. The hubcaps gleamed in the artificial
light and the crashing song of Mexico was beat out upon these
gleaming circles of chrome as we sped by.

"The El Rio was full. There was nothing available, not even

a broom closet. All the money in the world couldn't change the facts. And so we drove on, looking, worrying, frightened, excluded. In the middle of an enormous hedgerow we saw a dimly lit archway over a drive. We pulled in and Mexico talked to a sleazy-looking man who was stationed in a little booth under the arch. It must have been warm inside the booth because the man was wearing a T-shirt and drinking a bottle of beer. Money changed hands, hundreds of American dollars, and the man gave us a key and directions and let us pass. The compound did not look like Mexico. It looked like a suburban housing development. There were roads and intersections and trees and identical houses all attached to one another and American cars parked in all the driveways. Some of the wider roads were lit, and we followed them slowly through the village, every so often pulling off a main road to see if our hacienda was located on this or that dark and narrow lane. Finally we found our number and pulled into the short, steeply inclined driveway; it was so narrow we had to pull back out so I could open the passenger door and then pull back in. We unloaded the car as though we were returning from a vacation, put the key in the lock, and let ourselves into our little home. The front door opened onto a large living room with a studio kitchen at one end separated from the living room by a counter and doorway and some latticework. Off the central hallway we found a small bedroom with its own bathroom, a larger bathroom with a tub and shower and, at the end of the hallway, a master bedroom. Although the house smelled musty and unused, the rooms were clean and well kept and we were glad to be warm. We dumped our bags on the living room furniture without unpacking. There were upholstered chairs and couches and several end tables. French prints and romanesque sconces decorated the walls. In silence, we roamed the house and evaluated the remainder of the night.

"Thick fresh towels were piled in the master bathroom and I washed and dried myself with the biggest towel and then put on makeup and fixed my hair and stared into the mirror. I looked at home. I looked young. I reached into my blouse under my arms to feel the stubble of a day-old shave. Mexico would not like that I had shaved, but the damage had been done. When Mexico finished in the smaller bathroom, we left to find a restaurant. I waited to get into the car until after it was out of the driveway, and we drove back onto the highway, back to the El Rio Playa Hotel, where we knew we could get a good meal. We drove fast.

"There was a dance at the hotel. Young couples were crowded in the courtyard and the lobby, waiting to be admitted. The girls wore delicate white blouses and long, full multicolored skirts. The skirts were made from hundreds of carnations, all freshly picked and dyed and strung together for the big dance. They wore matching carnations in their silky black hair. Their young men wore tight pants and blousy shirts and pointy shoes. The hotel, described by the captain of the Marlin as 'modren,' was not modern at all. It reminded me of an old YMCA with mimeographed notices tacked to bulletin boards and handwritten placards on easels pointing the way to the dance, to dinner, to the other public offerings of the hotel. As we entered the lobby, the musicians were just beginning to warm up. I could hear them through the big double doors, still closed to the anxious young couples. The warm-up was raucous and improvisational and exactly what I had heard in my head and heart ever since we had crossed the border, Mexico and I, ever since the sweet mesmerizer of Los Angeles had turned into *los mariachis* of the cantina-by-the-sea. But we were not to go to the dance. And yet we would take their music back with us to our American hacienda, back to our master bedroom with the musty smell and the tacky watercolor hanging over the bed and the plump towels waiting to cool us down after hours of private dancing.

"The restaurant was busy, but we were shown to a good table right away. This time we drank a wonderful beer that was cold and mild and the color of our gold bracelets. It was served in champagne glasses and tasted like ambrosia. I do not remember the rest. Not the food. Not the coffee. Not the waiters and guests. Not anything. We drank beer and read the subtitles in each other's eyes and then suddenly we were home.

"Mexico called to me. Mexico sang to me. Mexico put its arms around me and began to undress me in the dark. I felt like a young girl about to be loved for the first time. I was incredibly aware of my body and the distinctive smells of my hair and breath and skin. One leg started to tremble and I realized I was standing on the toes, poised and trembling, on a nerve. But I knew what I was doing. I knew exactly and instinctively what to do, yet every move I made and every sound I uttered was one I had never made before. Mexico made me speak the unutterable. Mexico made me do the unthinkable. Claw and strangle each other. Shout and curse each other."

My God—Andrew began to toss and turn in the hide-a-bed at precisely this point in my reading of Victoria's file! My God! As though he were reliving it!

"Our private dance grew crazy and frantic. Whatever Mexico wanted, I obeyed. The slightest pressure—at my hip, the small of my back, beneath my legs—propelled me into the desired position. A rowdy verse of Mexico's song compelled me to answer in kind. Wetness met with wetness. Skin with skin. Nail against nail. Tooth to tooth. Salsa, fish, and lime commingled in our mouths. My incredible awareness of my body spread inside of me. I could feel my organs constrict and expand. I could smell their secretions. Shame went up in flame."

My God—he was clenching and unclenching his fists. He was stiffening his legs. He was writhing against the top sheet of the hide-a-bed, winding the sheet around his legs and arms.

"Everything I said or did, I said or did for the first time. It was an initiation. A ritual. At one point I escaped and watched myself from the ceiling of the master bedroom of the hacienda. I was a mirror over the bed watching myself slowly and violently change form. My hair grew thick and curly. My legs burst through the sheets. My breasts were flat and muscular. My arms wound out like tentacles. Mexico and the desire for Mexico dripped from my mouth, and my mouth was contorted, open, opening, wide, wider, in a constant exquisite howl."

My God—he was growling in his sleep, providing an unconscious commentary to Victoria's incredible entry.

"Mexico was inside me. Melted down. Smelling like game. Flowing like glowing red lava off the mountains. Dust, skulls, lizards, ruins, sequins, pennants, cactus, rattling tambourines—all melted and flowing and filling me and spilling over. In my throat, *los mariachis*. In my veins, rusted rivers. In my breast, the steamy flanks of charging bulls. In my stomach, a garden of jalapeños."

Jesus! He was getting bigger. His pants bulged at the fly. His hips rose and fell in a rhythm.

"Out of my howling mouth came the language of Mexico. The words poured forth, strung together like a thousand multicolored carnations. I screamed them, shrieked them, cried them. And then . . . at the very height of it . . . at the very depth of it . . . at the very moment of explosion—came silence. Came complete silence."

His hands held on to his thighs for dear life . . .

"We were a pantomime, Mexico and I. A silent enactment . . ."

. . . and the front of his pants darkened.

". . . and it was over."

The dark wetness on Andrew's pants spread like an expanding country—annexation, territory off the coast, a new cluster of tiny islands—while the great swollen continent itself, Andrew, lay breathless and undiminished, obscuring every horizon. I had to turn back to PENDING so as not to see him.

"To avoid traffic at customs, we left the hacienda before sunrise," PENDING continued. "We made good time and passed through without a hitch, although I had prepared several explanations in case we had been detained—explanations for the officers and explanations for my co-workers and friends and Roger. But none was needed. The drive back was quiet except for the car radio. On every station Eric Clapton songs were being played one after the other. I wondered if he had died. We listened to him sing about lost love and found love and being down and out and being on fire and being in trouble and going overboard and worrying about cocaine from five in the morning straight through to when we dropped the car off later that night, except for those times when we stopped . . . to be together . . . in complete, loving silence.

"We had plenty of time before catching the red-eye. We stopped at the San Diego zoo and watched the animals feed. We drove past the airport to Malibu and walked for an hour along the beach. We drove up into the hills to Blue Jay Way and Mullholland Drive and back down through Beverly Hills along Rodeo to see if the furrier had put a new coat in the window. In Westwood, we found a small cemetery, where Marilyn Monroe was buried. The cemetery was squeezed in behind a shopping complex. There was a fresh rose on her grave, as there is every morning, compliments of Joe Di-Maggio. We parked by the old Graumman's Chinese Theatre and stepped in the stars' footprints. We had dinner in a drive-in hamburger joint. I was twelve and shy and in love. On the plane back, the two of us were able to have three seats across, and I fell asleep in his arms, and it was tender and lovely and romantic, and I slept all the way. But I dreamed the truth.

"That ultimate moment of complete silence, of wild panto-mime, had been shattered by the ceiling mirror I had become. I came crashing down on myself. I was sorry. I was happy. I was lonely. I was embarrassed. I was in shock. But I was not guilty. Two contrary forces had existed in me simultaneously: complete abandon and complete control, each somehow fostering the other. I know now that I had plotted our journey to Mexico in order to lose myself along the way. I had arranged and rearranged the crescendos of desire to accompany the haunting music of *los mariachis.* I had gorged myself on food and drink and danger. Through an enormous effort of will, I had made myself a child again. Eleven. Twelve. Virginal. Verging on nothing. Remaining a child. Yet I was able to accomplish this transformation only because I was really three times that tender age. Three times wiser. Three times more experienced. Three times sadder. Like a painter who can think and feel and see in the abstract only after mastering the techniques of real-ism.

"Mexico, of course, had not been real. Mexico was abstract. There was nothing about Mexico's leering eyes and evil mous-taches and hot breath and fat belly and funny clothes that I wanted. What I wanted was *want* itself. Desire. Destiny. That it came along in Mexico's body was immaterial. That I have come along in my body is immaterial. And that I had to give my body to Mexico in order to give shape and freedom to my desire was not sinful. It was predestined. Once I was someone else. In the future I will be someone else again. All that remains constant and true is want. Unsatisfied want."

I looked back at Andrew, the sleeping continent of my wife's desire. He had taken her across more than a border. She had crossed a threshold into a newly discovered self, and he had been her guide and I hated him. I hated him for not being an entrepreneur or a millionaire or a genius or a celebrity or at least a tall, well-built, good-looking, blond-haired ski instructor with a thick Austrian accent. Then I hated him for buying her a fur coat. Then I hated him for making her howl in bed. But I hated him most for sleeping through my rage.

I folded the print-out in half, put it in my briefcase, and went to the hide-a-bed to wake up Andrew. I wanted to grab him by his wet pants and yank him out of the hide-a-bed by the same goddamn cock he had stuck into Goldie and then into my margarita-drugged wife, his sister-in-law, David's goddess, everybody's goddamn Marilyn Monroe all of a sudden. But I just stood over him.

What good would it do to fight with Andrew? He'd win anyway. Another round for Andrew. And I couldn't afford to lose another round. I was already on the ropes. And even if I won, even if I managed to come back and throw him out of the apartment, that would not be the same as throwing him out of our lives.

No. No hysterics. No dramatics. No grandstand fifteenth-round knockout. Instead I would do what I have done all along. Continue, to the very best of my ability, to live my life and let Victoria live hers. After all, Victoria's Mexico entry had not been intended for my eyes. She had not wanted me to suffer. There was no animosity in her. She had even deluded herself into believing that what she did in Mexico was not sinful.

No. I began rebuttoning Andrew's shirt. I had to be as cautious as before. It helped to know how dead to the world Andrew was. No, I decided, holding my breath as I closed another button, instead I will live my life ignoring facts that were never intended for me. I will go on with my work. I will see my friends. I will preserve the norm by believing in it. If we remain true to who we are and what we do and to the happiness created in the process, we cannot possibly make a wrong choice. It is right, *we* are right—our circle, our friends, our wife, our future. My God—nothing can ever compete with the future. It's all buttoned up.

25

I WAS ABLE TO SIT IN THE SAME room with my brother and ignore what would have driven others crazy. Others simply don't realize all they put up with in spite of what they insist they will not tolerate. They sublimate what is intolerable in their lives and pretend everything is okay. I face facts.

There I sat tapping out the finishing touches of appraisal number two while Andrew slept and snored and maybe even fondly dreamed of his filthy conquest in Mexico. If he had had his way, I would have attacked him and he would have murdered me. But in the end I will have my way. Victoria will be mine and Andrew will be no more important to her than a memorable teacher who imparted something that eventually benefited me.

Did I care that he slobbered all over her in the hacienda? Did I care that she fell tenderly into his embrace at the zoo and on the beach and in the car and on the plane? To be sure, I was not happy about it; but could Andrew have been happy that Victoria came home and did not announce that she was leaving me? Could he be happy that she reverted to her old self?

At the end of her first day in the office after returning from

Los Angeles, she came directly home and showed me her new coat before I could bring up the subject myself. She told me she just couldn't resist it. She told me she had finally talked to Lori from Los Angeles and Lori had clarified the message I had left. *(Lori says the coat is a lot of money. Roger.)* Yes, it was a lot of money, Victoria admitted, but that did not make it a bad buy. In fact, she argued, it was a great buy. An investment, practically. Then she sat me down and brought me a Kirin and told me how much her great buy had cost.

"Seven thousand." I repeated quietly. Quietness, I thought, was more in keeping with shock, and I was trying to pretend to be shocked. It seemed that both of us were doing our best to pretend that we were having a normal conversation. And we were.

"I'll get the money by borrowing against my whatchamacallit," she said. She could not call it her inheritance, which was what it was, although only a modest twenty-five thousand dollars from her maternal grandmother that had grown in interest over the years to more than one hundred thousand. Calling it her inheritance made it seem as though it belonged to her exclusively in case things didn't work out with me. Legally, she was not allowed to touch the money until she was fifty-two years old, the age at which her grandmother had given birth to Victoria's mother. But the sum had come with a provision allowing money to be borrowed against the principal, which could then be garnisheed in the event that Victoria's debt fell seriously in arrears. One night we tried to figure out the reasoning behind her grandmother's you-can-touch-it-but-you-can't-have-it-yet provision. Instead of serving as a lesson in fiscal responsibility, this condition encouraged buying on credit, paying out interest greater than the interest the inheritance could possibly earn, spending money as yet unowned, and ultimately never really knowing what specific gifts Grandma's money had actually purchased. Was it the TV and VCR we bought two years ago with the home improvement loan borrowed against Victoria's inheritance, or was it last year's trip to Vermont for the holidays, which was paid for with a personal loan? Or would it be the lynx coat or a trip to Pakistan or tuition for our future child's college education? By then we'd be able to take the actual inheritance out of the bank if it hasn't been garnisheed.

We never did figure out Grandma's motives. But Victoria's were more transparent. It was quite clever of her and Andrew to use a personal loan against her inheritance as a way of keeping me from seeing how the coat was actually paid for. All I'd ever see would be the monthly payments to the bank. But how did they buy the coat from the furrier without money? Certainly Victoria wasn't walking around with seven thousand bucks in her handbag. Which left Andrew. Andrew must have had enough money to buy the coat outright. How was Victoria going to get out of this one?

"I charged it on my expenses," she explained matter-of-factly, answering the question I never asked. "The bills won't go through bookkeeping for almost a month. By that time I'll have the loan and be able to repay my office."

How would I ever know if she had charged it on her expenses? How would I ever know whether she repaid the loan money to her office or to herself, keeping it, in small bills, stashed in some old handbag in the bottom of the closet? All I'd ever know for sure was that every month for the term of the loan, we would pay back the bank. The shop had its money. Victoria had her coat. The bank had its interest. Andrew had his way. All was right with the world.

Clever as Victoria's explanation was, her "real" reason for buying the coat was positively brilliant. She sat down on the floor next to my chair and told me how she had debated buying the coat for days and days and then finally decided because of something she realized about me.

"Me?"

"You are going to be a very rich man, Roger. We are going to be very rich people. You are going to be a huge success in your appraisals. I realized that, Roger. I realized why you did it, why you gave up your music and went full time into this, and the only way I could apologize for how I behaved when you told me you were going to do it, the only way I could think of to prove to you that I really am behind you, was to start spending some of the tremendous amounts of money I know you're going to earn for us. That's real proof that I believe in what you decided to do. Real proof that I believe in *you.*"

This was exactly what I wanted. It reminded me of one of those R. D. Laing poems: *Jill knows that Jack knows that Jill knows that Jack . . .* but the fact is, it worked. It always does. I knew that Victoria was acting. Probably she knew that I was acting. But that was exactly what we wanted. The normal acting out of our lives. Andrew did not have a chance. Andrew never had a chance.

"I would like you to think of this coat as ours, Roger."

"It's a little daring for me," I joked.

"Seriously. As a symbol of a major change in our lives."

"I understand."

"The inheritance is *our* inheritance, Roger. So the coat is *our* coat, symbolizing the time in our lives when both of us were brave enough to . . ."

". . . even change the way we strut our stuff."

"Seriously, Roger."

"Seriously, I understand. It's *our* coat, *our* inheritance. And it *is* daring. For both of us. I understand."

The week went well. Victoria was pre-NeAndrewthal. She was clean-shaven under her arms and on her legs. She ate heartily, drank no beer, and slept soundly. She was pleasant and home early and even interested in having sex in the middle of the week, although I was really too tired from all day at the Apple and had to say so. Victoria had energy to burn; she even rejoined her athletic club and started every day with a workout and sixty laps in the pool. She wanted our friends to come over every night, but one or the other of them couldn't make it and we all planned to see each other Saturday night anyway at Michael's bon voyage party.

Although no one could get in touch with Barbara, Victoria, who was the last one to see her, kept reassuring us that Barbara was fine, that she was away on business just like her office said, and that there was no reason to worry about her; she was her old spunky self and had come to terms with that whole awful business about Mohammad and his sister. The way Victoria talked about Barb sounded like she was talking about herself and Andrew and her own recuperation. Whatever injury I suffered from Victoria and Andrew's exotic liaison was healing rapidly and appeared to be leaving no scar. As for Andrew, he was forced to put up with us. He woke late and left the apartment and came home late and passed out. When we all happened to be in the apartment and awake at the same time, we ignored him and he ignored us. There was no rancor, only inevitable, invisible distance.

More and more, I wished that he would stumble home while we were awake. The one night that he did, he found us cuddling on the closed hide-a-bed watching *Remington Steele*. Victoria did not move. Her hand had been at the back of my neck, affectionately tickling me there, and she continued with no regard to Andrew's noisy, typically disgusting entrance. He burst in, in a desperate hurry to get to the john. Staggering across the room, he made it to the john and, as usual, peed without shutting the door. It was evident when he came back out into the living room that he was expecting to find his hide-a-bed opened and waiting for him. For a long minute or two he stood there swaying and looking down at the coffee table, which had not been moved out of the way. I waited for Victoria to do or say something, but she never moved. Finally I suggested that we go to bed, which we did. That was the night Victoria invited me to make love and I was too tired. First she had taken a shower, and I heard Andrew fall onto the coffee table. She came out of the shower completely naked except for a towel tied into a turban around her wet hair. The little hallway from the bathroom to our bedroom could not be seen from the hide-a-bed and so it was not surprising to see Victoria step into the lit hallway without a robe. But she paused and turned and went the other way out into the dark living room to get to the kitchen, where she poured herself a glass of spring water and then returned through the living room to our bed, where I pretended to be engrossed in the book of sci-fi short stories I was holding up in front of my face. Inevitable, invisible distance. Sitting on the edge of the bed, she loosened the turban and toweled her hair dry. Then she got in under the covers, drank her spring water, asked how my book was, shut her light, and put her hand on my chest. We spoke a little about my progress on the appraisals, which was good, and about the short stories, which were not. Without speaking, but with her actions, she asked if I felt like making love and I told her I was too tired, which she accepted with a goodnight kiss. In the morning I found Andrew passed out across the coffee table and the unopened hide-a-bed; Victoria had already left for the office.

I called Suzanne's house to ask if Angel was available to consult on the third movie. I had already prepared an outline, and now I was ready to watch the movie with Angel and finish off my first assignment as a professional. But there was no answer at Suzanne's. I suppose I could have watched the movie by myself, but I preferred Angel's company. I realized that the real reason I wanted to see her had nothing to do with the movie. She was a mystery to me and I hated unsolved mysteries. I wanted to talk about reincarnation and about her traumatic liaison with her father and about lunch that time with Victoria and "Nick," and about the three of them wearing matching gold bracelets. But there was no answer at Suzanne's; and I was annoyed.

In keeping with my new rules, however, I decided to watch the movie alone. I sat down on the unoccupied part of the hide-a-bed and stared at the TV monitor for a few minutes before I got up and got the cassette to put into the VCR. The remote controller was still missing, and I had to get up to turn on the VCR and fast forward the cassette to the beginning of the movie. Then I sat down again and watched without really watching, for I could not get Angel out of my mind. When I realized that I hadn't been paying attention, I silently reprimanded myself and rewound the tape to the beginning.

The third movie was a teenage comedy like all the imitations that followed the success of *Animal House*. This one was entitled *Be Prepared* and concerned a troop of bored and insubordinate Boy Scouts. Not even scouting was immune from satirization these days. The premise was simple enough. Traditional merit badges, awards, and honors had become far too tame and cornball for this sophisticated and horny breed of scout, so the troop decides to create its own merit badges rewarding more desirable accomplishments, such as tying knots in the cheerleaders' bra straps, swimming bare-assed

212 | Alan Saperstein

with a female companion for 150 meters, giving a girl mouth-to-mouth resuscitation, improvising an emergency sling for breasts, overnight camping endurance, *et cetera, ad nauseam.* It was pretty low comedy and I was glad Angel was not there to be insulted. Yet I called Suzanne's number repeatedly during the movie looking for Angel and never got through.

The music was the movie's only hope. Top rock performers had been hired, and the soundtrack already sounded like platinum. But the juvenile antics, poor performances, and inane plot all undermined the music, and midway through the film I shut it off. The sudden silence woke Andrew. He stuck a cigarette in his mouth, carefully separated himself from the coffee table and hide-a-bed, and made his weary way to the john. It was almost noon. It was raining. I didn't say a word to Andrew. When he came out of the john, he sat down in the chair across from me as though he were going to talk to me. But he never said a word. I haven't heard Andrew speak a single intelligible sentence since he first showed up at my door.

We sat there ignoring each other and then Andrew got up, went to his steamer trunk, and began rummaging in it for something. When he found what he was looking for, he came back and stood in front of me, close enough so that I could see every move he made. In his hands were three large silver rings. Like a magician, Andrew banged the three rings against each other to show that they were solid and unattached. Then he clashed the rings together—right in front of my eyes—and the rings were linked. With a flourish, Andrew shook the three rings and once again they were separate. Then he clashed them together again and they were linked. He tossed the linked rings onto the hide-a-bed next to me and left for the day. As soon as he was out the door, I picked up the rings and tried to unlink them. But they would not come apart.

Late in the afternoon, I began to worry about where Suzanne and Angel could have been. I called David at work and was told he was out.

"Can he be reached?"

"He's out on an emergency."

I played with the rings some more and still couldn't separate them. Victoria came home early, and we decided to try a new

Creole restaurant, even though we didn't have a reservation. In Los Angeles, Victoria had gone to a Creole restaurant and had had blackened redfish, which she said was the most delicious thing she had ever eaten. We got in without a reservation and had blackened redfish and blackened salmon steak, which was even better than the redfish, and got home later than Andrew, who was already asleep on the closed hide-a-bed. I looked for the rings and couldn't find them. I thought about trying Suzanne's again, but it was pretty late. I contemplated watching the end of *Be Prepared* but knew that I would fall asleep as soon as the picture came on. Victoria washed her face, brushed her teeth, brushed her hair, and came into bed wearing a linen nightgown. My book of sci-fi short stories was opened to my mark, lying face down on my chest.

"I love you, Victoria," I said, as though she had just done something particularly loveworthy.

"And I love you," she said sleepily.

It was hard to believe that only a few days before, she had been speeding down the San Diego Freeway in reckless pursuit of Mexico.

26

T HESE ARE MY FRIENDS, and I hurt for them. Just when things are going better for me and Victoria, my friends are having troubles. Barb is not her old spunky self, after all. Her personal problems have begun to affect her work and she's been taken off a new advertising campaign. Julia is depressed about her one-woman art exhibit; she feels that her work is not going well. The studio is not going to finance an extended stay in Peshawar for Dale and Phyllis, not even for Dale alone. The latest outbreak of terrorism in the age-old religious feud between the Sikhs and the Moslems has caused the United Nations to temporarily suspend its epidemic project in Pakistan, suspending Frank and Lori's trip along with it. There is still no answer at Suzanne's, or at David's either, and someone on the skeleton crew at David's office keeps reporting that so far as anyone knows, he's out on an emergency and can't be reached; but it's Saturday, and that makes me wonder if Angel has run away again. Only Michael, who is about to leave for one of the most traumatic operations imaginable, is in good spirits. His other friends have decorated his loft like Nirvana, the Indian restaurant that overlooks Central Park South from the penthouse of a twenty-story skyscraper. I've been there only once, but the decor was so exotic and vivid that Nirvana has become my idea of what India must be like: tented, mirrored, aromatic, panoramic, seductive, music floating in the air, dark-skinned servants with bright uniforms and unexpected English accents, which makes me think of civilized human beings trapped inside aliens like in *Invasion of the Body Snatchers.*

Dale arrived drunk and announced that he was finished going everywhere on an expense account anyway. "Fuck the studio if they won't pay my way to the Khyber Pass. I'll write the goddamn thing off a picture postcard if that's all they want." Then he regaled us with a wonderful story about a fellow he knew who wrote travel brochures for a certain well-known company. Of course, he would only reveal which company when we all swore we'd never tell anyone. The story wound up proving exactly the opposite point Dale set out to make.

"This guy was writing travel literature without ever having been to any of the places he was writing about. Good writer, though. Managed to get all the information out of Michelin guides and put it in his own words. Anyway, he finally talked his client into springing for a trip. He was going to write a special brochure and talked him into taking him to the key places, which happened all to be in Italy. So my friend got to meet his client in Venice, travel with him to Florence and then to Rome. Great, huh? Except the whole thing took about five days—and that included flying.

"Day one: Venice, a race around the doge's palace, a fast lunch with his client, who orders the two of them a half dozen ready made finger sandwiches because it takes too long for the tripe to cook, even though they really should try Venetian tripe, and then, zap, they're on their way to Florence. Day two: A look at the Duomo and the statue of David, a stroll across the Ponte Vecchio for some local color, dinner at a hotel that could have been anywhere, and then first thing in the morning, goodbye Florence, oh, with one quick stop at a lookout point so my friend can take a couple of snapshots of the sun coming up on the Arno. Day three: Rome. Maybe Rome wasn't built in a day, but it was going to be seen in a day.

"Now, let me ask you all something," Dale says slyly. "I want each of you to tell me—no, I want you to write it down; Michael, we need some paper and pencils—each of you write down the one thing in Rome that you'd want to see more than anything else. If you could only see one thing, what would it be?" When we're finished writing our answers, Dale unfolds each slip of paper and reads it like the foreman of a jury. "The Vatican. The Sistine Chapel. St. Peter's Cathedral. The Vatican. Michelangelo's ceiling. The Coliseum—good for whoever wrote that. The ceiling in the Sistine Chapel. The fountain Anita Ekberg danced around in in that old movie. The Vatican ceiling. The Forum—almost forgot the Forum, didn't you, folks? Another Vatican. Another St. Pete's. Well, the single most popular thing is Michelangelo's ceiling in the Sistine Chapel. It certainly would be my first choice. And it certainly was my friend's. Except he barely got to see it at all. Do you remember this story, Phyllis? This is a wonderful story. Touching, really."

Michael's friends are half listening to Dale while they dart around the loft refilling bowls of rice and dishes of sauces and glasses of Taj Mahal Pale Indian Ale. By the time Dale gets to the touching part of his story, Michael's friends are transfixed, hanging on Dale's every word. His friend and his friend's client have raced through the packed itinerary and arrive at St. Peter's late in the afternoon. They go inside and have a look around, the client pointing out a few of the things he happens to remember from the countless guided tours his occupation has forced upon him over the years. He points out the markings on the floor showing how far other great cathedrals of the world fall short in comparison to the overwhelming length of St. Peter's. He points out the Pietà, St. Peter's tomb, the grilled windows in the floor leading to the catacombs, "stuff an idiot would notice sooner or later," Dale says. Then they head out for the walk to the Vatican museum and the Sistine Chapel. Only it's getting late, and the client is suggesting that maybe they've seen enough; why don't they go back to the hotel and have a good meal and a good night's sleep before their early morning plane, which the writer knows is all his client really cares about.

"But my friend is not about to miss Michelangelo's ceiling. 'I'm not coming all the way to Rome and getting this close to Michelangelo's ceiling without seeing it,' my friend says, and he practically drags his client to the museum, and they get there just in time for the last tour of the day. What happens is a tour guide takes you down this seemingly endless corridor that leads to the chapel and every fifty feet or so along the corridor there's a huge poster showing the details of the frescoes. The posters are illuminated, so the colors are brilliant, and each tour guide uses one of these posters to explain to his group what they're about to see inside the chapel, because once you're inside, no one is allowed to speak. My friend is in the last group, and all along the corridor in front of him there are groups clustered around their guide and their poster, and each group is made up of a different nationality—Australian, Japanese, Indian, Chinese, American, whatever."

At this point, Michael's friends stop moving around and begin to pay stricter attention to Dale's story.

"This guide is a small, middle-aged guy, gray at the temples and balding, needs a shave, pot belly, polyester short-sleeved shirt, tomato sauce stains, could be a shoemaker or a waiter, but when he opens his mouth and begins his lecture, it's like Caruso has just begun to sing.

"He starts off slowly, explaining the overall scheme of the ceiling, how it's divided, heaven, hell, the creation, the fall, the saints, the patriarchs, the prophets, the great stories of the Bible, and slowly he starts to pick up speed and drama as he starts pointing out the real people in the frescoes—Julius II, other popes, the artist's heroes, rivals, loves, even Michelangelo himself painted onto the skin held up by St. Bartholomew, his heart and soul undisguised in the tortured or ecstatic figures of a fanfare of angels, sinners, and penitents, and then the little guide picks up more speed and more drama in his emotional explanations of why this foot is on this person's head or why this man is half serpent or that woman is being flayed— I'm making up most of it, it doesn't matter—what matters is that the tourists suddenly understand the mortal man behind the immortal ceiling. And who is bringing the ceiling and the artist to life? This simple little guide, whose voice by now is soaring as high as the ceiling itself. There are breaks in his voice, tremors and trills and gasps—Jesus, he's doing this for the thousandth time, the ten thousandth time—and each modulation, each catch in his throat moves his hushed audience closer and closer to tears."

And us, too, in Dale's drunken but passionate recreation. Arthur, one of Michael's other friends, has to mop up the Taj Mahal Pale Indian Ale he inadvertently spills over the top of a glass he's refilling.

"Finally the guide moves *himself* to tears. Everyone in the group can see the tears rolling down his cheeks and catching in the white stubble of his beard. His eyes are watery and red and his mouth is moving like Caruso's as he tries to make his tourists understand the majesty and humanity and holiness envisioned and executed by this one man—'this one man'—he keeps saying it over and over again to emphasize the stunning magnitude of such an achievement, and then he seems to slump while he's standing, deflated, wrung out, humbled—'the single greatest artistic achievement in the entire history of mankind,' he says, his voice down to a whisper. And everyone cries along with him. The tourists search their bags and pockets for handkerchiefs. None of them is embarrassed to have been so touched. They all thank the guide quietly but profusely, handing him a generous tip and whispering, 'Grazie, arrivaderci,' for the guide's job is over, and now all that's left is to continue down the corridor into the chapel to see for themselves."

Good storyteller that he is, Dale holds us all in suspense while he downs the rest of his ale.

"And then my friend and his client and the other tourists in their group go inside, and as soon as they enter, the client starts pulling on my friend's sleeve, telling him how late it is, how terrible the traffic gets in Rome at this hour, how much they have to talk about over dinner, how important it is that they get a good night's sleep so they're fresh for the plane in the morning. My friend is in the chapel for one minute, *less* than a minute, and his client is tugging at his sleeve, dragging him out. But my friend doesn't care. As far as he's concerned, the show was over when the guide left. Inside the chapel, there are a thousand people all jammed together. The ceiling is so high, few of the people are willing to strain their necks to look at it and others have purchased periscopes so they can view the ceiling without looking up, as though Michelangelo's master-piece were nothing more than the finishing hole in the United States Open. But it doesn't make much difference anyway because the lighting in the chapel and the darkness of the frescoes make it almost impossible to see any of the details that have been so beautifully reproduced and illuminated on the poster. For all the polite jockeying for position and up-periscopes and craning necks, there is really nothing much to see. One wall is obscured by scaffolding where workers have been trying to restore some of the original color by carefully washing the frescoes. The panels that have already been re-stored by this process are slightly more vivid than those still undone. Yes, of course," Dale acknowledges our unspoken pro-test, "there is a certain awesome presence in the chapel, the presence of Michelangelo himself laboring mightily in his old age, the palpable presence of passion and history and art and Renaissance and the whole Holy Roman Empire personified in Michelangelo's faded faces floating in the Holy See, the bulg-ing eyes and hooked noses and flared nostrils of the popes, the blind armies of the cross and their woeful victims, the olym-pian indifference of Adam, Moses, Noah, and the rest, the intangible presence of time and life and our famous western heritage—just like the TV commercial for the Time-Life Heri-tage Series says—but . . ." yet another swig of ale to punctuate his story, ". . . but this presence falls far short of the ceiling, far short of the magic that is undone by the actual existence of something that can only exist in the heart . . . like the little guide's aria."

Dale seems to be finished, and after we respectfully wait a few moments just to be sure, all of us break into spontaneous applause.

"Thank you, thank you. I thank you, Phyllis thanks you, my friend thanks you, my friend's client thanks you, their guide thanks you, if Michelangelo were alive today, I'm sure he would thank you . . ."

Do you see what I mean when I say that my friends are

always in the right place at the right time with the right answer? Here is Dale, drunk and disappointed because his travel expenses fell through, and yet he turns it into a virtual state of the union address on the dubious value of firsthand information—not that he even meant to. But when you're smart and eloquent, you can't help but be right. Even Michael's other friends seem to appreciate the moral of Dale's story, although they are impatient for us to return to the theme of the bon voyage—exotic India. At first these half dozen other friends do not seem very much different from ourselves, but as the evening wears on and they seize more and more control over the festivities, Michael's bon voyage becomes more exotic than any actual trip to India could possibly be.

First of all, Victoria, Phyllis, Julia, and Lori (Barbara hasn't arrived yet) are wearing saris and veils, and the men are wearing kurtas and shalvaars and tarbooshes, all of which were provided by a friend of Michael's who's a theatrical costume maker. Someone pitched a sort of dressing tent at the entrance to Michael's loft, and each of us was handed a costume as we came in, and one by one we went into the tent and put on our party outfits. It was a good idea. The loft itself is like Nirvana, and no one looks even slightly out of place lounging around in these strange clothes. In fact, we have all become part of the fabulous decor, and as we mingle, there's a willing suspension of disbelief as we pretend to chat with real natives in long shirts and balloon-bottom pants and sashes and gossamer wraparound saris. Victoria looks incredibly exotic and incredibly sexy in hers. Her transformation and its effect are so intriguing that I can feel myself summoning up courage just to go over and speak to her. Her sari is smooth and satiny, with a gold thread running throughout, and the loosely wound material is nearly transparent; you can see her bra right through it, with her breasts straining up out of the top of the bra looking larger and fuller than they do when she is naked. And the way the sari clings, her ass and the outline of her panties look incredibly sexy. Julia doesn't ever wear a bra. You can plainly see her longish, flat breasts with their tiny nipples, and they look like you'd expect the breasts of an Indian woman to look. Phyllis and Lori's builds are similar and both are wearing bras and their breasts look tiny and cute under their saris, Lori's cuter because her bra is one of those fancy frilly kinds with gauzy trim and an embroidered pattern and a little pink rosette appliqué in the middle. What amazes me is that I've seen all of these women stark naked on occasion—not terribly long ago at Big Tubs, for example—and I can't ever remember noticing their bodies—or, should I say, I can't ever remember not being able to keep from noticing their bodies until this very moment. It must be the saris and the sitar music floating through the air and the incense and the lighting, which is like moonlight.

Michael's other friends are all wearing the same baggy white suits as Dale, Frank, and me (David still hasn't arrived), but there's something about these people that is definitely not masculine. Their haircuts are greasy and long and their eyes look made up. They move too gracefully, and the parts of their arms that stick out of their flowing kurtas when they gesture or pour ale or spoon out more lentils are thin and delicate and seem to move in ways that male arms don't. And yet, they are not obviously feminine in manner or speech. They are neither here nor there but in some ascetic, antiseptic world of their own. Talking to any one of them is like talking to a servant, someone who is close without being intimate.

The food is elaborate and authentic, not just the typical curry and hot sauce. Michael's other friends do not seem to do anything halfway. We are treated to endless hors d'oeuvres, five different kinds of bread, a dozen or more fish, chicken, beef, lamb, and meatless entrees, vegetables that have been skewered, pureed, stewed, or immersed in heavy gravies, desserts as lush and colorful as tales of the subcontinent. Eliot, the most talkative, gloats over a drink called lassi, which is the most popular refreshment in India in addition to being a digestive aid. It tastes like bicarbonate of soda, and while we older, dearer, apparently less sophisticated friends of Michael's are gagging, Eliot is bragging about his having figured out how to approximate real lassi with skim milk and something else that I never heard of and am glad I haven't.

There are other drinks, too, and all of them go down so smoothly that soon we are mixing them without thinking.

"It's hot, isn't it, Michael?" I ask.

"India's hot," Arthur answers in a way that suggests he has set the thermostat for the party.

The lights are low and the temperature is up and the music is hypnotic, and we are mixing wines and Taj Mahal Ale and sweet liqueurs and green tea and even lassi after a while, and we are all growing lazier and lazier. I notice that the women are sweating and that the flimsy sari material dampens quickly under their arms and clings even more tightly to their hot hips and thighs as we all recline on the many pillows strewn around the floor of Michael's loft.

"We should have an elephant," Eliot says. He is flat on his back on a bed of several pillows, staring up at the high ceiling, which Oliver, the costume maker, has draped with thick red spangly fabric. "The moguls loved huge chandeliers and always tested the strength of the palace ceiling by suspending an elephant from the spot marked for the chandelier."

We are growing less and less alert except for Julia, who has had an anxious look on her face every time I've glanced her way. She is deep in contemplation, probably about her exhibit, which she now hates, and has been staring at Michael's other friends, making notes with her eyes. Our crowd is quiet, Frank and Dale barely saying a word, David and Barbara, two of our most dependable talkers, still not here, Victoria and Phyllis and Lori sort of draped around like the gaudy fabrics, indistinguishable from the pillows, damp and lazy and slowly losing their usual decorum. I can see in their faces the kind of drugged, faraway expression you see sometimes on the faces of the infirm—lost, weak, resigned to any indignity their condition is bound to force upon them next. Cute Lori's legs are spread apart so that anyone sitting where I'm sitting can look up an entire length of leg to a flash of white panties, but Lori doesn't care. From time to time Phyllis idly adjusts her underclothes, unsticking panties that have gotten caught, realigning the straps of her bra. Victoria appears to be dozing. She hasn't moved a muscle in the longest time. Her head is on Frank's lap. No one is talking much. Everyone but Julia is dazed by food and drink and atmosphere. When a conversation finally begins, it is between Michael's other friends and has to do with the practical arrangements of Michael's impending trip to

New Delhi. There is talk of what he should take with him, when and where to write or phone home news, how to judge the staff and facilities of the clinic, how to communicate without offending deep-seated cultural differences—which flies to catch with vinegar and which with honey.

"Do any of you realize what Michael is about to undertake?" Oliver suddenly says to us—*us*—Michael's oldest and dearest friends.

"I think so," Frank answers sharply. But Lori objects. As do Phyllis and Victoria, who I thought was sleeping.

"No," Lori says, "I don't think I really do."

"It's very, very strange," says Phyllis. Both of them say this to no one in particular, as though they are talking to themselves.

"I wish Michael would tell Roger and Frank and Dale," Victoria says. She, too, seems to be daydreaming out loud.

"Tell us what?" Frank insists.

"The meaning of this," Eliot answers for Victoria and Michael.

Arthur is pouring more sweet liqueur and we are drinking it without question. What we are doing is being orchestrated by Michael's other friends, one of whom, Ulysses, is busying himself by watering a jungle of tropical plants, some bigger than he is. I swear I can hear the water hiss and turn to steam when it hits the soil.

By now our tarbooshes are off and our baggy sleeves are weighing down our arms. A hookah is passed around, and the flexible pipe allows us to inhale without lifting our heads. A smoky lethargy fills the room. A hand is gently caressing the back of my neck, and my eyes are too heavy to see who the hand belongs to. A voice is whispering "chchchch." Victoria turns onto her side and slips off Frank's lap. Julia is moving into the circle of Michael's other friends. She is making her way toward Michael, getting to him by stepping over us. A phone is ringing. It may be David. It may be Barbara. No one gets up to answer the phone, and eventually the ringing blends into the sitar music. Julia is standing over Michael, staring down at him. "Chchchch."

"Do any of you believe in reincarnation?" Isaac asks.

Immediately, I think of Angel and David and Victoria.

"If you do, then you can appreciate that Michael is about to cheat his destiny," Isaac continues.

"No, I don't believe in reincarnation," Frank says like the doctor he is. I want to believe him.

"Well, even if the idea is too difficult for you to comprehend or too alien to Western philosophy—which it isn't, if you read your early Greeks—surely you have to admit that what Michael is about to do is at least an *act* of reincarnation," Eliot says, "and made possible by Western technology. But only dared to be practiced in a zealous country like India. Or in the immoral back streets of Denmark." His voice is calming. It sounds like the sitar music and makes me think of my symphony.

"If you knew, you would know it's not immoral," Michael says. "It is just all my time in one. All my feelings in one. All my desire and satisfaction made true."

Michael is the only one of us whose face is happy. I don't even have to look at him. I'm looking at the ceiling, at the dramatically draped fabric that is covered with tiny sequins and mirrors like the little mirror at the end of a dental instrument, and every time someone says something, it's as if his or her voice is projecting his or her face onto the ceiling. There are hundreds of deliriously happy Michaels in the mirrors on the ceiling. They are laughing through the wavy haze of smoke and steam and music and moonlight. Other faces enter the mirrors. My eyes are so heavy I'm sure they're closed, but the faces in the mirrors are so sharp.

Everything that I see now bears no resemblance to what I hear, yet this mismatch does not bother me. I hear one of Michael's other friends talking about princes and moguls and Akbar and Alexander the Great and Winston Churchill and Ava Gardner and Rudyard Kipling, and I'm watching hundreds of Julias standing over hundreds of Michaels in the mirrors. She is loosening her sari, unwinding it, stripping herself over Michael. Her long flat Indian woman's breasts are suddenly bare. Michael is looking up at the naked woman towering over him and he is smiling. Lori and Phyllis and Victoria are moving through the mirrors toward Julia and Michael. They, too, are naked, and as they crawl over the pillows reflected in the mirrors, I can see their asses and they look like the illustrations of asses that you see in the Kama Sutra. Each one is round and smooth, with a swatch of darkness at the base of the crack. The five of them undress Michael, who does not resist, and perform a different act on him in a different position in every mirror. Sometimes the four women perform acts on each other in the process of satisfying Michael. All this while Eliot continues to describe the geopolitical history of the subcontinent. "Chchchch."

I blink, and Barbara enters the loft. She disappears into the dressing tent and comes out almost at once, wearing a sheet that she has wrapped around herself like a toga. When Victoria and Lori and Phyllis see Barbara, they leave Michael and crawl across mirrors to talk to her. I can hear them talking. Gossiping. Barb is her old self, mocking Mohammad, mocking the account she lost, mocking Michael, mocking Andrew, mocking me.

"Why are you mocking me?" I ask her, but I do not hear my voice. I hear Eliot talking about the all-purpose nature of the sheet, how it descends from the days of Alexander the Great, how the peoples of the Swat Valley use it for shade, for warmth, as a prayer rug, to pitch a quick outhouse because they believe it is shameful to relieve oneself where one lives.

"Don't do it," Barbara is saying to Victoria.

"I won't," Victoria answers.

"Don't even think it."

"That I can't promise," Victoria sighs.

Barb says, "Andrew and Mohammad are cut out of the same cloth."

Victoria says, "I know."

"As soon as one of us tries to strike out on her own, it's a disaster. We need each other, Victoria, Roger included," Barbara warns.

"I love Roger," Victoria confesses.

"Then don't do it," Barbara is saying to Victoria.

"I won't."

"Don't even think it."

"Thinking is the control that I've lost. That's what I've lost," Victoria sighs.

"Destroy all evidence," Lori advises.

"Wipe the slate clean," adds Phyllis.

"Start with your diary," I tell Victoria, but I'm sure my lips haven't moved.

I blink, and David enters the loft. He, too, disappears into the dressing tent and comes out almost at once, wearing a long white shirt and balloon pants. The shirt is tied with a sash and on the sash is a leather holster for his beeper.

He walks through mirror reflections of rough frontier terrain. There are scorpions on the ground. There are carcasses and rotted fruit. David has the look of an outlaw, a man on the run. In every mirror he enters, he is alone.

"When he was stationed here, he sent articles back home calling this range 'the chipped teacup of the English empire,' " Eliot tells us, referring to Winston Churchill.

Someone puts the mouthpiece of the hookah between my lips and presses on my chest. Involuntarily, I inhale. I have lost all perception of the distinction between reality and fantasy, and it is not enjoyable. I want to close my eyes. I think I do close them, but I still see the reflections of my friends in the starry ceiling. Then these reflections begin to fade away. Suddenly they are dark and timeworn and I need a guide such as the one in the corridor of the Sistine Chapel to bring my circle of friends back to life. Soft, neutral voices provide this guidance. They are the voices of Michael's other friends. They are voices without gender. Without clue. The stories they are telling are foreign to me but also familiar, as though I'm hearing my own dreams narrated. I understand the language but not the reasoning behind the language.

There are hundreds of these stories, one overlapping the other. They are colorful and simple and evoke startling images of grotesque and mythic proportions. One is about a small mountain village that has been caught unaware by a sudden great flood. The villagers are very old, and for complex reasons of climate, diet, and fate, there are no offspring to continue the population. "It is a dying village of nothing but septuagenarians," Ulysses's neutral voice reports. "Yet these old men and women are robust in the extreme. All day they work energetically, then they eat heartily, socialize wildly and, before their usual sleep of no more than four hours, they make passionate love with their husbands and wives of forty, fifty, and even sixty years. The flood, which rushes in without warning, catches the villagers in the heat of this customary late night-early morning lovemaking. Muddy waters crash through the dirt-brick walls of their simple buildings. The interconnected hand-dug viaducts, channels, and gutters that distinguish the village by forming a lovely, tinkling labyrinth of practical plumbing for peasant and yak alike swell to a thousand times their size, demolishing everything in their runaway course until what had been a picturesque source of drinking water and civic pride becomes a torrential terror. One man, the youngest man, feels his wife of thirty years wrenched from his embrace by the unrelenting force of the flood. She is swallowed and stolen by churning waves. In her place, another woman is deposited into the man's embrace. And then this replacement is taken away by the flood and another woman is given to him. Again and again this happens during the course of the catastrophe, until every female villager has been thrown to him and taken from him." But before a simple sermonizing moral can be attached to this dramatic parable, another neutral voice is telling me about the moustachioed tobacconist from the banks of the Indus who . . . and the dancer born with a single breast . . . and the worm in the opium pipe . . . and the eunuch and the harem . . . and the robe made of foreskins . . . and the plagues of the guru . . . and the Bengal tiger who seduces the princess, and every story is holy and profane at the same time, fantastic and possible, and my circle of friends and one enemy star in these stories . . . Andrew and the princess, Michael and the harem, Frank on the banks of the Indus, David fighting household plagues, Dale hunting with the Pathan, Julia dancing behind a strategically arranged set of veils, the women all being tossed from wave to wave . . . and soon everyone is talking at once, telling his story at once, the neutral voices and the fabulous stories overlapping into a single continuous chattering "chchchch," the faces blurring into ecstatic and agonized frescoes, the air in the airy loft suffocating me with the smells of incense, lentil, curry, like a locker room after a grueling game, like a tabernacle after a grueling revival meeting, and then sleep comes, slowly and faster, and suddenly; and suddenly I am dreaming things I never knew about my friends, that Angel has avenged her fate by committing suicide, that Barbara has been fired, that Julia is throwing away the paintings she has been working on for more than two years, that Andrew has wormed his way into Victoria's opium pipe by taking over her diary, that Michael and his friends have performed sacrificial rites on animals, hung decapitated dogs and cats from the ceilings of imaginary palaces to test the strength of their convictions, and I do not know whether I am dreaming or witnessing, nor does anyone else, and the hand is still at the back of my neck and my eyes are closing, closed, shut tight, and now I am riding, and now I am ascending, and now I am unlocking a mystery that awaits behind the door, and now I am caught in a tangle of gold rings, first three and then two, and now the hand at the back of my neck must be Victoria's and her ass is like a drawing in the Kama Sutra and I reach out for it and see other arms reach out for it and I strain forward in protest and plunge into an abyss of sleep.

27

ANGEL HAS KILLED HERSELF.

Three o'clock in the morning. I wake up to the phone. It has been ringing quietly in my sleep and loudly as I awake and like an emergency bell when I'm up and out of bed and staggering through the dark bedroom around the foot of the bed toward the little telephone table that stands on Victoria's side of our bed. Victoria is sound asleep.

"Hello."

"Victoria . . ."

It is a voice I know but can't immediately recognize.

"Victoria . . ."

The voice is crying out. To Victoria. To no one. To itself.

"David?"

Sobbing.

"David? Is that you? What's wrong? What time is it? David?"

"Who's this?" a new voice asks.

"Who's this?" I want to know.

The new voice identifies itself as an officer, rank and badge number. I'm confused.

"Who'm I speaking to?" the officer insists.

"My name is Roger Abel. What's wrong?"

"Your wife Victoria Abel?"

I tell him.

"You two better get over here."

"Over where? Was that David?"

"David who?"

"David Mayo?"

"Right. Give me your address and I'll send a car over to pick the two of you up. Mr. Mayo here wants a Mrs. Victoria Abel."

"Why? What happened?"

"It's pretty bad, Mr. Abel. What's your address?"

The car is taking us to David's apartment. Victoria hasn't said a word since I woke her and told her why she had to get dressed. From her expression it appears that Victoria doesn't have to ask any questions, that she knows where she's going and why, that she knew whatever happened would eventually happen and is resigned. The driver says he doesn't know what happened, he was called by radio to pick us up and take us to an address. I think he's lying. There are police cars outside David's apartment building and uniformed police stationed in the lobby, at the elevator, on David's floor, at his door, inside the apartment. The officer I spoke to on the phone is in charge. He greets us at the door and holds us back from running to David, who is sitting on a couch across the room. David doesn't see us right away. He's hunched over, his head in his hands, a woman in a uniform talking softly and continuously to him, her hand on his shoulder. Finally David looks up and sees us and bolts from the couch. He runs to Victoria and stops just short of embracing her, teetering on his heels; he stands there swaying as though on the edge of a cliff, his toes hanging off the edge, Victoria looking back at him hard. He looks terrible. His eyes are black, his hair wet and unruly, his chest sunken. He's swaying and oblivious and helpless and pathetic.

"It's his daughter," I overhear the officer in charge whisper to Victoria. "In there." Gesturing to David's bedroom. "It's not pretty."

The words *not pretty* sound more ominous than the crime I'm imagining. I'm imagining a stabbing, a rape, Angel's young body mutilated in some unforgivable way, a nude and bloodied young girl's body like the kind you see in the movies, but somehow none of these visions lives up to the unimaginable horror suggested by the phrase *not pretty.*

When the officer in charge starts to lead us into David's bedroom, David just stands there. The uniformed woman approaches David and consoles him and leads him back to the couch as we follow the officer into the bedroom. At first I don't see anything unusual. I'm looking at the bed and there is no body in it. David's computer is on. Everyone is so quiet you can hear the fan whirring in the computer. The game Clue pops into my head, and I'm thinking I don't have enough information to solve the crime. I wonder if the officer in charge ever plays Clue, if he could beat Frank, who always wins, if Frank would make a good cop. And then, when at last I see what the officer had warned us was "not pretty," I wonder how I was able to have noticed the bed first and then the computer and heard the fan cooling the motor of the computer and thought about Clue and Frank and cops; how I could have missed seeing what now is crowding everything else out of the room, out of my head.

Angel's large, long body is absolutely still. It hangs as thick and dumb as a heavy bag in a gymnasium. There is no visible wound. The instrument of death is without menace: a short, strong length of rope, one end tied to a light fixture in the center of the ceiling, the other end innocently looped around her neck. The ceiling is strong enough to support a heavy chandelier, I hear myself think.

Victoria walks up to the hanging body and smooths the long skirt where the hem is turned up. Then she backs up to where I'm standing and presses herself against me for support. She reaches behind her and takes each of my hands in each of her hands and pulls my arms around her waist, holding them there. We stand like that until officials break in and ask us to step outside while they take down Angel's body.

There is nothing I can think of to say to David. Victoria, too, says nothing, but her silence is different from mine. Hers tells David something. Mine avoids David. Then David breaks the silence. He is distant, removed, as detached from the tragedy as is his daughter.

"I never saw a dead body before," David says.

"No," I manage to agree. My voice breaks and the word sounds like the first one I have spoken today.

"How was Michael's party?" he asks blankly.

Neither Victoria nor I say a word. I realize I don't remember the details of Michael's party.

"The food was good," Victoria remembers. But that's all she remembers.

"As a matter of fact," David says, "I never even knew anyone who died. My great-grandparents are still alive."

I'm still thinking about Michael's party, trying to remember something—anything—about it. I'm trying to remember whether or not David was there. One minute I think he was and the next minute I think he wasn't. And then I'm thinking that I have never known anyone who has died, either. Nor has Victoria, so far as I know.

"She's happy now, David," Victoria says.

Simple. Perfect. A thing most commonly said to the bereaved of people whose last days are agonizing or unconscious, a simple thing meant to paint a rosier than usual picture of death, to contrast a living death with the relief of the real thing, and Victoria and David seem to understand that this statement is appropriate in Angel's case.

We are not unmoved. God, we are shocked, literally, our feet and our emotions galvanized by a million volts of electricity. But such a shock can only be survived by an equal and opposite current of self-control and perseverance.

"I have to arrange the funeral," David says dutifully. "Suzanne is inconsolable. They had to take her home. They had to sedate her. I don't really know much about funerals and burials. I'm sure there's some kind of service. I don't mean a *service* service like mass, I mean a service I can call to take care of everything for me."

During the next hour, our friends arrive. I don't know how, but they know and they are here—Julia, Barbara, Frank, Lori, Dale, Phyllis—all of us crowded into David's small living room, all of us acting more serious than I can ever remember, talking quietly about funeral arrangements, offering to take care of this or that—flowers, food, announcements—all of us braver, smarter, more resourceful than usual, yet all of us feeling oddly out of place, slightly off our usual marks. Someone mentions never having known anyone who died, and that turns out to be true for everyone except Barb, who engineered the death of her terminally ill great-uncle. For this reason, everyone looks to Barbara as the unofficial director of our communal effort to put this tragedy behind us as efficiently as possible, and Barb basks in the unofficial glory. Things have not been easy for her lately.

"When did you leave last night?" I ask Dale while the women help David make a list of the relatives who should be notified immediately. The police have gone. Angel's body is gone.

"I don't know. Didn't I leave with you? I thought I did. I don't remember much. My titer was up pretty high when I got there," Dale says, half bragging.

"Did I have a good time?" Frank asks impishly. None of us remembers anything about the party.

It's left to Victoria to phone Angel's relatives with the tragic news. Each of us has an assignment. Because we are who we are, we can't help turn these assignments into a friendly competition, which will result in the best possible funeral for David's daughter.

By midmorning we're out of plans to make. We're also out of conversation. During this lull, Julia tells us she came to a great realization last night at Michael's bon voyage party and that it means throwing out everything she's done for her art exhibit and starting all over again, but she thinks she can still meet her deadline. Frank and Lori apologize for having to leave and then leave. Dale says that even though he doesn't remember a thing about last night's party, he woke up feeling that he'd just been in India and doesn't care that the studio won't foot the bill for his trip to Peshawar. "Fuck it anyway," he says. "There's no reason for any of us to go now that Barbara and Mohammad have split up and the Sikhs are up in arms and Michael's going to be too sore to schuss. You know where we should go?" he suggests as he helps Phyllis on with her coat. "We should go to the Planet Photon." "Not me," one of the women objects. Planet Photon is a sort of human video game in an indoor fantasy park somewhere in New Jersey where you're given special electronic weapons and armor and you zap each other with laser beams in a dark arena full of terraces and pillars and caves and other hiding places.

We have dwindled down to David, Victoria, Barbara, and myself. The others had to go. Victoria has to go, too, but doesn't want to. Only when David convinces her that there really isn't anything more she can do does she leave the three of us and go home to get ready to work the afternoon. Barb and I are still here. She's cleaning up. I'm trying to persuade David to take a few days to himself, go away, but he doesn't want to be alone with his thoughts. The mood is not gloomy, and the three of us are careful not to bring up Angel.

"I need some sleep," David says, and Barbara and I take his cue and leave together.

"Will you have a cup of coffee with me, Barb? You owe me. You wouldn't go to dinner with me the other night."

She says okay, and we go to the first coffee shop we come to.

"Have you lost your job?" I ask bluntly.

"This thing with Mohammad has made me useless. I needed my job to forget about him, and it didn't work. Not being able to forget about him made me useless at work, and I got fired. They took me off an important account, and I complained and I threatened, and they decided it was probably better for everybody if I looked for another job. You make friends and you make enemies. And when the enemies are in a position to do something about you, they do."

Barbara is trying not to look embarrassed.

"We're okay," I tell her, not sure I'm changing the subject. "Victoria and me, we're okay. You don't have to worry about anything."

"Is it my turn? Your plan, I mean. To talk to each of us as though we were working independently on another classified section of your problem?"

"How do you know that?"

"You told me."

"I did?"

"You told everybody. We all tell each other everything, even though we never talk about it. But I'll talk about it. You made me talk about me."

"Well, then you know it's all okay now."

"I was with her the day she came back from California and Mexico. She was talking about her new coat. She told me everything. She's under his spell."

"No, she's under her own spell. But she knows it. She keeps a diary in the Apple and I read it."

"Ask her. That's all."

"Ask her what?"

"Ask her if she keeps a diary. Ask her how her diary is different from what she told me. From what she didn't have to tell me."

"Believe me, she's working it through. Since she came back from California, it's been wonderful. I'll show you the diary."

"There is no diary, Roger. If there is, it's just to throw you off. She's fatally attracted."

"You're wrong."

"Then why are you telling me about it?"

Why indeed, I wonder, as I watch Barbara getting ready to leave the coffee shop. She's putting on her coat. I wave off her attempt to contribute to the check.

"I'll go to work for you," she offers, "since I'm temporarily unemployed anyway. I'll work on Victoria and get her to do the right thing before that stupid monkey insults her like Mohammad's sister and she goes up in flames. I've got the time now. You talked to me about it and now I have to do something. Julia can help, too, for what I have in mind. And the money Victoria's grandma left her. And Lori's connections with the stores. But she's the one who has to do it. Not me. Not you. Not Julia. Not Lori. Victoria. It has to be her own good idea. Hey, this is just like work. I'll get her marketing head on straight and everything will be okay again."

I keep staring at the door after Barb is no longer in sight.

Something is missing. The fact of the big, still body hanging in David's bedroom was overpoweringly complete, like the ending of a good sci-fi short story, yet something is missing. Something Angel took with her. Or left behind.

28

GRIEF IS ALIEN TO US. Except for Barb, who's so hard-boiled anyway, none of us has ever lost anything of value before. We have gotten rid of old cars and tinny-sounding stereo equipment and bell-bottomed pants and moved from apartment to apartment and even neighborhood to neighborhood, leaving behind smells, sounds, doormen, neighbors, shopkeepers, all of which faded from memory the moment each loss was replaced and none of which prepared us for anything like a full-blown funeral for the teenage daughter of one of our beloved friends.

Before the funeral I found myself at the office hoping to be alone, but finding Rich, who was more alone than I was. I let myself in with my key and went upstairs into the engineer's booth and saw Rich hunched over the studio piano, playing and swaying like an old black jazzman. The sound was not on, and I turned the switch and heard what he was playing. It was an original piece, not from our abandoned symphony. As he played, Rich moaned as though making love to his melody, good, clear, open-throated, open-hearted moans of irrepressible pleasure and pain. I stayed only a few minutes because I didn't want him to see me.

The funeral parlor is very plain. Drapes, chairs, a pulpit, the coffin center stage. I haven't been in a church or temple of any kind since we got married. I don't know if the room we have all crowded into has any religious affiliation. Barbara made the arrangements. It is small but austere and might be affiliated with any group depending on who stands up and what he wears and what metaphors he uses when he speaks.

David's family and Suzanne's family sit segregated on opposite sides of the room, like equal parts of the divorce settlement. I'm sitting on Suzanne's side. Victoria is sitting on David's side, near David and Barbara. Victoria and Barbara have done the lion's share of the work to get us all this far and for that they have been saved front seats. This morning, Victoria told me her work wasn't done yet.

"Angel left her own eulogy," she told me as I was shaving.

"You never told me that."

"I didn't know until last night. She requested that I read it to the mourners."

I turned to face Victoria. "You're going to read Angel's suicide note at the funeral?" I asked, dumbfounded, holding the razor an inch away from my face.

"It's not a suicide note. It's a eulogy. Remember when we went into David's bedroom and found her? Remember the computer was on? She wrote it on the computer. And never saved it. Just think, someone might have shut it off and lost it forever."

"I don't believe this," I said, the razor still frozen an inch away from my face.

"Why not? It's a beautiful eulogy. Very beautiful."

"Can I see it?" I asked, not knowing what else to ask.

"You'll hear it."

But first I must sit through the speech of the man Barbara has hired to conduct the services, the emcee. He enters briskly, running to the pulpit like the host of a game show. I don't know what he is; he isn't dressed like a holy man. He's wearing a dark blue suit and a dark tie and black shoes and tortoiseshell glasses in the middle of a friendly face that could be anywhere from twenty-nine to forty-nine years old. He could be an account man from Barbara's old agency.

Merely by entering, the emcee signals the congregation to begin mourning in earnest. Tiny cries and bigger sobs and the beginning of loud, long, inconsolable wailing break out on our side of the hall and quickly spread to the other side, which is not to be outdone. I notice Lori, who's sitting not far from Julia and not far from Phyllis; Lori is doing something to her nose, hiding what she's doing behind the fancy lace handkerchief she's holding up to her face. Before the funeral, we all agreed to sit apart. I think we were afraid we'd misbehave if we were close enough to encourage one another. None of us knew what to expect. Looking around for Dale and Frank has distracted me from hearing anything the emcee has been saying so far. When I find them, Dale way down in front and Frank way in the back, I tune in on a part of the emcee's talk that is about the youth of today. Surely if we were sitting together, we would be snickering or quarreling over the emcee's comments. But instead, I'm listening like a student to what's being said.

The emcee goes on and on. It occurs to me that a eulogy for a young person must be considerably longer than a eulogy for someone who has lived to a ripe old age. There is certainly much more that a person *might* accomplish than that which any person really *does* accomplish, and that is the emcee's subject now—the unfulfilled promise of Angel's aborted lifetime. But the emcee must be very careful. Angel's ailing and very religious great-grandmother has not been told the truth about the suicide and believes Angel died in an automobile accident. For that reason the coffin has been kept closed and the emcee has to be careful to avoid the unmentionable. But at the end of the emcee's speech, Angel's great-grandmother is led out of the hall, apparently as previously arranged, and the emcee tells us he has two announcements to make. The first is that Victoria will read a message the deceased herself wrote just before taking her own life. The second is that when Victoria is finished, the coffin will be opened for fifteen minutes for those of us who wish to pay final respects.

The congregation quiets down as Victoria makes her way to the pulpit. She looks very beautiful in her black dress and California blush. Beneath her stockings, her legs look firm and thin and graceful. She is not wearing makeup or lipstick. In her right hand she clutches the print-out of Angel's suicide note, the pages rolled like a diploma. I can hear a slight sound coming from her hand as it swings. A faint tinkling sound. And then the tinkling sound seems to be coming from the rear of the hall, and my head turns involuntarily.

Andrew is here. He is sitting in the last seat in the last row on David's side. He's wearing his dirty, rumpled, ill-fitting Nehru jacket, and his hair is messed up from his motorcycle ride and he needs a shave. He's wearing a pair of aviator sunglasses, which makes him look like an overage Hell's Angel. As far as Andrew is concerned, no one is here except Victoria. His head follows her movements and stops as she stops to wait for the emcee to adjust the microphone. There are several harsh noises and loud clunks while the emcee bends and twists and lowers the stand. Then he taps the microphone to make sure it's still working. Victoria clears her throat and it echoes throughout the hall. The emcee stands back. Andrew leans forward. The woman in front of him must lean forward to avoid his hot breath on the back of her neck. I look around for help. Lori is still working at her nose. I can't find Frank and Dale again. David will certainly not look my way.

"That I have come along in my body is immaterial," Victoria begins suddenly and dramatically. The sheets of paper have not been separated and flow down to the floor like tickertape during a major catastrophe. "And that I had to give my body to Death in order to give shape and freedom to my desire was not sinful. In the future I will be someone else again. All that remains constant and true is want. Unsatisfied want."

The words are not familiar right away. There is a slight delay. A slight tinkling sound. And then, when my head turns involuntarily and I see Andrew rocking slightly and moaning slowly behind the perfectly coiffed woman's shocked head, I remember these exact words from Victoria's Mexico diary entry, and Andrew is murmuring them along with Victoria, moaning along in pleasure and pain like Rich at the piano, making love to Angel's and Victoria's words.

"Death called to me," Victoria continues, "I heard Death calling to me all day and all night. Wherever I went, wherever

240 I Alan Saperstein

and whenever I made silence in my head, Death sang to me in beautifully orchestrated old love songs. If I closed my eyes and pretended to be dead, I could see a full orchestra and my father standing in front with his baton pointing, urging, threatening each section to give all it could. And always Death would step forward out of the orchestra and the instruments would stop and he would sing his tantalizing melodies a cappella, his back-up group harmonizing so gracefully, my father carrying the melody, voicing the old words. And always Death's group would then reappear in an explosion of smoke and light, wearing electric colors and aqua beards and clutching their blood-red guitars as though they had voltage running through their hands. And this too was Death's song, Death rolling up the sleeves of the frantic guitarists, Death squeezing out their arm veins and electrifying their veins and arteries until they were playing on their own bodies, the clanging, banging songs picked out on their own steel-wire veins."

I can hear Angel saying this at the same time Victoria is saying it and I cannot listen to them both at once.

"Death called to me," they continue, "pointing, urging, threatening me to follow him into the feeling of these songs, where bodies do not matter and time does not matter and only the music matters. Once I tried it and reached out for my father's baton and took it out of his hand and touched it to me and the music flowed through the me that was not my body. All the stringed love songs and the chanted a cappella gospel love and the electric madness of Death lifted me up out of my body and moved me through a mirror shining down on my body and from the other side of the mirror I could watch my temporary self box stepping with my father and fox-trotting with boys my own age and rocking with strangers in the strobe-lit darkness of the terrible age I have been stuck in. But stuck in no longer."

Victoria is reciting Angel's words without making a single mistake or faltering even slightly. She has read through evenly and confidently and her voice has not hesitated or broken even once. "I gave in to Death. I followed Death's melodies out of here. Out of this place that would not let me be obsessed with the present because of the pressure to be obsessed with the future. If you cannot feel the note when you play it, you cannot hear it when it sounds. That is how close and how far the present and the future are from each other. That is how close and how far I have come from Death my whole life long."

The congregation is confused. Some of the women are crying out of pity. They have diagnosed Angel's eulogy and think she was mad, and they're crying out of pity for her life rather than pity for her death. Andrew is still mouthing the words along with Angel and Victoria. He is still swaying in his chair. The faint tinkle makes me think of the finger cymbals one of Michael's other friends was wearing at the bon voyage party. I feel as though I am going to pass out. My heart is beating rapidly and it's hot in the funeral hall and I'm having difficulty breathing. David's beeper goes off, and he hurries out of the room with his hand inside his jacket, struggling to open the holster on his belt, trying to shut the damn thing off.

"Death called to me and I followed him to his hot and barren landscape. The heat is dry and the air is clean. The people you see along the rough roads are simple and friendly. They have American Indian cheekbones and East Indian hairdos and wear layers of animal skins and all of them are as proud as gurus and medicine men. There is music in their bones. And there is music in the rocks and dust and in the fat, juicy leaves of stubborn trees. And the other side of the mirror is a pool of cool water. I could look into the pool and see myself. I was young and old, like a girl and a woman, in love with the whole life of the man I loved before and will love again. From behind the mirror I watched myself curl up in his bed and make my love to his sleeping face and neck and hands, and I watchéd him twitch in his sleep and knew he was dreaming that he, too, was with me in Death's hot and barren landscape. Sometimes I was little and couldn't talk. Sometimes I was grown and wouldn't talk."

How could Angel have written this? How could Victoria have written her Mexico diary in the same way? How can Andrew know? How can Victoria recite every word without error, without shock, without blush?

"Death called to me from behind colorful masks, from the temporary mouths of the people behind these eternal faces.

He gave me all of my masks, a young one, an old one, a lover's, a daughter's, a mother's. And I wore one in Death's carnival, Death's farewell to flesh! This flesh. This life. This time. This foolish, corrupted, unappreciated standstill time within the course of all time. God, how I hated it. God, how happy I am to be free of it at last and able to look forward to coming back again at some other time when it is better and happier and no one cares who and what you are or who and what you know. In a sense I am already back. Part of me. In this. In the reading of this. It is me reading this to you."

Victoria did not so much as blink at this phrase. Whatever anyone believes about the state of Angel's mind when she wrote it, everyone—especially Victoria—is in that mind as she reads it; disbelief is unwillingly suspended as Angel's troubling diagnosis of her life and times continues. His phone call made, David returns in time to hear Angel and Victoria take us through landscapes reminiscent of Victoria's Mexico and of the India Michael's other friends talked about at the party. Every landscape is hot and barren and inhabited by unreal people, people neither alive nor dead but in some transitory state of limbo. For me the places are all too familiar and I can barely stand it, and I know that later I will have to confront Victoria about the eulogy and the diary. I can feel myself caught between the eulogy's hot and barren landscapes and my real world, which is so hard-edged that nothing can blur the immutable proportions of its truth. My mind wanders into the future, to a casual conversation with Barb. I take her up on her offer to use Julia and Lori and the inheritance to put Victoria's head on straight again.

Victoria ends the eulogy as suddenly as she began it. Only Andrew seemed to know that the end was coming. The rest of us are startled by the silence and by the calm, unemotional way Victoria gathers up the print-out and strides regally to her seat. Muffled sounds of confusion, pity, and disbelief simmer through the congregation. They are quieting down when the emcee lifts the lid of the coffin. The coffin is situated in such a way that the hinge is on the near side, and the opened lid obscures the view of Angel's body from the congregation. In order to see her it's necessary to go up to the coffin.

Not everyone goes. Many of the relatives on Suzanne's side

do not feel compelled to stare at someone I suppose they cannot easily forgive for causing one of them so much pain, first by birth and then by life and now by death. David's side forms most of the processional. And, of course, all of us, his beloved friends, are on line out of respect to David and, no doubt, out of our own fearful curiosity. To us, this is a first glimpse at real death.

I am right behind Lori in line and can't help asking what was wrong with her nose.

"I'll tell you later," she says, as though I should know better than to ask. But there's an impish quality to the frown Lori flashes at me. I'm glad Victoria is far away from me, at the beginning of the line. I'm not ready to say anything to her yet. Andrew has gotten on line way back at the end, almost as far away from me as Victoria.

As I move closer and closer to the coffin, I wonder what to do when I stand over it. Except for the lifeless form we found hanging in David's bedroom, I haven't seen Angel since watching the second movie with her, when she acted so strange and I thought she had fallen asleep. She had left me that day without explaining what she had been saying while I was on the phone with Victoria. And her face at the end of that last session is the face I remember now. It is so much a little girl's face that I am afraid she will be too small for the coffin, that somehow the rope around her neck choked all the growth out of her body along with the breath.

Lori is standing over the coffin and crying, her expensive handkerchief once again at her face, camouflaging whatever her hand is doing to her nose beneath the fancy lace. When she is done, I move up to the coffin and look down at Angel. I am not shocked. It helps that I remember her sleeping during the second movie. It helps for me to think that she is only sleeping now. Her face is prettier in repose than it was in real life, when she always looked so uncomfortable. The thick glasses I'm used to seeing on her face are missing, and her eyes are peacefully closed. Her makeup suggests a pleasant, almost rosy glow like the inner glow of someone waiting for a young man to pick her up and take her to a prom. The fingers of her right hand are gently closed over the slightly spread fingers of her left hand. The thin gold bracelet has been removed from Angel's wrist

244 | Alan Saperstein

along with other jewelry—the birthstone ring she wore and the one blue stone she kept in her one pierced ear. I assume David or Suzanne will keep this jewelry for sentimental reasons.

There will be no burial; Angel's body will be cremated. With Barbara's help the mourners are ushered out of the hall, and Angel's coffin is sealed and carried off to the furnace.

Of course, David and the rest of us gather afterward at our apartment. There are platters of Mexican food and pitchers of margaritas and a preprogrammed selection of jazz ready to play for ninety minutes per tape. The mood is not meant to be frivolous and only begins to turn festive after four pitchers of margaritas have been emptied. Dale suggests that this is a sort of wake and that we aren't supposed to sit around and mope, which no one is doing anyway. We are talking about the funeral and about the people at the funeral we would have ridiculed and laughed at if we had been sitting together and about the stupidity of ritual, and when the conversation starts leaning toward Angel, everyone steers it away from what she has done and the fact that it cannot be undone.

"What the hell were you doing to your nose, Lori?" I have licked enough salt off the lips of enough margarita glasses to finally ask.

"Shhhh," Lori laughs. "Oh, honesty is the best policy," she confesses, willing to confess to David, but happy not to find him in the vicinity. "I learned this on the set of that TV pilot I worked on last year," she confides in me. A very sober Barbara passes by with an empty platter. "You remember, Barb, I had to find all those stupid old fifties gowns and crinolines . . ."

"I remember," Barbara says as she continues on into the kitchen for another platter of quesadillas. But Lori is undaunted.

"If you really want to know, Roger," she tells me, "there was an actress in this one particular scene who was supposed to cry, and you know how she did it? You know the trick she used to make herself cry? I swear this is true, Roger, she pulled a hair out of her nose. It took me three hairs, but it worked."

Andrew came home without my noticing and is sitting quietly in the corner watching us all. He is different from us. He is the odd one. The others have maintained a link with their parents and that is what makes the world go on. Somehow I see the parents of my friends in them and know them better than I know my own. In growing up so brightly and progressively, my friends have still taken this or that more conservative characteristic from their parents and incorporated it into their stunning new lives. But they have taken the best— perspective, self-confidence, experience, some brio of the bones—and amalgamated it into their own personality. There is a trace, for example, of Victoria's father's demanding manner with money in the even more demanding way Victoria has always treated her inheritance. But Andrew is different. There is no trace of parental precedent in anything he does. He is able to go off drinking with Victoria's father and take Angel to lunch and Victoria to Mexico and me on a drunken tour of hell without having inherited anything other than some constant and spontaneous intuition all his own. Even now he is sleeping in the corner, bored with us.

David and Frank and Phyllis are starting an impromptu game of trivia, and it won't be long before our favorite game is out and everyone is playing for real.

"What two liners passed each other in mid-Atlantic for the last time at twelve-ten A.M. on September 24, 1967?"

"The *Queen Elizabeth* and the *Queen Mary.*"

I'm listening. Slightly dazed by the day. Not yet realizing that the slight tinkling I hear is coming from somewhere around the board game.

"What *Rebel Without a Cause* costar was stabbed to death in a still unsolved killing in Los Angeles in 1975?"

"Sal Mineo."

The slight tinkling is breaking through my subconscious.

"What doctor said 'There's no point in bringing up children if they're going to be burned alive?' "

"That's easy. Dr. Spock."

"Beam me up, Scotty."

The tinkling intensifies when Victoria rolls the die.

"How were Invisible Girl and the Human Torch related?"

"Brother and sister."

"Good guess."

"It wasn't a guess."

I have to ask to have my question repeated. I'm too distracted by the source of the tinkling sound coming from Victoria's wrist. Instead of her one thin gold bracelet, Victoria is wearing two. And they are interlinked. And I know it is impossible to separate them.

"The Doors," I answer correctly.

The question was: Who asked us to break on through to the other side?

29

"WE NEED TO TALK."
"What about?"
"You. Him. Her. Us."
"Do you want to make love instead?"
"Like in Mexico?"
"Mexico?"
"And Angel's eulogy."
"Is there supposed to be some kind of connection?"
"Have you checked your personal files lately? The one entitled PENDING?"

"It sounds as if *you* have. I don't like that. If I stay friendly during this little chat, don't think I won't be furious afterwards. That was a confidential file. That was for my eyes only."

"I don't want to know what I know. I'd be glad to delete it from my memory."

"It's been deleted in real life. People of good sense self-correct themselves. David understands that he was drunk that night and that drunkenness is not something he handles very well. He also understands, as I do and as you should, that there will always be something special between David and me. We started out that way and it'd be idiotic to think that we could ever end up without it. But it's completely under control. In fact, it never really got out of control. You read my file; you should know that."

"That and more."

"The other stuff is wishful thinking. There's a difference between willful and wishful. Even a paralegal knows the difference."

"I'm not a paralegal."

"You're acting like one. Interrogating me. Poking around in my personal files. Next you'll want to take my sworn statement."

"I'd rather just dismiss the case. I'd rather not talk about it at all. I'd rather you tell me you're completely innocent—"

"I'm completely innocent."

"—and that you were an unwitting victim of circumstances beyond your control."

"And I'm an unwitting victim of circumstances beyond my control."

"I think of you as innocent. I always have, Victoria."

"I always am. I was brought up that way."

"And Mexico?"

"What do you know about Mexico? Have you been talking to Barb? She's the only one I told how I felt."

"Was Mexico beyond your control? Were you innocent?"

"Of course. You know that. You have to know that."

"Mexico meant nothing to you?"

"It meant everything to me. It meant my life, my marriage, my sanity. There I go being wishful again. But it won't do any good. Mexico happened. It could happen again if the circumstances present themselves. I wish they don't. I wish I can promise myself that if they do, I'll be strong. But it's no good. Wishing doesn't make it so. It only shows where my heart wants to be. Not where it necessarily is."

"Where it wants to be is important."

"I'm sorry. Truly sorry. I'll make love with you if you want."

"If *you* want."

"I want too much. I'm trying to cut down."

"Well, then, get rid of one of us. Get rid of *two* of us."

"It took great courage for you to say that, didn't it?"

"More than I knew I had. I'm sorry I had to compromise it with that last bit of sarcasm."

"Although you're right."

"I don't want to be. I told you, I don't want to know what I know. It was hell to hear you read that thing today."

"Why? What does it have to do with anything?"

"It was Mexico all over again. Angel's loss of will kept reverberating in my head and reminding me of your own loss of will in Mexico. Only you've promised yourself to keep trying. The difference between Angel and you is that you recognize your loss of will for what it is and know that when you regain it, everything will be fine again."

"But I may never regain it. I may spend the rest of my life only trying."

"That's more than Angel did."

"Let's not talk about her anymore."

"Why?"

"It's too much like talking about me."

"You both love David. You both love me. You both love him."

"Forget love. It's too complicated."

"Can you forget what you wrote about Mexico?"

"I never wrote about Mexico."

"Should we punch up PENDING?"

"Let's punch up PENDING. Quietly, though. We don't want to wake him up."

"We won't. He wants to sleep. He needs to sleep. He's had a tough day."

"Promise you'll be quiet."

"I promise."

"What about the noise it makes when you boot it up?"

"He won't hear it. And if he gets up, we'll let him have his say, too."

"No. I want to keep him out of it."

"A little late for that, isn't it?"

"Here it goes. It's quieter than I thought."

"And it's over already. See? I told you not to worry."

"What else have you read?"

"Everything until I came to PENDING."

"It's going to make noise again loading the file. I hope it doesn't make that grating sound it makes sometimes. That one's loud."

"He doesn't want to get up. If he hears us, he'll pretend he's still sleeping. He won't mind a confrontation with his brother, but the last thing he wants is a confrontation with you."

"What is this? I never wrote this. Did you make this up?"

"I wish I had. Read it. Tell me it's a lie."

"I don't want to."

"Read it through to the end, then say it's a lie."

"I'm finished."

"Is it a lie?"

"No. But someone made it up and wrote it over my letter to David, and then they wrote the same kind of thing on David's computer and signed it Angel."

"Turn it off if it upsets you."

"I'm not upset. I'm fine. There, it's off. I'm fine."

"Well?"

"It's gone too far. Everything's gone too far."

"Including us?"

"I need to stop it."

"How can you do that?"

"I can do it."

"How?"

"I want to have a baby."

"What will that stop?"

"Some things. There will be things I absolutely will not do then."

"Are you sure?"

"Yes."

"And if you want to do those things anyway?"

"I won't. I will be willful."

"What won't you do?"

"Don't ask me that now. Maybe you won't ever have to ask."

"But I need to know."

"There are things about me and him that you will never know. And there are things about you and me that he will never know."

"Then who do you choose? How do you know which one?"

"I will choose the life that's good for me."

"How do you know which one is good for you?"

"The one that has the most momentum."

"And the baby, you're sure about that."

"The momentum is for having a baby. Soon I'll be too old. If I'm going to have one, I better not wait."

"A baby."

"Yes, a baby. You never thought of that, did you? But I have. It's been in the back of my mind for a long time. Maybe it's in the back of every girl's mind all her life . . . as a way to stop some things and begin others."

"It will make a very great change in all our lives."

"That's the idea."

"Not necessarily in our hearts, though."

"Did you hear me? I said, 'Not necessarily in our hearts, though.'"

"I heard you."

30

F OR THE PAST MONTH everything has been different. Even the color of the days has been different. It's as if a secret decision had been made the night of Angel's funeral that forced its own terms on everyone involved.

Victoria and I talked that night. I knew that I couldn't avoid a confrontation forever. We talked after everyone had left. Andrew was asleep when we talked, and then just as I fell asleep, I heard him stirring. Victoria may have talked to Andrew, too, after I fell asleep, for since then, her attitude toward both of us has changed. Something in the way she regards us has shifted as dramatically as if the sun had shifted in the sky. Morning, noon, or night, I look up and there it is, her sunlight, breaking through to fall upon me in sweet glances and peaceful smiles. Andrew has been Andrew, but something always creeps between him and this sunny side of Victoria's disposition to cast a blueness over him. He has always been a bit sorrowful, now even more so, humbled, too, as though he's lost something of tremendous value and must keep looking for it even though he knows it's lost forever. He gets on his gaudy motorcycle and roams the back streets and bars of the city looking for something he'll never find. When he's home, he spends most of his time going through his steamer trunk, sorting, rearranging, admiring the piecemeal shrine he thinks no one knows about. I choose not to say anything. I also choose not to say anything about the fact that he's wearing the carnelian ring I bought for Victoria, the one I later found in the trunk, although he had the stone reset. I can't prove it's the same carnelian, but it doesn't matter. I choose not to say anything to Victoria about the two interlocking gold bracelets tinkling on her wrist. Nothing matters except that life is more like it was before Andrew showed up. Every so often at an odd hour, he and Victoria are gone at the same time and I get the old sickening feeling in the pit of my stomach, but I'm sure that she's not misbehaving. She would not do that now. Not after our talk. Not after we began trying to have a baby. That is the biggest news. We try every morning before Victoria goes to work. We haven't told anyone yet.

I spoke to Barb, too, and now Victoria is involved in a project with her. It started right after I gave Barb the go-ahead. I don't know exactly what they're doing, it's mostly in the concept stage, but it seems to have animated Victoria in a way that her exercise and swimming used to. And she is back to the gym, too. And losing weight. She says it's because she's going to put so much on when she gets pregnant, but I sense that it's really another manifestation of the return of organization to her life.

My work has been going fine, too. I turned in the first two appraisals, and Simon was impressed. He told me I didn't have anything to worry about. The second appraisal was accepted last week and partial payment came yesterday. The first is very close to being accepted, Simon wrote me in the letter accompanying the check. The third is just a day or two from completion and, frankly, is not as sharp as the first two, but sharp enough, I think, to impress Simon and earn another check. Suddenly there's enough money to start saving in earnest, enough to warrant a CD account, enough to sock away for a rainy day even though our skies continue to be sunny.

In a few hours we'll have our traditional election night party. Although it's only a mayoral and not a presidential election, the mayor has aroused more than enough bipartisan antagonism to keep things interesting. No one thought he could lose if he tried, but he has tried very hard and may well succeed. We'll have our traditional closed balloting and melting pot smorgasbord and political movies, and it will be the first time all of us are together since the funeral. David's been away on business; otherwise we would have celebrated his birthday a couple of weeks ago. But he requested an assignment that took him out of town and away from the scene of the tragedy. Julia has been working like crazy revising her exhibit. Frank is back in harness at Johns Hopkins and helping a team of visiting French researchers study the AIDS epidemic in his spare time. Dale has broken with the studios over what he calls their "obscene pettiness" and has begun work on something original. He is also involved in Barb and Victoria's project. So are Julia and Lori. So is some of Grandma's twenty-five thou. Barb and Victoria are in the kitchen working on the project now, laughing a lot while they also prepare some of the dishes for our melting pot smorgasbord. Andrew is out looking for whatever he's lost. Michael has probably been operated on by now, but no one's heard from him yet. Arthur, one of Michael's other friends, promised to let us know as soon as he hears anything. All in all, I feel that the worst is over, that I was right in weathering what I could without sending up flares, that the storm or whatever it was has passed and made us all a little more seasoned but none the worse for wear. And it's tremendously satisfying every morning to wake up and try to make Victoria pregnant. It has added a brand new perspective to our lovemaking. There's a point to it now that was always lacking before. The feeling is different, not just because of the absence of her diaphragm, but because of the presence of something we feel but neither of us can really explain. Of course, one of the things that makes it better is that now our lovemaking is part of our regular routine. It's expected. It doesn't sneak up on either of us when it's inconvenient.

The aromas of all the different ethnic dishes, relishes, and spices are beginning to blend together into the one wonderful aroma of a street festival—onions, hoisin, coriander, curry, garlic, Jewish, Italian, Polish, Chinese, Indian, Irish, Spanish. Dale has brought his tapes of *Mr. Smith Goes to Washington* and

All the King's Men, which we always watch before and after the Channel 2 election report. Along with the kielbasa, dim sum, and blintzes, a discussion is heating up between Frank and Phyllis over the incumbent's habit of using street slang and ethnic idioms. Phyllis thinks it's a breach of the didactic political language that's always been part and parcel of our democratic heritage. "Would you want to hear a sermon delivered in slang?" she says. Frank thinks it's a brilliant technique. There will be many such discussions as the night wears on. We're not all in the same political boat. Some of us are slightly Democratic, some slightly Republican. But we're all issue-oriented and reserve the right to cross party lines on the basis of even a single important issue. But there are no real issues at stake in tonight's election and so our debates are on the candidates' styles, personalities and, in the case of the incumbent, vernacular.

David has just arrived, and there is an awkward moment when we all feel we're acting too glad to see him. But David heads right for a kosher hot dog and stuffs it in his mouth and everything is fine. "Yum!" he says with his mouth full. "They sure don't have anything like this in Atlanta." He's the same old David, knowing just what to do, just what to say, just how to put things right. How could I have ever doubted him and Victoria? They'd never hurt me.

"What's this mysterious project you're working on?" I ask Barb.

"You'll see."

"When?"

"Soon," Victoria chimes in.

"Sooner than you think, Victoria," Dale shouts across the room to us from where he's sitting on Andrew's battered steamer trunk. "I'm almost done with my part."

These are my friends and I love them tonight more than I have loved anything in a very long time.

After Jimmy Stewart has exhausted himself and us with his passionate filibustering, Victoria switches on the election report. The voting is still too close to call, which implies the possibility of an upset; everyone knows it, but the commentators refuse to speculate. The CBS bulletin logo suddenly flashes on the screen, but all heads turn to the door. Andrew comes barging through, drunker than I've ever seen him. He knocks down everything in his way as he takes the most direct route to Dale and throws Dale off his steamer trunk. We're too stunned to restrain Andrew, and Dale is too stunned to pop back up fighting mad. We all watch as Andrew drags his trunk across the floor toward the door and out into the hall, slamming the door behind him.

"Jesus. What the hell's the matter with *him?*" Dale says, picking himself up off the floor.

"Looks like he's gone for good," someone says.

"What, without saying goodbye or thank you?" Barb jokes.

"He's history," David says. And that seems to be the final word.

The CBS bulletin is being repeated. There's been a Sikh terrorist attack at a hospital in New Delhi. A private truck loaded with explosives drove into the front yard of the Kama Rawni Clinic and destroyed an entire wing of the hospital. There's no telling how many people have been killed. Almost immediately, the phone rings. It's Arthur calling to tell me that Michael's friends are trying to get through to New Delhi but that it would be difficult under the best of circumstances. "Sit tight," he says in parting. "What did he say?" Julia asks, her forehead all serious. "He doesn't know anything. He'll let us know."

The bulletin includes footage of the kind of truck that was used in the suicide attack. The foreign correspondent informs us that the wildly spangled, decaled, graffitied private truck we're looking at is as common in the streets of New Delhi as yellow cabs are in the streets of New York City. They're all privately owned transports whose independent owners vie to outdecorate each other with the kinds of gaudy, adolescent razzmatazz you see hung, strung, pasted, and painted on American hot rods, cycles, and vans. But, like our graffiti artists, each owner has a signature, and the correspondent suggests that a search of the wreckage may lead to that signature and the subsequent arrest of the madmen behind the attack. So far, however, the Sikhs are willing to take credit for the disgraceful murders of innocent patients and medical staff.

And yet even this news will not becloud the evening for us. Only Julia is truly anxious, something having to do with Michael and his friends having reinspired her work, but the absolute uncertainty that Michael is in fact a victim keeps this latest act of third world barbarism far removed from our happy little society, little more than conversation fodder. Not that we need more fodder. There's plenty to talk about: the election, the project, Julia's new work (which she talks around, not about), the book Dale has started (which he will not talk about specifically except to tease us into wanting to read because "it disinters a lot of things a lot of people want to keep buried, a lot of things I've been asked not to reveal," although we've all heard that before from Dale) . . . and beneath all this, still secret, still waiting for just the right moment to surface, waiting in the wings like a surefire showstopper, is the best news of all. Victoria and I are planning to have a baby. Andrew is history, and Victoria and I are planning to have a baby.

CBS is willing to announce that the incumbent mayor has lost. He spread himself too thin, the station's political analyst hypothesizes. He tried to be all things to all people. His opponent, on the other hand, went after the young, urban, upwardly mobile professionals who are forging new neighborhoods out of old and breathing new life into commercial districts the incumbent was not willing to invest the city's revenues in. His opponent, the analyst observes, was seen in all the right places, endorsed all the right enterprises, and probably turned the election his way when he promised that his first act as new mayor of the city would be to repave the entire Upper West Side. Our own closed balloting unanimously predicted the actual outcome, although we were all too busy to get to the polls. But we didn't have to get to the polls. We all knew exactly who was going to win. We all had the right answer written on our little folded up pieces of paper. We all won.

All the King's Men is over and I've been coaxed to the piano to play Randy Newman's "The Kingfish." David does an excellent impression of Randy Newman and everyone is singing along through most of the songs I'm playing from the sheet music to Newman's *Good Old Boys* album. The food is gone.

So is all the Chinese, Japanese, Mexican, Spanish, English, Irish, American, and Indian beer. There's a false lull and then an animated discussion about how fast the project can be executed.

"There's no point doing it if we're not out there in time for this Christmas," Barb says.

"Well, my part can be finished tomorrow," Dale brags.

"What do I have to do?" asks Julia, who's worried about her time and still worried about Michael. "Can I just make sketches?"

"That's all," Barb tells her. "Let me have the sketches and I'll get the thing made."

"You're not going to tell us what you're doing, are you?" I ask.

"It's a surprise," Lori teases. Then she tells Barb and Victoria that she's already talked to a number of store buyers and delivery can't be later than December first. "We've got to be in the stores by the first or forget it."

"We can do it," Barb says. "But I've got to get those sketches, Julia."

Everyone resolves to work her ass off. They make a timetable. They toast their resolve with seltzer, which is all that's left to drink.

"Hey, where are we going for the holidays?" Frank wants to know.

"I'd like to go back to the house in Vermont," Victoria says.

That seems to be fine with everyone, and I'm nominated to rent the house and work out everyone's responsibility.

"Is that all right with you, David?" Victoria asks, and suddenly we all remember that several seasons ago Angel came with us to the house in Vermont.

"Sure. Of course. It's a great house."

He'd absolutely kill himself before he'd do anything to hurt me.

The next lull is real and everybody leaves together, leaving me and Victoria alone with the party mess.

"Let's clean it up in the morning," I suggest.

"I won't be able to fall asleep thinking about facing all this in the morning. You go to sleep, I'm not tired."

All during the night I have a sense of being alone. My dreams inhabit vaster space than usual. The characters in my dreams, which I can't remember when I get up at seven o'clock in the morning, are tiny figures in wide open spaces. I can't remember the particulars of these dreams, but vaguely I remember that every character reaches out to touch something that appears close to him and realizes that what he's trying to touch is actually miles away.

When I wake up, Victoria is not in bed. My morning voice breaks as I call out her name; I'm not surprised no one answers the feeble cry. As I head for the john, Victoria calls to me from the living room, where I find her wide awake on the opened hide-a-bed. She is starkly, beautifully, naked and awake.

"Come," she beckons, and I go to her, flat-footed and groggy still.

It's a brilliant day, I know it is, the sun is streaming in through our two big windows, and then Victoria is so overwhelmingly upon me, on top of me, surrounding me, that everything goes black. My eyes are closed, but if I open them, I know that everything will still be black, her blond hair and blue eyes and fair skin and the sun and the windows, all black, as though we've been folded up inside the hide-a-bed, as though Victoria has swallowed me whole and I'm inside her body. And from inside of her, as though they were coming from another room, I hear screams of passion I've never heard in all my life. And my name is in her screams, ecstatic, agonized shrieks and moans of Roger! Roger! Roger! And the darkness is warm and wet and soft and wonderfully foul. Oh Roger! And the darkness grabs at me Oh Roger! and squeezes me Oh Roger! and turns pain into pleasure. Oh Oh Oh! And blood is drawn. And wetness from our mouths is drawn. And sweat and flesh and hair are drawn in rough involuntary spurts of pleasure and pain, in throaty shrieks of Oh Roger! Oh Roger!

"Oh Victoria!"

My own single violently sweet scream of gratitude resonates in my head. Nothing has ever sounded so loud, so mournful, so thankful. In my one cry, I have thanked Victoria for every wonderful thing she has ever done for me, for every smile, every caress, every sacrifice, for simply being Victoria and allowing me to be her husband and allowing me to be the father of the child I know we have just conceived on the sunny hide-a-bed.

31

B ARB, VICTORIA, JULIA, LORI, and Dale have done a fantastic job. Their million-dollar idea will be in the stores by December first. I still don't know what it is; they want it to be a surprise. But those of us who don't know are going to find out tonight at the "unveiling."

Andrew's motorcycle has remained parked across the street despite the constant risk of being stripped again of its dazzle of decals, reflectors, foxtails, and flags. Also, I'm not certain, but I think I've seen him in the apartment building across from ours. I think I've seen him standing at the window staring into our apartment. I haven't said anything to Victoria and I'm not certain it was Andrew, but I feel him watching us.

Vermont is all set. The house has been rented. Everyone has cleared the decks for Christmas week. Even Julia has made time. Her exhibit is nearly finished. She worked for two years on her first idea and then scrapped it and did as much work on her new idea in only two months. "Shows how fast you can produce when you're really into what you're doing," she keeps saying. Although she's been worried about Michael, she's turned her worry into energy in his behalf. Whether he's alive or dead, she has dedicated her exhibit to his memory. There still hasn't been any word on Michael. The Kama Rawni Clinic has become the unofficial headquarters for Moslem reprisals against the Sikhs, and all communications have been cut off. The fighting continues in living color on the nightly news. Gandhi or whoever the hell it is has declared martial law in New Delhi. When I think about Michael and the possibility that he's alive, I always think of that movie about the kid who gets caught trying to smuggle drugs out of Turkey and they throw him in prison for life and nobody can do anything about it, not his parents or his lawyers or the American embassy or his home state politicians, even though everyone with any intelligence whatsoever knows that the kid never got a fair trial and that he's being tortured and that the living conditions in the prison are worse than on Devil's Island. It really happened, too. The kid finally escaped and wrote a book about it and they made the book into a movie. That's the kind of book Dale should write. At least he's writing something original now. At least he's not writing a novelization. I always knew he had more talent than that. We all have more talent than we think we have. Or than we're willing to use.

For weeks, however, I've been assured and reassured that no talent was spared in creating and marketing the million-dollar idea. And now that everyone has arrived and the champagne has been uncorked and poured into plastic champagne glasses and the carton of first samples sits on the coffee table in front of the hide-a-bed like the lost ark, we who are still in the dark are about to behold the marvel that is lighting up the faces of its creators.

Barb wants Victoria to do the honors, but Victoria says it was really Barb's idea.

"It was *your* idea, Victoria," Barb corrects her.

Victoria looks uncertain, as though she's replaying original conversations in hopes they'll help her remember whose million-dollar idea it really was. In her reverie, she neither accepts nor denies authorship. But Barb does the honors.

"In this carton," Barb begins in a voice that is half snake-oil salesman's and half executive account planner's, "is this year's number one Christmas impulse item. This year's Pet Rock. This year's Lump-of-Coal-in-a-Stocking. This year's witty, adorable, affordable grab-bag bestseller. Wives will rush to give them to their hubbies. Secretaries will leave them on their bosses' desks. Old buddies will exchange them like old war stories. Ladies and gentlemen," Barb says to me, Frank, David, and Phyllis as she opens the carton, reaches in, takes out a black cardboard box about the size of a Walkman, "may we present to you . . ." and turns the black box so we can read the name and see what's inside through the cellophane panel on the front, "the one and only . . ." and holds it up for all to see, ". . . Andrew, the Mid-life Crisis."

I'm too amazed to respond, but the others tear the house down. They are laughing and cheering and fawning and congratulating each other over the funny little doll in the black box. Initially the plaudits go Julia's way, for the doll itself is her design and is a wonderfully funny yet sympathetic rendition of a middle-aged, out-of-shape, out-of-sorts, beleaguered, and bedeviled man on the make. The physical model for this raggedy specimen of mid-life plight and fright—as the name does not even care to disguise—is none other than my brother, although it could never be proved in a court of law, no more so than it could be proved that a certain head carved out of wood or a trunkful of various statues, sketches, photos, news clippings, and passages from obsolete books used Victoria as their model.

When the black cardboard box is opened and the literature is taken out and read aloud by Barb and Dale and Victoria (who looks as if she is still trying to remember whose idea Andrew, the Mid-life Crisis was), it becomes their turn to be applauded, for Andrew's pedigree and the accompanying questionnaire—both intended to convince the recipient that he *is* or *is not* suffering a similar mid-life crisis—have been written by them with a poisonously witty yet accurate pen.

"Are you still wearing your Nehru suit?"

"Does *far out* slip out when you mean to say *awesome*?"

"Are your friends' daughters starting to look good to you?"

"Do you go to every office party you're invited to?"

"Have you noticed that now you can mix your drinks without getting sick?"

"Do you go around telling everyone in your office that all the education in the world can't make up for your years of experience?"

"Has your wife aged two years for every one of yours?"

"Are you about to trade in the family wagon for a Z car?"

"Do you alternate between rigorous month-long physical fitness programs and eleven months of self-destructive gluttony, boozing, and idleness?"

"Do you hang around schoolyards?"

"Is your boss younger than you are?"

"Were you upset that Woody Allen didn't wind up with Mariel Hemingway in *Manhattan*?"

"Is your ass sore from kicking yourself?"

"Have you been tempted to quit your job in the last week?"

"Are you twenty in your dreams and forty in bed?"

"Do you keep a secret bank account so you can take off for parts unknown on the spur of the moment?"

"Have you been to every Club Med?"

"Do you carry your passport at all times?"

"Does everyone misunderstand you?"

"Are you teaching the old dog in you new tricks?"

"Do you believe that contemporary movies suck, theater sucks, TV sucks, books suck, and that rock 'n' roll died with Elvis Presley?"

On and on the questionnaire goes in that same jugular vein, everybody laughing and counting future proceeds. Victoria, too, is laughing. And her laughter is real. There was a time during these past few months when Victoria thought she was no longer indebted to me or our circle of friends. She had one foot out of the circle and the other one in the air. But her loyalty to me and to our friends and to her true purpose in life was so great that she could not escape. She did not want to escape. There was everything to escape from and nothing to escape to. Everything that was and is and always will be Victoria has been described by our circle. Outside, there is nothing. Inside, there is laughter.

Now Barb is reading Andrew's pedigree, how he spent the whole first part of his life in trivial pursuit of success, family, and material happiness only to give it all up because of a gnawing sense of dissatisfaction, an uncontainable wanderlust of the soul, an unslaked thirst for the true meaning of life, and an empty-headed twinkie named Dolores; and how he courted her and turned creaky cartwheels for her, and begged her to run off with him, for he had been waiting all his life for someone like her and a moment like this; and how she teased him and flirted with him and took him for all he was worth and left him with nothing more than his undying obsession for youth and truth; and how this obsession made him quit everything of value in his life—his marriage, his family, his position, his savings, his future; and how he plunged into despair, drowning himself in vodka and self-pity, living by his dulled wits, scavenging for food and warmth and a kind word; and how eventually he picked himself up and brushed himself off and began dating again, punishing all of womankind for the woes they had heaped upon him, loving them and leaving them, teaching them the same hard lesson someone had once taught him; and how one of these hopeful women—his own first wife, in fact— saw something salvageable in Andrew and helped him outgrow his second childhood and remake a place for himself in the real world; and how this time he recognized the true worth of such trivial pursuits and succeeded quickly and happily ever after.

Of course, the story is written in greater detail and with much humor and style. And there's more. As I stare out the window at the apartment building across the street, Barb tells me what else has been cleverly included to make the black box worth $9.95. First there are recommended books, self-help groups, and exercises—all of them bogus, of course—which the critically middle-aged should consult, join, or follow. "But an ounce of prevention is worth a pound of cure," Barb advises, and then she tells us about the preventive do's and don'ts, which, she reads, " 'if religiously observed, will serve as a good solid plank to throw across the inevitable pitfalls of middle age.' "

Well-worded, well-conceived, well-executed, well-marketed, altogether well done, I think as I gaze across the street at the shadow in the window.

When the doll comes around to me, I'm forced to examine it and love it as much as the others have.

"It's wonderful," I overhear Frank tell Julia.

"Who wrote what?" asks Lori, whose part in the project consisted only of setting up meetings between friendly buyers and Barb.

"Who do you think wrote the story?" Victoria teases.

"Not Barb, it's too sentimental," says David.

"Not Dale either, then," says Phyllis.

"I wrote all the funniest questions for the questionnaire," Dale kids.

"Let's guess who wrote which question," Lori suggests, and the game is on.

Is it possible that only I see the resemblance to Andrew in the glazed and lusty expression Julia managed to trap in the doll's eyes? Is it possible that only I see the same gnawing dissatisfaction, the same uncontainable wanderlust of the soul, the same unslakable thirst for true meaning, the same undying obsession for the youth and truth of a fair-haired young girl who is always laughing?

"Okay, who wrote this one?" someone challenges.

I look again; the face at the window is gone.

32

I DON'T THINK IT CAN EVER get better than this. Life.
There's been a steady snowfall for two days that has isolated this lovely house from the worries of the world even more than is to be expected from the huge Vermont maples and the absence of neighboring houses.

Inside, we have a good fire crackling away with its own blue, green, and red fireworks. The flames give out a palpable warmth, a warmth missing from steam heat.

A tall, full, healthy tree dominates the first floor; we cut down the tree ourselves and soon we'll hang homemade decorations on every branch.

Some of us are busy cooking up another wonderful dinner. The others are reading, playing backgammon, listening to tapes, waiting for the cooks to finish and come into the living room for cocktails.

Tonight, tomorrow, for the next few days, we who have everywhere to go and everything to do have nowhere to go and nothing to do except quietly or wildly celebrate the end of another year, the beginning of the next, and the sweet durability of our blessed friendship, a friendship as pure as our snowfall, as warm as our fire, as full as our tree, as intoxicating as our mugs of hot applejack. We're growing unabashedly sentimental as Christmas and the new year approach. We've been through a great deal this year, but as always, we've landed on our feet. The air here is charged with renewal. We're like characters in a TV series who've experienced every awful thing imaginable—murder, suicide, disease, infidelity, incest—and yet each week show up bright and handsome and ready to go on for as long as the series is renewed. Our lives continue to be renewed.

Even Andrew has capitulated. He did come back one more time. It was during the party we always give on the weekend following Thanksgiving. Everyone spends Thursday with family, so we host a Thanksgiving-leftovers party for our friends. Andrew actually knocked on the door. He didn't barge in. I opened the door and was amazed to find him sober. He was not so grizzly and less unkempt and his Nehru jacket was clean and pressed. Something about his posture made him appear unexpectedly civil, even gentlemanly. First he handed me an envelope, which I could feel contained money, lots of it. Then he reached into his jacket pocket and found the key I had given him to the apartment. He held up the key so I could see it and put it on the bookshelf over the Apple.

"We're just about to eat," I said dumbly. "Would you like something?"

He came in and walked around the room, shaking hands with each of us—using both his hands only for David's handshake—until he came to Victoria, who was sitting on the arm of the hide-a-bed. He stood in front of her for several moments. At last he took her hand and gently lifted her to her feet. He pressed something into her hand and I'm sure only I heard the tinkling from her wrist and only I noticed that suddenly, magically, there were three interlocking gold bracelets where once there had been two and before that, one, and before that, none. Her hand was closed around something else he had given her, too.

He held Victoria's closed hand for a long time while we all held our forks and glasses in mid-air, waiting for the scene to reach a climax. And climax it did, with something none of us, except Victoria, had ever heard before.

Andrew spoke. Not just words, but the most difficult words of all. Words I had always used too glibly, I suddenly realized. He spoke softly from someplace deep inside that was very old and broken, and yet the words soared as if on the wings of an eternal truth. In one simple statement, he asked for my understanding, my forgiveness, and for the compassion that was every brother's to give. Somehow I had beaten him. Without striking a single blow—without turning him away from my home, without condemning his obnoxious behavior, without using a marital advantage or moving Victoria to a limit of secret passion that was even more seductive than the limit to which Andrew had driven her—without in any way destroying Andrew's destiny, I had beaten him. Not because I was the stronger, but simply because . . . I was in place. And Andrew's place was long gone; the bloodstained, grown-over territory of the defeated.

Yet he knew that he, too, had won something. He had found his dream. He had chased it around the world and found it in his brother's house, where now he would have to leave it for safekeeping. He had sobered up and cleaned up and stood up as straight as he could to say goodbye. And when he spoke, he seemed to be saying to me, "Take this dream that I have cherished and cherish still, and make it real. Worship it. Recreate it in your heart. Love it as though nothing else in the world matters, not food, not money, not clothing, nothing." That is what he seemed to be saying to me. And I knew Victoria could hear this silent connotation.

He looked long and without blinking into Victoria's eyes, and there were tears in his own eyes, which could not be mistaken for the usual wateriness from too much booze, and he moved his lips a few times as if to speak, but the words were not there yet. Finally, when the words were ready and he could escape the terrible sadness that had transfixed his face, he said his piece and kissed Victoria on the cheek and turned away and left.

"I love you, Victoria," he said, and his whisper was louder than the closing of the door, louder than the churning of the elevator, louder than the gunning of his motorcycle on the street.

Andrew is history. At least a small section of it, anyway. And we are the future. And the carnelian, which must be what he pressed into Victoria's hand, is the sealing wax on the final chronicle. When she was brave enough to wear it again, she claimed that she found it, and I let it pass. I have no interest in revising history.

We had another unexpected visitor the day before we left for Vermont. She showed up at Julia's studio in the middle of the night after being told how worried Julia had been. And so we hosted a welcome home party at our apartment for Michelle at three in the morning and all left for Vermont eight hours later.

She looks . . . wonderful. She looks as if she has always been a woman. As it turned out, she was never in danger. She did not have to make a dangerous escape from the clinic. She wasn't even at the clinic when the truck drove into the front yard and exploded. By then she was recuperating at a nearby tourist house and making daily excursions to places like the Taj Mahal. Now she looks like some radiant work of art that she stole from the Taj. We loved her as Michael and we love her as Michelle. No, it does not get any better than this.

We've decorated the tree and opened small, meaningful presents. We've sung carols and eaten fruitcakes. We've tried to ski in the still falling snow and haven't had much luck. Six days ago, on Christmas Day, I walked by myself through the snow-covered maples and realized how close we might have come to wiping ourselves out. But I immediately reprimanded myself for doubting, even in retrospect, that we would bounce back. Glancing back, I saw that the falling snow already had begun to fill in my footsteps, and I realized that that was what life was like—that our momentum covers our tracks with its wake. In an oddly tender ceremony, Victoria and I had deleted our personal files before we left for Vermont. She booted up PENDING and I deleted it. I booted up RAWN and she pushed the button. A blank fullness like snow filled what was left of our impressions of the past few months and all that had happened. And what had happened? Nothing worth saving. Nothing worth thinking about again. And yet I thought about everything for one last time, realizing how simple and obvious the explanations were now that I was far enough away to see them.

Andrew had loved Victoria. He was obsessed with all her wonderful qualities, qualities he himself lacked. He saw in her the essence of good society and accomplishment and organization. And he tried to conquer her and all that she represented. He bought her an expensive coat. He gave her expensive bracelets. He courted her on his motorcycle. He got her drunk and sloppy. He even broke into her personal diary and wrote his own fantasy over her private entry. But in the end, he had failed. For a short while, Victoria's head had been turned. She let herself go. But she never let herself go all the way. The panties in the hide-a-bed had merely been mislaid. The coat was justifiable recompense for the anguish Andrew had forced upon her. Possibly, she really did lose the ring I gave her. And found it again. And Andrew's matching carnelian was yet another one of his desperate magic tricks, like the interlocking bracelets. Even magic was simple when you knew how it was done, and although I didn't know exactly how Andrew did his tricks, I did know that they were tricks and that somehow he had distracted me while he worked his hidden mirrors, secret compartments, and sleight of hand. As for the rest, Angel, Mohammad's sister, David and Victoria's innocent little crush on one another . . . these things happen. Madness, fanaticism, and romance run their course and lead where they must.

Last night we played old board games, Monopoly, Risk, Parcheesi, Life, and drank a Scandinavian punch called glug. Yum. When we got into our double bed, Victoria whispered to me in the cold darkness. The air smelled of the heavy woolen blanket we shared.

"Whether it's a boy or a girl," she whispered, "I'd like to name it Angel."

"That's lovely," I said, and we fell asleep touching.

Tonight we are playing our favorite game and finishing off the glug.

"How old was Lolita?"

"We had that one before. I know the answer," Frank confesses. "Twelve, right?"

"Jesus, have we gone through all the cards?"

I remember that Lolita's name was really Dolores, same as the young, empty-headed girl who almost destroys Andrew, the Mid-life Crisis.

The last of the glug has made us woozy and maudlin. We tell each other how much we love each other and decide to make our New Year's resolutions.

"I'm going to mine this new lode, kids," Julia goes first. "I'm really on to something in my work, and I'm going to mine it for everything I can get out of it." She tells us all about her new exhibit, that the theme is hermaphroditism, that all the statues have male and female organs, that Michelle and her friends inspired the idea of overloading the statues with double organs so that people will have to ignore the gender altogether and see that form is form and humanity is humanity. She is very proud of her idea and very humble at the same time. When she finishes speaking, she gets up, walks across the room to Michelle, and kisses her gratefully on both cheeks.

"I'm going to finish my book," Dale resolves. "I don't care if the studios call up and beg me to do their stupid novelization and wave a million dollars in my face, I'm going to finish this book."

"JFDI, Inc.," Barb begins. "That's the name of my new corporation. We're always coming up with great ideas and never doing anything about them. Except this time we did it, huh? We made that sonofabitchin' Mid-life Crisis! And we're going to do it again. We're going to Just Fucking Do It, Inc., from now on!"

"Speaking of doing it," Frank begins, "I've been invited to organize and head up an epidemic prevention authority under the auspices of the Massachusetts Department of Wildlife and I think I'm going to do it. I never thought about preventing epidemics *before* they happen. And I like the idea of helping animals. You know, when you stop to think about it, it's only human beings that are responsible for their own epidemics. Animals are always innocent victims."

"Me?" Victoria is surprised that she is next. "Well, now that Roger is making a lot of money with his appraisals, I've decided to take the entrance exams for law school."

I expected her to come to that decision.

"I looked at office space last week," Phyllis boasts. She is finally getting serious about starting her own women's research firm, an idea she's been toying with ever since she finished researching her women's history class and wound up with thirty double-sided double-density disks full of everything anybody could ever want to know about women from Eve to Mary Lou Retton. "I'm greatly encouraged by the responses I've gotten to a questionnaire I sent to publishers, periodicals, and independent writers. I think this is the year I do it, gang."

When it looks as if my turn is coming, the phone rings and I jump up to answer it. It's Victoria's mother calling to wish us all a happy and healthy New Year. I'm grateful for the interruption; I'm waiting for just the right moment to make my resolution, and I'm still searching for words that will give my resolution maximum impact.

While Victoria is on the phone, I bring out another six-pack of beer, and we all have a chance to congratulate Frank and ask Dale about his book and Julia about her exhibit and wish Phyllis luck and start coming up with ideas for JFDI, Inc.

Victoria looks bemused when she comes back into the living room.

"My mother just told me that my father got a Christmas present from his secretary," she states, "and it was the Mid-life Crisis doll."

"You're kidding!"

"I don't believe it!"

"We're a hit!"

"Did you tell her it was ours?"

"They said they were going to try to push it through to all the stores in the chain, and they did it!" Barb rejoices.

"What did she say when you told her it was ours?"

"I didn't."

"You didn't tell her?"

"No."

"Why not?"

"I don't know why. I guess . . ." The color is returning to Victoria's face. "I don't know why."

When we're done congratulating ourselves on the success of

Andrew, the Mid-life Crisis, we resume our resolutions, and Lori tells us her plans for the new year.

"I'm going into real estate. I got my license last week. Not regular real estate. Business real estate. The money is unbelievable. One deal a year, that's all you need. You know what one square foot of space in midtown goes for? Do you have any idea?" The fact that Lori has had no experience in the real estate business doesn't seem to bother her. She knows a director of TV commercials who started dabbling in this kind of real estate two years ago and has made almost a million dollars. Now he dabbles in making commercials, and he's willing to help get Lori started. "And the good thing is, if Frank goes to Massachusetts, I can start there. I mean I'm not going to get anywhere styling commercials in Concord, am I?"

"I guess I may have a new job, too," David says. "I've been talking to Solstice, which is a computer think tank sort of operation, and I think they're going to offer me something. It'd be completely different from what I'm doing now. I'd be programming. But not the kind of programming that gets airline tickets into passengers' hands. It'd be more theoretical. You know what think tanks do, they worry about things that are going to happen a hundred years from now. Anyway, it's a very prestigious company, and if they offer me something, I'll probably jump at it."

"Hey, not too many women animators out there," Michelle jokes when it's her turn to make a New Year's resolution. We all laugh, and everyone knows that Michelle has made the most dramatic resolution of all. But the rest of ours are not too shabby, either. In a month or two, none of us will be doing exactly what he or she was doing a few months ago.

"Your turn, Rog."

"Well, friends, my New Year's resolution . . ."

Timing is everything in this life.

". . . is to be the very best father I can."

Silence. The silent shuffling of information that does not seem relevant.

"You heard me, you jerks. Victoria's going to have a baby."

My God, they are on Victoria like a pack of wolves. Such joy.

Such remarkable vicarious joy. And slowly they trickle my way, hugging, kissing, laughing, slapping me on the back.

"Whatever made you decide?" Dale asks.

"Simple. What the world really needs is more people like us."

ABOUT THE AUTHOR

ALAN SAPERSTEIN's first novel, *Mom Kills Kids and Self,* won him widespread praise and the coveted PEN-Ernest Hemingway Award for Best First Fiction of 1979. He is the author of a second novel, *Camp.*